STATE OF CONTEMPT

RUINATION

STATE OF CONTEMPT

RUINATION

TYLER DEAN MILLIGAN

atmosphere press

Published by Atmosphere Press

Cover design by Dhiraj Navlakhe

Atmospherepress.com

PROLOGUE

KANSAS | APRIL 2035

"Ladies and gentlemen, this is your captain speaking. As we start our descent into Kansas City, please make sure your seats and tray tables are in their fully upright position. Make sure your seatbelt is securely fastened and all carry-on luggage is stowed underneath the seat in front of you or in the overhead bins. Thank you."

Captain Rice nodded his head in approval. "That wasn't too bad, Miller—and I've been doing this a long time. You do everything by the book. Even on the mic, it took me forever to memorize that crap." He held up a notecard as if to prove his point, and Miller smiled weakly in response.

"Yeah, me either," he said.

"Don't thank me yet; we still have to land this thing, and I hate night flights. Not sure why we have to train so hard when the AI programs fly these high-tech planes better than we can," Miller replied.

Just then, the lights and power in the cabin suddenly shut off, plunging them into darkness.

"What the hell?" Rice muttered as he scrambled with his seatbelt.

Miller gasped and felt sweat start to form on his forehead. The captain tried keying his mic to get ahold of air traffic control, but nothing worked—not even a single light illuminated the cockpit.

"What the hell is going on? It's dead—everything is dead," said Captain Rice calmly but with an edge of confusion in his voice.

"What? We're blind?" Miller started to panic as beads of sweat glistened on his face in the faint moonlight streaming through the windows of the plane.

Captain Rice rolled his eyes as he stood up and rubbed at his temples, trying to soothe away a growing headache.

"Calm down, first off I'm here," he reassured Miller. "I can land this shit any way I want to; we'll be manual but as moonlight is bright and the runway has lights, we are gonna be just fine, okay? Now I'm gonna check on the staff; you need anything?"

Miller shook his head nervously, watching through the window as Rice unbuckled himself from his chair. He rose slowly, his face twisted with pain as he clutched at his chest. Miller's hand flew to Rice's shoulder in concern, but before he could speak, Rice swayed and fell over on him.

The weight of Captain Rice's body pinned Miller down, pushing the control stick forward and sending the plane into a terrifying nosedive. Passengers screamed in terror as the ground grew closer and closer. Miller gasped for air and gritted his teeth as every muscle in his body strained, trying to push Captain Rice off him, but Rice was too heavy.

The captain's wheezing breaths filled Miller's ears as he fought to regain control of the aircraft. His fingers slipped on the slick controls as he tried desperately to bring the plane out of its fatal descent. But it was too late. The left wing clipped something hard, sending the plane tumbling end over end until finally, it slid into a mass of fire, metal screeching and passengers shrieking before everything went black.

CHAPTER 1

FORT LEAVENWORTH, KANSAS | MARCH 2035

The solid white cell door heaved open with a grinding and whirring of its electronic mechanism. Duke lay on the bottom bunk bed surveying his tiny, austere room; his view of the hall beyond the cell limited to a tiny window set in the center of the door. He stretched his arms out, feeling the rough, cold concrete wall against the back of his hand, and thought, *Another day in this hellhole.*

Duke walked over to where he had hung his calendar and with teeth still clamped around a black Sharpie uncapped it and put an X in that day's box. It was the same thing day after day but at least spring had arrived, which meant temperatures at Fort Leavenworth were finally starting to rise from the frigid Kansas winter.

Military prison meant Duke still had to shave every morning, so he splashed water onto his face from the metallic sink and dragged a plastic razor across his stubbled cheeks. His blue eyes looked tiredly back at him from the mirror, but his hair was as short and tidy as ever.

He settled into the only chair in the room and opened up his Bible for his morning devotional like he did every day before continuing on to another twenty-four hours of monotonous punishment within these walls. Duke Hollander had spent four long years in Fort Leavenworth Disciplinary Barracks. His thoughts every day were of his wife and children, who lived eight hours away in Colorado Springs. He was so eager to be with them again when he finished his sentence in two years.

Duke regretted the choices he had made that landed him in prison, but he knew that this was his chance to make something of himself. He held onto his faith and went to Bible studies, all while struggling with his PTSD and anger issues resulting from his service in NATO's spearhead into Ukraine to fight the Russians. Every minute felt like a battle between the guilt of what he had done before coming to prison and his desire for redemption.

Duke nervously drummed his fingers on the table, his gaze fixed on the ragged Bible in front of him. He was desperate to stay out of trouble and get out of the prison as soon as possible. His cellmate, John Roberts, hopped down from the top bunk and sauntered toward Duke with a smirk on his face.

"So, Duke, you in?" asked John, referring to an illicit deal he had proposed earlier that morning.

Duke rolled his eyes but kept them locked on the book before him. "You know my answer, John. Why do you even ask?" He tried to ignore the temptation and focused on reading his morning Bible verse.

"I'm pretty sure if Jesus Christ is as cool as you say he is, he'll want you to make money distributing porn to your fellow inmates," John said with a chuckle.

Duke shook his head in disgust but didn't take his eyes off the page before him.

"I'm just kidding, buddy. But you can't blame a man for trying." A small smile crept across John's lips, and he grabbed his boots to tie them up. "Anyway, I'll see you at the library tonight," he said over his shoulder as he left the cell.

Duke replied with a distant, "Sure thing," without looking up.

John clipped his EIB (electronic identification badge) onto the lapel of his dark brown uniform before leaving their white wall room. According to the older inmates, who had been locked up for a long time, Fort Leavenworth and other prisons across the nation have slowly integrated more sophisticated technology into the facilities over the years. Chipped badges, fingerprint scans, and facial recognition. Also, robots that help cook, clean, and monitor security cameras are now a part of the American prison system. Instead of having to do these tasks themselves, inmates were taught to operate and maintain these machines. Roberts hated these robots with a passion.

Duke would describe John Roberts as one of the most extreme far-right Republicans he'd ever encountered. With a close-cropped flattop and wide jawline, standing at six feet tall and 250 pounds, John was an intimidating presence. Religion, liberals, robots, and police were among his least favorite things. Ironically, John used to be a K-9 police officer in the military. He only had a soft spot when it came to dogs. He had been sentenced to life in prison for assaulting multiple officers and killing the one who was sleeping with his wife. Continuously being thrown into solitary confinement for fighting and provoking guards didn't help either. John Roberts was a handful, but Duke knew it was better to have him as an ally than an enemy.

✳✳✳

John held a "book club" to discuss post-apocalyptic books, topics, and strategies every night at the library. Before Duke was locked up, he had always been prepared for disasters by storing beans, bullets, and Band-Aids. Duke never did buy into all the conspiracy theories and far-fetched apocalyptic scenarios; John, on the other hand, did. He always said, "If you're prepared for a super-volcano, you're prepared for a winter storm blackout." Even though John had a point, Duke still thought it was silly. He considered himself a practical prepper; even though he had joined a community of like-minded individuals back home, it would be a while before he saw them again.

The topics of the "book club" that night were job loss from

automation and China taking Taiwan. These theories were very much in line with the usual fare for discussions and were made particularly polar by the lack of objective information that infiltrated the prison walls.

"I keep telling these grown children in here not to waste their time in college," John exclaimed. "Trade skills will pay the bills. Especially when you consider a post-apocalyptic world."

"Exactly." Duke nodded at John in agreement.

"But how do we survive after getting out of here?" Jeffers threw his hands in the air. "We have felonies! And companies don't need to hire us with so many jobs being taken over by robots or automated machines now. No training required, and they don't get tired or sick either. How can we compete with that? I had planned on driving trucks once I got out, but even that has been taken away from us—pilotless electric trucks have been around for years now!"

The people around the table murmured in agreement with Jeffers' statement.

Jeffers was tall and skinny, and he constantly twisted pieces of his small afro into little dreads. He referred to himself jokingly as the group's "token black man," suggesting every group of white people needed one. Duke appreciated Jeffers; he provided balance even though he was loud and excitable.

Duke sighed and pinched the bridge of his nose as he felt the conversation begin to spiral out of control. Jeffers' eyes had grown wider, and his lips pressed together in anger as he gestured with an open palm toward the others. John leaned forward, forearms resting on the table, a slight smirk playing on his lips as he spoke; Duke could tell that he was relishing the opportunity to stir up trouble and would revel in the attention it earned him.

The rest of the people gathered around the table watched silently, eyes darting between John and Jeffers expectantly.

"All right, with that, let's move on and agree to disagree. Okay?" Duke interjected, trying to keep the conversation from escalating further.

John scoffed in response, muttering under his breath before settling back into his chair. "Yeah sure, what-the-hell-ever."

Jeffers looked around at the other faces in the room before continuing. "Republicans are nothing more than greedy dick bags who only think of themselves and not the people," he retorted.

Duke's brow furrowed as he glanced down at his notebook, the anger and frustration in the room palpable. "Next topic: China taking Taiwan."

"I'll go first," said John, his jaw clenched.

Jeffers scoffed. "Imagine that."

John shot him a withering look before continuing. "We need to be backing up the Taiwanese, but those spinelesstard we had before, yet all those promises were for naught. Now they've got Taiwan, and we look like bigger fools than ever. We just showed the world that we can be pressured into submission and that we need a Republican president with some courage." His fists clenched as he finished speaking.

Jeffers' eyes narrowed as he pushed back against the table with an index finger raised. "They were threatening war! Possible nuclear war! What was he supposed to do? Let the world burn? If you hadn't noticed, the Third World War has become the Second Cold War! We are closer to nuclear destruction than ever before in our history. We spent time serving in Ukraine, remember?"

John shook his head. "Some people are cowards and don't understand honor or integrity! We gave them our word and now we've shown the world that we're willing to break it, that we'll back down if someone threatens us with enough force!"

Anger flared in Jeffers' eyes as he stood from the chair. "Da hell."

Duke quickly stepped between them, extending his hands with his palms out toward his friends. "Everyone relax," he ordered.

John jumped up, his chair scraping along the concrete floor.

He slammed his hands on the table and glared at Jeffers as he shouted. "You heard me. Don't know about y'all, but where I come from, if you give your word to somebody, you keep it."

Duke replied quickly in an attempt to de-escalate the situation, speaking in a calm yet authoritative tone. "I'm no Democrat, but John, people are tired of war and absolutely terrified of nuclear war. Everyone at this table has done their time in Ukraine. With that being said, I do agree with you that people need to keep their word. If the president had no intention of actually protecting Taiwan, he never should have said that he would."

John and Jeffers both looked over at the prison guards who had moved closer as soon as the shouting started. The two inmates nodded in silent agreement not to escalate any further and backed off, but they still cast heated glares at each other across the table.

Suddenly one of the guards yelled out, "Library time is over!" Greatly relieved, everyone quickly stood and made their way out of the room.

"All right, great conversation. Let's go, John." Duke rolled his eyes as he patted his friend on the back, making sure John was in front of him as they exited the library.

When Duke and John stepped into the hallway outside the library, Duke noticed it was much more crowded than usual. The heat from all the bodies made it hard to breathe. Everywhere he looked, there were strangers, and they were all talking over one another; it was difficult to make out any conversations.

"What is happening here?" Duke questioned while surveying the long corridor.

"Maybe the stories were true," John said, standing still and scrutinizing the unknown faces.

"What do you mean by 'stories'?" Duke asked, impatiently glancing at his roommate.

"You know those riots and fires that happened last month

at the other facility?"

Duke nodded as he shifted away from someone who passed too close to him.

"Well, obviously they weren't able to fix it, so somebody high up in command decided that it was too dangerous to remain there. So, they are transferring everybody here while repairs are being done. That means we will be living with room-mates for certain," John said, shaking his head sorrowfully.

"That sucks. Does that include Agigi too?" Duke anxiously rubbed his neck while looking around alertly.

"Yes, I considered that possibility too. What do you plan on doing?"

"I guess I'll just try my best to avoid him."

John shook his head doubtfully as they continued through the overly populated hall and toward their cellblock when a recognizable voice called out for Duke.

Isaac Agigi shoved through the crowd of inmates dressed in brown, all of them avoiding his gaze. He paused in front of Duke and John, a sneer on his thin lips. "Now there's the face I've been waiting to see. How ya been, Duke?"

Isaac Agigi was an intense, light-skinned Latino whose muscles rippled with each movement. He stood no taller than five feet seven inches, but his wiry frame more than made up for any perceived lack of height. His head seemed to be per-petually shaved bald, and his skin appeared to be kissed by the sun. His smile flashed like sharpened fangs more than it did teeth, and his dark eyes seemed to hold otherworldly secrets.

Duke's jaw tightened as he glanced around at the other pris-oners, realizing they were surrounded by six of Agigi's men. "What do you want?" Duke asked, dread spiraling in his gut.

Agigi laughed, a low rumble that made everyone around him tense up. "Well, how about my life back? But I guess since you can't give me that..." He smirked and stepped closer. "... how about you give me yours?" His six associates closed in like shadows, menace radiating from them in palpable waves.

John stepped forward with a warning hiss. "Fat chance, asswipe!"

The guards rushed in then, shouting for everyone to break it up. John and Duke backed away slowly.

"This isn't over," John said sternly, and Agigi nodded in agreement, a twisted smile of victory painted across his face.

****

Over the next several weeks, Duke found himself in an endless cycle of beatings at the hands of Agigi's goons. It didn't matter that he towered above them all at six foot three or that he weighed in at two-hundred-twenty pounds, or that he had MMA training ... it was all useless against their numbers. He knew it had to be more than a coincidence that the guards had to be allowing them to ambush him in areas without camera coverage. John did his best to shield Duke, but whenever he was away, Agigi's henchmen would seize the opportunity to catch Duke. Knowing John was already serving a life sentence, they understood he wouldn't. Duke had refused to seriously hurt anyone, even in retaliation, not wanting the possibility of additional jail time. Duke's bruised and battered body became a regular reminder of this predicament each time he stood before the mirror.

John watched helplessly as Duke nursed yet another set of wounds—a busted lip and countless bruises all over his body. He hopped down off the top bunk and handed Duke a toothbrush that had been sharpened into a makeshift weapon.

"I told you I'm not going that route; I can't risk getting more time," Duke said firmly, averting his gaze from the mirror.

"Knock it off with that crap! None of that stuff is going to matter if you're dead and you can't go back home to your kids!" shouted John in frustration. "Time to man up and protect yourself, Duke!"

Duke nervously said, "Just let me think about it," and hung his head.

A voice over the intercom system announced, "Delta block: chow time," and the electronic cell doors unlocked simultaneously. John shook his head and left the room as Duke followed him to the chow hall.

The prison cafeteria was filled with twice the usual number of inmates, their conversations echoing through walls splattered with graffiti. Duke and John waited in line until they reached a large touch screen, where they chose their meals from an automated menu. Duke watched in fascination as massive robotic arms prepped and cooked their food, while a few long-term inmates managed them from afar.

John's face twisted into a scowl as he glared at the mechanical figures. "I hate robots," he muttered. "Gonna turn on us one day, just watch."

Duke couldn't help but smile as he responded sarcastically, "What're they gonna do? Throw grease at us?" His teasing only provoked laughter out of John.

"Did I ever tell you how much I hate you?" John chuckled.

"Every day." Duke winked at his roommate.

The cramped dining hall was buzzing with chatter as Duke and John dug into their plates of undercooked baked chicken, soggy vegetables, and cold beans. Suddenly, out of the corner of his eye, Duke spotted Echo's cellblock lined up for lunch—Agigi's block. Duke could feel Agigi's icy stare from across the room. As if on cue, Agigi and two of his men strutted up to their table. The other men seated around them quickly dispersed without a word. Once they were alone, Duke nonchalantly took a bite of food before speaking up.

"You know, if you're going to kill me, stop being such a coward and get it over with," he said casually, not even sparing Agigi a glance.

Agigi slowly regarded Duke with his piercing eyes before responding. "Duke, we both know that there are worse things in this life than death. Like the choice to save your own skin or not."

A heavy silence stretched between them as everyone's attention was interrupted by a loud buzz and the lights flickering off. In an instant, absolute darkness engulfed the chow hall.

John's voice was loud and full of rage when he bellowed, "It's a trap! The hell you up to, Isaac?"

Duke raised his hands in a plea for calm, which momentarily got John's attention. Quickly, John spun around and threw an elbow with all his might into the face of the man seated beside him. There was a sickening crunch as the man's nose exploded in a spray of blood. Just as John pulled his arm back, the lights flickered back on brightly, dazzling those in the chow hall.

Agigi grabbed Duke and they began wrestling, exchanging punches amidst growing cheers from onlookers. Meanwhile, John had already shifted his attention to two other men, picking up a plastic cup from a nearby table and giving one of them a nasty cut with its open end.

Then suddenly, there came a high-pitched whine that steadily grew louder until it became unbearable. Amidst this sound were screams of fear and a surprised, "That's a plane!" right before a fiery explosion blew apart the back wall of the kitchen and sent everyone flying. Another explosion followed that shook Fort Leavenworth like an earthquake, and the deafening sound of metal twisting filled the air.

Duke felt as if the entire prison was shaking. Shattered glass scattered across the ground like glitter, and chunks of concrete were littered everywhere. Particles of brick and mortar turned into dust, drifting down from above like snowflakes, making it hard to see and breathe. The emergency lights flickered on and off in a frenzied sequence that created an eerie strobe effect within the chaos. The sprinkler system began to douse everything with water, Duke heard agonizing screams from injured inmates mixed with the wailing of sirens piercing through his ringing ears. His eyes stung from the fumes as he surveyed the destruction. He saw numerous guards and prisoners running every which way, bodies lying motionless on their sides, and robotic machines twisted into mangled piles of scrap metal.

John Roberts grabbed Duke's hand and pulled him up, and they stumbled their way toward what used to be the kitchen. John had sustained minor cuts and scrapes while Duke's legs felt so weak, he could barely walk. They stepped over body parts as they trudged through the debris-strewn room toward the gaping hole in the ceiling that now let sunlight stream in, illuminating the remnants of smoke and dust hanging in the air.

John's voice was barely audible over the blaring alarm as he shouted to Duke, "Watch my back; I'm going to check it out!" Fighting against the noise, John moved toward the danger with Duke trailing behind him. Without a word, Duke gave a thumbs-up in acknowledgment before turning to scan their surroundings for any signs of trouble.

Suddenly, Jeffers appeared from around the corner, looking as startled as Duke felt. "Jesus Christ, Duke! What the hell happened?" he gasped, struggling to catch his breath. The men stood frozen, staring at each other in disbelief.

The air was strangely still as John popped his head around the corner, into a gap in the wall. "Holy shit!"

Duke couldn't see what John saw until he pushed past him with Jeffers close behind. Before them lay a devastating sight—the plane they'd heard minutes ago had crashed like some giant metal bird. The prison courtyard was littered with twisted bits of metal and the sparking remains of smaller electronics. A jagged chunk of fuselage had torn through the fence like a knife through butter. "Yep, time to go," shouted Jeffers as the remnants of what used to be a wall started to crumble some more.

Duke and John knew it wasn't safe to be in the area any longer, so they hastily made their way out of the kitchen, through the cafeteria into the corridor leading back toward their cellblock. "Yo wait up, hold for me," Jeffers yelled, stumbling over chunks of concrete and steel.

On their way to their cell, they witnessed a scene of absolute chaos; inmates were running rampant throughout the facility, attacking prison guards who were desperately trying to contain them. As soon as they made it, Duke noticed that John had begun packing his laundry bag with clothes and food supplies.

"What the hell is happening!" exclaimed Duke.

"It's happening! SHTF is finally here! See, I told you I'm not crazy!" John replied, hurriedly cramming items into his bag.

"What do you mean? It was just an accident when a plane crashed down; it doesn't mean the world's ending!" Jeffers said nervously.

"Shut up, Jeffers! Are you really telling me none of this looks fishy to you? Our economy crumbling, our culture being ripped apart and divided, bad decisions from our government and then suddenly, the power goes out then comes back on minutes before a plane crashes in our backyard? That doesn't smell like an EMP attack to you?" John continued filling his bag without so much as giving Jeffers time to answer.

"Who the hell would have the courage to pull off something like this?" asked Duke with an uneasy glance around.

John took a moment to address Duke's question. "Well, I'm guessing the cold war with China and Russia just turned back into a hot one. But who knows? A lot of people hate us, lot of countries would have something to gain from us falling apart completely."

"Or maybe someone made a mistake, or was it an accident?" Pleaded Duke. "Like another 1983 Soviet nuclear false alarm incident."

John checked his pockets for anything else he might need and then slung his laundry bag over his shoulder. "Mistake or not, our power is out," he said gruffly. "The clock is ticking before everything is too far gone."

Duke looked up warily. "Clock? What the hell do you mean?" he asked.

John let out a heavy sigh and cast a glance toward the door. "If I'm right, and an EMP hit us, I need to get back home," he said as he started walking toward the exit. "If I stay here, they'll probably kill me rather than release me, so I'll be deciding my fate."

"What if you're wrong, and it was just a plane crash?" asked Duke, standing up quickly.

John shook his head and chuckled wryly. "Dude, I'm forty-five years old with practically a life sentence," he said with a shrug. "Do you think I give a shit?"

Duke slumped back down onto his bunk bed and muttered something under his breath.

"All right then, Duke. Whatever you plan to do, be it due to an EMP or airplane crash, I'm out of here." Jeffers glanced over at John. "I know we don't always see eye-to-eye, but I'm coming with you. Our odds of surviving will be better if we stay together. I'll go grab my things; meet me in the mess hall, okay?" He stared eagerly at John, awaiting an answer.

John nodded in agreement, then stepped closer to Duke and gave him a pointed look. "So, are you in this time?" he asked quietly.

Duke's eyes widened in shock. "Are you serious? I only have two years left! I can't take that risk!" he exclaimed as he stood back up.

John leaned in closer and softened his tone. "Well, I can guarantee if you stay here, you won't make it another two years," he said with an earnest look. "Not with this shit storm going on and Agigi hounding you every day." His voice softened even more as he added, "Don't you want to go home and be with your wife and kids? Who's going to protect them as society falls apart?"

John's words struck a chord in Duke's heart, and he longed to be reunited with his family. To hear his children laugh and play once more, to wake up next to his wife again. He knew John was right; it was too risky to remain in such a place and the promise of hope outweighed the danger of staying put.

"All right," Duke said, giving a subtle nod.

"All right what?" asked John, leaning in closer as if he had not heard.

"Let's go...now," said Duke solemnly, his face turning white with fear and anxiety.

"You serious?! Hell yes! You won't regret this, Duke!" John clapped him hard on the back, causing him to stumble.

"I doubt that," Duke muttered before packing up his things.

Treading through water mixed with blood, Duke and John made their way toward the mess hall to wait for Jeffers' arrival, heads turning sporadically, but the fire alarm and sprinklers had finally ceased working entirely. Every step they took echoed through the hallways, adding to their already heightened sense of dread.

John gasped in shock as he saw Jeffers slumped against the wall, his stomach pierced with multiple wounds and a stab wound on his neck oozing blood. Duke knelt beside him to check for a pulse and shook his head sorrowfully when he found none. He closed Jeffers' eyes before standing up again, wiping the blood from his hands on his pants.

They made their way into the bustling mess hall where Agigi and his men blocked their escape. "Are you trying to leave without saying goodbye?" he called out with a twisted smile.

"Yeah, well it seems that I'm not welcomed here," Duke replied curtly. But Agigi wasn't deterred, remarking lightly that Duke had plenty of friends present among the crowd.

With no other options left, John quickly snatched up an abandoned riot shield from the ground and turned it sideways. Winking at Duke, he shouted, "Run!" before charging toward Agigi's men. The shield quivered against assaults of fists and bodies while he knocked many of them down in order for them to make an escape.

Duke felt his heart sink as he watched the group of thugs

pile on top of John, their fists pounding into his body like relentless machines. He was frozen in terror, unable to move until a few seconds later when he heard John cry out, "Run!"

Without hesitation Duke snapped out of his trance and bolted. He ran toward the gaping hole created by the plane smashing into the building. Jumping over burning chunks of metal and piles of rubble, he made his way through the burning wreckage of the plane. The acrid smell of smoke stung his eyes and obscured his vision, but even through the haze Duke could make out the mutilated bodies that lay scattered around the site. The heat coming from the downed aircraft was almost unbearable as Duke ran for cover to escape the chaos.

Duke's fingers quickly rifled through the clothes and other belongings of a passenger's green hardshell luggage. He heard footsteps behind him and before he could turn around, he was tackled to the ground. A pair of hands lifted him roughly and Duke looked up to see Agigi grinning smugly.

"I'm impressed, Duke, you and that attack dog of yours are kinda hard to kill, or should I say were?" said Agigi with a smile.

Duke felt guilty for leaving John behind and muttered his name under his breath.

"Yeah, sorry, he was a bit of a problem," Agigi continued, shrugging his shoulders dismissively. He grabbed Duke's face firmly in one hand. His eyes flashed angrily as he spoke.

"Listen, I—" Duke started to protest but was quickly cut off by Agigi.

"I'm done listening, and I'm done with this nonsense," he spat as he pulled out a homemade weapon from his pocket.

The weapon gleamed menacingly in the dull light; Duke felt the chill of fear run down his spine as he anticipated being pierced by the weapon.

"Say hello to Roarke for me, I'm sure he'll be happy to see you." Agigi sneered as he raised his weapon above his head.

Duke felt a sudden impact from behind, and he was sent

sprawling to the ground. He rolled onto his back, blinking away the shock of the attack, and saw John bleeding badly from the head. He heard shouting and clanging metal as John and the other two men fought nearby. Then Agigi descended on him, the blade of his knife glinting in the fading light. Duke thrust his hips upward, pushing Agigi off, giving himself just enough time to stand up again. Before he could act, Agigi lunged at him with surprising strength and tackled him. Agigi climbed on top of Duke and started punching him in the face and choking him. With his airway closing, Duke's thoughts turned to better times—moments with his kids when they used to make puppet shows out of stuffed animals that would come alive in their laughter. He remembered those days when his wife used to smile at him with gentle eyes and his kids looked at him like a hero.

The desperation for survival snapped Duke out of his trance and away from the happy memory he had been indulging in. Reaching out blindly, he found purchase on Agigi's face, his fingers seeking his left eye socket. With a powerful thrust, Duke plunged his thumb into it, feeling as though it was sinking into jelly.

Agigi reeled back, clutching at his ruined eyeball and screaming in agony. Duke, fueled by rage, moved on instinct and leapt onto Agigi's back. He wrapped his forearm around the man's throat and squeezed tightly until Agigi's screams were silenced. Right before his lifeforce left him, Duke released his grip and stood up.

"Why didn't you kill me?" Agigi asked breathlessly.

"Because I'm not like you," Duke replied coldly before delivering an authoritative kick to the man's face that knocked him unconscious.

Duke met John's gaze across the carnage. John stood over two bodies attached to bloodied heads that looked like smashed pumpkins. They exchanged a silent nod; everything was okay now. Laundry bags slung over their shoulders, the two men walked away from the scene with several scrapes and cuts.

As they trudged toward the jagged hole in the fence, John glanced over at Duke. His face held a concoction of emotions, as if he were both relieved and guilty.

"Does it not feel good not to have to worry about Agigi?"

The question hung in the air until finally Duke spoke up. He kept his gaze trained on the ground and said in a low voice, "I didn't kill him."

John stopped walking abruptly and spun around to face his friend. "Duke, that's a mistake! Get your ass over there and finish it!" His voice was sharp with anger as he pointed back toward where Agigi had been left.

Duke shook his head sadly. "I can't. I promised God I wouldn't even do this to Agigi." Tears threatened to spill down his cheeks as he refused to meet John's eyes.

John grunted in frustration. "Cut the God crap out!" John let out a frustrated sigh. "Fine, I'll do it, hold this." He threw Duke his bag before storming off.

The two slowly made their way back to the spot where Duke had left Agigi. But when they arrived, there was no sign of him; only a smattering of disturbed dirt and uprooted weeds remained.

John cursed loudly in frustration, darting his eyes around nervously for any sign of movement. "Well, that's not good," he muttered under his breath. "Damn it! Let's get the hell out of here before he regroups."

They sprinted past the wreckage that had torn through the prison's fence, Duke pushing past the jagged coils of razor wire and chain link fencing. The sun was beginning to set, making it harder for them to see ahead. They chugged up the steep incline of a hill, hoping for a better view. What they saw next filled Duke with dread. It wasn't just the prison in trouble—stopped cars were scattered along the highway, their owners standing helplessly next to them as their electric vehicles were powered down. But a few of the older gasoline vehicles still drove around, weaving between the incapacitated ones.

John gazed out at the growing chaos before him with shock and awe. "I knew it! The shit has officially hit!" he blurted, grinning from ear to ear.

"Why are you smiling?"

"Don't you get it? We're free, free from it all. Our prison sentences, an overreaching government, Democrats—I bet even those stupid automation bots got taken out!" His eyes glowed in anticipation of the nightfall.

"Democrats? Really? That's one of your big concerns?"

"Yep, libtards will be the first ones to go. Those unprepared shitheads."

"You know that's not necessarily true."

"I know, but it's a happy thought of mine so don't ruin it. Now let's get into the tree line before anyone notices us," directed John as they scrambled into nearby thick foliage.

Duke and John marched through the dark, silent woods until John was satisfied they were far enough away from the prison and highway. John pointed to a patch of trees that were clustered together, allowing them enough space to build a fire pit without being seen from the road.

Duke cleared away layers of dry leaves and twigs as John used a stick to carve out a Dakota fire hole. With a makeshift knife, crafted by John during his time in prison, he shaped a fire spindle from found wood pieces and assembled a fireboard from additional wood scraps. John operated the spindle, initially moving his hands together slowly and then increasing the speed. In a matter of minutes, a tiny ember began to smolder. John placed this ember in a bed of dried grass and leaves, referring to it as a bird's nest. With every gentle breath, the ember in his hands intensified, ultimately illuminating the surrounding area as it erupted into flames.

The two scrounged amongst their bags and backpacks for whatever food they had managed to scavenge up.

"Peanut butter, Ramen noodles, and some water," said Duke, surveying their meager selection.

"Yeah, I pretty much have the same thing. Not very much to get by on," sighed John as he placed another stick into the hole and reclined against an old tree trunk. The light illuminated John's face—weariness mixed with satisfaction in his expression, streaks of dirt and dried blood lingering around his eyes.

"I appreciate you saving me back there, John," offered Duke, breaking the silence between them.

"Don't be gay, and you're welcome," chuckled John, showing off his teeth as if it was just another day in the forest.

"Sorry I left—"

"Shut up Duke, I told you to. I ain't crying about it; neither should you." John's voice was blunt and firm as he stared into the dancing flames of the campfire.

After a brief pause, Duke tentatively inquired, "Agigi made it sound like they killed you. How did you get out of that?"

John winced in pain, pressing his hand to his ribs as he leaned against the tree trunk. "Yeah, I thought they were going to get me for good," he said with a groan. "Agigi left two guys with me and took two guys to go after you. Right before they could finish me off, that big O-Indian dude they call Chief suddenly appeared."

Duke's eyes widened at this. "That Native American guy that's always locked up in the SHU?"

John nodded. "Yep, he came in and messed those guys up fast. He helped me to my feet and said nothing before he walked away."

The fire between them crackled, casting strange shadows on their faces as Duke processed John's story. "Why would he help you?"

"Don't know, mate." John shrugged his shoulders and shook his head in confusion.

Duke then changed the subject to something else that was concerning him. "I thought an EMP would take out all the cars, power grid, and everything with a computer chip. *If* that's true, that doesn't look like an EMP out there."

"Relax," John replied. "I still think so, but there has always been a theory that an EMP would not do that much damage to gasoline cars—only a small portion. So, I bet most of those cars that are stopped on the road are those fully electric vehicles."

Duke raised an eyebrow skeptically. "So, an EMP won't take out all vehicles?"

John hesitated before replying, "Not exactly." He paused and cleared his throat before continuing. "There has always been a debate about this," he began. "Some believe that an EMP would just wipe out any unprotected electronics, while others think only a certain percentage of vehicles would be disabled. But now, most of our vehicles are electronic, so I think most gasoline and diesel engines will still be running." He took a drink of water before continuing. "But cars or no cars, they all will eventually stop anyway due to the supply chain's disruption. Without the power grid, there's no technology; no gas; no internet; no medical lifesaving technology; no ability to reproduce medicine in mass quantities; no electrical pumps to pump clean water into the cities; and no mass food production," he said grimly.

Duke's eyebrows furrowed as he looked down at John. "No one thinks about that, do they? About how dependent we are on electricity?" he asked somberly.

"Hell yeah, we are," John replied.

Duke stood up abruptly and looked up at the moon. "What if it's not an EMP? What just happened?" he asked.

John glanced up at him, a mischievous glint in his eye. "If it's not, we just escaped from prison, and they'll hunt us like dogs."

Duke paused for a moment, looking back at John, dumbfounded. "I don't know which one is worse—the apocalypse or being hunted down for the rest of my life."

"Is that a real question?" John asked.

"It was rhetorical, John," Duke replied softly.

John smiled reassuringly up at Duke, still holding the peanut butter jar in one hand, and said, "Doesn't matter, buddy—we'll pull through."

Duke felt a hard lump in his throat; it was as if all the moisture had vanished. He shifted his gaze to John, who, having finished his meal, was now cleaning the remnants of peanut butter from his fingers on his trousers.

"So, what's the plan? What are we going to do?" Duke asked hesitantly.

"Well, I'm going home," John said with a sly smile as he licked his fingers clean, "and you are going home."

"You're gonna walk to Virginia?" Duke blurted out incredulously.

John chuckled. "Walk, run, ride a bike, hitch a ride, steal a car. Yep, I'll do whatever it takes to get home. You will be doing the same to get back to Colorado."

Duke felt his heart sink. It was true—tomorrow they would have to part ways. He took in John's scruffy face and remembered all the times that John had pulled him out of trouble over the years; without John he probably would have ended up dead by now.

"Will I ever see you again, John?" Duke asked quietly, dreading the answer.

John clapped him on the back and shook his head gruffly. "Don't start doing all that pussy-ass sentimental stuff! But no, I hope I never see you again because I'll be with my wife and kids, and you will be with yours."

John pulled debris from the surrounding area and built a makeshift bed for himself with thick branches tied together by vines, covered in an assortment of decaying leaves. Duke watched as John crawled into his new bed and soon started snoring heavily. Duke envied him, not only for how soundly he was sleeping, but also because of the warmth that seemed to radiate off John's makeshift mattress.

Duke lay on the ground and looked up at the sky. It was

beautifully illuminated by millions of stars twinkling brightly like little lights vying for his attention. As he stared out into the heavens, Duke's mind drifted back to camping trips he had taken with his children when they were much younger in Divide, Colorado. Those days seemed so long ago now. The reality of a 500-mile walk ahead of him weighed heavily on his mind, and there was no way for him to escape it. With the power grid down, Duke knew that problems would only worsen with each day that went by, and persistence would be key in getting back home. He eventually managed to drift off to sleep against all odds, his body drained yet soothed by the peace of the night.

✳✳✳

John gently shook Duke's shoulder and his eyes opened slowly. He could see the sun daring to peek out just above the horizon as he followed John's faint silhouette in the low light to a small creek. His friend rinsed his face with a rag and Duke joined him, soaking his own cloth before dipping it in the murky water of the stream.

The duo stood up and Duke reached out his hand for John to shake but instead, his friend pulled him in for an embrace. He let go of Duke's hand and looked into his eyes intently as he spoke, giving one final warning: "No more messing around, Duke. Things are gonna get bad. So, take care of yourself."

Releasing one another, they started on their separate paths, Duke taking careful steps west and John quickly making progress toward West Virginia.

All the while, Duke whispered to himself for reassurance, "Just one step at a time, Duke, just one step at a time."

CHAPTER 2

KANSAS | APRIL 2035

Duke trudged down the deserted highway, feeling a mix of dread and exhaustion. He was wearing a dark brown military uniform with bright yellow Fort Leavenworth lettering on the back, and he desperately wanted to avoid being seen by anyone. A surprising number of gasoline-powered cars still traveled along the road, but Duke mostly kept to the tree line and fields leading away from them, knowing he needed to stay out of sight. When he spotted abandoned vehicles, he checked them for supplies in his quest for something to replace his uniform and hide his identity from potential onlookers. The Kansas air was warm during the day, but at night it dropped into the low forties, forcing Duke to rely on his Army survival training to build primitive shelters and keep himself fed and warm. His thoughts kept returning to what could have happened: Was this an EMP? If not, what caused it? Did this happen locally or nationwide? And most of all—how are his wife and kids faring in all of this?

Duke's head was filled with questions as he walked down the Kansas highway. He had read about electromagnetic pulses, seen them in movies and TV shows, but this didn't look like any EMP he'd ever seen before. According to John's research, even the most powerful EMP might only affect a small portion of electronic devices, and those stored underground were safe from its effects. But what was really devastating were the implications for the power grid: a compromised electrical system could bring down an entire nation, something they heavily depended on in today's tech-driven world.

Desperate for hydration after his prison escapade, Duke had already drunk all the water he'd brought with him and found a few more bottles in some cars; now there was nothing left. Perhaps he should try his luck at one of the farms he'd come across—one he encountered stood out since it looked empty at first glance. However, upon closer examination, Duke spotted an older couple walking around, tending to their chores, seemingly unaware of what had happened in the outside world.

Duke had to take a chance to find food and water. He carefully made his way across the dewy grass, avoiding the chickens that scurried out of his path. He could make out the silhouette of an older woman putting gardening tools into a shed. He held his breath, waiting for her to disappear before running toward the well. Crouching down, Duke filled up his bottle with cold water and splashed some on his face.

Suddenly, a commanding voice thundered, "On your feet, and keep your hands where I can see them!"

Duke slowly stood and raised his hands in surrender. Water droplets ran off his hair and arms as he nervously tried to explain himself. "Sir, I mean no harm; just needed some water," he said.

The older man replied gravely, "I can't take that chance, 'cause it looks like you're not where you belong."

Duke pleaded for mercy, not daring to meet the man's gaze. He slowly turned around and saw an elderly man in his early seventies wearing faded coveralls and a sweat-stained trucker hat with patches of wispy white hair peeking out from underneath. The older man held a side-by-side double-barrel shotgun pointed directly at Duke's chest. His eyes narrowed as he scrutinized Duke suspiciously.

"Are you one of them rapists or molesters I keep hearing about at Leavenworth?"

Duke shook his head, about to explain what had really happened when an older, heavier-set woman ran up behind the man.

"Bert! What are you doing?" she said, her hands flying to her face in shock.

"Kathy, call the sheriff's office, sweetheart, looks like we got one of them Fort Leavenworth boys on the loose." Bert spat on the ground. "You do that, boy? You the reason why my power has been off? You've been casing my house?" He adjusted his grip on the gun, studying Duke intently.

"No sir. The prison's power is out too," Duke replied quickly. "And to tell the truth a plane crashed into the prison and I took the opportunity to get home to my wife and kids. Like I said before, I'm only here because I just needed some water."

"The truth? A plane crashed into the prison? Oh, baloney!" shouted Bert, his face flushing with anger.

Kathy placed her hand gently on her husband's arm, her voice soft and pleading. "Just let him go, honey! Please! Just make him go away."

Bert nodded slowly and tipped his head in the direction he wanted Duke to go.

Duke raised his hands slowly, an unspoken prayer that he wasn't about to get shot, and started walking past the older couple. As he passed, Bert spoke again in a stern voice. "If I ever see you again, you'll force me to have to shoot ya. Please don't make me do that."

Duke glanced back at them before starting down the gravel driveway toward Freeman Farms. But no sooner had he stepped onto the highway than Duke heard a sound from the woods. He stopped and stared into the tree line, feeling more paranoid by the minute as Agigi's men could be anywhere by now. Then he heard a woman scream, pulling his attention away from the woods.

Instinctively, Duke ran toward the woman's cries for help. He followed the sound of her voice to a small blue house with a dirty white garage. As he stopped and listened, he heard something fall inside. Duke rushed down the drive and threw open the side door of the garage. Light spilled into the darkened room as dust kicked up in the air. In that moment, he saw it all—one man trying to undress a young-looking blonde woman while two others held down her arms. She wore blue jeans and a white T-shirt that had been partially torn, exposing her pink bra. Her eyes were wide with fear and desperation as the men turned to Duke. They looked like typical midwestern rednecks, all three of them reeking of body odor.

"Help me!" the woman pleaded.

The shirtless man smacked her face and shouted, "Shut up!" Pointing at Duke, he demanded, "Who the hell are you?"

"Nobody," Duke said confidently, "but you should let her go."

At this they all laughed mockingly. "Or what? You gonna save her? You're gonna fight all three of us?"

Drawing a deep breath and silently hoping for courage, Duke muttered to himself, "Well, I'm going to try."

An axe flew through the air, hitting its target with a sickening thud and showering Duke with blood. The other two men scrambled backward but were quickly cornered by a large-bodied man, who wielded his knife expertly as he disarmed them and dealt swift justice. Duke heard desperate cries from the young woman in the corner of the room, and turning his head groggily to look at her, he saw the mysterious man crouching next to her, speaking softly as if trying to comfort her.

Through the fog of Duke's daze, he heard muffled sounds echoing through what seemed like an empty hallway in a bad dream. He felt a presence above him and opened his eyes enough to see a figure looming over him, holding a bloody knife. As the figure moved closer into focus, Duke recognized familiar features on the man's face.

"Wait, what? You?" Duke said as darkness swept over him.

✳✳✳

"Private Hollander, get up now!" a voice boomed.

"What? Where are we?" asked Duke, blinking in confusion.

"Wherever I say we are, private! You got air guard so keep your head

on a swivel," the voice ordered.

"Yes Sargeant," Duke said hesitantly, standing with difficulty due to the ice-cold temperature and the weight of his gear. As he surveyed his sector of fire, Duke could identify the city they were in—Kiev, Ukraine.

"Contact left! Contact left fifty yards!" someone yelled over the radio and then an enormous explosion filled the air with dust and debris. Duke tried to steady the 240B machine gun when the dust settled and he saw a small child lying on the ground with a badly injured leg, bleeding profusely. Duke tried to spring out of his seat to help him but was held back by several hands belonging to his fallen comrades.

"Sargeant! I need to go help that kid; he's hurt!"

"It's just a Ukrainian child; not worth risking your life for. Besides, you can't even help your own family." His sergeant gestured toward the back of the vehicle where Duke could see his wife and two children crawling around, desperately trying to find him while screaming his name.

Duke felt the tight grip of multiple hands restraining him, holding him back as he desperately attempted to be reunited with his family. His eyes finally finding them, he strained against the hold and shouted, "I'm right here! Let go of me! I'm trying! I'm trying to get to you!"

The hands let go, and Duke locked eyes with his wife, his two children, and the Ukrainian child. He could feel their hurt and see how much he had let them down by leaving them. His wife spoke quietly, her voice trembling but laced with anger. "If you cared about us, you wouldn't be doing this to us. You wouldn't have left us! We don't need you anymore!"

Duke felt something cold and damp pressed against his face, and his eyes fluttered open. A blurred figure appeared before him—a young woman with curly blonde hair and sparkling blue eyes. Her skin was pale, almost translucent. She smiled, her full lips curling upward. It took all of his concentration to focus on her words; he didn't want to look at anything but her face. Her voice was sweet like butterscotch.

"Hey, he's awake," she said, smiling down at him. "You, sir, are a dreamer, aren't you?"

"Where am I?" Duke asked groggily.

"You're at my grandparents' family farm," the woman

answered warmly. "And the good news is I think you're going to make it."

"How long have I been out?"

"A couple of days," she replied gently.

The room began to spin as Duke tried to get up in a panic, but his legs buckled beneath him. The young woman helped him back onto the cot, where he lay dizzy and disoriented.

"I need to get to my wife and kids," Duke muttered, clutching his head.

"I can appreciate that, but you have a nasty concussion and hopefully you don't wind up with an infection in your head wound," the woman cautioned, adjusting the bandage over Duke's forehead.

Duke looked around and noticed all the other bandages covering his body—both forearms were wrapped tightly. "You fixed me up?" He grimaced.

"I did." She nodded. "My name is Julie Freeman, and luckily for you, I'm a pretty good veterinarian. I used medical glue in your head and in your forearms." Julie handed Duke a bottle of pills. "These are your antibiotics; they are precautionary, so you don't wind up with an infection," she explained.

"Doxycycline?" Duke eyed the label skeptically.

"Yes, and I'm sure it can be taken by both humans and animals," Julie reassured him. "I promise you don't have anything to worry about."

As Duke lay back down, he couldn't help wondering if the same could be said about his wife and kids—he had to get back to them.

"Thank you for fixing me up, Julie," he said through clenched teeth, pain radiating from his shoulder.

"Are you kidding me? It's the least I could do; thank you so much, Duke, for what you did!" Julie said with genuine appreciation.

"I just couldn't stand by and...wait? How do you know my name?" Duke asked, perplexed.

"I told her," Karl Blackburn replied gruffly. He had short

but thick black hair, and his coal-black eyes were set into his Native American features; he stood at six-foot-five, 240 pounds of pure muscle. He was an old special forces soldier rumored to be in prison for murder—a rumor Duke had heard whispered throughout Leavenworth but had never been able to confirm or deny. After witnessing the brutal efficiency of Karl's attack on Agigi's men in the garage, Duke knew Karl was capable of unspeakable violence—yet here he was offering kindness and protection. Duke felt confused and curious why Blackburn would risk himself to save him and John Roberts, but decided it wasn't the time to ask questions.

"Thanks, man," Duke uttered uncertainly.

Karl only nodded.

"Karl here says you two are friends," Julie said questioningly.

Duke glanced at Karl then back to Julie before replying, "Yep."

The voice of Bert—the aged farmer Duke had run into days before—echoed from the next room: "Well, aren't you the lucky one? My father always told me it's about who you know."

"That's right," Karl called out.

"Hey Karl," the old man said with a warm smile. "Duke, is it? I just want to say that I am sorry for the other day. I shouldn't have been so harsh on you."

Duke sat up slowly and nodded in understanding. "It's fine. I would have done the same thing."

An older woman stepped into the room and patted her husband on the chest. "I'm Kathy, and this is my husband Bert," she said with a genuine smile. "We wanted to thank you both for helping our granddaughter, Julie. Please let us repay you; we don't have much but can at least give you a proper supper and have you stay here as long as you need until you feel healed enough to be on your way."

Duke and Karl exchanged glances before Duke shook Bert's hand. "Yes ma'am, we would appreciate that."

Kathy smiled in response before scurrying off to the kitchen.

"Come on, Bert, let's start getting things ready and you boys sit back and relax."

✳✳✳

As the sky began to dim, Duke and Karl settled into an awkward silence in the living room. Duke was too exhausted to form words. His mind raced with memories of the past few days: the fight with Agigi, his wife and children back home, and a lingering concern for John's safety. Eventually gathering the will to speak, Duke asked Karl the question that had been weighing on his mind. "So, how long have you been following me?"

Karl answered plainly, "Since your fight with Agigi."

Duke felt annoyance bubbling up inside him; he didn't know why Karl had chosen to lurk in the shadows without offering aid. "You've been following me since then? How come you didn't help? Or at least link up with me instead of following me?"

Karl shrugged. "I wanted to see what type of man you were, how you conduct yourself, and what you were capable of."

Taking a moment to digest this, Duke finally asked his next question. "Okay, fair enough. And? What's your assessment so far?"

There was no mistaking the air of judgment as Karl replied dryly, "You're not a bad guy, but way too nice. Your intentions seem admirable. It seems that you'll likely put others before yourself. You're decent at one-on-one fighting but are complete shit when it comes to anything more than that. Good enough?"

Duke nodded slowly in agreement before Karl added another comment which made Duke wonder if they had really saved anyone at all: "Yeah, that's all fine and dandy here and now, but what the world is going to develop into, those traits are going to get you, or someone, killed."

Pointing toward the kitchen where Julie stood with her grandparents, Duke argued weakly, "But I...well...we ended up saving that girl in there."

Karl shook his head. "No, I saved her from being killed. You put her in jeopardy. Yeah, she would have been assaulted but alive. You busting in there trying to play the hero changed that. They would have killed her afterward because of you."

Duke shook his head and said, "Thanks for the lecture but why do you care?" He furrowed his brow in confusion.

"I overheard you and John talking. Heard you were going to Colorado Springs; that's where I'm headed. So, I figured I'd have better chances getting back if I had someone to watch my back but found out you're an amateur." Karl gestured with his hands as if weighing something on an invisible scale. "Can barely fight, minimal survival skills, and takes unnecessary risks. Yeah, amateur."

The room fell silent, and Duke started fidgeting nervously. His gaze shifted from side to side as if searching for an exit, finally settling on the figure beside him. The candlelight illuminated Karl's face—not quite a smirk, but not a smile either.

"So, what do you make of all this?" Duke asked, gesturing vaguely around them.

"Do you ever stop talking?" Karl replied with a hint of amusement in his voice.

Duke smiled sheepishly and said, "I haven't talked to anyone in days."

Karl chuckled softly before replying, "Except when a seventy-year-old man sticks a gun in your face. Hell, you were almost singing." He smirked as he took a sip of water before continuing. "From what I've seen, the evidence would say EMP. No power and the majority of electric vehicles shutting down. I don't know what else it would be. Doubt it was a CME."

"CME?" asked Duke, unfamiliar with the term.

"Coronal Mass Ejection from the sun," Karl explained before glancing up at the sky outside their window. The darkness seemed to overcome the room more quickly than before.

"Oh yeah, I remember John talking about those."

"Yeah, I know. He would never shut up when he was in the SHU."

Duke smiled fondly at the memory of John's constant chatter before asking another question. "Why were you in the SHU for so long?"

Karl sighed audibly before answering. "By request. It was quieter ... unless John was in there."

***

The antique oil lamps flickered and the shadows they cast danced around the room. All five of them were seated at the dinner table in the dark, eating quietly until Bert disturbed the silence with a groan.

"Ain't it just our luck that we gotta eat like this? I haven't had my power on in a few days now, don't know what's going on!" He threw his hands into the air before continuing, "My phone won't even turn on anymore either; reckon it's something to do with all these electrical problems."

Duke immediately jumped in. "It's an EMP; kind of like a big pulse of energy that scrambles electronic circuits and shuts everything down."

Kathy put her fork down as she listened, eyebrows raised in shock. "That sounds so scary—is it true?"

Bert scoffed. "Oh, don't worry too much, we've been through worse than this—Great Depression, World War Two ... all kinds of wars. America will survive. We always do; God provides for us if we let Him," he said confidently and crossed himself quickly at the end of his statement.

Duke smiled politely and then directed his attention to Julie. She looked young but, according to Bert, she was successful enough to own her own home. "How old are you, if you don't mind me asking? You seem rather young to already be a homeowner."

"I'm twenty-six, but I've been working with animals since I was a kid on my grandparents' farm—that's where I got my love for them from. Being a vet pays very well. Unfortunately, my parents passed away when I was still quite young, so I inherited it instead of buying it outright. Still though, some good came out of it I guess," she said somewhat awkwardly with a forced smile.

Kathy nervously cleared her throat before asking, "So, how long have you two known each other?" realizing too late that she shouldn't have asked.

Karl glanced over at Duke before responding with an awkward, "A few years."

All eyes drifted to Bert when he blurted out, "What did y'all do to get put in there?"

Julie and Kathy both reprimanded him for the inappropriate question.

Karl's nonchalant answer shocked them all. "I murdered someone who deserved it, and I think he stole some stuff or something of that nature. Never really got the whole story."

Kathy choked on her water at the confession as Julie patted her back. Everyone seemed relieved when Kathy caught her breath and suggested they talk about something else. "Would anyone like a drink?" she asked, then quickly left the room to get a bottle of wine and two beers.

"Bert, how is this cold without any power?" asked Duke before he took another sip, his taste buds rejoicing as the cold brew hit his lips after so many years without one.

"Oh, thank you for reminding me," said Bert. "I need to go to town to get more gas; been blowing through our fuel reserves."

Karl then asked when the last time Bert had gone into town for gas was.

"I imagine it's been over a week now; why do you ask?" inquired Bert as his eyes moved between Karl and the others at the table.

Karl took another sip of his beer and looked at one of the flickering flames inside an oil lamp. "Like what we were saying. If we're right about the EMP, the world is going to be a different place."

Bert adjusted his glasses and peered at Karl. "Not much crime around here, but I always put my old shotgun in the truck when I go to town anyway." He ran his hand through his graying hair.

"So, where are you boys headed to? And when will you be leaving us?" asked Kathy from the end of the circle.

Julie shifted closer to Duke. "Duke, you said something about a wife and two kids, right?" she asked, turning to look him in the eye while he answered.

He nodded and smiled slightly. "We're both headed for Colorado Springs, and we are trying to get home as soon as possible. I haven't seen my wife and kids in a long time."

"What about you, Karl? You got anyone special at home waiting for you?"

Karl fiddled with a beer can and avoided eye contact with everyone else. "Nope, hopefully just a bed with my name on it," he said without looking up from his plate.

Everyone exchanged a few more stories before they finished their drinks and cleaned up for bed.

✳✳✳

Ava and Michael stared wide-eyed at their mom, silently asking if it was true that their father was a bad man. Sarah could feel the tension in the room rising as she hesitated, unsure of how to answer her children's questions. She opened her mouth to speak when a sharp knock on the door interrupted her.

The kids gasped as Sarah went to answer the door. The man standing there was unfamiliar to them, and they scrambled behind Sarah for protection. His gaze seemed to search the room before he stepped inside without being invited. All three occupants screamed in unison.

Duke jerked awake, the suddenness of it causing him to gasp. His chest heaved with relief as he realized it had only been a nightmare. He glanced around and noticed Karl seated in a chair by the window, his features barely illuminated by the moonlight peeking through the curtains.

"Bad dreams?" Karl murmured from across the room.

"Yep," Duke replied, rubbing his eyes before sitting up straighter on the couch. "What about you? Can't sleep?"

Karl shook his head slowly before replying in a low voice, "Nah, haven't really slept in years."

CHAPTER 3

KANSAS | APRIL 2035

The morning sun streamed through the kitchen window, casting a soft golden glow on the assembled group. Duke and Karl smiled thankfully as Kathy served up a steaming plate of eggs.

Bert cleared his throat and set down his fork. "We wanted to talk about something over breakfast," he began, making them awkwardly shift in their chairs.

Julie glanced at him before turning her gaze toward Duke and Karl. "How did you two sleep last night?" she asked gently, her voice barely above a whisper.

Duke lied and said they had slept fine, and Karl chimed in with thanks. Julie glanced back at her grandparents, then looked to Duke again. "Do you know when you'll be heading out?" she asked quietly.

Duke told them that they would most likely leave that day, and Bert smiled broadly. "Well then, let Julie change your bandages and give you a few more for your journey." He paused for a moment before continuing, "Kathy and I talked about it last night, and we prayed about it, and God put it on our hearts to help you out." His eyes glimmered with warmth. "We have an old spare truck y'all can have."

Karl's jaw dropped in surprise, while Duke muttered his thanks, stunned by the generosity of the elderly couple who just days earlier had threatened him at gunpoint.

Bert was quick to speak up. "Don't thank us—thank the Lord! He works in mysterious ways through His faithful servants." Kathy leaned across the table and took Bert's hand in hers as he emphasized his point with a single finger tapping against the wooden surface.

Duke sat back in his chair, feeling the weight of Bert's words sink in. His heart was heavy, and he wasn't sure if he deserved such kindness.

Kathy worked quickly to prepare sandwiches for their travels, while Bert filled up old water jugs from a nearby faucet. Julie changed Duke's bandages, replacing them with fresh ones from a small brown bag.

It was time to say goodbye. Bert shook hands and hugged them both, then told the story he planned on telling the sheriff's office—that a couple of good old boys had rescued his granddaughter, and he didn't know where they were headed. Karl and Duke shared a silent nod of approval before Duke handed Bert a piece of paper with his address written on it. He explained that if they ever needed help, they could find him at that address.

Julie ran up to them again, tears streaming down her face as she thanked them one last time for what they had done. Before they could climb into the truck, Bert reminded them there was one last surprise waiting for them inside. With a big grin stretched across his wrinkled face, they said their final farewells.

Duke felt his stomach twist as he watched Julie turn to walk back into the house. As she stood paralyzed, Duke traced her line of sight and discovered Bert and Kathy in the clutches of two menacing figures, each wielding a blade pressed to their victims' throats. Agigi stepped out of the shadows, a makeshift bandage covering his injured eye and bruises marking his lips and other eye from his fight with Duke.

"You know, you really ought to lock your doors these days," he said.

"What do you want? We don't have much," Bert replied.

"Oh, little did you know, you have everything I want," Agigi said, pointedly turning his gaze to Duke. "Duke Hollander, so this is where you've been hiding! You're getting good, but I must insist that you stop playing hide and go seek on the account that it's pissing me off! Now Dookie, be a good little boy and come with us."

Duke pleaded with him to let the Freemans go but Agigi only laughed. "Oh, that's right, thank you for reminding Dookie. Sir and ma'am, you have been found guilty of harboring a fugitive, and I hereby sentence you to death," he said sinisterly before kissing Kathy on the cheek.

Julie screamed in protest while Karl stepped forward with an icy stare. "Let them go," he said.

Agigi grinned wide at the sight of him. "Well, look at what we have here, folks! Fort Leavenworth's very own super savage!" He spread his arms out as if presenting Karl. "You stay out of this; this isn't your fight. This isn't your problem, Chief."

Karl didn't waver. "Well, you just made it my problem—let them go," he commanded.

Agigi's icy gaze swept over the small crowd, and he let out an unpleasant chuckle. Bert stood next to Kathy, whose body trembled with fear. Duke stepped forward, determined to rescue them from Agigi's wrath.

"Don't do it, son; I'm an old man who's lived his life, and I know where I'm going," said Bert confidently. Tears rolled down Kathy's face as she bravely held her husband's hand.

"Come on now, let's talk about this, Isaac, just let them go!" pleaded Duke.

"I was done talking the moment you ratted me out and took that plea deal to save your sorry ass! Hey Sweetheart, you can thank Duke there for this," said Agigi, pointing at Julie. "Kill them!"

Agigi's men started to stab Bert and Kathy. Julie screamed as Duke quickly grabbed her and threw her in the back of the truck. He tried starting the old farm truck. After what seemed like an eternity, though only a few seconds, the truck fired up. Duke quickly released the clutch, and the truck launched forward. As Duke drove down the driveway, he realized two of the men were in the back with Julie. Duke made a hard left out of the driveway, causing the vehicle's back end to fishtail. The motion sent one of the attackers flying out of the truck and into a speed limit sign with a sickening thud. Duke started to slow down to help Julie.

"What are you doing? Don't stop, we don't know if Isaac has a vehicle or not. Keep going!"

Duke saw what Bert had prepared for them. Karl was loading an antique double-barrel shotgun, and in the rearview mirror, Duke saw Julie being pummeled by a large man. He stamped on the brakes, sending the man careening into the back of the cab. His head crashed through the back window, spraying glass across the cab. Duke accelerated away, throwing the man back towards the tailgate, giving Karl enough time to aim his gun at the assailant. The man regained his composure and pinned Julie down in the truck bed as he strangled her. Karl pulled the trigger and the old shotgun roared next to Duke's ear. He felt a concussive wave that made him swerve slightly as a 12-gauge buckshot ripped through the man's face, disintegrating it into a pink mist that washed away with the wind. Julie lay underneath the motionless body, blood covering her.

Duke slowed to a stop and jumped out of the truck, opening the tailgate. Julie lay on her back in a pool of her assailant's blood. The cool air caused her to shiver violently, and she stared up at them with hollow eyes. Her once-blonde hair was now matted and dark with blood, giving her an eerie resemblance to Carrie from the horror movie after the bucket of pig's blood had been dumped on her.

***

Duke drove the old truck, feeling awkward every time he had to shift gears with the stick shifter wedged tight between Julie's legs. Karl and Duke exchanged a few words occasionally, but otherwise the cab was filled with a heavy silence as

Julie stared out the windshield, her sunken eyes empty of emotion. The only break in her trance-like state came when they stopped at a small pond so she could wash off some of the blood and grime caked onto her skin. Duke wasn't sure if it was better for him to smell the stagnant pond water or the metallic odor of dried blood, which seemed to linger no matter how many miles they drove away from the scene of violence.

Karl seemed unfazed by what had happened, but Duke couldn't shake the images from his head. He had been through plenty during his time in the military, yet nothing could have prepared him for what he had witnessed these past couple days—Julie's captors being killed brutally, and her grandparents murdered right before her eyes.

Karl suggested that they siphon gas from abandoned vehicles whenever they came across a gas engine. But nothing ever worked out—the tanks were already empty, every gas station had a sign stating they were out of fuel, and even the stored fuel Julie got from her grandparents was running out. The old truck didn't get great gas mileage, so Karl suggested that they only drive at night to save fuel. When they found an area suitable enough, Duke would build a temporary lean-to with branches and moss while Karl foraged for food and water nearby. Julie would sleep across the seats in the truck during the day until it was time to move on again. Through a couple hundred miles of driving, Julie had only said a few sentences.

Duke was filled with despair and confusion as he looked around the empty Kansas countryside. It was hard to believe that within a week, their beloved United States had been brought to ruin. While it was peaceful in the small towns, Duke knew that the true chaos would be found in the larger cities. There were some who refused to believe that all this destruction could be possible, but Duke knew better. He feared that when the chaos set in, most people wouldn't survive it.

The thought of how many people had already been killed

haunted him day and night. Duke couldn't help but imagine the hundreds of thousands of lives lost on the first day from plane crashes alone. When it came time for Duke to sleep, his dreams and nightmares kept him awake. In prison they had given him pills to suppress his PTSD-induced dreams, but now he was left to confront them every night without any form of escape. His restless nights only heightened his anxiety further.

Fortunately for Duke, Karl started opening up a little bit more as time went by. So at least he had someone to make small talk with while he dodged his nightmares.

"Tell me about this group you're a part of," Karl said, his gaze flickering across the flames.

"It's a tight-knit community focused on preparing for emergencies and providing for our families with others who are like-minded," Duke replied. "I don't know what's become of it since I was locked up—no one has been in contact with me for a while so I'm not sure if they even want me back." He paused and looked away sadly, thinking of his family.

Duke asked if Karl had any such support system himself and Karl shook his head. "I'm in the same boat—not sure if they'll welcome me back either."

Duke smiled hesitantly and said, "Maybe if everything works out all right, our groups can join forces and help each other out."

Karl scoffed. "These guys don't play well with others."

***

Over the next couple of days, Duke drove. It was mostly spent in near silence. The road was clogged with many broken-down cars, and they had to drive slowly. Karl estimated they were about halfway home.

Duke saw a woman in blue waving him down with a flashlight and standing next to a car with the hood open on the side of the road. He started to slow down out of curiosity and kindness, not responding when Karl spoke up.

"What are you doing? I can understand wanting to help people, but this isn't going to end well," Karl said with suspicion in his voice.

The truck came to a stop, and Duke rolled down his window as the woman smiled and came closer.

"Hey, what seems to be the matter?" Duke asked her with a friendly smile.

She thanked him for stopping and explained that she thought her car was out of gas or something was wrong with it before requesting that he take a look at it. Getting out, he agreed, but just as he moved toward the front of the car, two men jumped out from behind it and pointed assault rifles at Julie and Karl. Duke froze for a few seconds, then tried to run across the street, only to hear another gun cock behind him.

"Turn around there nice and slow," said the woman.

"Really?"

"Oh, don't feel bad; you're not the only one. This used to belong to someone else," the woman said with a smile. She was a beautiful brown-haired, brown-eyed woman in her late thirties, Duke guessed. But she was as crooked as she was beautiful, standing there with a revolver pointed at Duke's face.

"What do you want from us?" Duke asked.

The two men forced Karl out of the truck and led him over to Duke's side.

"We'll be taking the truck, your supplies, and the girl," the woman said.

"No, you will not," Karl said calmly.

"What makes you think that? You're the ones with guns pointed at you, you stupid spic!" The woman sneered.

Suddenly, they heard the truck roar to life and saw Julie behind the wheel, driving off.

"That's why," Karl said with a short-lived grin.

"Okay, say what you want; that silly girl just cost y'all

your lives! Move it!" the woman barked.

They ordered Duke and Karl into the ditch while the woman and her two men stayed on the road, all of them shining flashlights in their faces.

"Why are you doing this? Kansas girls don't seem like the kind to steal or kill," Duke said to the woman.

"First of all, I'm from Chicago, and people like you two are going to help us get back to LA. But like I said, your little girlfriend just forfeited your lives." She paused. "Well, it's been fun, boys—any last words?"

Karl answered, "Native American."

"What?"

Karl continued, "I said I'm a Native American, not Mexican, you ignorant bitch!"

The woman replied in a patronizing tone, "Ohhh, so you're a savage then?"

"You have no idea." Karl looked at the woman with an icy glare.

The woman and her men aimed their weapons.

"Hold up, Nancy, we got a couple of cars coming. Let's wait for them to pass," said one of the men.

"So, while we wait, you have any other smart-ass things to say?" asked the woman.

Two cars passed the group. Their headlights shined brightly. A third vehicle came into view. Karl recognized the sound and shape of the third one.

"No, I'm good," Karl said with a smile.

When the woman and her two men turned to see the truck speeding at them, Julie plowed into them, smashing them into the back of their broken-down vehicle. The impact seemingly made their bodies explode. Both vehicles flew into the ditch with tremendous force. The sound of crunching metal and glass echoed across the empty farmland that surrounded them.

The air was thick with debris. He saw shards of glass mixed in with supplies and pools of blood spattered across the destroyed wreckage. He searched frantically for Julie, and to his surprise he found her slumped over in the passenger seat. She was unconscious and bleeding, clearly not wearing a seatbelt. Duke climbed through the window and carefully pulled her out, passing her to Karl who quickly brought her away from the car to a nearby field.

"Stay here with Julie; I'm going to see what supplies I can salvage from the wreckage," Karl said before taking off at a sprint into the darkness.

Julie had already regained consciousness. They assessed their losses and gains, noting that while they were missing some essentials like water, they had acquired two backpacks, a buck knife, a small hand axe with a broken handle, an intact double-barrel shotgun, a 357 revolver with five rounds, and a box of 12-gauge shells from the glovebox. With frustration Karl remarked how it could have been worse.

By the time Karl returned after searching for freshwater unsuccessfully, Duke and Julie had changed each other's bandages near the warm light radiating from the Dakota fire pit John had taught Duke to construct earlier.

"Do you want to talk through it?" Duke asked.

"I have a better question, what were you thinking?" Karl yelled.

"Calm down, man."

"Calm down? I just wanted to get back home safely with you two. But that doesn't look like it's going to happen," Karl continued.

"What do you mean?" Duke asked.

"You need to be tougher, Duke. When you fought Agigi, you could've killed him; instead, he probably went on to kill who knows how many people. That girl over there will be forever changed because of this situation. Does God's law not matter anymore? Thou shalt not kill? Newsflash: that doesn't work now. And now with that lady back there. I told you it wasn't going to end well, and now look at us—we almost got killed!"

Karl then redirected his attention to Julie. "I understand everything you've been through, but your suicidal attempt cost us our supplies and vehicle. We don't have any water now, so we'll have to go into town and risk getting some. I'm not here to babysit you—if you're no longer useful then I'll leave without a second thought," he barked at her.

Julie nodded, just gazing at the fire, seemingly in a trance. Duke took Karl's words to heart—they were difficult to hear but accurate. He realized that it was his fault: many had died due to his decision not to kill Agigi, and many more had their lives altered. His return home was already challenging, but with Agigi hunting him down, it seemed almost impossible. Back in jail he had promised God he would never take another life again, but Agigi was making it arduous to abide by that solemn vow. Duke had made a lot of bad decisions throughout his career, getting tangled up with Isaac Agigi being one of the most shameful ones.

CHAPTER 4

KANSAS | APRIL 2035

The next morning, Karl announced that they had to press on right away if they wanted to find water before they became even more dehydrated. Duke nodded in agreement, but Julie just gave them a nonchalant gesture as if it didn't bother her either way.

Duke adjusted his stride accordingly so that Julie could keep up with him and Karl's steady, military-trained pace. He noticed how she winced each time her feet touched the ground and he silently thanked himself for packing a few extra pairs of socks that she could use.

The trio finally saw the faint outline of Hays, Kansas, on the horizon. Before making their way to the town, Karl wanted to look around from the overpass above. Duke was shocked at how many people and vehicles were scattered across the small truck stop town below them. Even though cars were everywhere, the crowd had gathered around a fuel truck, and they could clearly hear their desperate cries for fuel echoing in the air.

They maneuvered cautiously down from the overpass, advancing stealthily towards the closest gas station that didn't have anyone near it. Karl signaled to Duke, both halting beside the shattered glass door of the establishment. Silently, he mouthed the word "slow," counting down from three with his fingers. Taking a deep breath, he navigated over the fragments of glass and stepped into the interior of the store, with Duke trailing closely, his shotgun elevated.

The shelves were nearly empty, faint traces of rot in the air. Karl quickly checked each aisle while Duke stood guard at the entrance. They found an employees-only door that was locked but could smell something coming from within—a putrid odor indicative of death. Julie arrived soon after, cringing at the smell.

"Dead body," said Karl as he gestured to the door.

Duke and Karl looked at each other, their years of military experience allowing them to intuitively and silently communicate their plan. Duke nodded his head in agreement and pointed toward the locked employees-only door. With a single powerful kick from Karl's size 15 boot, the door splintered open. The trio stepped inside, waves of rot and decay hitting them like a wall. Julie retched while the veterans pulled scarves up over their noses against the smell. The sound of a million flies filled the air like bees as they noticed the white middle-aged man slumped in a chair with his head tilted back in death. A revolver lay spent on the ground with bits of brain, bone, and hair spattered across the wall behind him. It was obvious that he had been holed up in this office for some time—there was a bucket of feces and urine in one corner and wrappers from various food items littered around.

"You ever wonder what it takes to drive someone to take their own life?" asked Julie, her voice flat.

The two men exchanged glances before Duke replied, "The man probably could not handle what had happened to his livelihood or simply no longer had the will to want to live."

"Starting to understand that more and more every day," said Julie without emotion.

Karl laid a hand on her shoulder before quietly instructing her to stay put as he made his way toward a clothing rack.

Duke watched Julie slowly nod her head, her shoulders sunken and her head hanging low.

"Here, these should fit you." Karl tossed Duke and Julie each a gray T-shirt.

Duke, Karl, and Julie carefully scanned their surroundings as they left the gas station sporting their new "Welcome to Hays" T-shirts. The three of them scurried through Hays, their eyes darting from vehicle to vehicle in search of supplies. Duke couldn't help but feel sorry for his fellow countrymen as they scanned the abandoned streets of a city where electricity and infrastructure no longer existed. He knew this was nothing compared to the larger cities like NYC, Chicago, or LA where millions would be forced to go without basic necessities and with no survival skills or supplies.

After what seemed like hours of scavenging, they heard shouting in the distance. Duke saw a hulking lifted truck with a rebel flag billowing behind it as it approached a large mob of people that had gathered around a fuel truck. Four burly men exited the cab with an assortment of weapons and one of them shot a gun into the air. The crowd hushed as he spoke. Karl stepped forward cautiously and Duke and Julie followed close behind.

Duke surveyed the scene and immediately knew what was going on. The men were stealing the fuel truck, but they were also actively robbing innocent bystanders. He saw people in the crowd holding up cash offerings as the men moved around them. Despite their attempts to appease them, Duke knew that those notes of currency were worth nothing in the current state of eastern Kansas.

"What's the plan?" Duke asked Karl, a silent observer of the crime taking place.

"We are not going to get into a firefight over them robbing people. So, the plan is to stay out of it," Karl replied somberly.

Duke sighed heavily; he wanted to help others, yet the situation was not their problem, and they had no business involving themselves. Then he noticed Julie was missing. "Hey! Where's Julie?!"

Karl nodded his head in disbelief as he pointed toward Julie, who was sprinting toward the large fuel truck.

Duke and Karl raced after her, car to car, trying to remain unnoticed by the criminals as they closed in on their target. To their surprise, Julie opened the door of the truck with caution and carefully shut it once inside. She started up the engine, which roared loud enough for everyone to know someone else was getting away with their stolen property.

"Hey! Get out of my truck!" one of the men shouted as he began to chase after her.

Julie floored it in reverse until she reached Duke and Karl, who had just caught up to her.

"C'mon, get in!" Julie yelled, revving the engine of her newly acquired vehicle. Duke and Karl leapt into the back of the truck as Julie quickly sped off down the road. With a loud bang, the men fired their shotguns at the tailgate of the truck, shattering the back window. Julie's whoops and hollers filled the air as she drove faster and faster away from danger. Their group drove a few miles more until Karl finally banged on the side of the pickup and shouted for her to pull over.

"Let her off easy, Chief," pleaded Duke.

Karl shot him an icy stare before turning his attention to Julie. He approached her with anger only to find her curled up in a tight ball, sobbing quietly. He realized no words were necessary; she was overwhelmed by what had just happened. His heart softened at the sight of her fragile state, so he picked her up and held her close. Soon enough they all piled back into the truck and continued down the road toward their destination.

✳✳✳

Daddy, when are you gonna come home?

As soon as I can.

Do you still love us?

Yes, of course, I do. Why would you ask me that?

Because people tell us that you don't.

Are you a bad man, Daddy?

No, I'm not—who's telling you these things?

Then why are you in prison?

Duke was jolted awake by the squeal of the truck's brakes. He felt Julie slumped against his shoulder, snoring softly. Carefully, he shifted her to the other side before she could wake up.

"How long have we been out?" he asked groggily as Karl looked ahead through the windshield.

Karl pointed at the overpass in front of them and Duke squinted to make out what had stopped their truck: Vehicles were lined up in a barricade across the road, arranged in such a way that allowed small cars to pass, but left no room for big trucks like theirs.

"I don't like the way this feels. Is there a way around it?" Duke asked, rubbing his eyes.

"What about the off-ramp?" Julie piped up.

"That's blocked off too," Karl replied. "The sign said Goodland, Kansas."

The group paused to consider their options before Duke spoke up again.

"You want to take a closer look?" he suggested, peering into the darkness ahead.

Karl inched the truck forward, ever so slowly, and soon they were parked at the beginning of the blockade. Through the remnants of the shattered back window, a faint noise reached Julie's ears from behind them.

Karl and Duke spun around, their eyes wide with shock. Illuminated in the headlights was a gray unmarked car pushed into place behind them, followed by several men carrying assault rifles trained their way. A man with a bullhorn boomed instructions from the overpass above.

"This is Goodland Police Department; proceed through the checkpoint for further inspection and instruction."

Julie turned to Karl, her voice trembling. "It's the police; maybe they could help us?"

Karl shook his head slowly. "I don't think that's a good idea.

Hate to remind you, but besides us being felons who escaped from a federal military prison, if they have some type of martial law in place, they will probably confiscate this truck, our supplies, and our weapons." His voice was tight with worry.

"I'm really not enjoying this whole end of the world thing so far," Julie said sarcastically.

Karl sighed heavily. "Then you're definitely not going to enjoy this next part." He braced himself against the wheel as he called out: "Fuck it, everybody get down!"

He slammed his foot onto the gas pedal and the truck roared backward, crashing into the car behind them, sending it spinning out of the way. The men on the overpass opened fire on Julie's newly commandeered ride as Karl sharply pulled off a 180-degree spin, slamming the stick shift from reverse into first gear and flooring it forward. Bullets ripped through the windshield, showering glass shards everywhere and making it difficult to see. Karl expertly maneuvered them away despite the barrage of bullets that battered the truck's hood as smoke started pouring out of it.

Julie screamed in terror as Karl steered the truck into the cornfield. She held onto the armrests for dear life, her knuckles turning white. The truck bounced over the uneven terrain, and Duke could barely make out the path ahead through the thick dust that had settled on the remains of the windshield. When Duke looked over at Karl, he was beaming ear to ear.

"Are you enjoying yourself there?" he asked.

"Yep; reminds me of growing up in the country in Missouri," Karl said with excitement in his voice.

Duke smiled, understanding what Karl meant—back home in Iowa, Duke and his friends had done plenty of crazy stuff like this too.

"As fun as that was, we have a problem," Karl said, his expression sobering.

Julie groaned. "Now what?"

Karl pulled the car up to the side of the road and jumped out, popping open the hood. Duke approached cautiously as a hot rush of air filled with aromas of burning oil and grease blew out. Thick, white smoke billowed into the air while Duke rummaged around inside.

"They shot the radiator, and it dumped all of its fluid," Duke assessed grimly. "It's probably not going to last much longer."

Duke had studied automotive technology in college, but he disliked it. Fortunately, his knowledge was enough for him to repair his own car when needed. However, now that the apocalypse had hit, not even the best mechanic could have saved the truck.

So, they made the decision to drive until their vehicle died—which it did after five miles. The trio abandoned the truck and unloaded their supplies onto the side of the road. Karl pulled out a map and said, "Looks like we got around fifteen more miles to the next town; you ready?"

Julie responded dryly, "Do we have a choice?"

Karl shook his head and said firmly, "Not really."

✳✳✳

Julie's foot pain had become too great to go on any further, and they had to take a few rest breaks. She used the bandages Duke had given her to patch up her injuries as best she could. The trio were ever vigilant during their eight-hour, fifteen-mile journey west, taking care not to be seen by anyone.

The sunrise eased across the sky like a brush of pastels. Duke, tired and dirty from the journey, still felt elation as he saw Kanorado, Kansas, right on the border of Colorado and Kansas. The sight of it was closer to home and his family than he had ever been before.

They reconnoitered the small town from afar, making sure not to be detected lurking around. A crisp breeze blew across the barren farm fields, carrying with it the smell of moist earth—a scent that reminded Duke of his childhood in Iowa with its endless cornfields and soybeans. But this smell also evoked memories of his mother, the florist and gardener who instilled in him a love for plants and gardening.

I hope you're okay, Mama.

Duke peered through the foliage and saw a roadblock with two vehicles manned by armed guards patrolling the only entrance into the town. Karl quietly surveyed the scene behind him, his brow wrinkled in concentration as he counted out loud. "One...two...three...four of them."

Julie squirmed anxiously next to Duke. "Can't we just ask for help?" Her voice was strained with desperation.

"I get it, we're all tired, but we have to make sure it's safe and that we know what we're getting ourselves into," Karl responded gruffly.

"Can't we just walk around this?" Julie persisted.

Karl sighed heavily. "We could, but last night's trek used up the majority of our food and water. So, to keep going wouldn't do us any good, not until we can resupply."

Duke placed his hand on Julie's shoulder soothingly while looking at Karl. "Listen," he said softly, "Karl's right. We need to resupply no matter what, but we can't afford any unnecessary risks." He paused, locking eyes with Julie to ensure she understood his words. "But if there's a chance to ask for supplies without stealing or someone getting hurt, I promise we'll make that call together."

The sound of tiny rain droplets hitting the leaves above them started off slow then began to pick up tempo.

"Okay, sounds like a plan," replied Julie, finally relenting.

"All right, let's move in, on me," declared Karl.

CHAPTER 5

KANSAS | APRIL 2035

Karl crept into town, examining every abandoned dwelling he could find. The rain intensified as the trio drew nearer to the city limits. Silently darting from shack to house, they tested each door for a way in. Even with the rainfall blanketing their movements, something about this place felt off. Duke wished for a thick layer of fog to settle over the eerie atmosphere.

As the drizzle developed into a full-on downpour, Karl and Julie began to race against time, frantically searching for an unlocked door. Duke knew that any roaming vehicles could spot them—not knowing what their reaction would be—so speed was key.

"We need to hurry," he warned.

Just then, Julie stopped.

"What? What is it?" Duke asked, following her gaze to a nearby window where a little boy stood staring at them. Caught off guard, the trio awkwardly waved and forced a smile in his direction, which he reciprocated before quickly disappearing inside his home.

"That was creepy," Julie uttered.

Karl's gaze flew around the area in search of a place to hide as they ran away from the kid, who was threatening to rat them out. He noticed a small, metal shed that was locked and tightly shuttered, surrounded by a bed of wilted flowers struggling against the pouring rain. Karl took a few steps back and kicked at the wooden door until it creaked open. Duke wrinkled his nose at the pungent smell of gasoline and oil that filled the tiny shelter, knowing that it would be tight and uncomfortable, but it was still better than being outside in the pouring rain. They used a cinder block to hold shut the damaged door and watched helplessly as small droplets weaseled through the roof and spattered against the tools. The sound of heavy rain pounding on the metal roof made it difficult to hear anything else.

"So, what's the plan?" Julie asked over the noise of the storm, her voice barely audible.

"We should catch whatever rainwater we can with whatever containers we have," Karl suggested, motioning to an old tin bucket that sat abandoned in one corner of the shed. "It'll help us rehydrate before finding somewhere else safe."

Duke nodded in agreement, looking around for any other objects he might find useful. "I was thinking about hunkering down here and getting some sleep instead of doing shifts on guard duty," he said tentatively.

"That would be nice," Karl replied thoughtfully, "but I think it's best if someone stays up on watch just in case something happens. I'll take first shift." He moved a rake behind him as he settled into his seat.

Duke was haunted by the memories of his deployments in Ukraine. Fifteen-hour patrols and missions, followed by hours of radio guard and rooftop watch each night; in between he had to burn and stir everyone's poop in a small barrel with a metal stake and JP8. It was pure misery, yet Duke never got a full night's sleep.

Julie had already drifted off into slumber, while Duke was still wide awake. No matter how exhausted he felt, his mind kept racing and wouldn't rest. It became a routine for him to talk to Karl when he couldn't sleep anymore, even though he knew he should be getting rest.

The oppressive humidity of the shed made Duke's skin glisten with sweat. He wiped his hand across his forehead, but the beaded moisture quickly gathered again.

"I'm trying to adjust to this world," he said. "I'll do whatever I have to in order to survive—but killing is going to be tough for me."

"You were in the military, though," Karl interjected. "You must have taken lives while you were in Ukraine. What makes this any different?"

Duke paused and shifted uncomfortably before responding. "There's a lot of guilt ... things I did that I shouldn't have—or should've prevented."

Karl nodded understandingly and looked away, giving Duke some space. Then Duke stood up and moved aside a cinder block, revealing an improvised rain catcher—a plastic two-liter soda bottle with the top quarter cut off and inverted inside the bottom half. Water was already steadily collecting in it.

"Looks like we'd all have enough to drink soon," Duke observed, taking a small sip from the container before offering it to Karl. Then he glanced over at Julie and sighed heavily. "So, what are we going to do about her?"

Karl slowly scratched his chin as he considered the question. "I really don't know," he said in a low voice.

"Like I said, I may not even be allowed back in my group. They're private and exclusive, so they'll probably decline her request to join. As for me ... well, I have no idea."

"What did you do? Go to prison or something?" Karl asked sarcastically.

Duke smirked and nodded silently before continuing. "The group is Christian based; it began with people from our church but grew much bigger than that over time. I wouldn't blame them if they didn't take me back since I went against their rules by breaking the law. Rules are rules after all."

Karl snorted. "Forget them," he said darkly, his face twisted in disgust.

Duke shifted uncomfortably, not sure if he agreed or not. "What do you mean?" he asked carefully, hoping for an explanation.

"They sound like a bunch of hypocritical pricks," Karl spat. "Didn't Jesus break bread with the thieves and prostitutes? I hate people who preach one thing and then act differently."

Duke couldn't deny it. His only hope was that the church would take in his wife and children. In desperation, he looked to Karl.

"You could stick with me," Karl said, but there was an edge to his voice that gave Duke pause. "But to be honest, I'm not sure if I can trust you long term or not."

Duke's brow furrowed as he asked, "What do you mean you can't trust me?"

"No offense, Duke," Karl replied slowly, "but you're too nice. Soon this world is only going to speak one language: war. Where people must eat, think, sleep, and breathe like animals. Niceness won't help anyone survive then."

Duke felt a chill run down his spine at the thought of such a bleak future. He shook his head grimly. "What if a man is capable of great violence but chooses not to be violent?" he asked quietly.

Karl pondered the question for a moment before answering. "You need to figure out something—what is better? A man who is capable of violence but chooses not to be or a man who is capable of violence and knows when to use it or not?"

Duke considered carefully. "After everything that's happened, I made a promise to God," he said solemnly. "I'd rather be a man who is capable of violence but chooses not to be violent."

Karl emitted a heavy sigh. He wiped his forehead of the never-ending accumulation of sweat. "Yeah, but what if that promise gets someone close to you killed? Throughout my many years, I've learned two things for certain: one, most people are stupid."

Duke couldn't help but chuckle at Karl's comment.

"And number two," Karl continued with an intense gaze, "I'd rather regret something I've done than something I haven't."

Duke averted his gaze and shifted uncomfortably as painful memories of past mistakes rose in his mind. He knew he was capable of much in this new world they were living in, thinking maybe his past would serve him well. Still, he wished he didn't have to participate in it all. Duke often dwelled on the past—it was a way for him to punish himself when no one else did. Perhaps he felt he didn't deserve to move forward or live in the present.

❉ ❉ ❉

Duke felt as though his chest had been caved in as he was sat up by an unknown Ukrainian soldier. His rifle lay forgotten in the dirt and his helmet lost in battle. He dragged his hand over his face, only succeeding in grinding the hot sweat and dust into a gritty paste that glued itself to his cheekbones. "You okay?" the soldier yelled.

Duke could hear the shouts of men and gunfire growing ferocious. He scrambled to his feet with the help of the Ukrainian soldier and opened his eyes to see nothing but a thick cloud of dust lit by blinding rays of sunlight. His ears still rang loudly as someone over the radio shouted, "Contact left! Dismount and get that 240 over here and lay down some suppressive fire!"

Without hesitation, Duke limped toward the thirty-pound machine gun. He rolled the dead soldier that had previously been manning the gun away. Duke threw on an assault pack that was full of belts of 7.62x54 ammo and sprinted toward the deafening sounds of war, ignoring the stinging sensation of sweat dripping into his eyes as he searched for his men. An explosion went off to his right and knocked him off his feet. A large man in a US uniform stood over him.

"You okay? Wake up, hey, wake up, Duke."

Duke opened his eyes to find Karl shaking him awake. His voice was a harsh whisper, and each word sent a chill down Duke's spine.

"We have a problem. Julie is missing," Karl said, looking out the broken door.

Just then, Julie came in with a look of confusion plastered

on her face. "Did I miss something?" she asked.

"Where the hell were you?" Karl snapped, gripping her arm tightly.

Julie yanked her arm away from him and replied, "I had to pee. Is that okay with you? Let me go!"

Karl ignored her and raised his eyebrows as he asked, "Were you followed? Did anybody see you?"

Duke heard birds chirping nearby, brakes squeaking to a stop and multiple truck doors slamming shut. His heart raced as he looked through a small hole leading outside. Sure enough, six armed men had gathered outside their hideout.

Karl quickly grabbed his revolver and muttered under his breath, "Damn it."

Duke peered out of the small shed, his heart sinking. He heard one of the men bellow a warning: "Y'all come out with your hands up!"

Karl shot Duke a glare and immediately began assessing their options.

Quickly, Duke swiped his shotgun and bag out of sight, tucking them underneath a heavy tarp in the corner. "Karl, put your gun and backpack under here."

"No, we got to sacrifice half of it by leaving it out in the open." Karl paused and exchanged reassuring looks with Duke and Julie. "So, they don't come in here and feel like they must search this shed. Better to lose half our stuff than all of it."

The trio walked out cautiously, hands raised in surrender. The men grabbed zip ties from their pockets and trussed the three of them up with their hands behind their backs before another truck pulled up with four more armed men.

Karl was the first to speak up. "What do you want?" he said, only to receive an ironic inquiry from one of the men in reply: "I was about to ask y'all the same thing."

The armed men stood in a semi-circle facing them. One short, fat, middle-aged man asked who they were.

"We're just passing through," said Duke. "It was raining,

and we used that shed for cover." He tilted his head in the direction of the shed. "Didn't think it was a big deal. We mean no harm."

"Those are some llies you are spewing over there," said another man with a large hunting rifle slung across his chest. "If you meant no harm, why do you have a gun? If you're not up to anything, why all the sneaking around and trespassing?"

Duke shrugged and looked down. He watched as his shadow played across the cracked asphalt of the street. It looked like he was walking on water.

Duke wasn't very good at lying, so he decided to stay silent.

"Incorrect answer," said one of the men as he jabbed Duke in his ribs with his gun for emphasis. "I can tell you are lying about something."

Karl raised his voice slightly so everyone could hear him clearly. "There's no need for that. We're being peaceful here."

"What are you going to do with us?" asked Julie.

"That's not for us to decide; that's the mayor's job."

"The mayor?"

"That's right, the man that takes care of the people. He makes all the big decisions around here. He makes everything run a little smoother."

Duke, Karl, and Julie were put in the back of a beat-up green truck. The sun hid behind a dark overcast that still loomed in the sky. Duke thought the only benefit of being zip-tied and thrown into the back of a truck was that the ride provided temporary relief from the heat when cool air blew across his face. As they drove down the main street of the town, Duke noticed businesses' windows were boarded up, most likely from looting. Others were converted into more seemingly useful spaces. A few dozen people stood in line at those buildings. The people turned their heads and gawked at the latest trespassers paraded down the main street. The truck finally came to a stop in front of a big white house with a covered porch, guarded by yet more armed men. Long flowerbeds lined both sides of the sidewalk, starting from the entrance to the building and stretching all the way up the huge flight of stairs leading to a door.

Karl shook his head at the sight in front of him. "Seems a bit excessive for such a little town," he commented to one of the men, who wore a long-sleeved flannel top with a grubby white shirt underneath.

"I guess you can never be too careful nowadays," the man replied.

The guards brought them into a large office where they were met by a tall, portly man in his sixties. Small, circular glasses perched on the bridge of his nose and short, salt-and-pepper hair lay flat against his scalp. His white shirt was tucked into dark gray slacks which were held up by suspenders. The room was filled with bookshelves crammed full of tomes of varying sizes—so many that even though it was bright out, no natural light filtered into the room and only oil lamps provided illumination.

The man let out a chuckle and spoke with a thick Southern drawl. "You must be the intruders I heard about. You don't look like much trouble to me, though I'm usually wrong in situations like this. People have taken advantage of my trust too many times before. Won't make that mistake again." He grinned and sat down on his leather chair. "My name's Henry Miller, and I'm the mayor of this town. Don't worry about my men; they're just doing their job; can't be too cautious these days."

Karl scoffed.

Duke stepped forward. "We don't mean anybody harm; just trying to get home, sir."

One of the guards slowly placed Karl's revolver on a desk and Henry spoke up. His deep voice boomed in the enclosed space. "Well, that tells a different story, mister ..."

Duke cleared his throat before introducing himself. "Duke Hollander. Just trying to be cautious in these uncertain times, sir."

Henry let out a loud, rumbling chuckle then gestured toward Julie. "Is someone going to introduce this lovely young woman?" he asked.

"I'm Julie Freeman, sir," she replied with a slight nod of her head.

"Well, Julie, I am very glad y'all have stopped by our small town." The mayor glanced around at the group before continuing. "Which one of these men do you belong to?"

Julie's eyebrows furrowed. "Excuse me? Belong to?"

Duke stepped forward and quickly interjected, "Nobody, we're all friends here."

Henry nodded. "Right, I see..." The mayor shifted his gaze to one of the men. "Donny, have everyone lower their weapons. These people are now our guests; they will be treated as such, you hear me?"

The man Henry spoke to—Donny—was statuesque, with deep, hooded eyes and lips like a cupid's bow. His shoulders were strong but sloped forward, probably from years of bending over doing manual labor. He wore a plain white long-sleeve T-shirt, sleeves rolled to the elbow, which contrasted with his tanned forearms. His blue jeans were worn thin on the knees.

"Yes, sir," Donny replied briskly.

Turning back to Duke, Henry asked curiously, "Where y'all headed to if y'all don't mind me asking?"

"Colorado," Duke answered firmly.

Henry's eyes twinkled with amusement as he said fondly, "Colorado? Heading to the high mountain country, are we? I'm fonder of the coastline and being at sea level. I was born and raised in Savannah, Georgia, you see, but the good Lord told me the end of days were coming and this place is where HE needed me to be. Told me that HIS people here were in need. Being the good and faithful servant that I am, here I be." With his arms spread out wide, he smiled warmly at them.

"Y'all must be hungry." Henry tilted his head back toward

Donny. "Donny here will take y'all and get you some grub. He and a few others will even fetch you some warm water so y'all can get washed up and a change of clothes as well. Also, I'm going to give y'all temporary living quarters until you're ready to leave."

"Thank you so much; we don't know what to say. How can we ever repay you?" asked Duke

"Oh, we can figure that out later, but for now, let's just say you owe me one." Henry cleared his throat and adjusted his glasses before speaking again. "And another thing—all I ask is that you abide by a couple of rules we have here for guests."

"Yeah, of course," said Duke.

"You stay in the house at night and don't come out. That means no more snooping around, you hear? Don't go talking to locals; they get spooked easily by outsiders. Lastly, what I say goes. Agreed?"

The guards escorted them down the street, locals suspiciously pausing their yard work and chores to watch them pass by. When they finally reached the house, Duke received a bucket of hot water, a bar of soap, and a washcloth before changing into donated clothes. Though it wasn't a hot shower or a bath, Duke appreciated the comfort that came with being clean. By the time he was done, both the white washcloth and the water were murky brown.

They all changed into a new set of clothes provided for them. The mayor's men even managed to find clothes for Karl. The smell of chicken, rice, and beans wafted through the air as Julie eagerly devoured her meal like she hadn't eaten in months.

Duke took the moment to look over at Julie and saw her smile. Seeing her smile was infectious. He felt his own grin stretch across his face as Julie hummed with pleasure.

Catching him looking, she asked, "What? Am I eating like a pig?"

"No, no, not at all," Duke replied. "Just glad to see you

doing better is all." He turned his attention to his food, seeing Karl smirking in the corner of his eye.

Karl looked down at Julie's feet, which were in stark contrast to the rest of her body; they were swollen and covered with painful-looking white blisters. The backs of her heels had been rubbed raw, and faint traces of blood could be seen on the soles of her boots. "So, Julie, how are your feet doing?" he asked.

Julie winced as she tried to flex them. "They hurt like hell, blisters all over the damn place," she said. "I lost a couple of toenails too."

"We'll see if Henry has better supplies than what we got to fix you up."

Julie shook her head. "I appreciate it, but I just need to get our supplies, and I can do it myself," she said with a trace of pride in her voice.

Karl's face hardened as he spoke. "We can't draw attention to that shed again, not until we're ready to leave."

Duke snapped his head in Karl's direction, eyes narrowed as if studying him. "Speaking of Henry, is it just me or is there something off about the guy?"

Karl cocked an eyebrow with a wry smile. "What? Don't like the religious zealot types? Thought you were into all that stuff."

Duke shook his head. "No, I just don't like the way he was looking at Julie. Every time their eyes met it looked like a lion staring at its next meal."

Julie smiled softly and rested a hand on Duke's shoulder. "I appreciate the concern but he's harmless, Duke; I've dealt with men like him all my life. Old bachelor veterinarians who flirt and make inappropriate comments while trying to pet my arm as if it were some kind of animal they could tame. Yes, they are perverts, but nothing more. With him, I'm nothing more than eye candy, so don't worry about it. Promise it will be fine."

They finished eating and their conversation dwindled to an intimate silence. Suddenly, a loud knock shook the entire house. Duke jumped to his feet and opened the door to find the mayor, Henry, surrounded by five armed guards.

"Howdy folks, y'all get settled in just fine? How was the food?" boomed Henry in his baritone voice, looking around at each of them with a wide smile on his face. "May I come in?"

"Yes, please." Duke gestured with his hand for Henry to enter. "The food was delicious. Thank you!" he said nervously.

"Well, I'm glad to hear that—just doing what I know the good Lord would have me do." Henry looked around the room for a few moments before turning back to Duke, smiling widely.

"Were you just seeing how we were doing or was there something else you needed?" asked Karl, speaking up from across the room.

The mayor shifted his gaze to Julie. Swallowing hard, he cleared his throat before continuing. "Well, both. I must admit I came here to cash in on that favor. I was wondering if Miss Julie would accompany me this evening."

"I'm not so sure that—" started Duke before Julie cut him off.

"I can think and speak for myself, thank you," she said firmly as she rose from her chair. "What would this evening entail?"

"I have to admit I'm an old man who would enjoy the company and conversation of a beautiful young woman like yourself," he said with a smirk spreading across his wrinkled cheeks. "I mean no harm, just some wine and some words, that's all."

"That sounds fun to me."

The mayor seemed taken aback for a moment before regaining his composure and holding out his arm for her.

Duke felt sick to his stomach as he watched Julie take the

mayor's arm and walk down the street with him, but she was determined—it was the least she could do for all they had done for her.

CHAPTER 6

KANSAS | APRIL 2035

One hour later, Duke kept pacing back and forth, his gaze never leaving the window. No matter how much he tried to ignore it, the sickening feeling in his stomach would not go away. Karl had been rummaging around the house for items of use, but all Duke could think about was Julie and her safety.

"Bingo!" Karl shouted from across the house, bringing Duke out of his thoughts. He ran to see what Karl had found, only to be faced with a bottle of bourbon.

"Really?" said Duke, disappointment evident in his voice.

"I think you could use a drink," replied Karl as he poured the bourbon into two glasses.

"I don't get drunk anymore, Karl," said Duke softly.

"I said 'a drink,' plus it will help stop you worrying about Julie. It'll take the edge off."

"I'm not that worried," Duke lied.

"Oh really? You have practically burned a spot in the carpet by the front window."

Dammit, I can't stop thinking about it; I know that creepy old man's intentions aren't honorable, but do I have any say about it? Maybe Karl is right; there's nothing else I can do at this point.

"All right, fine, pour me one," Duke relented.

"There we go. Julie's a big girl and it was her choice," Karl said excitedly as he raised his glass.

"What are we drinking to?" asked Karl.

Duke wanted nothing more than to forget all his worries and drown himself in alcohol, but he knew better than that.

"How about getting home," he suggested instead as he raised his glass.

Karl's face slowly split into a grin. His blue eyes brightened, and his teeth shone like pearls in the lamplight. "I like it. To getting home it is. Whenever the hell that ends up being."

***

Duke and Karl traded funny military stories and jokes back and forth for about an hour before Duke looked over and realized they drank the whole bottle. Duke thought it was interesting seeing Karl cut loose. He was not used to seeing the big man joke and laugh like that.

"Okay, that was pretty good, but I got a better one," said Karl with a drunken smirk. "An Army Major visits some sick soldiers, right? Goes up to one private, and asks:

'What's your problem, Soldier?'

'Chronic syphilis, Sir.'

'What treatment are you getting?'

'Five minutes with the wire brush each day.'

'What's your ambition?'

'To get back to the front, Sir.'

'Good man,' says the Major. He goes to the next bed. 'What's your problem, Soldier?'

'Chronic piles, Sir.'

'What treatment are you getting?'

'Five minutes with the wire brush each day.'

'What's your ambition?'

'To get back to the front, Sir.'

'Good man,' says the Major. He goes to the next bed. 'What's your problem, Soldier?'

'Chronic gum disease, Sir.'

'What treatment are you getting?'

'Five minutes with the wire brush each day.'

'What's your ambition?'

'To get the wire brush before the other two, Sir.'"

Duke's laugh echoed through the room, and he was suddenly overcome with emotion. It had been so long since he'd laughed that hard, he thought to himself, and it had been even longer since he'd felt like there was something worth laughing about. His head spun from all of the alcohol, and his thoughts started to drift. Was his wife, okay? Did she miss him? Would his children recognize him when he got home? He was sure his nine-year-old son would remember him, but his daughter hadn't seen him in four years. When Duke first went away, his wife visited often; after the first year, she stopped coming and eventually stopped taking his phone calls.

"You doing all right there, mate? You disappeared on me for a second," Karl asked.

"Yeah, I'm fine," Duke chuckled. "Are you getting soft on me?" he added with a smirk.

Karl let out a drunken sigh and leaned back in the chair. "At the end of the day, everything will turn out as it should," he said.

"I sure hope so," Duke murmured, glancing down at his feet. He paused briefly before continuing. "Do you think Julie's okay?" he inquired, casting his gaze toward the window.

"I think so," Karl replied, gesturing to the armed guards outside the door. "But what can we do?"

Duke shrugged his shoulders.

"She's certainly an attractive woman though," Karl noted, raising his eyebrows suggestively.

"Yes, she is," Duke responded uncomfortably. "What was your point?"

"Nothing really, just an opinion," Karl replied casually.

Duke knew why Karl had made that comment; even if he still felt loyal to his wife, he couldn't deny Julie was beautiful.

They remained silent for a few moments as Duke kept looking out the window. Duke could tell Karl wanted to say something.

"I understand what it feels like to be isolated, but getting too close to people will put you and them in danger. It's true—nice guys don't always come first," Karl said.

Duke sighed audibly. "What are you implying?" he asked irritably.

"That if we want to make it back alive, I need to know that you can use your weapon again," Karl said bluntly.

"It isn't that easy."

"Yes, it is," Karl insisted. "I can see it in your eyes; I've seen that look many times over my military career. Even though I don't know exactly what happened to you, you must either forget it or embrace it."

"Karl, you don't know me," Duke retorted.

"Oh, yes I do," Karl scoffed. "You were a soldier who made a mistake, went to prison, found God, and promised to turn his life around. Does this sound familiar?"

"Go screw yourself! I'm telling you; you don't know me. Yes, I made a mistake and maybe I just want to be a better person."

"You're full of shit!" Karl slurred loudly. "Do you really think being religious makes someone superior? Get real, buddy! Sorry, but in this new world you can't simply go through life without getting your hands dirty!" His face contorted with rage. "I kill with a purpose! It protects us and it is necessary."

"Ah, so you are 'protecting' people by killing them? That sounds strange coming from the man that killed his own teammates and ended up in prison for it!" Duke scoffed.

"You know nothing! Shut the hell up," Karl snarled. "And don't forget, you were in the same prison as me!"

"That may be true," Duke replied defiantly. "But I wasn't in there for killing people I had sworn to protect!" His voice rose to a thunderous cry.

Karl let out a deep sigh before he slumped his shoulders in defeat. He sat down and rubbed his face wearily. "Do you want to know the truth?"

"Karl please, I didn't mean—" Duke started to apologize but Karl cut him off.

"One of my men had tried to rape a Ukrainian girl, and we fought over it. I hurt him badly; I wanted him to stop but I went too far. He later died from his injuries," Karl said with a distant expression on his face.

Duke was filled with remorse. "Karl, I'm sorry I didn't know."

"And that's why I went out of my way to help you and Julie. You reminded me of myself, just trying to help." Silence lingered between them for several long minutes before Karl finally spoke again. "Duke, you need to trust me; this world is not going to be kind to us so promise me that when the time comes, you'll pull the trigger out of necessity and not out of malice."

Duke nodded slowly in agreement even though dread crept through his veins at the thought.

"It's been a few hours now; do you want to check on Julie?" asked Karl without betraying any emotion in his voice.

"I thought you said..."

Duke's voice failed to finish his sentence as the door swung open, filling the room with a gust of cool air. Standing at the entrance was Julie, holding a beautiful blue dress that matched her eyes. Duke froze for a second before he lunged forward and embraced her tightly. For a split second she was too bewildered to react, then she returned the hug half-heartedly.

Duke quickly pulled back, cheeks growing red from embarrassment. "You okay? Did he touch you? Did he hurt you?" he asked, trying to hide his intoxication with slurred words.

Julie answered with a perplexed expression on her face, "Yes, no, and no?"

Duke attempted to save face by asking if she was all right before Julie shot him an inquiring smirk.

"Duke, are you drunk?" She glanced over at Karl. "Are you both drunk?"

Karl smiled wide, chuckling a bit under his breath as he sheepishly admitted, "Well ... yeah, little bit."

****

Julie recounted her evening to Duke and Karl. She had been certain the mayor was going to make unwanted advances, but she admitted she was pleased by his perfect conduct. They talked about their jobs prior to the apocalypse, drank wine, and listened to music on an old Victor phonograph. Julie said he was strange, dull, yet incredibly polite. Duke sighed with relief upon hearing this news and inquired about the blue dress.

"Yeah, I thought that was a little weird, but I guess they're having a little party in a few days," said Julie.

"A few days? Party? Julie, we need to get on the road," said Duke.

"He's right, time is essential right now."

"I know, but honestly, guys, I kinda need this. I need a break from walking; let my feet heal. Let my head heal a little bit too. Please?" Julie pleaded.

Duke felt his heart lurch as Julie batted her lashes and widened her bright blue eyes at him. He found himself taking in every detail of her appearance: the gentle curves of her body, the softness of her lips, the delicate hue of her skin, and the way her golden hair cascaded around her shoulders. He wanted to reach out and comfort her, but he felt a wave of guilt that he had become attracted to her when he was already married. The guilt amplified when he realized it was his fault she was dealing with all these problems. If he had just killed Agigi, she wouldn't be suffering like this.

Duke looked at Karl and queried, "What do you think?"

"Why don't we meet halfway and spend a few more days here so that we can recuperate and get our hands on some supplies?" Karl suggested.

As Duke reclined in bed, he reflected on the oddness of life—how he and Julie had met under such unpredictable circumstances. He tried to remember everything Karl had said earlier that night; logic told him it was true. The world was disintegrating into a state that would require desperate measures from its inhabitants. People would have to do things they never imagined or expected themselves to do.

Duke felt his heavy eyelids start to close as he battled with inner turmoil and exhaustion. His head swirled with all the possibilities before him, aware that he may eventually be forced to make choices no one should ever have to make.

****

The early morning light poured through the window and touched every inch of Duke's body as he lay on the couch. It slid gently across his skin and warmed him, coaxing him from sleep. He heard cabinet doors being shut in the kitchen. The loud, metallic bangs shrilled through the house, sending vibrations all along his body. His head pounded with a hangover and his stomach hurt. His hands were shaky and sweat rolled down his face.

Julie handed Duke two ibuprofen and a glass of water, watching as he stuck his nose in the air and sniffed like a dog.

"Do I smell coffee?" he asked desperately.

"You do, courtesy of the mayor," she said with a smile. "See? I told ya he's not a bad guy."

"Fresh coffee? Well then, I'll take it all back," Duke joked weakly as he gingerly stood up to face his hangover head-on. His body felt shaky, and he remembered why he stopped drinking so many years ago.

Julie took him by surprise when she hugged him tightly.

"What is this for?" he asked quietly, still confused about her gesture.

"For caring," Julie said softly as she rested against his chest.

"It feels good; after everything we've been through, it just does."

It most certainly does.

He felt a warmth wash over him as they embraced. It had been so long since he had been hugged by a woman. Duke's guilty conscience told him to break the embrace and his cheeks flushed slightly as he did. He stepped out of the room and into the kitchen where Karl stood hunched over an old camping stove, heating up eggs. The smell of smoky bacon mixed with fresh spring air that came in through an opened window.

"Good morning, Karl," Duke said softly.

But Karl held up his pointer finger and hushed him quietly. "No, it's not."

Duke couldn't help but laugh, shaking his head at their shared discomfort.

Karl poured the thick, dark liquid from the French press into a mug hand-painted with "World's Greatest Boss." He set it in front of Duke, who grabbed the mug. The heavy steam rose from the cup and tickled his nose as he cautiously brought it to his lips. Aromas of sweet roasted hazelnuts and bitter citric acid engulfed him, bringing back memories of when he was free of military duty—when quality coffee was accessible on a regular basis. He took a sip and felt instantaneous relief from his hangover as warmth spread through his body and into his stomach.

Duke paused for a moment, feeling the heavy weight of the conversation. He glanced up at Karl, whose face was etched in frustration, and saw he had placed a paper plate full of eggs in front of him.

"So about last night..." Duke began, but Karl put his hand up to stop him mid-sentence.

"I haven't drunk hard liquor in years. I need you to stop talking, but we're good. Just eat your damn eggs," Karl said gruffly.

Duke nodded in understanding and quietly reached for a fork as Julie suggested they see if Henry needed any help.

"Yeah, it wouldn't hurt," Duke agreed quickly before turning to her with a serious expression. "But first I really should shave this thing off my face. It itches like crazy." He ran his hand over the coarse black stubble that was growing in on his cheeks.

Julie smiled and shook her head. "You should keep it. It looks good on you."

Duke felt himself blush as he scratched the back of his neck awkwardly.

Trying to break the tension between them, he gave a mischievous wink and continued, "Okay then let's get going—where to? To schmooze your sugar daddy, of course!"

Julie gave an exaggerated eye roll and playfully punched his arm as she replied, "Ewww gross! Don't call him that."

***

Duke stepped onto the porch and slowly inhaled the crisp morning air. His headache was still pounding, but for a moment the beauty of the small town made it seem almost non-existent. He gazed around at the vibrant green fields, peaceful blue sky, and cheerful yellow wildflowers that lined the fence, until he spotted something out of place. As they walked farther down the main street, his once peaceful view shifted to a scene of dystopian despair. Every shop window was barricaded with boards and locks, some cracked from recent break-ins. The sidewalks were filled with people whose faces were drawn with fear and worry.

Duke and Julie continued down the street, approaching the King's Cafe.

"What a shame," Julie said as they passed by the small cafe. "It looks like it's seen better days."

"Looks like more of a hang-out place versus a cafe." Duke looked ahead and pointed to the large building in front of them. "Let's check that out Scotty's Motor Co.," he said. "Looks like there are a lot more people over there."

Julie and Duke set out toward the building, their steps echoing against the broken pavement. The sun shone down on the weathered sign bearing the words "Scotty's Motor Co.," its once vibrant colors faded. When they stepped through the entrance, Duke noted that the place had been abandoned, and what used to be a motor shop had now become something else entirely; an edifice of makeshift stalls lined with goods available for bartering and exchange.

A doomsday flea market—who would have thought?

To the right of the building, a hubbub of activity was taking place as people queued up to receive food from half a dozen people ladling out bowls of soup and stew. Armed guards scoured the area, ever vigilant for any potential danger. They brought back memories of Fort Leavenworth prison for him, where all inmates were warned to follow the rules, or their good behavior time would be taken away. AI bots, security cameras, and guards combined to make sure this happened. The town of Kanorado didn't have any advanced automation technology or high-end electronics. However, it was still vulnerable to the precarious American supply chain.

Duke and Julie made their way up the cobblestone path to the mayor's house, and Duke cursed silently as his pounding head made every step a struggle. As they approached, they saw Henry sitting on his porch swing in his usual Sunday suit, smiling and waving them forward.

"Good morning, you two," he said with a deep baritone voice that did nothing to soothe Duke's headache.

"Good morning, Henry," Duke replied. "We were wondering if there was anything we could do to help around here?"

Julie smiled sweetly at him.

Henry adjusted his bowtie and leaned back in the swing. "No, no, no, you all are our guests. But I thank y'all for offering." He regarded the pair with a fond smile. "Did y'all get a chance to see the town yet?"

"Yeah, we did a little bit on the way here," Duke replied. He gestured toward the warehouse in the distance and continued, "Saw the food line and trading store slash storage building."

"Ever since God took the electricity away," Henry began, "the people here needed direction and guidance. What better man than an ambassador for God? I prayed for His will, and God showed me that we needed to ration everything. We gathered up volunteers and started storing everyone's food, water, fuel, and supplies in that warehouse."

"Good idea," Duke remarked with interest. "But why the armed guards on it? Isn't it everyone's food?"

Henry nodded sagely. "It is. I'm just trying to keep people honest. People are used to having rules and they know if you break the rules, there are consequences. Without that there would be anarchy."

Duke nodded his agreement before saying, "Well, I suppose we should get going. We'll be at the house if you change your mind on us helping with things."

"Okay, good to know," said Henry as he stood from the swing. He looked directly at Julie and asked warmly, "Oh, Julie, are you still coming over this evening?"

Julie smiled and nodded, replying, "Indeed I am."

Henry grinned broadly. "Make sure to wear that blue dress I gave you. We want everyone to look their best."

"Yeah of course." Julie smiled as she walked away.

As Duke and Julie headed back toward their house, they could feel curious eyes watching them from windows and yards.

"Why is everyone staring at us?" she asked, tucking a wisp of hair behind her ear.

"Small town, socially awkward," Duke responded with a shrug. "Henry's a bit of a weirdo, huh? Wants you to wear that dress?" he added, ducking his head in sympathy.

"I know. Better than walking until my feet bleed again. He's weird but harmless, I guess," Julie sighed.

A few yards away stood a man with stringy blond hair and sunken cheeks. He caught Duke's eye and seemed as if he was about to approach them when an old guard truck came rumbling down the street. The man quickly ducked out of sight and disappeared into a nearby alleyway.

Julie looked around in confusion. "What the hell was that all about?"

Duke shook his head worriedly. "I'm not sure. This place keeps on getting weirder."

***

Later that night, Julie nervously strode up the walkway to Henry's house. She had taken extra care with her hair and dress in anticipation of the dinner party. She was the first one to arrive. Plates loaded with cheeses, fruits, and other delicacies had already been set out.

"Miss Julie, it is always a pleasure to see you," Henry greeted her with a warm smile as he bowed slightly from the waist.

"Yes, it has been nice, and a good change of pace actually," Julie said genuinely. "Henry, where is the rest of the party?"

"Oh, people have been in and out. I'm sure more will arrive soon."

The conversation was interrupted when one of Henry's guards came in and whispered something urgently into his ear.

"Please excuse me, Miss Julie, it seems I need to attend to some problem," the mayor said with a tight-lipped glare at his guard before heading off down the hallway.

As the Mayor left, he turned up the music so that it filled every corner of the room; Julie was left there eating by herself. She took a sip of wine then paused as a faint sound reached her ears through the din of music—like air rushing through vents. Her brow furrowed as she stood up and turned off the music, then stood, silently listening intently for the sound again. After a few moments, she heard it—coming from the vents.

****

Duke and Karl were hunched over their crude map, debating the merits of a pit stop at a farmhouse on I-70. A frantic tapping on the window broke Duke's concentration. He peered outside to see the man from the street, this time with an even more harried look about his face.

"Are you okay?" asked Duke as he cracked open the window slightly.

"I don't have much time, but just know he's not who he says he is," replied the man breathlessly.

"Who?" Karl quizzed.

"Henry, or the mayor, whatever you want to call him. He is not the mayor; we had a mayor, and she was far better than him," said the man with intense urgency. "It happened so fast; he came in with a bunch of men from somewhere else, saying he was here to help during our time of need. God's name was dragged through the mud as he made up all kinds of laws and rules." His voice trembled as he continued, "He confiscated all food and weapons in the town, did it under his own authority. A lot of people went along with it since they thought it was for our own good."

The man then described how their beloved mayor had gone missing ever since Henry arrived, and now lived in Henry's house—along with several missing women, including his daughter Stephanie.

Karl cursed under his breath while Duke felt an icy chill run down his spine: Julie! She could be in danger too!

"We need to get her out of there!" Duke yelled desperately.

"I agree, but first, we need a plan!" Karl took a deep breath and began formulating a strategy.

Duke looked at his friend, shrugged, and said, "Okay, you're right, got any ideas?"

Just then the heavy wooden front door slammed shut, jolting them both. Julie walked in, her eyes puffy and red from tears. She wore the sparkly blue dress that Henry gave her. She went into the bathroom and emerged a few moments later wearing her usual clothes. She threw the blue dress across the room in disgust before collapsing into Duke's arms. He held her tightly as she sobbed.

"You were right," Julie sobbed.

"Are you okay? Did he hurt you? What happened?"

Julie tried to collect herself, but the pain was still fresh. "We were having dinner, and he left to go do something. I heard a noise coming from the vent. It was a young woman, along with a dozen other women. She said they were being held captive in the basement, chained together like animals." Her voice cracked as she spoke, her terror palpable.

Karl's brows furrowed and his voice rose to a pitch of urgency. "We need to leave now!"

Julie gasped, her eyes widening in disbelief. "What about those girls, Karl? How can we help them?"

Karl shook his head sadly. "I'm sorry, Julie, but we don't have the tools or manpower to do that."

Julie felt tears welling up as anger and frustration overwhelmed her. She shouted at Karl. "You coward! I'm not going then."

Karl sighed and gave her an apologetic look. Duke sat down next to Julie and placed a gentle hand on her shoulder.

The sound of the front door opening and slamming shut made Duke's heart jump; it was Henry, accompanied by four armed guards.

"Ah, Miss Julie," he said with a smirk. "I see you changed out of your dress. Somewhere to go?"

"I didn't think you'd be back so soon, and I'm more comfortable wearing jeans and a T-shirt," she replied, wiping her eyes with the back of her hand.

"Well, technically I told you to stay in the dress, but … you can put it on again now if you want," Henry said with a false smile.

"Hey! Easy there!" Duke shot him an angry look. "She doesn't want to wear the dress, just let her be."

"I'm guessing you already forgot the rules; what I say goes. Julie, dress now," said Henry as he snapped his fingers.

Julie reluctantly grabbed the dress off the floor and started for the bathroom.

"Where do you think you're going?" Henry barked.

"Getting changed like you asked me to," she mumbled timidly.

"What? And have you run off again," said Henry. He laughed and took a seat on the couch. "No need for that; you'll get dressed right here. You'll show us that tight little body God gave you," he said in a low voice.

"But I don't have anything underneath," Julie stuttered in disbelief.

"You can't do this!" Duke yelled, stepping between her and Henry. Karl followed suit, standing at his side.

With a clap of Henry's hands, the armed men pointed their weapons straight at them. "Sit down or else I'll send all three of you to meet the Almighty himself!" he threatened, pointing toward Duke and Karl. His face turned a deep crimson as he screamed, veins bulging in his temples. His spittle flew like a fountain as he pointed at Julie and shouted for her to put on the blue dress.

She stood still with embarrassment, tears streaming down her cheeks as she slowly began to undress. The room felt heavy with humiliation, even though Duke and Karl had the decency to avert their eyes.

But Henry didn't show any mercy—he made Julie spin around in circles so that all the men in the room could get an eyeful of her.

"There, see? That wasn't so hard, was it? All right now,

let's go, we have a date to finish." Henry stood, buttoning his overcoat.

"She's not going anywhere," Duke said, his face contorted with rage.

Henry snapped his fingers at one of his men. The man walked over to Duke and hit him in the head with his gun, knocking him to the floor. The mayor walked over to him.

"Seems to me you keep forgetting, YOU DON'T MAKE THE RULES!" screamed Henry, bent over Duke. He barked orders and grabbed Julie by the wrist, dragging her away. He left two guards behind to watch over Duke and Karl.

With blood dripping down his face, Duke clenched his fists in anger as he watched Henry take Julie away.

Jaw clenched tightly, he declared, "He can't get away with this!" His body shook with fear and rage. "We can't abandon her like this!"

Karl put a comforting hand on his shoulder and looked him in the eye. Karl's eyes were vacant, devoid of emotion, yet still instilled Duke with assurance. As time went on, the look grew more intense, cold and filled with anger, like a stormy sea in the dead of night. Duke felt as if death itself was staring at him.

"I promise you that we will not leave her behind," Karl said.

CHAPTER 7

KANSAS | APRIL 2035

Duke and Karl sat in the dimly lit room, the tension thick enough to cut with a knife. Duke had his hands clenched into fists, fearful of the plan he was about to make. He felt sick to his stomach, knowing it would likely require him to break his sacred promise to God—but it was the only way to save Julie from being a sociopath's plaything.

"Duke, I know it's hard," Karl said softly, "but I need you to focus. Can I count on you to do this? My life and Julie's life depend on it."

Duke closed his eyes and nodded his head slowly.

"And also, sorry about this." Karl suddenly lunged forward, tackling Duke into the wall and sending objects clattering onto the floor as the house shook. They made as much noise as possible. Two guards rushed in, trying to separate them.

"What the hell is your problem?!" Duke shouted back, wiping his mouth with the back of his hand.

"You dumbass!" Karl yelled, pointing at Duke.

"What the heck is going on here? Do we have to put you two in the corner?" one guard asked as the other stared menacingly between them both.

"Not a bad idea," said Karl as he head-butted the man.

Duke punched the other man, knocking him out.

Armed with AR-15s, Duke and Karl waited for more guards to arrive. Moments later, two men emerged from different directions carrying hunting rifles and began sweeping through each room. The larger of the two stopped when he saw his unconscious comrades on the floor bleeding.

"Hey, we got a problem here, at guesthouse four," he cried into the handheld radio.

"Go ahead, what's going on?" came a voice from the other end of the line.

Duke stepped forward and pressed the barrel of his weapon against the guard's forehead. "Drop your weapon and call it off. Tell them it was a false alarm or I will shoot," he said in a gruff whisper.

The man complied and slowly lowered his rifle to the ground before speaking into his radio. "Hurry, they're trying to escape!" he yelled before Duke clubbed him across the jaw with the buttstock of his gun, sending the man falling to his knees, unconscious. A few seconds later, Duke heard a gunshot from across the house. He ran over to see Karl standing over an unconscious body with a smoking gun in one hand and a radio in the other.

Duke and Karl heard the sound of a car skidding to a stop outside. Duke quickly grabbed the unconscious man's radio off of the side table. Karl saw his face harden as he spoke. "We need to go, my guy called for backup."

Karl raised an eyebrow. "Yeah, I heard. I'm going to grab this guy's radio. I didn't hear a gunshot, but you took him out, right?"

"I knocked him out," said Duke shakily.

"You do realize you're going to have to kill people tonight as we planned; I can't see any way around it. Who knows how many people are coming here right now. So better now than later."

"I know, I just couldn't shoot an unarmed man."

"This isn't the time to play the honor card. We are out-manned and outgunned so we need to fight dirty and…"

Their conversation was interrupted when bullets ripped through the front of the house like an artillery barrage. Glass and wood exploded all around them as shards ricocheted off of furniture and walls, creating a deafening cacophony inside the tiny room. One of the kerosene lamps was shattered in the chaos, setting curtains and furniture alight in seconds.

Karl shouted above the din while ducking for cover behind an overturned table, "What about now?" he asked sarcastically with a smirk on his face.

Duke's breath was labored and sweat beaded on his forehead, but he still managed to grin when Karl asked if he was good. "Yeah, I'm good," he replied.

Karl barked for them to make their way to the back of the house. The flames licked at the walls with a roar and smoke billowed through the hallways. Duke tried to use his sleeve to cover his face, but it did little to help him as they blindly felt their way through the darkness.

When they finally burst through the back door and into the open air, Duke's eyes widened as he took in the sight of a bright, full moon above them. But before he had time to appreciate its beauty, three men came around the corner and pointed their guns at them. Karl and Duke reacted instinctively, firing off shots that found their marks with alarming accuracy. As soon as Duke realized what he had done, nausea hit him like a wave, as he remembered what it felt like to take another person's life.

Karl flipped the selector switch on his rifle to safe before turning to Duke. "You good?" Duke nodded slowly. "Good, because we're not done yet," Karl said, slapping Duke on the back as he scanned the area for other assailants.

Karl bellowed, "Three o'clock!" as a mass of men surged forward. Duke and Karl lay down in the prone position to open fire, blasting through their magazines with lightning speed. When the bullets were gone, they stood up and ran. As Duke sprinted away from the building, he felt the heat emanating from the raging blaze and saw people gawking at the house fire. He knew some had seen him and Karl retreating; there was no going back now.

The sound of their feet slapping against the pavement echoed in the air as they sprinted toward their destination—the shed they had stumbled upon when they first arrived. There, tucked beneath a tarp, was Duke's double-barrel shotgun. After loading it with shells, he looked up into Karl's eyes.

"I know you want to be better than this ... but we can't take it back now. We've got to do this for Julie." Karl gave his shoulder a reassuring squeeze. "I need that man I see behind your eyes—brutal, dangerous—if we're going to make it out alive."

Duke's therapist had given him a method to help him control his emotions. He could use it to make the painful memories ever-present in his mind bearable. This time, Duke was determined to channel that rage into a corner of himself he kept hidden away.

He thought about when he was a child and observed his father beating his mother, about how he tried punching his dad as a five-year-old but it did nothing. He remembered the taunts of school bullies calling him names, beating on him, making him feel worthless, and then recalled the day he almost brought a gun to school to kill them both before realizing that someone in his family had already been murdered, and he could never do that to anyone else. This memory made him think of his cousin who had stabbed their grandmother sixty-seven times.

He replayed all the heartbreaks and betrayals of the women he'd loved throughout his life. Then came the vision of the Ukrainian boy whose life faded right in front of him—it was just one of many haunting moments from past deployments that Duke still carried with him.

He dug deep into his mind, revisiting the memory of when he was ten years old and heard his mother's screams. That was the day Duke walked in on his stepfather raping his mother. As a five-year-old he couldn't do anything to stop his dad, but being ten years old he had a plan. He crept toward Jeff, clutching the kitchen knife tightly, and thrust it into his back. The pain from being stabbed only seemed to make his stepfather angrier as he reached out and backhanded Duke down the wooden steps that led up to his mother's room. The pounding of Jeff's footsteps followed him down as he beat Duke worse than ever before. Luckily Duke's mother came to the rescue—she had picked up the knife and finished what her son had started by stabbing Jeff to death.

Duke felt like his skin was on fire and his heart beat wildly in his ears. Fear mixed with a sense of relief as Karl watched with awe at the rage burning in Duke's tear-filled eyes.

"Now that's the man I'm looking for, and that's the man I need right now."

Karl grabbed an old rusty hammer off a wall full of tools. They both crept around the side of the mayor's house, taking great pains to avoid detection. The two guards were on alert and Duke could make out Henry's figure in one of the windows on the second floor. He whispered urgently to Karl, who nodded in agreement as they approached the guards with determination. Duke swiftly butt-stroked one guard with his shotgun, and before the other guard could react, Karl had already thrown the hammer with deadly accuracy. The man fell to the ground with a sickening crunch. The man attempted to scream only to choke instead on his blood and teeth. Duke picked up the hammer and hit the fallen man with two more blows before his body went limp. He dropped the rusty hammer in a pool of blood that gathered on the sidewalk.

Karl crouched down and whispered, "We need to be as quiet as possible."

"Get down!" Duke barked, swinging the muzzle of his shotgun toward Karl.

Karl obeyed, dropping quickly onto his stomach as Duke fired a shot over his head. The buckshot caught the other guard who had just regained consciousness in the chest, sending him tumbling limply to the ground.

"Well, I guess we can forget about being quiet," Karl mused, grabbing one of the hunting rifles from a guard.

Duke and Karl strained against the door handle, but it was locked tight. Voices rose on the other side of the door as confused guards attempted to make sense of what was happening. Before they could break through, two more men came sprinting from around the corner. Karl sighted with his rifle and pulled the trigger once, taking both targets out with a single shot.

Duke focused his attention on the door again and kicked it wide open, catching an unsuspecting guard in its path and knocking him flat. Without hesitation he brought up his weapon and discharged a shell right into the man's skull, splattering blood and brain matter across the floor.

Duke called out, "Reloading!" as he leaned against the dining room wall. He quickly drew two 12-gauge shells from his pocket and reloaded the firearm in one powerful motion while Karl stood at the bottom of the staircase leading to the second floor. The man on the stairs above them shot down at them, grazing Karl's arm; Karl dropped his rifle and ducked to the side to avoid further injury. Duke returned fire. His shots missed, tearing chunks off the wall and leaving a cloud of dust behind when the man rounded the corner.

"Thinks he's reloading!" one of the men yelled from the top of the stairs. As two figures rushed down single-file, Duke saw Karl leap out from the shadows like a panther and snatch the first man around the waist. He yanked away the assailant's gun and bashed it repeatedly against the stunned victim's face while Duke released another round of buckshot at their second assailant. The man screamed with pain as the shot blasted through his right shoulder, enveloping him in a fountain of blood and tissue. In awe, Duke watched as Karl snapped the man's neck like a twig.

He hurriedly reloaded his weapon as Karl reached for a fallen handgun with one hand and motioned for Duke to take the low position at the corner of the hallway. Peeking out from cover, Duke fired at an unsuspecting figure just ahead. The blast took off part of his leg, and with one final shot to the head from Karl, they advanced forward room by room until they found nothing else alive.

Finally, they came to one of the last doors and found it locked. Karl kicked the door open and saw Julie tied to the bed. Her dress looked as if Henry tried to rip it off her but stopped halfway through. She had a cloth gag in her mouth but was trying to yell something. Duke's desire for blood-lust was immediately extinguished when he saw her. Without hesitation, he set his gun down and took the gag out of her mouth.

"I got you," said Duke as he took the cloth out of her mouth.

"Look out!" screamed Julie.

Henry came out of the closet with a revolver pointed at Duke. "Well, well, looks like the knight has finally come to rescue the princess, but I have a feeling this fairy tale ain't gonna end with happily ever after," he said with a low, grizzled voice.

Karl shot Henry in his hand, making him drop the revolver.

"God? I can show you God real fast!" Duke yelled. He picked up his shotgun and aimed it at Henry.

Julie shouted desperately for them not to kill him. Duke turned to Karl and softened his voice. "Okay."

Henry looked up at Duke and Karl with terror; he knew this was it for him.

"Nope," said Karl coldly as he blocked off any possible escape route for Henry, "it's time to pay for your sins, preacher."

"I'm an ambassador of God! My sins are already forgiven!" Henry said with bits of spittle flying out of his mouth.

Duke untied Julie, and she promptly jumped out of bed in her torn blue dress. She picked up the revolver that Henry had dropped. Duke noticed it was the revolver that was confiscated from Karl when they first arrived.

"Take off your clothes," said Julie with a quiet, trembling voice.

"Do what?" asked Henry, confused.

"I said take off your fucking clothes!" Julie screamed with tears running down her face, pointing the revolver at him.

"I will not do such a thing," said Henry.

Julie fired the revolver, missing Henry's head by a few inches and shattering the window next to him. "Now! Or next time I won't miss!" she screamed, gun trembling.

Everybody stared at Henry in stillness as he clumsily stripped down. He shivered with shame.

"Feels nice, being put on display for all eyes to see." Julie spoke softly.

"Now listen, I'm sorry. Can you find in your heart to forgive this old preacher?"

"I thought you were already forgiven? I guess you'll find out if it worked."

"Please don't, please!"

"Too late for sorry. Go to hell!" Julie screamed in a bloody rage.

The revolver roared, and Henry's body jolted backward as the bullet tore through his groin. He grabbed at the wound with both hands and screamed in pain, but no sound escaped him as he writhed on the floor. Julie was standing just feet away, tears streaming down her face as she emptied the remaining bullets from the gun into Henry's lifeless body. Duke quickly moved to take the weapon from her hands and placed it aside before drawing her close in a comforting embrace. Julie felt numb; she stopped crying. She simply looked on at what remained of Henry, shock numbing any emotion that may have come otherwise.

Karl's voice echoed through the hall. "We have company."

The sound of chattering voices wafted in from outside. Duke peered out the window and saw a mass of people that seemed to stretch on for miles. Not one person carried a weapon, leaving him with a sense of relief.

"What do you want?" Karl yelled through a broken window.

"Is he dead?" asked someone in the mob.

"If you're talking about Henry then yes, he is, and he deserved it. Your mayor was a monster!" Karl shouted back.

"Good, he wasn't our mayor; he never was," replied the man.

Duke sighed in relief, grateful they weren't dealing with incensed killers.

Karl turned to him and Julie. "I'm going to go talk to those folks and get some more information. You two should see if you can find anything about those girls."

Julie led Duke toward the basement door. He kicked it open and heard screams coming from below. A nauseating smell filled his nostrils as he moved down each step cautiously. Once at the bottom, he could barely make out over a dozen young women chained together in the center of the room. Buckets full of human waste were scattered throughout their makeshift cell. Their wrists were rubbed raw from being bound so long, and they had not bathed in days.

"Don't worry, we're not gonna hurt you. Let's get you out of here," Julie said with tears streaming down her face.

As the morning progressed, the sky lit up with the first glimmers of sunrise. The girls were cleaned up and reunited with their families.

"Why didn't you guys fight back?" Karl asked. "You had the numbers."

"Well, when everything went down, Henry said he was a Baptist preacher on furlough. Our mayor vouched for him. But she ended up disappearing."

"That's not at all suspicious; why did he take over?"

"He told us that our mayor left to go find her children in Missouri. We didn't question him. In our culture, a preacher usually makes a good leader. Unfortunately, we were incredibly wrong with Henry. He suggested that the town pool its resources together. Food, water, guns were all given."

"Why did he have so much help?"

"Those were not people from here. All was well for a few

days, then we had a significant influx of trouble-making refugees. But it seemed like Henry got them under control and on board if they helped. Slowly but surely, young girls and women in this town began to disappear. When people started questioning it, those people slowly began to disappear. Every time someone asked where their daughter was, she was found dead somewhere in town the next day. It quickly became apparent what was going on. But without our guns, there was nothing we could do. We didn't want them killing any more girls, so we just went along with it. We tried formulating a plan a few days ago, but they found out about it, and we found more dead girls. Then you three showed up and handed their ass to them." Tears welled up as he finished his story.

"Well, hopefully, this town can hit the reset button and protect each other now. Just glad we could get those girls out of there."

"We're gonna try."

Duke saw Julie talking to one of the girls and walked over to see how she was doing.

"How are you holding up?" he asked.

"Despite the circumstances, good actually. I'm happy to see these girls free." Julie looked around at the families hugging their daughters. "Even compared to our last couple weeks, I can't imagine being in their shoes."

"You want to talk about it? You know, our last couple weeks? What happened here? Any of it?" asked Duke.

"Maybe someday, but right now, I just want to not have to think. I'm tired and I'm sick of...feeling." Julie looked at Duke with a sigh. "But if I ever need help or talk about anything, I promise you'll be the first one to know," she said as she kissed his cheek.

He knew the kiss wasn't sexual, but he also knew she meant something—he just wasn't sure what it was. Duke hadn't connected with a woman in a long time, even as a friend like Julie.

Duke tried to hide that his cheeks turned a crimson red.

"What was that for?"

"I wanted to thank you and Karl for everything done for me, especially you. You're a good man. Having to do what you did here, I know it wasn't easy for you. I know you broke your vow to God, but I promise you it was not done in vain," she said, her voice thick with emotion.

Duke nodded solemnly and smiled warmly at Julie, his heart swelling with pride despite the heavy toll the night had taken on him. The townsfolk offered them a pickup truck full of supplies to aid them on their journey—clothes, food, water, fuel, and ammo—and a compact 9-millimeter pistol for Julie before bidding them farewell. The group decided to stay one last night in Kanorado before departing in the morning.

***

Duke lay on the couch, his breathing slowing as he drifted into slumber. He felt the sudden presence a split second before he heard the telltale creak of the floorboards. Suddenly, he felt a shiver run down his spine and he slowly opened his eyes. He was met with Julie's silhouette standing in the doorway, a long T-shirt barely reaching her thighs.

"Julie, what are you doing? Are you okay?" Duke asked almost desperately.

"I'm fine," she said in a low, soothing voice. "I want to show my gratitude for your kindness."

Duke tried to object, but she put her finger to his lips, silencing them with a soft touch. He sat up on the couch. She knelt between his legs as they trembled nervously beneath her. His heart beat wildly as Julie leaned forward and their lips collided in a passionate embrace. Duke's fear quickly faded away as he stood with Julia. They were clawing at each other's clothes with reckless abandon, unable to keep their hands off one another.

"Duke...Duke? Time to get up," Karl said.

"We need to get on the road," Julie said, staring down at him. She stood beside the bed, her arms crossed and her brow furrowed.

Duke jolted awake at the sound of her voice, his heart pounding as he realized what he was dreaming about. His skin felt hot with embarrassment as he scrambled to sit up.

"Yeah, okay, thanks," he said, unable to meet Julie's gaze.

She studied him intently for a moment before asking, "Bad dream?"

Duke paused for a moment before answering. "Not exactly." He struggled to hide his discomfort and willed his blush to disappear.

"Good, let's get going," said Julie with a renewed smile.

CHAPTER 8

Colorado | April 2035

Billowing smoke carried by the wind told Duke he was getting close to Colorado Springs. He couldn't see much as they sped along Route 25 toward the municipal airport. The rain pounded like so many soft, fluffy hammers on the old pickup truck's windshield wipers. Each swipe dislodged more of their ragged blades until it became almost impossible to wipe away the rain.

As they drove through the Colorado countryside, they were met with a depressing sight. Everywhere around them, homes and farms had been reduced to ash and rubble. Further on the horizon, there were several crashed airplanes. Some of them looked intact, like they had landed safely, while others had clearly collided with trees or buildings; their wings had been torn free. Still more planes had attempted to land but had found their final resting place in a blazing inferno.

Duke couldn't help but notice all the people walking on the road, heading west. Men, women, children—anyone and everyone was trudging along, their eyes dark with fatigue and hunger. Mothers and fathers pulled their children in wagons or carts. Duke felt helpless as they drove by them.

"It's hard to drive by and not do anything," he said to Julie.

Julie sighed heavily, feeling sorry for the refugees they were passing by.

"We've talked about this before," Karl reminded them from the driver's seat.

"We know we can't stop," Julie replied sadly, sounding defeated.

Duke wanted to help, and he knew Karl did too. But they had agreed not to stop. They couldn't risk being overrun and losing their truck or supplies—or worse, their lives. As Duke looked out at the sea of people, he noticed dead bodies rolled into the ditch. He wondered what these people had died from—sickness, dehydration, medical reasons, malice?

The highway was disappearing beneath their tires as the orange, dusty twilight of Colorado's plains faded into a deep purple night sky. As they drove past Peyton, Duke's sharp eyes spotted what looked like a roadblock up ahead. Karl slowed down and the group peered out of the windows. The signs of military presence were unmistakable: canvas tents fluttered in the breeze on both sides of the highway, each lane blocked with intricately woven coils of steel, and men in camouflaged uniforms moved around with haste.

Spotlights blazed from towering generators, illuminating the scene with an artificial white glow and casting harsh shadows over huge signs that declared: "Colorado Springs under martial law, no weapons or entering without ID & proof of residency, must register all incoming & outgoing vehicles."

Karl whistled softly. "Looks like the National Guard has already been deployed—makes sense, I guess. It's been a couple of weeks since this started."

Julie strained her neck to look beyond the roadblock. "What's with those lights over there?"

Duke squinted through the windshield at the distant silhouette of Peterson Air Force Base. "That's where US NORTHCOM is located."

"They also have Army Space Command and Missile Defense there," Karl added.

Duke glanced at the fortified military base, his eyes lingering on the tall barbwire fences and heavily armed guards that patrolled the grounds. He thought about those inside, struggling to keep order under immense pressure while chaos reigned in the streets beyond their walls. The thought of being trapped in there made him shudder—how did they cope with a never-ending barrage of responsibility?

"Well, we definitely don't have any of that stuff, plus we're not about to give up our guns," Duke remarked, gesturing to the convoy behind them. "Plus who knows what the military knows about us taking off. Maybe they still have communication with Fort Leavenworth." He directed his gaze to Julie, whose face twisted in concern.

"That's true," she murmured. "What are we going to do then?"

"I know a back road we could take. It will take a lot longer, but I doubt they have a roadblock there." Karl turned off the highway. His fingers tightened around the steering wheel as they turned onto the back road, eager to avoid the checkpoints that had been set up for miles. But as they rounded the corner, their hopes were dashed; a checkpoint lodged itself between them and their destination.

Julie spoke up, worry lacing her voice. "What now?"

Duke responded with an air of confidence. "Just back up."

But Karl knew this was impossible—the road was too narrow for any 180-degree maneuver. He clenched his jaw and took a deep breath as he rolled down the window. "Everyone just relax, let me handle this."

Their vehicle got the attention of the checkpoint guards. A spotlight pierced the truck windshield.

"Turn off ignition and put your hands on the dashboard!" shouted the soldier through a megaphone.

The guard's flashlight shone in their faces as he slowly approached the vehicle. In one hand, he held the megaphone, while the other grasped an electronic tablet for logging travelers' information. The soldier barked his demand: "Name and residence!"

Everyone in the truck froze, not knowing what to say.

"You deaf? Name and residence."

None of them wanted to give up their identities; Karl and Duke were on the run from military justice. Karl glanced over at Duke, who nodded slightly, letting him take lead on this situation.

Fake confidence oozed from his voice as Karl replied, "Hey there, we were just passing through trying to check on the family to make sure they are okay. If we can't come in, then is it all right if we turn around?"

"You have to let us search your vehicle for contraband."

"What's the deal? We're not even coming in," Duke said, leaning forward.

"It doesn't matter. We've got orders to apply martial law procedures to anyone who stops at our checkpoints. Everybody needs to exit the car."

Duke, Karl, and Julie reluctantly stumbled out of the pickup.

"Look what we have here," said one of the soldiers behind them.

"Holy crap! You three are packing!"

"If we lose our weapons, it'll be a death sentence," Duke whispered anxiously.

Karl stepped up and said, "I guess I'm gonna have to take a chance with this."

Julie started but was quickly pushed back by a soldier with an M4 rifle pointed in Karl's face.

"Back off, pal!" the sergeant shouted.

"What the hell? You can't just—" Julie exclaimed before being shoved to the ground.

Duke ran over to help her up but was driven down abruptly after being hit in the stomach with an automatic rifle. He hunched over, unable to take a breath.

"Go ahead, cowboy, make your move." The soldier scowled at Karl. "Take them away! Put them in the detention box until I decide what to do with them. I'll run them through a scan and see if they're on file already."

Thick black zip cuffs were placed on Duke's wrists, behind his back. He was brought to his feet. Duke, Karl, and Julie were led to a shipping container. A metal door swung open, causing a light to flicker on. The shipping container was outfitted with an office area with filing cabinets and desks and computer terminals. A holding cell stood inside the office area. They were instructed to sit on the metal benches inside the cell.

"This place is already hard enough with what's going on, and you gotta cause more trouble?" The black, middle-aged sergeant set the forest green helmet on the table. He ran his hand over his hairless scalp and shook his head at Duke and his group. "You all gonna behave now?"

Karl let out an audible sigh. "Karl Blackburn."

"What? No, Karl," Duke said with knitted brows.

"What was that?" asked the sergeant.

"My name is Karl Blackburn, how about you look that up?"

"Hey, Perez."

"Yes, Sargeant?"

"Look up the name Karl Blackburn."

The sergeant walked away with the fat specialist who pulled out a thick handheld device, but Duke could still hear what they were saying.

"This thing is heavy and ancient. Wish we still had the micro scanners."

"Yeah, well, tough shit, Perez, all those things got fried."

"So it looks like there's only three people that go by that name."

"Are there pictures of the people?"

"Only if we scan them in. We can check an address."

The sergeant walked back over to the holding cell. "What's your residence?"

"Site Z ops group four."

"What? Is this some type of joke to you? What is your address, asshole?"

"Call up to your chain of command and have them contact

the US Northern Command at Peterson Air Force Base. Tell them that you have an operator from Site Z ops group four that goes by the name of Karl Blackburn, call sign Chief. Then they will contact the...appropriate set of people. Let me know what they say." Karl spoke firmly.

The sergeant walked away with a confused but intrigued look on his face and whispered to Perez. The two men left the shipping container. After a few seconds the lights turned off, plunging the container into darkness.

"What the hell was that about? Why did you give them your actual name?" Duke asked in a loud whisper.

"I don't know if you noticed but our weapons and supplies were confiscated. To top it off they are going to put us in some jail during all this shit." Karl inhaled deeply and exhaled slowly. *I had no other choice*, he thought.

"What did you mean by Site Z?" asked Julie.

"Please, I'm not going to play twenty-one questions with you. So don't waste your breath," Karl growled.

"Sorry, just curious." Julie turned away slowly.

Karl let out an audible sigh in the darkness. "Listen, the less you know the better, okay?" he said, trying to sound apologetic. Julie didn't respond. "Well, who knows how long we'll be here. Try to rest your eyes while you can."

Yeah right, like I could sleep.

***

Duke was jolted awake when the lights in the container suddenly flickered on. Squinting his eyes against the sudden brightness, he could see the bald sergeant approaching their cell door. Duke sat up from the cold metal bench, unsure how much time had passed since they were thrown into this dark, cramped space. Julie and Karl were already alert and waiting to hear what the man had to say. The sergeant's face betrayed a glimpse of defeat as he looked up from his clipboard, a scowl deepening the wrinkles on his forehead as he spoke.

"Looks like you're free to go, Blackburn."

All three stood up from the metal benches.

"No, just you, big guy. They didn't say anything about them."

"These two are with me." Karl's gaze was steady, unwavering.

"I don't care! They are staying, I've got my orders!" He jabbed the papers in his hand for emphasis.

Karl stepped forward, bristling with anger. "Listen to me, you bald, fat piece of crap, you don't know who you are dealing with. They are coming with me and that's it."

The sergeant blinked, taken aback by the outburst, then recovered himself and sneered. "Who the hell are you?"

"I'm the man who holds your career in his hands ... Sargeant Kent." Karl read the man's name tag on his uniform. "I'm also the man that holds your life in his hands. You see, if they don't leave with me, I'm gonna come back for them. But not only for them—also for you. The only difference is they'll get to see their friends and family again."

Julie seemed shocked, her mouth agape as she looked sideways at Duke. Duke was also taken aback.

The sergeant released them and escorted them back to their truck. A faint, misty glow crept over the horizon as the sun slowly rose. Shadows of rocks, trees, and shrubs cast long, dark lines against the makeshift shipping container.

Karl barked the order for the soldiers to put everything back where they had found it, including the weapons. He could feel the sergeant's reluctance as his men went about putting all of the pieces back in place. Karl started up the truck engine with a roar and threw a wink at the soldiers before pulling away. Duke let out a chuckle when he saw Julie quickly stick her tongue out at them.

"Karl ..." Julie said with furrowed eyebrows, "who are you?"

Karl sighed and rolled his neck. "Tired and hungry," he replied simply.

***

The morning sun cast an orange glow on the chaotic situation that had engulfed the city, like a veil of light surrounding it. Even though everything was in disarray, it still gave Duke a sense of familiarity, a sense of home. The city was a disaster. Thousands of people lined up at the FEMA tents set up around the perimeter, like ants marching to a new mound. Every business building was ransacked, their glass fronts smashed, or the windows punched out and replaced with boards. Burn marks surrounded empty buildings like halos.

Duke tried to contain his alarm as he saw the carnage of the front doors kicked in around him. He thought of his wife and kids, imagining their terror, and then pushed forward with a burning sense of urgency.

Duke stared out at the desolate landscape before him. People were rummaging through what was a once thriving society, now reduced to rubble and dust. He knew how fragile their world was; how quickly it could all come undone. Only a few weeks ago, the streets would have been brimming with life. But now, without technology, law and order, or anything resembling the supply chain ... everything had fallen apart. It was as if the members of society had reverted to their primal instincts—find food or starve, find shelter or sleep in the rain, find clean water or perish, kill or be killed. This was the new norm.

The engine of the truck echoed through the empty streets. As they turned the corner, onto the street where Duke's home lay, his throat became increasingly dry. He didn't know what kind of welcome he would find there, but he hadn't expected what greeted him—a scene of carnage and destruction. His wife's vehicle sat in the driveway with windows missing, broken glass glittering on the ground like stars. The front door hung open, its frame splintered from some terrible force, foreboding a sinister fate that had befallen his family within. Duke leapt from the truck before it came to a stop, shotgun clenched tightly in his hands as if it was an extension of himself, and raced toward the house with bated breath. All that awaited him now were the echoes of tragedy.

Karl flung open the truck door. "Duke, wait! We don't know what we're walking into! Dammit," he shouted as he hopped out of the truck and stomped up to the front porch, his revolver clutched firmly in his sweating hands. Julie stayed back by the truck, her heart pounding against her ribs as she watched Karl disappear into the ransacked house.

A deathly silence hung heavy in the air, only to be broken by Karl's labored breathing as he stepped inside. He felt a chill crawl up his spine as his eyes adjusted to the dim light. He quickly scanned the room that reeked of death and saw two bodies sprawled out on the floor. Tables were overturned and drawers had been ransacked, but one thing remained in place: a portrait of Duke and his family from years ago.

"Duke, I'm here," Karl called out. But no response came. Fear gripping him like a vice, Karl slowly inched down an adjacent hallway until he heard sobbing coming from a back room. He crept inside to find Duke sitting on the ground, tears streaming down his face. His grief was soon made apparent when Karl noticed three figures lying motionless on the bed, shrouded in bloody sheets; two little ones next to an adult figure. Falling to his knees, Karl placed a hand gently on Duke's back.

The room had a stagnant smell that seemed to stick to the walls like glue. Duke stared, uncomprehending, at the bodies. He couldn't seem to tear his gaze away from them. He felt his heart sink in his chest and he began to shake uncontrollably.

"Man, I'm so sorry," Karl said softly.

"We were too late..." Duke's voice was barely audible. "This is all my fault. We took too long."

His words felt hollow and meaningless in the stillness of the room, and they hung heavy in the oppressive air. Karl didn't seem to know what to say.

"There's nothing to say," Duke said between sobs. "I have nobody left ... I have nobody to blame but myself."

Karl tried to sound hopeful with his next words, but it fell flat. Nothing would take away Duke's pain now; all he ever wanted was to see his wife and kids again, but they were gone. Suddenly Karl stood up and carefully lifted the sheets off of the bodies.

"Don't you touch them!" Duke shouted angrily, his eyes blazing with rage.

"Hold on a second," Karl said cautiously, "didn't you say you had a little girl?"

Duke nodded silently as tears rolled down his cheeks. "Her name was Ava," he managed to whisper between sobs.

Karl looked over at him before turning back toward the corpses; after a few moments he spoke again. "Duke ... this is two little boys."

Duke's hand trembled as he tentatively reached for the bedsheets. His heart racing, he yanked them off, only to feel a wave of relief upon realizing that it was not his wife and kids buried underneath. No, these were Justine—his wife's best friend—and her two sons. Sarah and Justine had been inseparable when Adam, Justine's husband, was deployed with Duke over in Ukraine. But unfortunately Adam never made it home from Ukraine.

As blessed as he felt with his fortune, guilt overwhelmed Duke as he realized how relieved he was that it wasn't his loved ones. It meant there was still hope that he could one day reunite with his family once more.

"Do you know them?" Karl asked from behind him.

"Yes," muttered Duke, "I did." He had a sudden urge to rush toward the basement.

"What are you doing?" Karl shouted.

But Duke was already down the eerie, steep steps, standing tall before a large safe adorned with scratches and dents from thwarted attempts to break into it. He inserted the combination and pulled open the door of his long-standing collection of weapons and ammunition, much to the chagrin of his wife.

To Duke's surprise, the safe was empty. But taped on the inside of the door was a single piece of paper. Duke read the note aloud: "Duke, if you're reading this, I have the kids and our supplies. We're going to Mountaintop with Jake for now – April 14th 2035." Duke passed the note to Karl who could only utter an astonished "My God!"

"Who's Jake?" Karl asked, followed by other inquiries about what exactly Mountaintop was and how Duke knew when specific days were.

With a smirk, Duke replied simply: "Jake is my best friend; Mountaintop is where we're headed; and also, I've been tracking every day and every hour for the past four years, counting down to the day I was supposed to get out."

✳✳✳

Duke drove Karl and Julie up Highway 24, heading toward his old prepper community.

"So I'm curious about this property," said Karl.

Duke smiled wide with renewed energy. "Well, it used to be called the North Pole."

"Wait, you mean that Christmas-themed amusement park?" Karl asked, incredulous.

Duke nodded with a big cheesy grin.

Julie added, "Must've cost someone a pretty penny."

Karl continued to inquire, "How and why?"

"Well," Duke began slowly, "the original owner died and left it to one of his family members who didn't want to deal with taking care of it and ended up selling it. The community leader is Paul Jones—though that was almost five years ago when I was being investigated. When I was hiding from them so they wouldn't look at Mountaintop. Who knows if Mr. Jones will take me back in."

Julie looked at Duke with worry as she nervously asked, "How many people are there? Do you think they'll let me stay?"

Duke softened his gaze as he smiled reassuringly, saying, "I think around thirty people. And like I said, I may not even be allowed back in. But I will plead your case on your behalf as well."

"What if they say you can stay and I have to go?" Julie asked, her voice tight with fear.

"Jules, no matter what they say, I'm going to help you. I promise," Duke replied, steeling himself for whatever the community decided. He had grown fond of Julie; she had become a good friend and the thought of her being homeless devastated him.

Karl glanced around coolly, his smirk evident even in the darkness. "Okay, I think this would be a good time to tell them who YOU are," he said sarcastically. "Don't think my name will work here."

The sudden call from the guard tower was as unexpected as it was loud. An authoritative voice boomed from above.

"Shut off the truck! Everyone out with your hands up!"

Time seemed to stand still, and then crawled slowly as the group emerged from the vehicle. They shuffled closer, their eyes wide with apprehension.

"Wait! Hold on—Duke? Is that really you?"

As the man lowered his weapon, Duke's heart halted in his chest. His eyes widened as recognition bloomed within him. It could be none other than Jacob Anderson, Duke's best friend. His bald head and ruddy beard were as bright as a cardinal's wing and his face was pale like the moonlit night sky. Jake advanced with cautious steps, as if approaching a specter from beyond the grave.

"It's really you!" Jake yelled, disbelief and excitement clear in his voice as he wrapped his jacked arms around his friend. "I can't believe you're here, and how?" Jake released Duke from his embrace.

"That, my friend, is a very long story, but somehow I managed it," said Duke with a weary smile.

Jake shook his head, unable to fathom what his old friend had gone through over the past four years. He opened his mouth to speak when he noticed two strangers standing behind Duke.

"Oh wow! Who are these people?" He extended a hand to them both.

Duke glanced back. "These are Karl and Julie, my new friends. Truly, they are the reason why I made it home. They saved my life more than once," he said before turning back to Jake with an exhausted expression that spoke a thousand words. "Without them I wouldn't be here now."

"Wow, sounds like one hell of a story. Nice to meet you both." Jake shook hands with both of them before turning his attention back to Duke. His old friend had changed, grown beyond recognition. "You look jacked, man," Jake remarked as he squeezed Duke's arms appreciatively.

Duke chuckled weakly as he stared Jake in the eyes. "Yeah, four years in a military prison will do that to you." He paused before adding, "You look thinner though ... I'm guessing fast food isn't an option anymore, huh?"

Suddenly Jake was rubbing his shoulders with enthusiasm as he pointed toward one of the large gates surrounding them. "Come on, man, I got so much to show you! Much has changed since you've been away ... you won't believe it! You two can come in for now." He waved his hands gallantly toward Karl and Julie, still trying to wrap his mind around having his dear friend back home again after all this time. "Let's take a stroll and catch up."

The air seemed to stand still, and Duke's heart raced as he stared at Jake with dread. "Just tell me you have them. Where are they?" His voice was so desperate it was almost unrecognizable.

Jake shifted his gaze to the ground, avoiding Duke's plea. "About that, Duke ... there's something we need to talk about."

The words knocked the wind out of Duke's lungs. He knew what this meant. His eyes welled up with tears as he spoke haltingly. "What do you mean? What happened to them? Just tell me if something has happened—"

Suddenly, the most beautiful sound in the world pierced through the tense silence.

"Daddy? Michael, it's Daddy!" Ava shouted in joy as she and her brother ran toward him, wild with glee.

In moments, all of Duke's worries and anger drained away like water in a sandcastle. Nothing mattered in the world anymore but his children clinging to him tightly, their happy tears spilling onto his sleeve.

Duke's six-year-old daughter Ava looked up at him with wide, trusting eyes. "You get to stay? Are you with us now?"

A lump rose in his throat and tears rolled down his cheeks like a river overflowing its banks. "Daddy is never gonna leave you again," he vowed.

Behind them stood Sarah, Duke's wife, her face a mask of shock. "I can't believe you actually made it ... you're actually here." She pulled him into an embrace but there was stiffness to it. She quickly let go and stepped away, her expression unreadable.

"I went to the house first," Duke said, taking a deep breath. "Read your note." A cloud of guilt crossed his face. "Sorry about Justine."

Sarah winced at the mention of her friend's name. Turning away from Duke, she replied in a low, harsh voice, "Please don't. I don't want to talk about that." When she looked back at him, her eyes had hardened. "I still can't believe you're here... After all this time?"

He reached for her hand but she pulled away. Taking a

step back, she shook her head. "What's wrong?" he asked, not understanding her hesitation.

"What's wrong? You gotta be kidding me." Her voice was tight and strained with emotion. "I'm happy that you are home and safe, but did you forget where you were? You left us! Not for training, not for a deployment, but for being greedy and selfish. We had to fend for ourselves for four years, Duke."

Sarah spoke without turning her head. "Plus, there's something else."

"Mommy is Jake's girlfriend now," Ava blurted out.

"What? What do you mean?"

"I was trying to tell you myself, brother," Jake said stepping forward.

Duke glanced between Jake and his wife before exploding with quiet rage. "What?!" He spat out the words like venom. "How long?"

Sarah calmly explained that she and Jake had been seeing each other for almost two years. An icy chill spread through Duke's body as he looked into his children's eyes and reassured them, "Honey, I will always be your daddy." Then his cold gaze turned to Jake. "No matter what."

After a moment of silence, Duke turned back to his son Michael, who had remained silent throughout it all. He spoke in a soft voice while tousling his son's hair. "Hey buddy, did you miss me?"

Michael quickly nodded before bursting into tears, burying himself in Duke's embrace.

As Sarah gathered up Ava and Michael for their departure, they shouted out their love for their father in unison. Julie and Karl stood by, watching with sorrowful eyes, then Julie gently hugged Duke with concerned affection. Her voice trembled as she asked the obvious question. "I know this sounds stupid ... but are you okay?"

Duke watched his children and wife walk away before turning back to his friends. In a broken whisper, he replied,

"As long as they're safe ... that's good enough for me."

"Is that who I think it is?" Charles Ferguson asked. His voice was raspy and disbelief was clearly etched in his face.

"Yes, sir, it is me, Duke Hollander," Duke said, shaking Charles' hand with a tear rolling down his cheek.

"I am glad you are back home, with your family," Charles said.

Duke glanced over at Sarah before he answered. "Yeah ... me too."

Charles paused for a moment; he had suspected something but opted to do nothing so far.

"Has Paul said anything about it?"

The sorrow on Charles' face was unmistakable as he shook his head. "I regret to inform you that Mr. Jones died last year from colon cancer; it took him fast. The people of Mountaintop voted on it and put me in his place; being the owner of the property, it just made sense."

Duke clenched his jaw and muttered under his breath, "That's too bad; I wish I could've said goodbye."

Charles patted his shoulder in understanding as Duke continued. "As for Sarah, it hurts but as long as she's happy I don't care. It may be hard to accept right now, but I have my children to consider; I don't need a wife for that."

"That's a good man right there, and a good father." Charles smiled encouragingly. "Come with me, son, much has changed since you were here last and I would like to know who you brought with you," he said with anticipation.

"That's a long story," Duke said wearily.

CHAPTER 9

COLORADO | APRIL 2035

The moonlight illuminated Mountaintop like a beacon of hope in a landscape that was otherwise sad and dismal. Duke couldn't help but be amazed at what the place had become. Although the power was knocked out only weeks before, Duke appreciated the lights more than ever before. Laughter echoed in the night air as Michael and Ava ran around with the other children. People gathered around small fires, discussing their plans for tomorrow. The walls around Mountaintop seemed to block out the harsh reality that existed outside its gates.

Charles' tour of Mountaintop was like a ghost from his past. He barely recognized it. A small remembrance of the old Christmas-themed amusement park still lingered, the old tourist shops turned into cabins. The Ferris wheel turned into a lookout tower was Duke's favorite part. A metal ladder ascended to a sturdy wooden platform perched atop the metal structure. It revealed an incredible view of the mountains and the forests below. It enabled community members to look beyond the walls that surrounded them.

As the evening wore on, Duke filled Charles in on the tale of Julie and Karl; how they met and what they went through in order to get home.

Charles was an old man of sixty-odd years of medium height and an out-of-shape physique, though you'd never know it from the way he moved. He seemed to have the energy of a much younger man; up early every morning, checking on everyone, taking care of business. His wardrobe choice for such tasks consisted of a wide-brimmed straw hat with a white band around the crown, round glasses, and a well-kept short white beard. Duke always joked that Charles looked like Dr. John Hammond from Jurassic Park—minus the Scottish accent.

Charles sighed wistfully as he surveyed the flourishing settlement. "We're lucky to be alive, Duke," he said slowly. "And you won't find troubles like that here. Everything from hydroponic gardens, a blacksmith, construction crews, medical teams, and security—we have it all. When you left us we had thirty-ish people—now, thanks to me lettin' in some folks over the years plus those from FEMA camps with specialties, we got more than 150."

Duke's brow furrowed as he asked, "Did they bring food? I hope you don't mind my asking."

"Some did," Charles replied hesitantly. "But between our food stores, gardens, and the Colorado forest, we can certainly get by." He tried to sound optimistic but couldn't help feeling a chill of dread at the question.

Before the power went out, getting into the community of Mountaintop was an intensive process. It was invite-only, extended only to those with specific skill sets. But that wasn't all—to continue to gain entry, one must also contribute to the monthly food and ammunition stores. Before Duke's stint in prison, he served as third in charge behind Charles and Mr. Jones, two powerful forces who seemed to share an unspoken understanding and bond. Though they had never spoken it aloud, each held the others' respect in the highest regard.

"So what do you think?"

Duke's gaze shifted to the people passing by as he muttered, "Not sure they'd even want me in a leadership position after prison..."

Charles' eyes hardened. "Don't tell me you don't want your old position back? Mountaintop has been divided since Sean got voted in; I mean, the man barely scraped through already."

Duke sighed heavily. "The thought never crossed my mind. Just being able to be let back in is luck enough." He looked around as more people passed by and shook his head. "With thirty people it was hard enough before, but with this many? I don't envy you at all, Charles."

Charles pursed his lips. "Come now, Duke. We need good leadership here—someone that can work well with everyone. Someone who isn't in their own world making decisions without consulting me first or putting it to a vote." He lifted an eyebrow. "Plus, you have my endorsement; if we put it to a vote, I'm sure the people would vote in your favor."

"I don't know. The idea of running a community just seems so daunting."

Charles' voice boomed through the air. "You would be great! Even some of the original members weren't too keen on Sean when he was voted in."

"Well, I'm not sure if I even want it," Duke said, his voice low and sullen. "It's a lot of people to take care of, and I'm no CEO with a multimillion-dollar company." He shot Charles an incredulous look, but the man seemed oblivious to Duke's sarcasm.

"Oh, but you do get perks!" Charles exclaimed, gesturing energetically with one arm. "Like extra food rations and access to important information and decisions."

"If I ever got this old job back—and that's a real big 'if'—I still intend to share equality when it comes to food rations. There is no doubt that it will become an issue, given the increase in population."

Charles nodded slowly. "Yes, yes, I know. All right then, the choice is yours of course," he said with a knowing smile.

Duke took a deep breath before continuing, "I think Sean might not take it well either. We didn't exactly get along..."

"That's precisely why I want him to lead the hunting party and nothing else," Charles declared adamantly. "He can be quite the hothead when things don't go his way; he's even tried intimidating me before. He should stay out there look-ing for game and leave leadership matters alone."

"Some people may not like the idea of someone who escaped from military prison helping run this place," Duke added darkly.

Charles stared into Duke's eyes, a glimmer of curiosity in his gaze. "True," he said slowly, lips pressed firmly together. "No one knows why you went to prison, Duke; it was a closed courtroom. Was always curious though. Sarah would never talk about it. Said it wasn't anyone's business."

Duke sighed and glanced away as if drawing upon an invisible strength from the distance. "She only knows a por-tion of what happened. She wasn't even there for the trial. Sarah stayed home with the kids."

Charles' brow furrowed and his voice dropped lower in volume. "What did you do?" he asked cautiously.

"I'll tell you soon enough. Right now is not a good time," Duke replied, his words cutting through the air like a rusted blade through flesh. He shook his head slightly, adding, "Plus, it's a really long and complicated story."

Charles nodded solemnly at the response, clapping him on the back in reassurance. "I understand, all in due time, I sup-pose," he said with a smile.

Duke began to walk away with heavy boots and an even heavier heart. "To be honest, sir..." He stopped and turned back toward Charles, exhaustion evident in his stance and hollow stare. "Right now all I want is just to be with my kids and not have to worry about anything else."

The corner of Charles' mouth perked up slightly into a kind smile. "Well, let me know if you change your mind; we'll put it to a vote." Then he said more softly, "Oh, and Duke, you can tell Julie and Karl they are more than welcome to stay, as long as they can pull their weight."

✳✳✳

Duke stepped into the orange light of the campfire. Julie and Karl were seated on logs, chatting happily until they noticed him. His face was a mask of somberness.

"You okay? What's wrong?" Julie asked.

"Julie, I'm sorry, but we need to find the medical station," Duke said softly.

Julie furrowed her brows in confusion. "Why do we need to do that?"

"To meet your co-workers," Duke said gravely.

Julie balked, covering her mouth with her hands. "What?"

"Looks like you're going to be working there as an assistant. Mr. Ferguson said you're more than welcome to stay," he added, turning toward Karl. "You too, Karl."

Julie grabbed Duke, tears streaming down her face as she hugged him tightly then kissed him on the cheek. She pulled away awkwardly with a red face.

"Sorry," she squeaked out.

Duke chuckled at her nervousness. "It's okay." He diverted his attention toward Karl, who shook his head sadly. "I appreciate that, Duke, but I can't stay—I have to figure out things with my unit."

Duke and Julie exchanged murmured goodbyes as Karl stood and took a few steps back from them. In that moment, he seemed larger than life; his gaze was firm and determined as he spoke directly to them both.

"I think it's safe for you two to call me Chief now," he said with a wink.

The next morning, Karl reluctantly accepted their offer of the truck.

Julie pressed herself against the window, her forearms perched on the frame as she asked him when they would see him again.

"That's a good question," Karl replied as he pulled out a piece of paper with a frequency written on it. "This is a radio channel that my group should be monitoring still. Use it if it's an emergency. Call for Badger base." He paused, his eyes drifting away briefly. "Take care." With that, Karl turned and drove away, leaving them to watch his departure.

***

Duke felt the warmth of his children near him, and he allowed himself to savor every moment—having been in prison for so long, he knew not to take them for granted any longer. He spotted Julie sitting by a campfire, seemingly lost in thought.

"You okay, Jules?" he asked her.

She nodded without looking up, simply saying, "Just trying to relax and take it all in." She gestured toward the other people around the fire, laughing and joking as if nothing had ever happened. As if people weren't dying outside the walls of their camp.

"I know what you mean," Duke said with a heavy sigh. "But at least WE made it. WE are safe." He immediately wished he hadn't said anything as Julie muttered, "For now."

The silence between them was broken by someone calling out to Duke—it was Jake.

"Sorry to interrupt," Jake said sheepishly, "but Duke, can we talk?"

Duke eyed him suspiciously before finally turning to his kids and telling them that Daddy would be back shortly and that they should watch over Miss Julie while he was gone with a smile. Duke followed Jake away from the group where they wouldn't be heard or seen.

Before Jake could even say what he had come to say, Duke spun around and punched him square in the jaw, sending him toppling to the grass.

"I guess I deserve that," Jake mumbled from the dirt.

"You think?" Duke snarled.

Jake looked up at Duke. "Look, I said I'm sorry."

"You're sorry? This is what I get after everything? I didn't rat on you; you get to walk away and this is how you repay me? By having an affair with my wife!?" His voice was low and filled with an intensity like none other.

Jake shifted uncomfortably in his spot on the ground before stammering out an apology. "I will always be thankful for you not ratting on me," he said, rubbing his sore jaw. "But it just happened; she was always scared of being alone. One night it just happened—we didn't plan for this to happen." Jake stood and kept his voice down. "Plus, after everything went to hell we thought you would be trapped there ... we didn't think you could escape and make it all the way home." His words trailed off as desperation crept into his tone.

Duke glared at Jake with a mix of rage and contempt. "So, does she know?"

"Know what?" Jake replied, trying to remain calm despite the tension.

"That you were involved with me and Agigi?" Duke asked, his voice low.

Jake shook his head. "Of course not. Nobody knows that, and trust me, I would know if she knew."

A heavy sigh escaped Duke's lips. "Speaking of Agigi, I'm not the only one that escaped. He killed Julie's grandparents in front of her, so he's been after me for a while—but I think we lost him. Who knows, though? He's a relentless son of a bitch."

Jake raised an eyebrow at him. "Yeah, I know. So was it you?"

Duke's expression turned guarded. "What do you mean?"

"Isaac's courtroom was closed because they had a witness that saw him killing Roarke," Jake said slowly. "There were only his two goons, you, me, and Roarke. He sent me away before killing him—so I'm guessing his own men didn't give him up."

Duke hesitated for a moment before finally admitting, "Yeah ... that was me."

Jake nodded approvingly. "I knew it—good on you, man! I know you got time for it but without you, there would be no justice for Roarke. I don't care if he was narcing on Agigi or not; that kid didn't deserve to go out like that."

Duke quickly changed the subject as if to avoid the awkwardness of talking about it further. "What happened with you on this? I couldn't find you anywhere."

"Nothing really," Jake replied softly. "I went silent after they questioned me—after that I tried to lay low and stay out of the spotlight."

Duke cast an incredulous look at Jake. "They knew you were working for Agigi too—I'm surprised they didn't try to use you after Roarke disappeared."

"Why do you say that?" Jake asked, an uneasy feeling beginning to form in the pit of his stomach.

"I'm just guessing that Roarke probably gave them our names too," Duke replied, a tinge of fear creeping into his voice.

"No, Roarke was solid. I don't think he would give us up. The feds asked me questions about you, Agigi, and Roarke. After I told them I didn't know what they were talking about, they left me alone. That's how I knew you didn't rat on me. I got to walk away."

Jake let out a sigh of relief, but Duke pressed him further. "Are the caches still out there?"

A look of panic washed over Jake's face. His eyes darted around before settling back on Duke. "Probably, but I have no idea, man. Like I told you last time I talked to you, they are buried and I'm not going anywhere near them. The feds were watching me like a hawk." He shook his head slowly, guilt weighing heavy on his conscience.

Duke ran a frustrated hand through his hair as he tried to process the information. "All right, well we eventually need to go see if the caches are still there."

"That might be problematic," Jake replied with a humorless laugh. "I buried those things a long time ago," he continued, pausing for effect, "and I was really high."

Duke stared at him incredulously. "Really? You idiot!"

"I'm sorry," Jake said sheepishly, "but I was a little stressed."

Duke took a deep breath and looked off into the distance, shaking his head in disbelief. "How was smoking weed going to help you?" he muttered under his breath.

Jake gave him a sly look and replied with mock innocence, "Never said it was weed."

"Really?" Duke said. "Smoking meth again?"

Jake looked away and cleared his throat awkwardly. "It was one time ... okay, maybe two times."

Duke looked at Jake, dumbstruck.

"Okay fine, it was two weeks." Jake rubbed his face aggressively before explaining himself. "I used my cousin's excavator and put those things in the ground super fast. Didn't I mention I was a little stressed?" he finished lamely, unable to meet Duke's gaze.

Duke simply stared at him, dumbfounded by Jake's complete disregard for common sense. After a few moments, he sighed heavily and asked, "Who else knows where they are?"

"Only me," came the reply, a hint of resignation in Jake's voice.

Duke nodded grimly and muttered, "All right, we'll figure out something." He paused for a moment before looking at Jake slowly and somberly, asking in almost a whisper, "Do you love her?"

Jake blinked in surprise. "What?"

Duke enunciated every word. "Do—You—Love—Her?"

After considering this question carefully for several moments, Jake finally allowed himself to admit the truth. "Yeah, I think I do, man."

Hearing this admission visibly upset Duke, who clenched his fists in frustration and exclaimed, "I swear to God, don't hurt her or the kids! God knows I've already done enough damage to them."

"I don't intend to, brother," Jake whispered.

"Don't call me that," Duke muttered as he turned away from his old friend and returned to Julie, who was still sitting near the blaze. The sight of her made him smile; she had carved herself a place in his life, and when Duke discovered Sarah and Jake's dastardly deed, that space became firmly rooted in his heart.

"Hey there." Julie looked up from the fire and gave Duke an inquisitive glance. "What was all that about then?"

Duke shrugged nonchalantly. "Just settlin' things between us is all."

Julie followed his gaze down to his hand, now rough and red from punching Jake. She reached out and gently probed the wounds on Duke's knuckles.

"So I take it you two boys didn't exactly get along too well?" Her tone held a hint of amusement as she gazed into Duke's eyes.

"Well enough, I guess," he replied gruffly.

The corners of Julie's lips curved upward and she clasped Duke's hand in hers. "You think you'll be all right?"

Duke felt something stir inside of him as Julie steadily met his gaze. He replied confidently, "Yeah, I think so."

His arm intertwined with hers as she leaned her head against his shoulder.

CHAPTER 10

Colorado | April 2035

Duke awoke from yet another night of fitful sleep, his body heavy with exhaustion. It was a painful sight to watch Jake and Sarah together. Instead of feeling sorry for himself, though, he quickly inserted himself into the community to be helpful.

As Duke stood in the community food line, he thought about what Charles Ferguson said about being his number two. He didn't want the extra responsibility, but he did pledge to these people once before. But now there were five times as many people; it was a huge responsibility. Duke wanted a simple life where he could watch his kids grow up safely.

Duke's serenity was shattered when he heard the menacing voice of Sean Myers behind him. He turned to face what could only be described as a walking nightmare, standing in front of him with an evil smirk on his lips. "The notorious Duke Hollander," he said mockingly. "I don't know why Mountaintop would take in an escaped prisoner, but I'm sure we can find something for you to do here that won't make you completely useless—like cleaning, cutting wood, and digging. Maybe then you won't be a complete waste of space. Especially if you're going to be eating the food that I provide." Each word felt like acid dripping on Duke's skin, and he knew the man was far from done.

Sean was a bantam of a man, thickly muscled, a rough-looking white redneck with dark features. His hair was black and closely cropped. He sported a short black goatee. Black eyebrows rose above dark eyes filled with the mischief of a schoolboy who had been told he could not hold back any more information. He had a chaw of tobacco tucked into his lip—it gave him an unsettling protrusion like some kind of juicy growth—and he wore tight blue jeans, sheathed a long buck knife at his side, and always finished off the ensemble with a baseball cap and squared-toed cowboy boots.

Rage bubbling within him, Duke attempted to think of a way to best Sean without having to physically harm him. His gaze never leaving Sean's face, he said, "Charles, is your offer still on the table?"

Charles replied tentatively, "Having a vote? Yes, it is, but only if you're doing it for the right reasons."

Duke nodded.

"So you're saying you want to put it to a vote?"

"Yes, I do," Duke bit back with a hint of maliciousness in his voice.

Sean protested loudly, "You can't do that; I got voted in fair and square."

Charles stepped in to explain further, "Oh yes, we can. Duke was never fired from his position and he never quit, therefore he should have been second in command when Mr. Jones died. Then Mr. Jones died, leaving his position to me. But since Duke was not here to be my second, we had to vote someone else in. Duke would need to be voted in if he were to get his position back since there are so many new people at Mountaintop."

Seething with anger, Sean bellowed, "This is bullshit!"

"That may be so," Charles reasoned calmly, "but it's fair. We will bring it up in the nightly announcements. Spread the news, people; there will be a vote in one week."

The crowd murmured discontentedly before eventually dispersing. Charles turned to Duke and said hopefully, "Can't say you're going to win, but you have a chance, I think. Sean has a lot of followers backing him up; I don't know how many will actually vote for you instead."

Duke nodded in thanks before walking away. His future—as well as Mountaintop's—was now in the hands of fate.

Weighed down by the burden of his decision, he exhaled heavily and dropped his head in despair.

You really stirred up a hornets' nest now, Duke, he thought to himself.

Julie shot Duke a sideways glance. "Man, you make friends real fast, don't you?" she said, all jest and no sting.

Duke smirked. "Yeah, something like that."

"What the hell is that guy's problem?" Julie's question hung in the air for a moment.

Duke released a heavy sigh and ran his fingers through his hair as he began to explain the situation. "Long story short," he said wearily, "that was Sarah's sister's ex-husband. I confronted him about his drinking and abusing his wife."

Julie shook her head in disbelief. "Wow, he sounds like a real winner. You really want to help run this place?" She gestured around at the inhabitants of Mountaintop. "It's an organized zoo."

Duke thought carefully before answering. "Yes and no. At least I'll have a say on what goes on. But not sure how the community will respond... This could backfire. All the new people will know I was in prison."

Julie laughed lightly. "Well, at least you'll have my vote." She smiled.

He grinned appreciatively. "Thanks, I appreciate that." After a few moments of silence, he asked, "How are you settling in?"

"Dr. Kelly welcomed me with open arms and got me a spot in one of the women's bunkhouses," she replied with warmth in her voice. "So again, I can't thank you enough for what you have done for me."

"I'm happy to hear that," he said gratefully.

Julie looked away as if she had to go back to work then turned around quickly and said with a wink, "Stay out of trouble, Mr. Hollander!"

"I'll try," Duke chuckled before she walked away. Just as she started to fade out of sight, he called out to her softly; "Hey, Julie?"

She stopped and faced him again. "Yeah?"

"I was wondering if you were wanting to hang out by the fire tonight again?"

A small smile tugged at her lips as she nodded in agreement. "I would love that."

✳✳✳

One week later

An atmosphere of excitement and anticipation filled the air as the citizens of Mountaintop assembled to cast their ballots for Charles Ferguson's new second in command. Duke, Sean, and Charles stood upon a raised ledge, looming five feet above the heads of the crowd that had gathered below them where a food court had once been. Duke gazed languidly down at the bustling throng, his arms propped against the railing.

Charles barked to the assembled, his voice rising over the murmurs of the crowd. "It's time for a vote, but first we must hear from these two men. Who would like to go first?" He gestured to Duke and Sean, eyes flicking between them.

"I'll go first," said Sean, stepping forward, the sound of his boots echoing off the buildings that surrounded the food court.

"Listen up, people," he said, drawing himself up tall as if to intimidate everyone present. "You know who I am, right? But who the hell is this?" He jabbed his finger in Duke's direction. "Don't worry, I'll tell you—he used to be second in charge when Mr. Jones was around. But why isn't he now? Because he went to prison! A prison that he had to escape from in order to get here!"

The crowd erupted into an uproarious chatter that seemed

to shake Duke's bones. Sean looked back at Duke and smiled triumphantly, then turned back to face the mob with an air of confidence. He gestured for them to calm down so he could talk.

"Did I mention that he did it when he was in the service? If someone like that can dishonor the uniform he was wearing, what's going to stop him from dishonoring this community? I'm not perfect by any means, but what's better? The devil you know? Or a dishonorable convict?"

The crowd erupted again, voices carrying wild accusations in all directions. Sean walked back toward Duke smugly and whispered with a smirk, "All yours, sweetheart."

Duke's steps were heavy, filled with dread and trepidation. His glance swept across the crowd to land on Julie in the front row, her presence offering him a modicum of solace. He waited for the hush of silence before he began to speak.

"It's true. I did escape from prison. But I did it to get home to be with my children." He paused to gather his thoughts. "But that doesn't excuse the reason why I was there in the first place. I got myself into debt and looked for ways to get out of it. So I got myself tangled with the wrong people. I helped them steal things from the government. I paid for those mistakes with my time. I also lost my career, my friends, and now my marriage." Duke caught a glimpse of Sarah standing with Jake in the crowd before continuing. "But instead of dwelling on why Sean would be wrong for this position, let me tell you why I would be a good choice. Let's get one thing straight. You won't work for me—we'll work together." He paused again as he got an idea. "Matter of fact..." Duke jumped over the railing and down into the crowd, right next to Julie, who smiled wide and gave him a thumbs-up before he continued. "This is where I'll be; among you, not above you. With me, you'll have someone who will actively listen to your needs and concerns and fight alongside Mr. Ferguson so we can create a safe place for our children to grow up in—one where we can be in a position to help our country get back on its feet!"

The crowd erupted in fervent applause, then began to hush as Duke took a confident step further into the crowd. His voice was unwavering and serious. "I'm a firm believer that everyone deserves a second chance," he declared, determination etched into his face, "and I need one myself. So if you vote for me today"—his gaze swept the crowd like a lighthouse beam—"I swear to do everything within my ability to see that Mr. Ferguson gives Mountaintop the opportunity it needs to not only survive but also thrive!"

The crowd erupted in a frenzied cheering.

Within the hour, a long line had formed entering Charles' command room. His hand-picked security guards silently watched from the doorway as two ballot boxes sat atop the desk, Duke and Sean's names written on each side. Every voter was handed half of an index card and instructed to drop it into one of the boxes. The process went faster than expected, and multiple people tallied the votes for accuracy. In no time at all, they had come to a conclusion.

"Are you anxious?" Julie asked.

"Pretty much, yeah," Duke replied. "Would you mind standing with me?"

"Of course not," Julie answered.

Duke and Julie stood alongside Charles as a piece of paper was passed to him. Julie held Duke's hand, and he smiled after looking down at their clasped hands and then into her eyes.

"The winner is Duke by a vote of ninety-two to Sean's sixty-four," Charles announced with a grin.

The crowd erupted in a mixture of shouts of joy and booing.

"This is bullshit!" shouted Sean.

Sean's people huddled around him, still trying to encourage him.

"Duke, come up here and say something."

Duke couldn't believe that he'd won by nearly thirty votes. He walked to the podium as Sean stormed out, still surrounded by his allies.

"I was going around telling everyone that you were a better choice—glad you're here, Duke," Charles whispered in his ear.

Duke hated addressing public gatherings, but his years in the military had somewhat alleviated that fear. "Look, I'm grateful to those who chose me. For folks with doubts about my background, let me clarify; I'm not a bad person. I'm just a dad wanting to make this town safer for both my children and all of us living here. I'll do my best to help Mr. Ferguson achieve that goal." A lump formed in his throat as he awaited the crowd's response.

As everyone clapped and cheered, Duke stood there reflecting on what he had said to the community. He hadn't lied outright but neither had he told them everything; the complete truth would have been too complicated.

Charles reached out and firmly shook Duke's hand, his voice booming. "You're the right man for the job, Duke. We'll make great things happen," he said, the corners of his eyes crinkling in a cheesy smile.

"Thank you, sir," Duke replied haltingly, "but there is something I must be honest with you about."

Charles' expression was one of worry. "What's wrong?"

Duke inhaled deeply and exhaled slowly. "We need to talk about someone called Isaac Agigi."

✻✻✻

Agigi stood outside of Duke's old house, holding a piece of paper that read: "Thank you so much for everything, Bert and Kathy. Here's our address: 101 South Street, Colorado Springs, Colorado, 80917."

Agigi and his men opened the front door slowly as glass crunched beneath several sets of feet. His men rummaged through the house looking for Duke and anything of importance. A thick, pungent smell saturated the air—a mixture of death and decay, a foul odor that hung like a fog. The windows were broken and shattered, allowing the curtains to flutter in the breeze, wafting the scent through the whole house. It was enough to make one gag and overwhelmed the senses. Two lifeless bodies lay sprawled on the ground, their skin pallid and eyes glassy, as if frozen in time. Maggots crawled around them, feasting on what remained of their flesh.

Eventually, one of Agigi's men emerged from the basement, a single slip of paper clutched in his hands.

"Duke, if you get this," Agigi began, voice almost a whisper but with an unmistakable air of menace about it, "I have the kids. I'm going to the Mountaintop. Blah, blah, blah." He read the rest of the message aloud with a mocking growl. "So this is where you've been hiding?" He sneered, looking at Duke's family portrait. "I can't wait to meet your family, Dookie. Just gotta figure out where this *Mountaintop* is."

CHAPTER 11

COLORADO | MAY 2035

The early morning air was ripe with expectancy when Charles rapped his knuckles against Duke's door.

"Duke? Duke, it's Charles. You're needed."

The door cracked open to reveal Duke, looking unkempt and sporting a broad grin.

"Duke, it's nine o'clock. I haven't seen you all day. It's been like this for almost a week now. Is everything okay? What has been going on?"

An unmistakable figure appeared behind Duke, hair disheveled and cheeks aglow. Julie smiled shyly at Charles.

"Ah, I see," he said thoughtfully, surveying the young couple. "Good morning, Miss Julie. Duke, we need to have a word—there are a few matters that require your attention."

"Charles, if this is about Julie and me…"

Charles chuckled softly and laid a hand on Duke's arm. "Oh no, I'm happy for you two—it's been over a month since you've been here and it's nobody's business but yours. This is something else entirely."

Duke pursed his lips and nodded slowly before pressing a kiss to Julie's lips. "I'll be right back," he said matter-of-factly before turning away from her embrace.

"What's going on?" he asked Charles as they began walking in the fresh morning air together.

"Let's walk and talk," Charles replied.

Duke's boots scuffed on the concrete as he trailed Charles into the command center. Years ago, this place had bustled with people getting their tickets to the amusement park; now, it was used as Mountaintop's command center. It was filled with radio communication hardware. It also was where Charles held his meetings—though Duke suggested that their time not be wasted on meetings but doing their jobs, which everyone appreciated. Charles agreed, so now Duke went around to all the "department heads" individually. It was a lot more work for him but he knew it was better that way.

Duke entered the room and saw Sean sitting at the table. Since Duke came on board, Sean was now only the head of Mountaintop's hunting party.

"Good to see you finally show up, Duke," said Sean.

"Mind your own business," Duke growled in response.

Charles cleared his throat and spoke up. "You two done? We have a couple of potentially serious problems. I called you two in here because someone radioed in that there's a fire way up north, and it has the potential to eventually reach Mountaintop."

Duke furrowed his brows. "Who radioed it in?"

"Some man calling himself the voice of the mountains," Charles replied. "I'll have to ask Eric and Patrick what his call sign was, but apparently this guy has been updating people in the area about things he has been hearing."

Sean shifted uncomfortably in his seat and spat tobacco-stained saliva into an old glass bottle. "Fire, huh? That would explain the heavier smell of smoke and the lack of animals around these parts."

"That brings us to our second problem—go ahead, Sean, give us the rundown," said Charles.

Sean took a deep breath before beginning to explain. "My team is going out every day and we're seeing fewer and fewer large game animals. We're still bringing back some deer, rabbits, and squirrels but nothing compared to what we used to get. Not only that, but more and more people from the city are coming through here looking for an easy hunt because of hunting season. If the fire smoke gets worse like I'm expecting, it's going to drive away whatever game remains."

He then turned and asked Charles what he suggested should be done about the situation. "We need meat in this community," Sean said firmly. "It'll make our food reserves last longer and give everyone a morale boost. Even if I have to push my team farther out into dangerous territory, that's what needs to be done."

Duke didn't care for Sean, but he was a great hunter. He knew Sean knew what he was talking about and agreed with what he was saying. It wasn't unusual for Mountaintop to smell like campfire smoke, but Duke noticed the hint of smoke was stronger than usual. Not supplementing the community with enough meat would create many future problems. Like going through their food reserves too fast.

With the meeting over, Duke set off to complete his daily walk through the small mountain community. He passed people tending to their areas, gardens, and animals; he smiled as he watched Michael and Ava play tag in front of small cabins with the other children.

He knew that beyond the walls, chaos and suffering still held sway—but his focus remained on the work he had found here. He smiled as he passed chattering groups of people, all busily engaged in the tasks of keeping the community running smoothly. As the days went by, Duke found himself thinking less and less of his life in prison, a concrete existence void of any meaningful purpose. Slowly but surely, that part of his life began to drift away.

Duke made it a point to conduct his "rounds" throughout the day, checking in with each group and department head to ensure their needs were met. One of his favorite people to check on was Joe, who was the head cook—a white middle-aged man from Texas with a chubby frame and a big smile. Joe's passion in life was feeding and making food for people. He greeted each customer with a big smile and friendly conversation.

Duke pushed open the metal door of one of the food court buildings that served as Mountaintop's kitchens. As he walked in, the warm scent of freshly baked bread mingled with the sharp tang of diced onions and garlic. He saw Joe checking his clipboard, ticking off tasks and calling instructions to his team spread out across a dozen workstations, all humming in unison. Duke got Joe's attention and waved for him to join him. Satisfied that everything was under control, Joe stepped outside into the light of day.

Duke strode under the kitchen's low-hanging metal rafters, grinning when he heard Joe's hearty greeting. "Hey, boss man! What can I do for ya?"

"Not much—just making my rounds. You need anything?"

Joe smiled. "Not really." He gestured to the bubbling black cauldron on the side of the building. "Want to taste my stew? Meet me around the side."

The tantalizing aroma grew stronger as Duke approached the fire pit. Joe stirred a huge pot with a long wooden ladle, ensuring that each scoop would contain at least one small piece of meat.

"Wow, what is that meat in there?" asked Duke.

"There's bits of venison, rabbit, and squirrel in there," said Joe. "But my real secret ingredient—the thing that makes it so delicious—is organs from the animals." He made a face. "Most folks turn their noses up at it but it adds a ton of flavor and calories."

Duke chuckled and thanked him for the sample before heading back to work. His mouth watered with anticipation as he imagined eating Joe's stew later that evening.

Next, Duke approached the only blacksmith in Mountaintop, Mr. Colfax. He could hear rapid-fire hammering from the forge as he approached. A rush of sweltering air greeted Duke. Mr. Colfax was a massive black man. Duke estimated him to be in his forties and standing at least 6'4". He had a bald head with drops of sweat cascading over it, no matter how cool the mountain air was. His large hands expertly worked the metal, hammering it forcefully on the anvil with each movement. An African accent fell from his lips as he spoke few words. His face always had the same stoic expression.

"Mr. Colfax, how are you doing today?" asked Duke.

"Good," he said without looking up from his work.

"Is there anything that you need?"

"No," Mr. Colfax said flatly.

"All right, I'll see you around, I guess," said Duke, taking a step back before turning and walking quickly away from the building with its familiar clanging sounds. *Well, that was fun...*

Next up on Duke's daily rounds was Greg Arrowood, the Mountaintop's lead mechanic. With his weathered face and graying ponytail, the eighty-year-old Vietnam vet stood tall despite an unruly hip replacement—a testament to his lifelong experience tinkering with combustion engines.

"Dammit boy, I said ten-millimeter socket, not nine!" the old mechanic barked as he tossed a socket wrench in the direction of the skinny shop assistant, who scampered to retrieve it from the concrete floor.

"You know, he will be even less helpful if you kill him," Duke said sarcastically as he stepped forward.

"Oh hell, what do you want, Duke? I got nothing for ya."

"Well, good afternoon to you too," Duke said, shaking his head. "Just stopping by to see if you need anything?"

"Yeah, I could use some competent help!" Greg glared at his young shop assistant.

"Yeah, I know, but the turnover rate is kinda high working for you. That kid is your third one this month."

"That's a bunch of bullshit; kids just don't know what hard work is these days. Back in my day, we went to school and then went to work and listened to the radio and that was it. No internet, no cell phone, no fancy-ass help robots or any of that shit! We either played outside or read books. We worked our asses off and listened to our parents or they would whoop your ass," said Greg, taking a swig of whiskey out of the flask.

"I agree, but times have changed, Greg. Even people my age didn't grow up without that stuff."

"You damn right they have—and at least you ain't soft, these kids are soft. I'm glad the world went to shit. Everything will go back the way it's supposed to be," Greg grumbled. His weather-beaten face looked tired as he raised the flask to his lips again.

"And how is it supposed to be?" Duke asked.

Greg slammed down his flask and began ranting: "It's supposed to be simple and not complicated. Food, water, shelter, someone to talk to. That's all you need. But, most importantly, to have a purpose. Kids in the modern age have had everything handed to them. Physical labor didn't exist anymore. Never having to work for nothing. The internet, robots, and all that automation bullshit did everything for them! People couldn't even drive themselves anymore. Then they started talking about that universal income bullshit!"

"Well, all right, I think—"

"Participation trophies watering down the sense of real achievement. America's youth is a joke! They're being taught to think like a victim instead of pulling themselves up by their bootstraps like they're supposed to. Hate to break it to you little shits, more government doesn't mean more freedom!" Greg shouted at his shop helper.

"Can't disagree with that, Greg. I'll let you two get back to work."

The kid that was helping Greg jokingly mouthed the words, "Help me." Duke shrugged his shoulders as he smiled and walked away.

"Boy, where the hell is that nine-millimeter socket at?!"

Though Duke thought Greg to be a drunk, cranky old man, he agreed with him for the most part.

Next up was Tracy Furne. Tracy was a stout woman with cascading curly brown hair that reached her shoulders. As storage manager, she kept track of the community's entire food supply. Her job was to ensure everyone got their allotted share while carefully calculating how many supplies remained. Duke entered the room and found Tracy counting countless sacks of beans, rice, and other goods in containers along the wall. Sweat dripped down her face as she calculated how long the supplies would last.

"Afternoon, Tracy," said Duke.

"Hey Duke," Tracy replied without looking up.

"What's wrong Trace?" Duke already knew the answer, but he was being polite. Tracy had volunteered for this responsibility, not understanding how complex the task would be with more people living in the community. She had helpers, but the weight of providing enough resources still weighed heavily on her.

"Oh, you know, just counting the countless sacks of beans, rice, and everything else in here," Tracy said with a deep sigh. "Charles is wanting a weekly update on our food storage. But he wants it in years and months."

"Like a countdown?" asked Duke.

"Yep." Tracy nodded as she continued counting. "Well, there are a lot of variables—the amount of wild game brought in foraging, and that doesn't include the food we will get when Ed starts harvesting his potato crop." She paused to add up some calculations then added grimly: "Initially, with the group that we had, we had over five years' worth of food. But with all these extra people Charles allowed in, I give it one year before we are fully out."

Duke gasped at her words. "Really? Only a year?"

"Now, mind you," Tracy explained, "that's if we don't produce any crops and stop eating wild game."

Duke swallowed hard before asking, "Does Charles know that we only have a year?"

Tracy nodded. "Yeah, I told him that; he's just one optimistic guy and says everything will work out the way it's supposed to."

"I guess all we can do is pray for rain and wild game."

"Yeah, especially with that wildfire up north," said Tracy.

"How did you hear about that?"

"Small place, little to talk about." Tracy smiled.

"Yeah, that's true." Duke scratched at his beard. "I'll let you get back to it; try not to work too hard, Trace."

Tracy forced a smile and went back to counting.

Next up was another one of his favorite stops, Dr. Kelly Sako. Dr. Kelly was very blunt and direct. She was a beautiful middle-aged Indian woman with dark brown eyes. She always wore her jet-black hair loosely in a bun. The main reason Duke loved Dr. Kelly's stop was because it was where Julie worked.

Charles had made the mini-hospital out of six forty-foot storage containers; three on the bottom and three on top. Duke was amazed every time he walked in. It looked like a small hospital with gurneys lining the space from wall to wall. Charles had poured a lot of money into it. Everything was framed in, supported, drywalled, and painted. The whole bottom floor was almost completely open except for the spaces between the gurneys. An all-encompassing curtain hung at the door for privacy.

Duke saw Dr. Kelly, Julie, and one other assistant when he walked through the door. He nodded to Dr. Kelly and her other medical staff before his gaze met Julie's. A wide smile cracked across his face as he opened his arms, and she ran into them with a delighted squeal. She kissed him, then pulled away with a regretful look on her face.

"Afternoon, ladies," said Duke with a big smile.

Julie apologized, her cheeks burning with embarrassment. "I've got a patient I need to attend to; I have to go. Bye!"

"Is there something that you actually need, Duke, or are you just here to distract my P.A.s?" said Dr. Kelly, her eyebrow raised in amusement and disapproval.

"Well, not all of them, just one," Duke said with a big cheesy smile.

Dr. Kelly threw her used gloves at him in a playful manner, smirking.

"Do you need anything, Dr. Kelly?"

"Yeah, for you to stop distracting my Julie." Dr. Kelly smiled and crossed her arms over her chest protectively.

"All right, I'm leaving," said Duke with a chuckle as he stepped out of the room.

Just before the door closed behind him, Dr. Kelly stuck her head outside and fixed him with a stern glare, her voice low and serious as she spoke. "And Duke, Julie is a wonderful young lady... If you break her heart, I'll break your nuts—got it?"

The door clicked shut before he could answer. *Good to know.*

Next on the list was visiting Patrick and Eric. These two brothers, still in their early twenties, were real tech whizzes when it came to all things electrical and radio-related. They both had round figures and short, dark hair. They helped assemble and set up Mountaintop's massive solar panel field. Their workstation was inside the command center—Patrick and Eric practically lived at the radios. They said they would do permanent radio guard as long as they didn't have to do anything else.

Patrick shouted, his voice charged with indignation, "No it's not!"

Eric shot back, "You're smoking crack, old man!"

"Old man? I'm only two years older than you!" Patrick roared.

Duke rolled his eyes. "Hey, fellas, what seems to be the problem today?"

Eric glanced at him before questioning, "Duke, which is better? Dungeons and Dragons 4th or 5th edition?"

Duke sighed. "I don't know what that means. I honestly don't wanna know either."

The sweet notes of music emanating from the radio drew Duke's attention away from the argument. "Hey, what was that?" he asked in wonderment.

"What's what?" Eric questioned.

"The radio, it's playing music. Is there a radio station that got up and running again?"

Eric explained, "Oh it's some guy here in Colorado playing his old vinyl records on a dedicated channel. He even plays the national anthem at night. In the morning he broadcasts himself saying the pledge of allegiance. He calls himself the Voice of the Mountains."

That's the second time I've heard about this guy.

Duke flashed a grim smile at the thought of someone out there clinging to hope for the relic of America. Music had always been integral to American culture, and this person refused to let it fade without a fight.

"He's even been broadcasting news reports from around the world," Patrick added. "He was first to report about the fire in the north."

"The fire, yes, but news from other places too? Does he know what caused the power outage? What does the rest of America look like? The world?" asked Duke.

"Operators have asked him that stuff, but all we've heard is something about it happening in all fifty states. He's given his opinion on why and some other folks have thrown in their ideas."

"What are people saying?"

"EMP blasts, solar flares, cyber warfare—you name it. Even one guy's suggesting our own government was behind it."

Duke stared off into space as he assessed the countless possibilities.

"Do you really think our government could do that to us?" Patrick said skeptically.

"No," Duke sighed heavily, "I don't think they did it, but then again—our government didn't stop whatever it was, either."

"Sounds like typical government work," Patrick mused. "Overstepping their authority here, not taking enough action there..."

Sounds about right.

Next up was the security building, where Jake was the head of Mountaintop's security. The command center also housed the security barracks, so Duke walked toward the security side of the building, down the hall to Jake's office. A couple of security personnel meandered out of their stations.

Duke reached Jake's door and tapped it twice. "Hey, Jake, you in there?"

"Yep, come on in," replied Jake.

Shutting the door behind him, Duke waited for Jake to finish his conversation on the radio.

"All right, I'm out. Anderson over and out." Jake set the handheld device on the desk and looked up at Duke. "What can I do for you?"

"Still hard to wrap my head around how all this equipment didn't get fried," said Duke.

"That was a big conex with great protection—practically a forty-foot Faraday cage, brother." Jake smiled.

"Look, our relationship is strictly business—so knock off with that 'brother' stuff, okay?" said Duke sternly.

"Yeah man, of course," sighed Jake in resignation.

The room filled with an awkward quiet until finally Duke spoke up again. "You need anything from me?"

"Actually yeah, mind if you take a walk with me?" said Jake.

Duke followed Jake to the Ferris wheel, an old relic of a forgotten time. The wind rushed past them as Duke ascended the ladder leading to the observation platform. Once at the top, Jake handed him a pair of binoculars and pointed down the mountain.

"According to Sean, it's another FEMA camp," he said grimly. "If they know about Mountaintop, then the authorities might try to intervene."

Duke felt his stomach flip as he realized what Jake was implying. With a hesitant nod, he asked, "Like martial law?"

"Yeah, pretty much," Jake replied. He gestured for Duke to give up the binoculars before continuing. "We need to find out more information without drawing too much attention to ourselves. Figure out how many people are in this camp and how they operate so we can avoid them."

Duke pondered this for a moment. "So how do you suggest we do that? I don't think spying on a federal agency is something in this community's repertoire."

"I agree." Jake smiled as he looked off into the distance. "That's why I think it's time to test Eric and Patrick's new project out."

CHAPTER 12

COLORADO | MAY 2035

As Duke approached the command center, he heard a familiar sound. Looking to his left, he spotted Michael and Ava, who had been waiting impatiently for his arrival. Before he knew it, he was being embraced by both of them in a flurry of joyful laughter.

"Daddy, can you play with us?" Michael asked eagerly.

"Absolutely," Duke replied with a smile, "tonight after Daddy is off of work, I promise."

Their disappointment was quickly interrupted when they saw some other kids walking nearby and ran to join them. All Duke could hear were faint echoes of "Love you, Daddy!" as they vanished around the corner.

"Love you, too," Duke murmured.

Jake turned to Duke. "They talk about you all the time, Duke, how much they missed you. Just know that I've been good to them. Always will be," he said sincerely.

Duke wasn't interested in hearing Jake's words and quickly changed the subject. "Anyways, are we going in?" He opened the door and stepped inside, leaving Jake behind.

Duke saw Charles talking to Eric and Patrick, their heads bent together as they intensely discussed something to do with the radios. He waited for them to wrap up their discussion before stepping forward.

"Charles, can we run something by you?" Duke asked.

A perky smile spread across Charles' face. "Absolutely."

"There's a FEMA camp set up in Cascade," Jake said.

Charles frowned. "Well, that's getting awfully close, isn't it?"

"Yes, it is. We were thinking we needed to see FEMA's setup and see what's going on there," Jake replied.

"To be honest, we can't risk people going out there to spy," Charles stated firmly. "That could just draw their attention to us."

Jake cleared his throat. "Oh, I know, that's why I was gonna ask if you think it would be all right if we let Patrick and Eric try out their drone?"

Patrick's eyes widened with excitement. "Heck yeah! Hear that, Eric?" he shouted.

Eric furrowed his brows in overjoyed disbelief. "We get to take baby out on her first mission?"

Charles eyed him skeptically. "Is it ready to fly?" he asked, his voice tinged with concern.

Eric gave an apologetic smile. "Yep, and no more accidents. Promise."

Nodding slowly, Charles said, "All right, everyone follow Eric and Patrick." His tone was filled with a sense of impending danger.

Patrick and Eric guided the group toward the electronics bay in the back of the room. Amidst all the hardware and wires, their drone was massive. It was over five feet long and wide. It had six arms with their own propellers resting on top of it. The main body of the drone looked like a carbon fiber spider from another planet. It was propped up by four metallic arms extending downward. In the middle of the body was a big camera of sorts.

"This is our baby; it has a Watts Prism Quad motor system. Position lighting system. These legs act as a pick-up and drop system." Eric pointed to the various components on the drone.

"We custom-built a sky echo mobile ground control station. Gimbalized Radiometric Thermal camera with RGB zoom camera. We also integrated it with my old V.R. headset," Patrick said with pride.

"You might as well have said that in Chinese because I did not understand a word you said," chuckled Charles.

"It's a huge drone with badass capabilities," said Eric.

After five minutes of bickering, it was decided that Eric should fly the drone. Clad in his headset and goggles, he held the remote control firmly in his hands.

Patrick ushered everyone to the electronics room as Eric prepared for takeoff. Once there, everyone gathered around a computer monitor.

"With this monitor, we should be able to see whatever Eric sees," Patrick announced.

The telltale hum of the hovering drone could be heard outside. Duke could feel the vibration of its powerful motors against his palms as it hovered in place. It seemed to echo through the valley like a swarm of locusts. The drone left their line of sight, soaring down the treacherous mountainside, past trees that stood like sentinels watching over their precious land.

"That thing was so loud—wouldn't people in the FEMA camp hear it?" asked Charles.

"No, not necessarily. That camera can easily see things up close a mile away. That's far enough away that they won't be able to hear it," Patrick assured him.

Once the drone was about a mile away from the FEMA camp, Duke marveled at the computer screen as the camera zoomed in. He could see even the smallest tattoos adorning some of the survivors' bodies. The camp was alive with all sorts of activity as workers scurried about carrying out tasks and taking care of those unfortunate enough to have been caught up in this mess. There were about a dozen buildings in various shapes and colors; everywhere people shuffled in orderly lines. The camera captured it all with remarkable clarity.

A deathly stillness pervaded the air as Patrick peered at the landscape below. "That place is bigger than I thought," he muttered into the silence.

Charles gave a wry smile, eyes squinting in the bright sunlight. "Mountaintop is bigger," he said with a knowing smirk.

Duke's gaze lingered on the scene, jaw agape in wonderment. "Did you see the FEMA camp in the Springs? It's way bigger," he chided, almost reverently. Abruptly his attention was drawn to something else, and he exclaimed with a jerky gesture of his head, "Wait! Stop! Have him zoom in on the bald guy!"

"Eric, zoom in on that short bald man on the bench."

Charles looked to Duke and asked, "Who is that?"

Duke stared intently at the figure becoming sharper by the second as Eric obliged him.

Jake's jaw hung open. "No, that can't be him." His eyes widened to saucers filled with terror.

"I assure you it can be," Duke stated firmly yet all too regretfully, looking back at Jake.

Jake stammered incomprehensibly as he pieced together what Duke had said previously about Isaac Agigi being nearby. With panic rising in his voice, he finally managed to ask, "So you're telling me that Isaac Agigi is about a mile away from our community?"

"Yeah, it looks that way ..." Duke shook his head in despair.

"So this is the man you were telling me about?" Charles inquired.

Duke nodded reluctantly, sadness casting its long shadow across his face.

"What are we going to do?" Jake gulped visibly as he awaited Duke's response.

With a heavy sigh, Duke said, "Try to remain hidden for as long as possible, and hope for the best."

✳ ✳ ✳

The first streaks of gray morning light had just begun to break over the horizon when Sean and his hunting crew gathered in the parking lot.

"No trucks this morning—we're going on foot," Sean barked, setting off down a steep incline with nary a glance behind him. His compatriots followed without question, always looking toward their leader for guidance—even Dale, Sean's right-hand man, though slower of wit than the others.

"Hey, Sean," said Dale as they clambered through thick undergrowth, "what you gonna do about Duke and Ferguson?"

"Don't know yet," replied Sean as he crested a rise and surveyed a sight that made him pause. "But I'll figure something out—sooner the better."

Dale peered over his shoulder. "Where are we going anyway? This way sucks, way too steep."

Sean pointed toward the FEMA camp about a quarter of a mile away.

"What, why? The emergency team camp thing?"

Sean stopped and faced his men. "First of all, it's called FEMA," he began, scanning their faces with a glare that spoke of years of experience and understanding. "And if they catch wind of Mountaintop," he continued slowly, emphasizing every word for effect, "the feds will be all in our business trying to tell us what to do." A pause for breath came with a collective sense of understanding as everyone in the group realized exactly what he meant. "Is that something you want?"

A fierce chorus met his words: "No!"

"Good, because I overheard those idiots talking about it. They used Tweedle Dee and Tweedle Dum's drone. And they are right; this does pose a threat. But something in that camp scared them and I want to know what. If there is a real threat to Mountaintop, we're going to take care of it like a real security team would." Sean spat a long stream of brown saliva on the ground. "That jackass Jake doesn't know shit about security. Maybe if we pull this off and stop whatever the threat is, we can get voted in for me to be in charge of security. Dale and y'all can run the hunting parties. We'll have more power and more say on what goes on in that place. Are you with me?"

"Hell yeah, boss. We got your back," Dale replied, his eyes darting to the huddle of men around him.

Sean gestured for them to split into teams and fan out across the area before leading his own group toward the FEMA camp. As they crept closer and closer, he peered through the trees ahead of him until a man from another team suddenly squatted down beside him.

"Hey, Sean," he whispered. "Looks like somebody's lit a campfire beyond the FEMA camp's perimeter ... quarter mile up that way."

Sean marched his men toward the campfire, drawn in like moths to a flame. A distant figure could be seen, lounging against a log. As they drew closer, they were met with the pungent aroma of cooked meat. When only fifty yards remained between them and the lonely figure, Sean raised his rifle warily.

"You there, keep your hands where I can see them," he called, his voice stern and sure.

The man ignored him, chomping loudly on his beefy offering.

"Hey numbnuts, I said hands in the air," shouted Sean even louder.

The man finally looked up and wiped glistening grease from his chin. His face shone in the firelight; he was covered in grease, like some sickeningly luminescent mask. His pants were stained with brown splotches as if he had been wiping greasy fingers on them for days. He stared at them with tired eyes, yet his expression remained calm as he spoke.

"Hey friend," he said around a mouthful of food, "please sit down and join me."

Sean bristled. "I promise you I'm not your friend," he barked back, adjusting his rifle on his shoulder.

"Well, that's unfortunate," sighed the stranger, "friends are hard to come by these days, especially in these trying times." He stretched out his greasy hand. "Please sit down and get that thing out of my face. There's no need for that. I'll answer your questions."

Reluctantly, Sean motioned for everyone to lower their weapons and take a knee.

The stranger flashed his teeth in a wide grin. "That's what I like to see—discipline. These men obviously respect you. That tells me you're a good leader."

Sean was getting impatient. "Who are you? Are you with the FEMA camp?"

"Ah, that can wait a moment. Right now it looks like your men could use some grub. Here, help yourselves to these bowls of meat here." The man handed a couple of bowls to Sean, who sniffed it suspiciously before taking a bite.

"See how much easier this is when we get along?" The stranger leaned back, stretching his legs out in front of him casually. "Name's Isaac, what's yours?"

"None of your damn business," growled Sean.

"There's that rudeness again." Isaac *tsked*, shaking his head before taking another bite from his bowl.

"Where did you get pork? There haven't been feral hogs in Colorado since 2018 or something like that. I know FEMA camps are not serving up roasted pork loin. So where in the hell did you get this?" Sean hungrily chewed another bite.

"Oh, that's because it's long pork, my friend," said Isaac, tearing into another bite.

Dale looked from one man to the other in confusion. "Long pork? What's that?"

"Human," Isaac said nonchalantly.

At those words, both Sean and his men immediately spat out the meat and pointed their guns directly at Isaac. "You sick freak!" shouted Sean.

The hungry man spoke with his mouth full, eyes glinting in the orange light of the fire. "Sick? Try smart. As you can probably tell, hunting around here is running a little thin. That FEMA camp's gonna run out of food eventually." He paused and turned to look at Sean. "Every time I see them cart away a dead body, or feed some useless fat piggy of a man, I can't help but think how they're just wasting food. It's a win-win for everyone," he said before popping another greasy morsel into his mouth and chewing slowly. "Plus, a little salt, little pepper—it's tasty, right?"

A chill ran down Sean's spine as Isaac rose to his feet with an unimpressed look on his face.

"I should kill you, you sick psycho," Sean said as he stepped closer.

"That's a good way to get yourself hurt," Isaac replied with an icy stare.

"How do you figure? There are twelve of us and one of you."

Isaac gestured around them and Sean felt dread rise up in his throat. His crew had been surrounded by more than twice their number—all looked bloodthirsty and desperate.

"Looks like we're both dying today, Isaac," Sean said, trying to sound confident despite the terror creeping through him.

"Maybe," Isaac replied coolly. "But that's your call." He fixed Sean with a cold gaze before continuing, "I want what every man here wants: To find, give in, and fulfill our most primal instincts—eating, drinking, sleeping, mating, and the occasional need for revenge." He paused as he looked around the circle of faces illuminated by the flames. Then he laughed with a deep, rumbling chuckle that sent shivers down Sean's spine. "These are basic needs of every man."

Isaac took another bite from the remains of his meal and addressed Sean again with greasy lips stretched into a sinister grin. "It doesn't have to be this way between you and me. Because I know good character when I see one—and I would love it if you and your squad would join my crew."

Sean cleared his throat. "Why would I want to do that?" he asked cautiously, trying to stay on the psychopathic killer's good side. "What's in it for us?"

"Why join me? Look at us! You'll never go hungry. You and your boys with your bellies full every night. I'll treat you with the respect that you deserve. We'll rise in power together and create a large and powerful community of survivors and soldiers. We get to recreate the United States to our liking. And destroy those who stand in our way and those who did us wrong."

Isaac's words lingered in the air like a whispered promise of hope, yet Mountaintop still held a grip on Sean's conscience as an ever-present reminder of all that could be lost if he accepted Isaac's offer. He looked up from thought, aware that everyone was waiting for an answer.

"So, what do you say ... what did you say your name was?" asked Isaac.

"I didn't say," Sean replied, his throat tight as he shifted uncomfortably under their gaze, "and if we say no? What happens then?"

"Well, nothing," Isaac said flatly, unwavering. "I'm not holding a knife to your throat." The group around them shifted uneasily, weapons ready to raise again at any sign of aggression.

"No," Sean responded quickly, "but THEY are pointing guns at us." He slowly turned toward the men surrounding them silently with deadly intent blazing in their eyes.

"True," Isaac growled as his face darkened in anger at Sean's challenge, "but you are not being held prisoner. So you are free to go no matter your answer." He paused briefly, looking each man in the eye as if willing them to accept his offer.

"Any answer?" Sean finally asked after moments of tense silence stretched out between them.

"Yes," Isaac answered with a wicked smile growing on his face, "no matter what."

"Then the answer is no." Sean declared confidently as he stared down Isaac menacingly across the small campfire.

Everyone waited for what felt like hours for some sign of reaction from Isaac; only silence settled over them like a thick haze until finally Isaac spoke up.

"That's too bad, friend," Isaac remarked without malice.

Sean and his men slowly gathered their belongings and began walking back to Mountaintop while eyeing over their shoulders with fear of being followed.

As they began moving back the way they came, Dale spoke up nervously, asking, "You think they're going to follow us?"

"Not sure," Sean replied, glancing back at the receding campfire, "but let's get back."

With that, they hastened their pace, still looking over their shoulders in fear.

✳✳✳

Isaac Agigi's men stood around the campfire, their faces bathed in the orange and yellow light. They waited for him to explain why they had allowed their enemies to escape.

"Why did we let them go?" asked one of Agigi's men. "We could have easily taken their weapons and ate for days."

Agigi sat in silence for a moment, cleaning his fingernails with a makeshift knife before he beckoned the man forward.

"You want to know why?" Agigi said in a low growl.

The man nodded and stepped closer to his leader. But before he could utter another word, Agigi moved his hand faster than lightning, thrusting the blade deep into the man's chest several times before he fell back gasping for air.

Agigi knelt beside him and spoke in a hoarse whisper close to his ear. "Because I said so!"

Agigi then rose to address his men, rage burning in his eyes.

"Everything I do is for a reason," he shouted, pacing back and forth as he tried to look each man in the eye. "I need you to trust me, never to question me!" He jabbed a finger at two of his men. "And you two—go and follow that group, see where they are headed. Think you can manage that without being seen?" His tone was almost mocking, as if he were addressing a couple of children.

❋❋❋

Making his rounds for the day, Duke strolled around the perimeter of the compound, an ever-watchful eye on his men. In the distance, he saw Sean and his group of mercenaries shuffle through the back gate.

"How did this morning's hunt go?" Duke questioned in a perfunctory tone.

"How do you think it went?" Sean replied, voice dripping with sarcasm, panting heavily.

Duke noticed that there was something off about him. "Why are you all sweaty and out of breath—don't you drive everywhere?" he asked, genuinely perplexed.

"We were hunting nearby and decided to hike on foot. We raced each other on the way back as a morale boost," Sean replied cheekily while patting Duke's shoulder. "You should join us sometime," he said with a smirk.

Duke tried to shake off Sean's words but couldn't help feeling uneasy anytime Sean was around.

Suddenly, Jake appeared behind him. "Sean still pushing your buttons?" he asked knowingly.

"Yeah, but there's something else going on," Duke responded, looking concerned.

"What do you mean?" inquired Jake skeptically.

"I can't put my finger on it exactly, but Sean seemed spooked or something."

Jake scoffed dismissively. "I doubt it, man. Sean's not one to get spooked so easily."

CHAPTER 13

Colorado | June 2035

Duke had been trying to wake up early, even before the sun rose, in order to make the most of his day. He attempted to read his Bible every morning, but his concentration was often broken by Julie's gentle snores. His reading light illuminated her golden hair, making it appear as though it were glowing.

"Thank you Lord for granting me a second chance with my children. Thank you for Julie; she has been nothing but a blessing in my life. I honestly do not deserve them but I am so grateful for having them in my life. I know that I have made mistakes, and I understand that I am far from perfect, so please forgive me for failing You," Duke whispered.

Suddenly, he heard a knock at his door.

"Amen," he muttered before turning around to face the door. He opened it to find Jake standing there, his face creased with worry.

"What do you need?" Duke asked impatiently.

"Charles called a meeting," Jake replied. His voice quaked slightly. "He asked me to come get you."

Duke went over to Julie and kissed her on the forehead. "See you tonight?" he whispered.

"Okay," she responded, still half-asleep.

Duke and Jake jogged over to the command center and could hear raised voices before they entered the building. When Duke opened the door, the sound of people talking loudly in disagreement assaulted him. He could feel the heavy tension in the air.

"Good morning everyone," Duke announced.

Everyone stopped their grumbling temporarily and nodded their heads, acknowledging Duke's presence.

"What's going on, Charles?" Duke inquired.

"The Voice of the Mountains—you know the guy who's been playing music and giving updates over the radio?" Duke nodded. "He got ahold of us saying said that due to wind change, the fire up north had turned and was heading in our direction."

Duke had never seen Charles Ferguson distraught. He usually held an optimistic outlook about any situation they were faced with.

"Duke, do you have any ideas? Or do you think you can call up Karl and see if his group can help in any way?" Charles sounded desperate.

"Yeah, sure," Duke answered uncertainly. "Though I haven't heard from him, so I'm not sure if he's even there."

Charles let out a loud whistle that seemed to pull everyone back into reality momentarily. Finally people stopped and looked at him.

"Thanks, Charles," Duke began. "Hey everyone, just listen to me for a second: We are going to be okay. Do you hear me? We'll figure something out, don't know what that is yet but we'll figure it out." Although his tone was confident, deep down he wasn't sure whether his words would prove true.

The message was received but failed to bring the group solace like Duke had hoped. They were all too aware that hope alone was not going to be enough this time.

"This news about the fire stays in this tent," Duke declared.

"Or what?" Sean challenged him.

"What do you mean?" Duke cocked an eyebrow.

"What would happen if we told our friends and family? Are you seriously asking us to lie?" asked Sean.

Eric asked gruffly if it was too early, even for him, to start being a jerk.

Sean shot up from his seat and bellowed, "Shut your mouth! The grown-ups are trying to talk here!"

"I'm not telling anyone to lie," Duke explained with a sigh, "I'm just asking everyone not to say anything until we have a concrete plan, otherwise this whole town will descend into panicked chaos."

After a few moments of silence, Dr. Kelly spoke up. "Duke is right; please let's not tell anyone outside of this tent about the fire. It'll only cause trouble."

Everyone stood up from their chairs and began to filter out of the room. Charles halted Duke with a wave of his hand, signaling for him to stay behind after everyone else had left.

"Duke, I need you to hop on the radio immediately and see if you can arrange a meeting with Karl and his group," Charles commanded.

"I'll do it right away," Duke responded, already fumbling with the communication device. "Eric, do you still have that paper I gave you with Karl's camp's frequency?"

Eric was already punching in the frequency.

Duke took a deep breath. "Badger base, Badger, this is Mountaintop, over," he said hesitantly into the mic.

A few moments passed before Duke tried again.

"Badger base, Badger base, Mountaintop looking for Chief, over?"

"Mountaintop, this is Badger base, wait one, over," someone responded on the other end of the line.

"Roger that, Badger base," Duke said with barely contained relief.

Several minutes went by before someone identifying as Chief finally responded. "Mountaintop, this is Chief."

"Hey brother, how's everything going?" Duke asked nervously.

"What do you need from me, Mountaintop? The radio isn't meant for idle chatter—over."

A pause hung heavy in the air.

"Are we done here? Or do you actually have something important to say?" Chief growled impatiently.

"Chief, Mountaintop needs your assistance with fighting that forest fire that's heading our way—over."

Time seemed to drag on endlessly as they waited for a response.

"Our unit has been discussing this possibility for several days. I'll talk to command about linking up; we can discuss the possibility of sharing responsibility for fire mitigation—over."

"Hopefully they'll agree; where should we meet?" Duke asked. "Over."

"Don't get ahead of yourself. We haven't received an answer yet. If it does come through, we'll send you grid coordinates—over."

"Thank you, brother. Mountaintop out," Duke said with a celebratory grin spreading across his face.

***

The following morning, Duke and Charles were talking when Eric suddenly bolted out of the command center.

"Duke, Mr. Ferguson. It looks like we got ourselves a rendezvous with Karl's pack."

"That's great news!" Charles exclaimed.

Eric handed Charles a piece of paper, gesturing for them to go inside. "Here, I'll show ya."

He directed them to the back wall where a large laminated map hung.

"They want to meet on the west side of Manitou Reservoir," said Eric, indicating the spot on the map.

"When?" Charles inquired.

"Today at noon."

"Patrick, I need you to inform Jake that we require him and a squad of four security members to be ready within the hour," Duke commanded.

Within the ensuing two hours, Duke, Jake, and four people from Mountaintop's security group readied themselves and went over their plans.

"Is there anything that we should anticipate from these individuals? What do we know about them?" Jake questioned.

"Well, if they are anything like Karl, they will be blunt, calculated, and dangerous," Duke said with a lazy smile.

"So people we need as friends. I know you trust Karl, but can we really trust his group?"

Duke hesitated before saying, "Yeah, I do trust Karl but ... I don't know anyone from his group."

"So what are you saying? This could be a trap?"

"No, I'm just not sure who I was talking to," Duke replied nervously, rubbing the back of his neck. He took a deep breath and continued, "But we have to take a chance because that fire is coming and we need to do something about it."

Jake's eyes beseeched Duke with an expression of dread. "So we're trusting people we don't even know?" he muttered, as if the words themselves carried a heavy weight.

"I get it. Trust is hard to come by these days, and it's a fairly easy thing to break. Wouldn't you say?" asked Duke, eyeing Jake.

"Yeah, I suppose so." Jake was unable to look at Duke.

"The good news is it's also an easy thing not to mess up," Duke said, walking away from Jake and starting toward the truck, a heavy backpack slung over his shoulder.

Jake followed him quickly, desperation in his eyes. "When are you going to forgive me?" he pleaded.

Duke whirled around, anger flashing across his face. "Forgive you? You can't honestly expect that, not after what you did!"

Jake swallowed, suddenly quiet. "I said I'm sorry..."

"It doesn't matter! Personally, I want nothing more from you—never again—but this community needs us all to work together and put out this forest fire." Duke dropped the bag into the bed of the truck with a loud thud. His voice softened as he looked at Jake. "Can you do that?"

Jake gave a single nod. "Yep, sure can." Defeat laced his voice as he watched Duke turn away from him again.

"Good." Duke called out to the rest of the group, who stood by waiting. "Let's get loaded up and head out."

The convoy had two vehicles, each with a driver, a passenger, and one person in the bed. Jake was in the lead truck, Duke's following behind close enough for them to communicate via handheld radio.

"We're taking Pikes Peak Highway down," Duke said, looking at a map, his voice crackling through the speaker on the walkie-talkie.

"Roger that," Jake responded.

They wound down a dirt road flanked by mountains and trees, the fresh mountain air carrying the scent of pine and earth through Duke's open window. Having done time in prison, Duke realized he should never take little things like this for granted. Countless people must feel the same about their changed lives, living in a world devoid of electricity, unable to turn on the tap for water or flush a toilet without a thought.

Duke felt grateful his children didn't have to suffer like so many others because they were part of the Mountaintop community. His mind then turned to his parents; his mother who was a nature-loving hippie, and his dad who hunted game and taught respect for wildlife. They had both instilled in him an appreciation of the natural environment he found himself surrounded by.

It was such a beautiful day, Duke thought. Driving to the mountains, it was hard to tell that the world around them was falling apart because nature didn't seem to care. He thought it was crazy how nature did its own thing and would flourish regardless of human suffering. Nature was perfect before people, and it would be just fine after they were gone. There was a way to live harmoniously with the earth, but humans tried to dominate it instead, much like they did with each other. Human beings were intended to be the nurturers that helped nature thrive. But they ended up being a virus that made it sick. A parasite that takes more than it gives. A species hell-bent on destroying itself.

Jake knocked on the truck's hood, taking Duke out of his nature-induced hypnosis.

"Hey, we are out of road. What do you want to do?" Jake asked, leaning on the door with both hands.

"We walk around to the other side, I guess—nothing else we can do really," said Duke.

"We're heading out on foot," Jake called out to the crew.

Duke, Jake, and the other four men skirted the five-acre reservoir through the pine trees. Duke looked over at Jake, trying to command his men into a wedge formation. Duke shook his head in disappointment.

"Now what?"

"How the heck do you mess up a wedge formation?" asked Duke.

"What? They're doing fine. It's a V shape," proclaimed Jake.

"True, but it's backwards. We need to train these guys properly," Duke scoffed.

"What is this WE you speak of? I thought you wanted nothing to do with me," Jake said.

Duke spoke with urgency. "Listen up: Agigi has people just beyond our walls. We need to protect Mountaintop, so it's time to get our people properly trained."

"How in the blazes are we gonna do that?" Jake asked incredulously.

"It's going to take time, I guess." Duke shrugged.

The two made haste toward the meeting point only to find it empty when they arrived. Jake looked at his watch, his anxiety rising. "It's noon, right?" he asked, expecting a confirmation from Duke, who was now pacing, worry lines creasing his forehead.

Suddenly one of their associates shouted, "Movement!" All heads turned as one in the direction the voice had come.

Two figures emerged from the dark; an older, short, burly black man with a shaved head, dressed in tactical gear, and beside him, a tall and broad white man with short brown hair and a steel-gray goatee. The air around them crackled with potency as they strode up to Duke's group.

"Stop right there!" Jake yelled, his gun pointed at the two men. The rest of his group mirrored his gesture with their own weapons.

"Where's Karl?" Duke called out.

The reply came in a low growl from the older black man. "He couldn't make it, sorry 'bout that."

Duke stood his ground as he answered. "Well, we're here only to do business with Karl, and if he's not here I'm afraid we wasted our time."

The tension crackled in the air like lightning. The black man narrowed his eyes and spat, "What? You don't want to do business with me because I'm black? You a racist?"

The white man echoed him in agreement, adding scornfully, "Yeah, he looks like a racist."

Duke quickly backpedaled. "No, I just don't know you. As far as I know, you did something to Karl."

The black man showed no emotion as he replied. "Maybe we did, maybe we didn't."

Duke asked cautiously, "You don't mind us leaving then, do you?"

A sinister smile spread across the black man's face as he said, "Nope, not at all, but before you go, I got a surprise for you."

Everything seemed to happen in slow motion. A shrill whistle pierced the air, and the group was surrounded by what felt like a dozen guns pointed directly at them. Goosebumps rose on their skin and fear crept up their spines like icy fingers.

"Put your guns on the ground," guffawed the black man.

Jake shook uncontrollably but managed to growl through gritted teeth: "Never."

Duke knew it was useless to resist and spoke calmly but firmly to the group. "Just do what he says."

The strength seemed to have been sucked from them and they reluctantly put their weapons down on the ground while holding up their hands in submission. Their guns were collected in one swift motion.

Duke's voice quivered as he asked hopefully, "What do you want?"

With a menacing glint in his eye, the white man replied, "We're here to give you Karl."

The black man unslung his backpack from his shoulders and set it gingerly on the ground. In slow, deliberate motions he unzipped the bag and plunged his hand inside. He then pulled it back out, giving Duke's group the middle finger.

The white man smirked as he pointed to a patch of dried grass at Duke's feet. Duke was about to ask what the guy meant when there was a sudden *whoosh* and the grass seemed to come alive. Stiff blades of grass rose up like a wave, flipping Duke off his feet with one powerful brush. His group scrambled to their feet just in time to see Karl, camouflaged head-to-toe in a ghillie suit, rolling over onto his back and grinning up at them.

The black man fell into hysterics and the white guy leaned forward slightly, eyes gleaming with amusement. "I bet they actually pissed themselves!"

Duke felt heat rush to his face, but Karl cut through the laughter with a booming chuckle. "All right, all right, enough fun. Let's get down to business."

Duke and the group approached the hastily constructed campsite where Karl's men had gathered. The air was thick with laughter and banter, and everyone introduced themselves.

"Name's Jones, they call me Havoc," said the black man with a broad grin.

"Is that your call sign or personality trait?" Duke quipped.

The white man chuckled. "Oh, come on, Duke, you got to admit that was pretty good." He cleared his throat. "And you can call me Patch."

"Why do they call you that?" asked Jake, eyeing Patch curiously.

"My last name is Adams. Patch Adams? I'm a medic? No? Nothing?" Patch stared at them blankly before exhaling heavily in disappointment. "Gen Z."

Karl, unable to contain his amusement any longer, burst into laughter. "Sorry, Duke, we couldn't help ourselves."

Duke rolled his eyes but still managed to crack a smile as he shifted back to reality. "Ha ha, yes, okay, that was really good ... Now what are we going to do about this forest fire?"

Karl's expression became serious again as he explained their plan of action. "A firebreak of some sorts needs to be created. We have chainsaws and trucks. We also need as many people as you can spare and some heavy-duty machinery."

"I'm not sure how many personnel we can give up," Duke replied thoughtfully, "but I can ask."

Jake chimed in too, remembering Greg's project while passing through earlier in the day. "I think our mechanic, Greg, is currently fixing up a backhoe. When that's fixed, I'm sure Mr. Ferguson will allow you guys to use it."

Karl nodded solemnly in appreciation for their efforts. "Good, because we have a lot of sensitive things we don't want to get fucked. We will need all the help that we can get."

The conversation trailed off until Duke was left alone with his own thoughts—thoughts that began to spiral out of control as he contemplated the upcoming battle against nature.

Karl noticed Duke's mental absence. "You got something on your mind, Duke?"

Duke nervously shifted his feet and rubbed his beard. "Ya know, actually. We need to train Mountaintop in firearms training, hand-to-hand combat, battle drills ... you name it."

Karl nodded in agreement. "Go train 'em. You have the knowledge and supplies to do so."

"We need help," Duke said hesitantly. His eyes darted around the group, searching for support. "Only a few of us have that type of knowledge. Was wonderin' if you and your men could help us out."

Karl remained silent, studying Duke with narrowed eyes as if attempting to probe into his thoughts. The air was thick with anticipation until he finally broke the silence. "We all have our hands full with this fire situation. So why is this an issue right now?"

"We spotted Agigi in Cascade," Duke began with worry in his voice, "inside the FEMA camp there. That's a mile away from Mountaintop."

"So what? Y'all should be safe at Mountaintop," Karl said nonchalantly, not showing any concern.

"It looks like he has over a few dozen men already followin' him," Duke continued, shaking his head in disbelief. "You saw how relentless he is ... you know that number is gonna grow."

Jones piped up, confusion written on his face. "Who's Agigi?"

Duke sighed heavily and looked down at his feet before looking up again with grief in his eyes. With resolve on his face, he replied slowly and quietly, "A psychopath that's seekin' revenge on me."

"Revenge? Revenge for what?" Patch asked.

Duke closed his eyes tightly as memories came flooding back to him—memories he would want no one else to experience. He took a deep breath. "Was working with him ... got busted by the ATF and FBI for smuggling packages for him. They busted me and then showed me that I had been carrying crates of weapons, so I cut a deal with them to help bring him down for domestic terrorism." He swallowed hard at the memories. "Agigi caught wind that there was a leak somewhere and thought it was a friend of ours ... Agigi shot him in front of me ... so I also helped bring him down for murder."

He ended the story somberly, looking at Jake, who gave him an understanding nod.

The room went quiet save for Jones' snarky comment which pierced the silence like lightning across the sky. "Spare us da sob story," he spat out angrily, waving away Duke's sadness with a disdainful gesture. "How could ya mule for domestic terrorists and wear the flag at the same time? Sounds like treasonous behavior to me."

Duke shouted in desperation, "I didn't know what was in those packages! He paid me a lot of money not to ask questions!"

The whole camp seemed transfixed on the scene and Karl waved to everyone, trying to ease any concerns. Jones stepped in and coldly stated, "Well, the way I see it he's your problem. Why should we help you fix your mess-up?"

Jake said, "Because if he gets ahold of one of those packages, he'll be a problem for everyone."

Karl shifted his gaze slowly toward Jake as if sizing him. "You were a part of this?"

Jake slowly nodded in response.

Patch took an uneasy step forward and inquired nervously, "Wait—there are some weapon crates cached out there?"

Again, Jake only nodded as if already knowing the consequences of his actions.

Karl further probed, "What type of weapons are we talking about?"

"The military-grade kind," Jake grumbled quietly. His face gave away how ashamed he felt revealing what he had discovered. "I had to take a peek. There were various assault weapons, machine guns, rockets, grenades, etcetera. Not to mention thousands of rounds that go with them," he added solemnly.

For a few moments the camp was enveloped in complete silence. The birds chirped peacefully as Karl and his men seemingly contemplated what it meant if those weapons fell into the wrong hands.

Finally Patch spoke up. "You know we need to bring this to the Colonel, right?" he said to Karl.

Jake tried to break the tension by offering a solution. "Okay, let's go talk to him."

Jones quickly cut in, shaking his head violently while exclaiming, "That's not gonna happen there, cowboy!"

Duke glanced around, dumbfounded. "Why not?"

"The colonel doesn't like surprise visits," Patch said, "to say the least."

Karl paused briefly before letting out a loud whistle, giving a signal to wrap it up. Everyone immediately scurried around putting out fires and packing their gear while Karl reaffirmed his point. "No one outside of our group knows where our base is, and it will stay that way."

"So what are we supposed to do then?" Jake asked, a tinge of hopelessness in his voice.

Karl shoved his equipment into the back of an ATV, eyes narrowed. "I guess you'll just have to wait," he said. "We'll give you an answer soon."

Jake scoffed and gestured wildly at their surroundings. "By all means, take your time; we only have a forest fire and some psychopath on the loose nearby."

"Please hurry, Karl," Duke stated sincerely.

Karl nodded sharply before climbing into the vehicle. "I know, but in the meantime, let us know when that backhoe is fixed and when you got your firefighting personnel picked out," he said before driving away with his group.

Jake stood there, his arms dangling at his sides as he watched them vanish into the mountain forest. An overwhelming sense of dread descended upon him as he turned to Duke and asked, "Now what?"

Duke sighed heavily and met his gaze. "You heard him—all we can do is wait and see what this Colonel has to say."

CHAPTER 14

Colorado | June 2035

The Mountaintop folk stood around their nightly bonfires, and voices of praise filled the air as Sean and his hunting party returned with fresh meat. For the past week, the hunters had been returning with sizable catches each evening.

Julie glanced over at Duke, who seemed lost in thought. Trying to break the silence between them, she said with a flirtatious tone, "I like you with a beard. What's on your mind?"

Duke hesitated before speaking. The whole trip home, Jake and Sarah, his kids, the fire, helping Charles run the camp—it all felt like too much to take in. He cleared his throat and tried to explain. "It's a little bit of everything." He started rubbing his eyes. "Everything that happened on our trip home; good, bad, and ugly; this camp; Agigi practically at our doorstep; no longer having a country; and doomsday actually happening. It's just ... a lot."

Julie nodded in understanding, squeezing Duke's hand tightly in support. "You forgot one thing," she jokingly said with a wink. "Dealing with your annoyingly hot blonde girlfriend."

Duke laughed exhaustedly and grabbed Julie by her waist, pulling her onto his lap. "Oh yeah, how could I forget about that?" he joked. "How can you have such a good attitude after everything? Your parents? Your grandparents? All of this?"

"Don't know if you remember but I wasn't okay with everything, and quite frankly I'm not still. My grandfather always told me that every day we can wake up and make the decision to do everything in our power to have a good day regardless of what happens to us." Julie smiled at the memory. "Said that life was ten percent what happens to you and ninety percent how you react to it."

"Are you our new mom?" asked Ava, awkwardly staring at Duke and Julie.

"No, honey, of course not," said Duke.

"You want me to be your stepmom?" asked Julie.

Ava shook her head no.

"Okay then, I don't have to be. How about I be your friend or big sister?" said Julie with a smile.

"Oh yeah, I always wanted a big sister!" squealed Ava. She gave Julie a big hug and ran away.

Duke and Julie both noticed that Michael stood watching them.

"You should've never left! None of this would have happened!" He shook his head in anger before he stormed off.

"Come on, buddy! Michael!" shouted Duke.

"Just give him some time, Duke," said Julie, placing a hand on his face.

"I know, he's taking his mother and I breaking up really hard," said Duke rubbing his face in frustration. "Did you ever think about having kids?"

"Absolutely, I always wanted to be a mother. But I don't think I can have children—my ex-husband and I had tried for years," Julie said somberly.

"I didn't know you were married before."

"I sure was. Married my high school sweetheart, Danny. Turned out to be a huge mistake. I'm glad, because I think he's some type of Mormon now." Julie laughed. "That's all I have to say about that."

"Sorry to hear that."

"Unfortunately, I think the time has passed for anyone to responsibly have a child right now."

"Yeah, I think so too. I'm truly grateful to have Mikey and Ava."

Julie let out an audible sigh.

"So tell me, how are you truly holding up, Jules?" Duke asked. "You know, despite your grandfather's wisdom."

"Like I said, I'm doing better than I thought I would be. But still, a lot has happened. Still trying to learn how to cope with it. I can still see my grandparents' faces," Julie said, getting choked up.

"I know," said Duke, kissing Julie on the top of her head.

"I mean, I dream about them almost every night. Still hear my grandmother's screams ringing in my ears," Julie said with tears rolling down her cheeks.

Duke pulled away from Julie and looked her in the eyes intently. "I promise you Agigi will get his. I just need a plan," he said firmly.

"I hope so." Julie nodded silently in agreement, hoping he'd find a way. She looked up at Duke as a single tear raced down her cheek. "You wanna know what bothers me the most?" Her voice quavered, barely audible above the fire.

Duke shook his head; there were too many options to hazard a guess.

"I enjoyed killing him," Julie whispered, her voice trembling, "I enjoyed hearing that fat sociopath scream! Doesn't that make me a monster?" She was shaking now, and her tears shone like diamonds in the firelight.

Duke ran his thumbs across her cheeks, wiping away tears as he looked into her eyes. "Everything that has happened in this new world is fair and just," he said confidently. "We must hold onto our humanity while still changing ourselves to survive this world." He pulled her close and kissed her gently, feeling her tears soak through his beard.

Charles interrupted their moment with words slurred by wine. "Hey, you two lovebirds!" His cup was raised in one hand, the other gripping a plate of meat.

Julie chuckled despite herself as she replied. "How's it going, Charles?"

"I have a drink and food in my belly: What more could a man ask for?"

A cacophony of cheers from Sean's pack captured Duke's attention. Out of the corner of his eye, he observed Sean wildly displaying to a young man who wilted in humiliation—it was plain that he was having a rough time. A peculiar look of apprehension spread across Duke's face.

"What is that?" Julie asked.

"Simply Sean being Sean," Duke responded with a shake of his head.

Charles tried standing still, but faltered as he spoke. "I feel like I've had too much ..."

"Mr. Ferguson, would you like some help getting to your room?" Julie inquired.

Joe, the community cook, wandered by and intervened, gently grabbing Charles. "I got him, Miss Julie."

"Thank you, Joe." Julie smiled warmly.

"Of course," Joe replied. "What did all of you think about the dinner tonight?"

"It was magnificent!" Julie chirped.

"Truly delicious, Joe," Duke added.

"You all should be thanking the man right there for this food," Joe said, pointing at Sean.

Duke nodded his head whilst fumbling around with a stick in his hands.

"I know that you don't have any affection for him, Duke, but he and his group are gonna be necessary for our long-term survival in this community. He has been bringing in deer meat, small game, and even a calf."

"Yes, Joe, I'm aware of that ... thank you."

"Please try to reconcile with him," Joe implored.

Duke took a deep breath. "All right ... I could do that," he uttered as he threw his stick on the fire.

Julie gave Duke a wink and quipped, "Play nice."

"Can't make any promises," Duke mused as he kissed Julie.

Duke trudged toward Sean and his gang, apprehensive. Instantly, the murmurs ceased, and the crowd parted for him to make his way to Sean. The stench of alcohol filled Duke's nostrils as he neared; Sean's face flushed crimson from all the liquor he had consumed.

"Looks like someone lost." Sean mockingly grinned.

"I'm not here to quarrel or fight with you, Sean. I'm here to give thanks for all the hard work your men have put in," Duke said sincerely.

"What? Am I hearing correctly? Is the notorious Duke Hollander saying thank you?" Sean slurred.

"So what do you say, Sean? Can we try and let go of the past?" Duke asked, extending his arm.

Sean paused for a moment, casting dubious glances toward Duke's hand before looking into his eyes. "What game are you out here trying to play?" he questioned.

"No games, just an olive branch and my gratitude for helping out the neighborhood," Duke answered honestly.

Despite not liking Sean, Duke understood that Joe was right—if the community were to make it long-term, people such as Sean and his hunters had to be around.

Eventually Sean reached out and shook Duke's hand firmly.

"So are we good now?"

"Guess so ... for now," said Sean warily.

"Glad we can move on from this. And seriously, Sean, great job. All y'all are doing an incredible job." Duke looked around at everyone.

The raucous singing and wild celebration continued, but Duke noticed the young man Sean had been antagonizing hadn't joined in with the others. He made his way toward the youth and put on a calm yet imposing front.

"My name is Duke," he said with a steady voice.

The kid glanced up at him quickly, then averted his gaze. "Yeah, no shit," he spat.

Duke's brow furrowed, and he surveyed the kid suspiciously. "What's your name?"

"Timothy," came the taut reply.

"Well, Timothy ... I hope you don't mind me asking, but do you need any help? You seem out of sorts."

Timothy peered behind Duke before looking back down at the ground.

"He's fine," answered Sean firmly from behind them. "Timmy here had too much to drink."

Timothy nodded in agreement, though he seemed distant. "Yep, what he said, I drank a little too much. Sorry." He looked at Sean. "I should go lay down."

"Great idea, why don't you go lay down, Timmy?" Sean clapped the kid on his back as he walked by. "Don't worry, Duke, I'll make sure he gets to where he needs to be."

"All right, y'all have a good night," Duke said without probing further.

Something was wrong. Duke could feel it, but he resisted the urge to investigate and risk ruining Sean's new treaty. He smiled at Julie when he returned to their campfire.

"So how did that go?" asked Julie.

"It went really well, actually," he replied.

"I sure hope it works out." Julie sighed.

"Me too, but I won't be holding my breath," Duke said with a wry smile.

The two sat there for a few moments in silence before Duke announced his intentions to retire for the night. "You ready?" he asked Julie.

She shook her head as she gazed into the flames of their bonfire. "Not yet," she said softly, "but I'll be there soon." She smiled up at him.

Duke leaned down to kiss her before heading off toward his shelter. As he passed through groups of people who greeted him, Duke felt grateful for the kids and Julie in his life—grateful for Mountaintop.

At last, Duke made it back to his shack and prepared to drift off to sleep until suddenly his door opened slowly and a male voice called out in a loud whisper: "Julie? Duke?"

The voice was unfamiliar to Duke's ears. Before he had time to respond, three figures barreled into the room. They pinned Duke down on his bed and put a cloth sack over his head as he attempted to break free. Panic rose within him as he inhaled deeply, trying to fight his assailants. Noxious vapors emanated from the bag, slowly taking the fight out of Duke.

Julie eventually walked into their shack. She was surprised not to see Duke lying in bed waiting for her. She figured that he was still talking to people and having a good time. She didn't want to ruin that for him, so she drifted off to sleep.

CHAPTER 15

COLORADO | JUNE 2035

The following morning, Julie sat up in bed and realized Duke was still not there. She thought that maybe he had come back already and woke up before her. Perhaps he was at a meeting already. But her gut told her something was wrong. She quickly got dressed and walked as fast as possible to the command center.

When Julie arrived, she almost burst through the doors in her anxiety. Everyone stopped their discussion and stared at her inquisitively, confusion etched across all of their faces.

"Miss Julie? Everything okay?" Charles asked hesitantly, standing up slowly from his chair.

"Has anyone seen Duke?" Julie responded urgently, scanning each person's face for any sign of recognition or answer.

Charles broke eye contact with her and an expression of worry crossed his features. "Actually, Duke and Jake are both running late this morning."

Panic began to fill Julie's chest as dread overwhelmed her. Suddenly, she noticed Sean sported a sly smirk on his face as he shook his head in disbelief.

An eruption of emotion spilled from Julie's mouth before she could even think twice about it: "What the hell are you smiling at, you ugly little prick? Swear to God if you had anything to do with this, I'll kill you myself!"

Charles' jaw dropped in shock while Sean held his hands up defensively. "Take it easy there, killer," he said calmly. "Duke and I might not always see eye to eye, but we made amends last night. So if he's gone, I had nothing to do with it."

Julie felt despair flood through her veins as tears welled in her eyes. She stared pleadingly at Charles and whispered hoarsely: "Charles, we need to find Duke; I can't lose him too!"

The radio suddenly crackled, and Eric jumped to attention. "This is Mountaintop, over."

Charles shifted his glasses on his face. "Julie, I'm sure there's an explanation for why Duke is gone." He put a hand on his hips. "Him and Jake probably are off somewhere having another talk or something."

Julie said nothing, choosing instead to pace nervously around the room.

Eric replaced the mic, speaking softly. "Mr. Ferguson ... it's about Duke and Jake."

Charles' face drained of color as he looked at Julie. Her expression was one of fear and panic. Stepping hesitantly toward the radio, Charles cleared his throat before pressing the mic button. "This is Charles Ferguson."

✻✻✻

Duke's heart raced as he looked down at the document in front of him. He glanced up to meet the eyes of the special agent. "So, if I sign this, I'll get less time, and you guys will protect my family and myself?"

The agent gave a curt nod. "Yep, all you gotta do is sign."

This was the third meeting between him and the special agent. Duke licked his lips nervously and scratched the back of his head before finally giving in. His hand shook slightly as he put pen to paper. "And you'll leave the other two out of this?"

The agent nodded again. "That's right—we don't want Jake and Roarke either."

Duke took a deep breath before finally signing. "Now what?" he asked, trying desperately to keep his voice from trembling.

"Now you help us take down Isacc Agigi. Just keep doing what you were doing for him, picking up those crates and dropping them off. You'll

be our eyes and ears. We'll do the rest." The agent glared at Duke with an intensity that made him want to flee from the room—but instead he held firm and returned the gaze.

"Okay, I can do that," said Duke meekly.

The agent stood up abruptly, locking eyes with Duke one last time as he said, "All right then, go do your thing—oh, and Duke...don't screw this up."

Shaking off the fear that had settled in his bones, Duke stepped outside into freedom once more. Soon he found himself walking through the door of his housing on Fort Carson. He heard a chorus of excited voices call out for their father before they emerged from their room; little Michael running first followed by Sarah holding infant Ava close to her chest.

"Daddy, you're finally home!" Michael blurted out between breaths as he reached Duke's side.

"I've been trying to call you. Where have you been?" Sarah asked her husband, feeling relieved yet exhausted.

"I told you this would happen, honey. Becoming an NCO is a lot more responsibility, which means more paperwork and more of my time," Duke pleaded.

Sarah let out a loud sigh. "Our time," she corrected him sternly.

Duke couldn't help but smile at her determination not to let him forget despite her exhaustion and accepted her correction with humility. "Yes, I know, our time."

"Sorry, I just need a break from these kids," she said, slumping onto the couch, allowing herself some much-needed rest while she still could.

With a playful voice, Duke offered an alternative solution, grabbing both his children close to him. "Well then, let me take over!"

"Thank you," Sarah said with a sigh. "Dinner should almost be ready."

His children squealed with delight at the prospect of spending time alone with their father while Sarah smiled contentedly at being released from her duties as a mom, even if it was only temporary; allowing her some peace before the chaos resumed come morning.

The vibration in Duke's pocket disrupted the serenity of the moment. He pulled out his phone and read the text: "Pick up: 9 AM"

Sarah glanced over, arching an eyebrow as she asked, "Who's that?"

Duke sighed. "My courier gig, have a pickup for tomorrow—sorry, hon."

"It's the weekend," Sarah whimpered pleadingly.

"I know—I just need to do it a little longer, then I can finally pay off those credit cards." Duke shook his head slowly.

Sarah reached out, gently stroking Duke's arm with understanding. She had no concept of what sort of packages he was delivering—nor did he; they were secret until he was apprehended by federal agents on his way to a drop-off point. What Duke didn't know was that inside those packages were weapons being smuggled across state lines for FEAR, a domestic terrorist organization led by one Isaac Agigi—who was suspected for the murder of his wife and unborn child.

The following morning, there came a knock at their door—two men leaning against the frame, grins plastered across their faces.

"Good morning, sunshine," said Roarke with a mischievous smirk.

Jake followed up in a sarcastic tone, "And where are your manners, Duke? Aren't you going to invite us in?"

Duke playfully lunged at them, trying to loop an arm around each neck as he joked, "No, you two are embarrassing enough!"

He kissed Sarah goodbye. "I love you," he whispered.

When Duke and his friends hopped in the car, he noticed something bizarre in the back seat. It was Roarke with a young girl.

"Who the hell is that?" growled Duke.

"Chill out, bro, this is my girlfriend, Amber," Roarke replied.

Duke glowered at him. "How old are you?" he demanded of Amber.

"Sixteen," she whispered hoarsely.

"What the hell, dude!" Duke snapped at Roarke, unable to contain his rage any longer.

"Relax! I'm nineteen; it's perfectly legal." Roarke smirked.

But that wasn't what Duke was worried about. With furrowed brows, he asked, "Does Amber know what we're doing?"

Amber glanced around nervously before replying, "You guys deliver packages or something ... right?"

Roarke gave her a reassuring wink as he answered smugly, "That's right, babe. See, Duke? She knows exactly what we do."

Duke looked over at Jake, who just shrugged his shoulders—there was nothing to be done now but move forward with their mission, no matter how uncomfortable they all felt about the situation. He let out an exasperated sigh and reluctantly put the car in drive.

They arrived at the pickup location and noticed that the package was larger than usual. The package consisted of several wooden crates stacked and strapped down to a flatbed truck. A rough-looking man gave Duke the drop-off location on a piece of paper.

Jake put the address into his GPS. "It's in Pueblo; that's not one of the usual spots," he stated.

"Doesn't matter—we gotta deliver it anyway. These things can't be late," said Duke, releasing the truck's air brakes.

Upon arriving in Pueblo, Colorado, they found themselves deep in the middle of nowhere where two men stood alongside Isaac Agigi, each one holding a shovel. As Duke and the others warily got out of the truck, Jake asked in a trembling voice, "What's going on? Are we burying all these things?"

Agigi smiled menacingly. "Oh God no, that would take forever. No, we are here to dig for something," he said as he gazed at Amber.

"She's my girlfriend," Roarke uttered meekly.

Agigi flashed an evil smile. "She's cute. Start digging," he commanded coldly, tossing three shovels on the ground.

Duke, Roarke, and Jake began to dig, and soon they were about four feet deep into the earth. "Okay, that should be good enough," Agigi said with a smirk.

Roarke looked up with confusion and exasperation. "But we didn't find anything."

Agigi let out a sinister chuckle. "No, not yet ... but we will." He then turned his gaze toward Amber. "Sweetheart, why don't you go down there and join them?"

Amber shivered nervously and stammered, "I'd rather not; it looks really dirty."

His voice was like ice as he replied, "That's adorable, but it wasn't a suggestion."

Roarke grabbed her hand reassuringly. "It's okay, Amber, I got you," he said gently.

Duke looked up at Agigi and his men with dread. "What the hell is going on?" he croaked.

Agigi grinned maliciously. "We have a rat in our midst ... I've known about it for a while but I just didn't know who it was ... but I've narrowed it down." He narrowed his eyes at the three of them. Everyone in the hole shouted over each other in protest but Agigi silenced them with a wave of his hand and continued speaking through gritted teeth. "First up is Jake," he seethed icily. "Sources say that more than likely you are not the one due to an alibi they have for you, so step out of the hole."

Agigi's men helped Jake out and handed him the keys to the truck along with a new drop-off location. He drove off alone, leaving his friends behind with mounting terror in their hearts.

Agigi's gaze seemed to pierce Duke and Roarke, as if he could read their minds. "So it's between you two." His voice echoed in the darkness. He shifted his attention to Roarke, who shook with fear. "I caught wind of Roarke here, wanting out of our arrangement. How would he do that, Duke? Don't worry, I'll tell you." Agigi's eyes narrowed on the man before him, his grin wickedly stretching across his face. "The best way is to make a deal."

Roarke reached out to Agigi, pleading for the girl next to him. "At least let Amber go, she has nothing to do with this," he begged. But Agigi remained unmoved.

"Sorry, darling, nothing against you," Agigi spat. "Just look at this as being in the wrong place at the wrong time with the wrong guy." He motioned for his men to haul Duke out of the hole, then ordered them to point their guns at Roarke and Amber.

Suddenly, Duke spoke up again—a last-ditch effort to save his friend and Amber. "You don't have to do this," he said, panicking, knowing full well that the rat was him and not Roarke. "Maybe he's innocent ... and she definitely has nothing to do with this."

Agigi slowly turned to face Duke, searching his eyes for some hidden truth or secret lurking beneath them. "Why? You have something to confess?"

But fear gripped Duke, forcing him to shake his head no.

The reek of ammonia seeped through the air, slowly but surely assaulting Duke's nostrils. He felt a slap on his face, its intensity gradually increasing until he opened his eyes and found himself staring up at the rugged visage of Patch, the man from Karl's unit. To his left stood an old man wearing black and gray military fatigues. His gray flattop haircut was sharp and neat. The man's dark eyes bristled with secrets.

Duke started to struggle as he realized he was tied to a chair in a closed room. As he looked around the room, he noticed he was not the only one in the same predicament. There was another person bound to a wooden chair next to him, with a black sack on their head. His eyes widened as Patch pulled the black sack off Jake's head. Patch then proceeded to examine Jake as he did with him.

Duke felt fear knotting his insides. "What the hell is going on? What do you want?" he yelled in terror, frantically trying to free himself from the restraints.

"Sir, they're awake," Patch announced to the old man.

Something sinister stirred in the air around them, and Duke knew he was about to find out what was going on.

CHAPTER 16

COLORADO | JUNE 2035

Pain seared through Duke's head as he gritted his teeth. His mouth was dry, tongue caked with a coat of pungent morning breath. The world spun around him in nauseating circles, and his head throbbed with the misery of a thousand drums, each beat threatening to rip him apart from the inside out.

The room was awash in the eerie glow of a solitary light that hung down in the middle of the room, casting its otherworldly light on the older man and his two captives. The man stood ramrod straight, filling the air with an aura of intimidation—or perhaps confidence. A tendril of smoke wafted from the cigar clenched between his teeth, dispersing like cobwebs in an old haunted house.

The man took a few steps toward Duke and Jake, still manacled to their chairs. "I apologize for the abduction—it was necessary and unavoidable. You can trust my motives; I am a friend," he said warmly yet firmly, as if trying to reassure them without letting them suspect anything else.

Duke snorted in disbelief. "If you were our friend then why are we tied up?" he asked sarcastically.

The man smiled knowingly and gestured at Patch with a wave of a hand. "Patch didn't want you to fall out of your chair. I can understand your confusion. My name is Colonel Roy Campbell. I assure you our interests are one and the same," he said, taking a drag from his cigar.

Jake groaned loudly and with eyes shut muttered something about having the "world's worst hangover."

"That will wear off soon," Patch assured him.

The colonel stood before them, his form a silhouette against the feeble orange light. His whisper seemed to echo throughout the dank, small room as he uttered a few mysterious words. Patch suddenly got up and left, leaving Duke alone to survey the morose environment. The air was dense with cigar smoke, and all Duke could make out were dimly lit cement walls, a small table off to one side, and Patch's medical bag perched atop it. Then, moments later, a dark figure emerged from the shadows with Patch leading him. Karl staggered into the room alongside his old friend, sending a wave of dread through Duke's body.

"You're part of this, Karl?" Duke growled, his headache intensifying every second.

Karl sighed heavily before replying. "Keep your panties on, it's not what you think. For the record, I wasn't okay with how they went about it, but no one can know where this is." He looked around cautiously as if someone was watching them. "So you got to understand that, Duke."

"Yeah, I guess I can understand that," Duke said with disdain festering in his voice. "Doesn't mean I have to like it." He squinted as if trying to keep his headache at bay. "Can someone untie us?"

Karl paused for a moment. "I know. But come on, you two, we have things to talk about."

Karl, Patch, and Colonel Campbell marched Duke and Jake through a dimly lit hallway. The walls seemed to go on forever, like a never-ending labyrinth, each corner bringing with it another bend or turn in the dark abyss. Their steps created a cacophony of echoes that bounced off the walls, seeming to get louder and more disorienting as they went. Every now and then, the stillness was broken by the flicker of lightbulbs above them.

"I know you two must have a lot of questions, and remember there is no such thing as a stupid question." Colonel Campbell's deep voice echoed through the frigid hallway, sending shivers down Duke's spine.

"Why is it so cold in here? Where the hell are we?" demanded Jake, his words punctuated by chattering teeth.

"I stand corrected; that's a stupid question. It's a government black site, and that's all you're getting."

Duke looked over at Karl, who was chuckling silently.

"What about you, Duke? You have any non-stupid questions?" asked Colonel Campbell, glancing away from Jake.

"You said we have the same interests; what did you mean by that?"

A smile played across Colonel Campbell's face as he pointed his cigar at Duke. "There we go, that's a question I can actually answer."

They stopped at a set of metal doors with a digital access pad and camera.

The colonel turned toward the camera. "Excuse me for a moment, gentlemen." He placed his hand on the neon red pad below the display screen, his face illuminated in the harsh light. The screen flickered to life, scanning his features before turning green and sliding open with a metallic groan.

"Welcome to the rabbit hole, gentlemen." Colonel Campbell grinned as he led them in. "Try not to gawk too much."

The chamber was rife with chaos; radios crackled with static, and computers hummed with activity. Glittering screens adorned the walls, broadcasting a wretched tapestry of desolation from all corners of the city. On one screen, a family huddled around a campfire, their faces obscured in sooty shadows. On another, people scavenged for resources amidst the ruins of bombed-out buildings. It was obvious the office personnel inside had been working overtime, heavy eyes watching screens filled with an American dystopian nightmare. The assignment had taken its toll on the inhabitants of the room, leaving their faces etched with sorrow and despair.

The colonel stood in the center of it all, eyes narrowed

through a cloud of smoke issuing from the cigar clamped between his teeth. Drawing two soldiers to his side with a mere gesture, his craggy face reflected an authority that had been earned through blood and sweat. The duo followed him to a far corner of the room where a stout door barred entry. With a single push of a button, the big door opened. The colonel led the group inside, and the door clanged shut and sealed itself behind them.

The colonel cleared his throat before his booming voice filled the room. "Shopia, secure the room."

A digitized female voice replied, her presence as opulent as it was robotic. "Room secure."

A brilliant emerald light filled the chamber, emanating from where crown molding should have been, indicating that all was secure.

Jake's eyes widened in disbelief as he surveyed the sheer decadence of the room. Expensive leather furniture, fine art adorning the walls, even shelves brandishing top-shelf bottles of alcohol.

"Holy moly!" Jake exclaimed. "I thought we had it good. How freaking cool is this? What is all of that?" he asked with childlike wonder in his voice.

The colonel's weathered hand snaked out and grabbed a bottle off the shelf. Duke squinted, trying to make out what it was. *Forty-year-old Macallan.*

The grizzled man slowly poured himself two fingers of the scotch, admiring its amber color as it swirled around the crystal glass. He dropped in two metal cubes that clunked against the side of the glass. Taking a sip, he answered: "Expensive."

"I'm a bit curious now," Jake continued. "Do you know what happened to us?"

The colonel replied with a wink, "Depends on what you are talking about." He paused for dramatic effect. "If we're talking about you, I'd ask your mother. If we're talking about our country, I'd say all signs point toward an EMP."

Duke crossed his arms and leaned forward in his chair. "From a nuke?" he asked cautiously.

"There are several ways to achieve the same effect—everything from nukes to weaponized satellites," the colonel answered as he twirled the metal cubes around in his glass.

Duke looked on intently, hanging onto every word like they were gospel. "Any idea who did it to us?"

A sly smile crept across the colonel's face as he took another sip of scotch. "That's the million-dollar question, isn't it?" He glanced over at Karl before continuing. "We've made so many enemies over the years it's not actually easy to point our finger at just one—take your pick: terrorists, Russia, North Korea, China, Iran. Hell, you're better off spinning a globe and throwing a dart at it... But if I was a betting man, I would put my money on either Russia or China. People in our government seem to forget that World War Three armistice was only temporary." Finishing off the last drop of scotch in his glass, he looked straight at Duke with an expressionless face and said, "I think China or Russia finally hit the un-pause button."

A wave of exhaustion and disappointment washed over Duke's face.

"Listen, son, government assets like ours were well protected, but we gathered that most state governments have collapsed for the most part. So whatever is left of the US federal government, it's struggling to survive."

"You call this struggling?" Jake blurted out.

"Just drop it, Jake. So let's get to why we're here," said Duke, trying to change the subject.

"Good, let's get down to business."

There was a thick, black, glass-topped table in the middle of the room. The colonel touched the corner of the table and Duke realized the entire tabletop was a screen. It showed a digital map of the surrounding areas.

"Wow, can't believe all this made it through an EMP," Duke said in awe.

"How do you think I felt when I first saw all this after Leavenworth?" Karl said, shaking his head. "I haven't been in a normal ops setting in years and now everything has changed. Seems like there's artificial intelligence in everything."

"This is a normal setting?" asked Jake sarcastically.

Duke started studying the map and noticed many locations were highlighted and labeled. One of those places was Mountaintop.

"Okay, you have my attention—now what do you got?" asked Duke.

"We need to get this fire under control, and Karl here tells me you have an enemy. Agogo or something," said Colonel Campbell.

"Agigi—yes. Fire is definitely our biggest problem right now," Duke said grimly. "But luckily we have some chainsaws and a backhoe that will be useful in creating firebreaks. We can also assemble a team quickly if needed."

Colonel Campbell nodded slowly as Duke finished speaking. "Now, to be quite frank, whatever it is between you and Agigi, that's your problem. But Karl says that Agigi has assembled a few dozen people, and there's talk of a weapon cache out there. Our intelligence did confirm that. He has roughly given orders to around forty people. Not that big of a deal, but with military-grade weaponry in the hands of that amount of people, he can do some serious damage—but again, that is your problem," he said.

A ragged cloud of smoke hovered in the air like a ghastly apparition. The colonel glanced between Duke and Jake with a hardened expression, like he'd seen it all before and was tired of having to explain himself.

"What do you mean it's just our problem? The man is a maniac; you have no idea what he's capable of," exclaimed Jake.

The old timer leaned back in his chair, savoring the thoughts rattling in his head and taking a moment to light up another cigar before continuing. "Son, I've been alive for over sixty-five years, and about half of it I have worn some type of uniform or patch for this government, with over fifteen combat deployments. So I'm quite aware of what a human being is capable of when properly motivated." He paused for effect before adding with icy authority, "If this man has chased you for over 600 miles, has assembled dozens of people, and can get his hands on weapons cache ... I'd say that's pretty motivated."

Duke stepped forward fearlessly despite his trembling heart. "So will you help us find this weapon cache so it doesn't end up in his hands?"

Shaking his head slowly yet firmly, the colonel answered him bluntly. "Help you fight him? No. Help you find it? Yes."

But before Duke could plead any further, Jake jumped in to add an important detail they had not yet revealed. "Actually, it's caches—as in more than one."

"What?" asked Duke, though he heard him clearly.

"Yeah, it was way too much to bury in one spot, so I put them in three separate locations," Jake said nervously.

"How the hell did you manage to bury all that? Those crates were pressured, treated wood, and full of who knows what. There had to be over a hundred of those things," Duke said, amazed.

"I will tell you exactly how I did it. I may have borrowed Mountaintop's backhoe. And the thought of being busted by the feds. Also, smoked meth for like a week," said Jake, sounding exhausted, having relived the memory.

Everyone stopped and just stared at Jake, waiting for him to say he was kidding, but he didn't.

"All right then, ya crackhead, point on this map where those locations are," said Karl.

"It was meth!" Jake cried, making his rebuttal.

"You say it like it makes it better," said Duke.

"Well ... it's better than crack."

Duke looked at Jake with doubtful eyes. "Is it though?"

Jake let out a loud huff. "Dammit, let me look at this map." He studied the map and made three large circles.

"What the hell's that?" asked Karl.

"They should be in those areas," said Jake as if it wasn't a big deal that he just drew half-mile circles on the map.

A heavy silence hung in the air as everyone looked at Jake in disbelief. Duke, still unable to believe what he had heard, uttered a disbelieving "What?"

The only sound heard was an old wooden antique clock ticking away on the wall and Jake's labored breathing. He nervously cleared his throat before speaking up again.

"Yeah, it was way too much to bury in one spot, so I put them in three separate locations." A bead of sweat rolled down his forehead as he spoke, emphasizing his discomfort.

"You don't have grid coordinates?" asked Colonel Campbell.

"Like I said, when people started going to prison, I took the merchandise and got rid of it as fast as I could. The ... drugs ... didn't help the paranoia or my memory, but it did help me put them in the ground really fast."

Duke looked at the most northern cache on the map and realized something. "Karl, how far away is that fire?" he asked.

"From Mountaintop?" asked Karl.

"No, from that cache area," said Duke, pointing to the northernmost cache on the map.

"The fire is several miles northwest of Woodland Park, the cache is just a few miles north of Green Mountain Falls. So the fire is not that far away," said Karl, realizing they didn't have much time.

"Well, gentlemen, looks like we got a lot of work to do. When you get back to your camp, Duke, get that firefighting team ready with the backhoe. We need to make a firebreak a mile above the cache. We also need to get a search party going for those caches," said Colonel Campbell.

"I have a question," said Jake, raising his hand.

The three men carefully looked over at him, wondering what now.

"Don't worry, it's a legit question," said Jake.

The group stood silently.

"Who gets the weapons if we do find his caches?"

Duke looked at Karl and the colonel, realizing it was an excellent question.

"Well, I wanted to talk to you boys about that. I think it would be fair to help you find these caches to make sure this Agigi doesn't get his hands on them. But the finder's fee would be the contents of those caches," said Colonel Campbell.

"Now wait a second!" Jake exclaimed. "That's not—"

Duke interrupted him. "That seems fair, but only if we get hunting rifles and ammunition. If there is any. Also any handgun ammo." He looked at Karl and the colonel. "So y'all get all the fun military-grade weapons and ammo and we get everything else. What do you say?" he asked, holding his hand out.

Colonel Campbell paused for a moment, staring at Duke. Duke could tell that the older gentleman was mulling over the deal in his head. Campbell looked over at Karl and then back at Duke with a big smile. Finally, he grasped Duke's hand with a thick, callused paw.

"You got yourself a deal, son. Let's get to work."

"Can you do me a favor? Can you reach Mountaintop and let them know that we're all right?" asked Duke.

Already having reached out earlier in the day, a smile creased the colonel's leathery face. "Already did, and talked to a Charles Ferguson. Then I was forced to talk to an outraged young lady who apparently ripped the mic away from Mr. Ferguson. She proceeded to tell me that, and I quote, if one hair on Duke's head is harmed, she would hunt me down and gut me like a fish." The colonel shook his head with a smile. "Lots of fire in that one," he chuckled approvingly.

Duke's face lit up with a thousand different emotions, from joy to relief and back again. He couldn't help but steal a glance at Karl, who had his own grin plastered on his face.

"Let's get you back to your camp, before we lose our beloved colonel," joked Karl, giving Duke a pat on the shoulder.

Duke and Jake were guided through the hallways toward a rumbling elevator. As they entered the metal box, it lurched upward for what seemed like an eternity until it arrived at its destination. When the doors opened, their eyes were met by a motor pool filled with military vehicles of all makes and models. They walked over to an old-style Army cargo truck surrounded by thick canvas.

The two were about to climb into the back of the vehicle when Jones and Patch approached them with black cloth sacks in hand. Karl hopped in casually and said, "Sorry, boys, you know the rules, you still can't know where this base is," said Karl as he grabbed a bag and slipped it on his head.

Just as Jake started to protest, he suddenly slumped over, falling to the ground with a thud. Everyone burst into laughter; this jocularity went on for a good few minutes until finally someone spoke up.

"I said they didn't need it this time," chuckled Karl between breaths, trying to contain himself.

"Yeah, I know," replied Jones, wincing in pain from laughing too much, "but you said he talks too much!"

Everyone erupted into laughter once more; even Patch chipped in with an unsettling imitation of Jake toppling over that only served to heighten the mirth.

With everyone still in stitches, Duke tentatively reached for a sack before freezing mid-motion. He cautiously surveyed the merrymakers before turning his attention to Jones.

"Don't worry, son," Jones said, seeing Duke's hesitance, "we only doused his hood—Chief here vouched for ya!"

Duke looked around at the men skeptically before letting out a sarcastic chuckle and slipping the bag over his head.

The sound of a rusty diesel engine rumbled through the night as Duke, Jake, Jones, and Patch rode in the back of a military transport truck. Karl drove the rig. It was obvious to Duke by now that Karl and his men were a part of some type of black ops unit. They were highly trained combat personnel whose joviality was only exceeded by their ability to carry out orders with precision and without hesitation.

Karl spoke up from the driver's seat, trying to be heard above the noise of the diesel engine. "So I've spoken with Jones and Patch here," he shouted over the clatter of the old truck. "I know what the colonel said—Agigi is not our fight, and he's right. But the three of us agreed to help train the Mountaintop community," Karl continued, looking into the rearview mirror for approval from his fellow comrades-in-arms.

Duke partially lifted the sack from his face in order to talk. "I really do appreciate it, guys," he said in a muffled voice. "We're going to need it. Especially if Agigi gets his hands on those caches before us."

As they drove on into the night, they all were aware of how much was resting on their mission, yet still managed to exhibit their trademark dark sense of humor as they joked around and playfully ribbed each other. Time seemed to almost stand still as they traversed an unknown course through darkness, until eventually something jostled them awake. The truck had finally stopped with a telltale hiss of air brakes; Duke had lost track of how long it took them to reach their destination, but by now knew better than to guess.

"You're good to go, man," said Karl, telling Duke to take off his hood.

The cold Colorado night air felt like a blanket against Duke's skin as he removed his hood. The sky was alight with a brilliant moon and an array of twinkling stars, casting an ethereal glow upon them—a mesmerizing sight.

"When will you guys come to start training?" Duke asked.

"Fairly soon, but we have caches to find and fires to fight," Karl answered.

Duke nodded in agreement and extended his hand for a

shake. They heard someone stirring and Jake slowly sat up, holding his head as if in pain.

"Get me down. I'm going to be sick," Jake managed to say.

Patch eyed him playfully. "What's wrong, friend?"

But all Jake could do in return was give him the middle finger before being overtaken by a wave of nausea. The rest of the group couldn't help but laugh at his misfortune while they started up the truck and drove away, leaving Duke and Jake alone.

Mountaintop security personnel were moving swiftly about the property, clearly having been alerted by the engine noise.

Jake, now standing with Duke, staggered slightly before blurting out, "How come you didn't get sick from it?"

Duke smirked. "Just lucky, I guess."

"They didn't do it to you, did they? Duke? Why?" Jake asked, still clueless about what was going on.

"I always did say that you talk too much," Duke said with a hint of laughter in his voice.

"Good to hear you laugh again, Duke. Listen, I can't apologize enough about everything—"

"If you hurt them—I mean physically, emotionally, mentally, hell, even spiritually—you call them one unnecessary hurtful name, lay one finger on them—I'll break that finger and rip out your tongue to start with. You understand me?" Duke grumbled while staring at Jake, envisioning the things he would do.

"Come on, man, you know I would never hurt them," pleaded Jake.

"Answer the question. Do you understand me?" Duke said forcefully.

"Yes, of course, brother," said Jake.

"Again, I am not your brother," Duke snapped.

"Can we at least try to be friends again?" asked Jake.

"Hell no, you lost that privilege the moment you betrayed me."

Duke could see the defeated look on Jake's face. So he decided to give him something.

"We live in a messed-up world now. Things change, people die, and people change. So if she's happy, the most I could ever do is forgive you. Slowly over time, I could forgive you. But I promise you I'll never forget."

The men and women of the security force finally reached Duke and Jake. Duke just held up his finger, motioning to give them a minute.

"Fair enough. Truce?" asked Jake, holding out his hand.

"Truce," said Duke, firmly gripping Jake's hand. He then pulled Jake toward himself and placed a hand on Jake's shoulder so he could say something without the security personnel hearing it. "Don't make me regret this," he said in a loud whisper.

Jake nodded his head.

Duke walked with Jake up the rest of the driveway with the security personnel. Everyone was happy to see Duke and Jake back. The community shook their hands, hugged them, and asked them many questions. Duke and Jake walked through the big metal doors and were greeted by the Mountaintop community. They both were getting swarmed with questions and love.

Duke let out an ear-piercing whistle that got everyone's attention. "Listen up, I know y'all have questions. So everyone, let's meet up at the community fire pit in one hour so Jake and I can try to answer those questions."

"Daddy, where were you?" asked Ava.

Before Duke could answer, he could see his son Michael sobbing by himself. He picked up Ava and knelt to talk to his son.

"Daddy's fine, I promise," he said.

"I thought you left again," Michael said through tears.

"I told you, buddy, Daddy isn't going anywhere. I promised you two, didn't I?" asked Duke, looking at his children as he got teary-eyed.

Charles made his way toward Duke. "Are you okay, son?" he asked.

"Yeah, absolutely, they meant no harm. Just very secretive is all," Duke said. Taking a deep breath, he gently put his kids—who were almost recovered from shock—down and they ran off.

"Love you, kids!"

"Love you, Daddy!"

"Well, I got a bone to pick with that colonel of theirs. Coming into our community and abducting our people," said Charles, his face turning red.

It was the first time Duke had ever seen Charles get really angry and thought best to defuse his temper. "Honestly, Charles, I'm fine, and rest assured it won't happen again. I can promise you that. Plus they are some high-level people in the government."

Charles let out a hard breath, studying Duke as if looking for signs of distress. "Did you give him hell at least?" he asked with a smirk on his face.

"Have you seen Julie?" asked Duke.

"Yeah, she was in the crowd when you all came in, then she headed back in the direction of the shelters," Charles said with furrowed eyebrows.

Duke thanked him then began walking away as Charles called out, "Hey Duke—she took it really hard... Not sure what's going on, but she needs you."

Duke nodded in understanding and continued on his way with determined footsteps. As he crept along the cobblestone path back to his shelter, he took a moment to marvel at how much this small corner of Mountaintop had become like his own home. Its safety and assurance were an oasis in a world that had become chaotic and unpredictable.

Duke made it to his shelter and felt silly for knocking on the door, but he didn't want to startle Julie if she was in there.

"Jules, you in there?" asked Duke, but there was no reply.

He walked through the door and saw Julie pacing back and forth. Duke took a step forward and her body convulsed with sobs. Turning swiftly around, she leapt toward him and buried her face in his chest.

"It's okay," Duke cooed, stroking her hair.

But suddenly Julie ripped away and slapped him hard on the cheek before pounding her small fists into his broad chest. Tears cascading down her cheeks, she shouted brokenly, "It's not okay! Everything is not okay! I thought you were dead!"

Wrapping Julie in his arms again, Duke said firmly, "I'm not going anywhere, Jules."

Taking a deep breath, she pulled away, and looking up slowly at Duke with eyes full of anguish yet glimmering with love, she spoke softly:

"You want to know the worst part? How alone I felt? Even though I was surrounded by dozens of people, I felt alone. The thought of you being dead created this empty cavity inside me. No matter how much I tried to fill it with positive thoughts, that void consumed my every thought. I've been alone for most of my life ... but this time it was overwhelming. Losing you would be too much for me to bear—I love you, Duke, don't ever leave me again!"

Duke's body went rigid the moment he heard those three little words; his heart raced, his mind numb. Did she really mean it? He had grown so fond of her over these past few weeks, yet could love be blooming between them? All he knew was that when they were together all of his worries seemed to fly away and the only thing that mattered was her.

He mustered up his courage and spoke for the first time in minutes: "I love you too, Jules."

His heart thumped like mad against his ribs, and he moved toward her on pure instinct. He took hold of her delicate frame and pulled her close. Duke could feel her curves pushed against his body as his lips sought hers in an urgent kiss. She responded hungrily and wrapped herself around him, sending wild sensations coursing through his veins.

Duke scooped Julie up and carried her across the room until they reached the bed. His hands fumbled impatiently to undress them both as if nothing else mattered in this moment—no failures from before or worries for tomorrow. Within moments the two were enveloped in a wave of pleasure and bliss that seemed to wash away all of their troubles for a single night.

✳✳✳

The sun rose, painting the land in a dazzling display of light and warmth. Duke and Julie stepped into the new dawn, their eyes slowly adjusting to the incredible brightness that surrounded them. They made their way to the gathering crowd standing around Charles, who commanded their attention with an air of calm authority. Duke and Julie were filled with a sudden sense of hope as they listened attentively to what Charles had to say.

"See, I told you, there he is. All right, Duke, the floor is yours," said Charles.

Duke stood on a table and projected his voice, informing the Mountaintop community why Karl's group took him and Jake the way they did. But he did not mention how they did it. It was probably a bad idea to tell the crowd that they put black sacks on their heads and chemically rendered them unconscious. Duke also told them that both groups were going to collaborate to create a firefighting team to make a massive firebreak.

"So what I need from y'all is volunteers—we need able bodies who can work chainsaws and help clear a path, so this fire can't make its way down here. So who's going to volunteer?" he asked, holding up his hand.

To Duke's surprise, dozens of people raised their hands. Greg Arrowood, the mechanic, said the backhoe was good to go. He even volunteered to run it because he didn't want anyone to mess up his handiwork. A clipboard was passed around to gather the names for the firefighting team.

"Also, one other thing we worked out: my good friend Karl and a few others have agreed to come in and train our community to help us out to better prepare for this new world that we live in," said Duke.

"Why do we need something like that?" someone shouted from the back.

"Help us with what?" shouted another.

"All great questions. First, we live in a quickly evolving world, and we should never stop learning, especially when it comes to honing certain skills. This brings me to my next point—our skills. We all have our specialties, but these men that I'm bringing in will teach everyone how to shoot properly, move as a unit, and hand-to-hand combat."

There was a mixed response. Some people liked the idea, and others did not.

"Why does everyone need to learn that stuff? We already have a security team. Why not just have them get trained up?" asked a lady from the crowd.

"What's your name?" asked Duke.

"Carol."

Duke tried to choose his words carefully. "Well, Carol, those are very valid questions. I know it seems safe inside this community, but there's a world out there that is falling apart rapidly. Even though we have a security force already, there may come a time when we need to call on the whole community to fight," he said.

At this point the crowd erupted, fear in their voices. "Sounds like you're trying to prepare us for war," someone shouted from the throng, and another echoed them with "What are you not telling us?" followed by another saying, "I thought we were safe."

Duke could feel the tension rising in the air as if it was

tangible. He tried speaking up over the din, but it was no use. Then Charles' sharp whistle cut through the noise like a knife, silencing those who remained.

Charles Ferguson stood tall atop the courtyard platform, his stern face illuminated by the Colorado sun. He took a deep breath before addressing them again. "Everyone, please calm down," he said as he held up his hands in a calming gesture. "We all understand your concerns. But this is purely a precaution—there's nothing wrong with being a little cautious these days."

He paused to take stock of the crowd. The murmurs slowly faded away, but an air of suspicion remained. He scanned the people one by one until his eyes locked with those of Carol, whose arm protectively encircled her daughter.

"Carol, did you happen to carry pepper spray or a pistol in your purse before all this happened?" asked Charles.

"I carried both," she replied firmly, not breaking eye contact with him. "My daughter did too."

Charles nodded slowly. "That's good; everyone should always be protected," he said. "Let me ask you a question: did you take classes to get your concealed carry? Did you go to the shooting range to practice?"

Carol swallowed hard before answering. "Yes, we did."

"Carol, did you or your daughter ever have to shoot anybody? Or pepper spray them?" he asked in a commanding voice.

"Thankfully, we never had to," sighed Carol in relief.

Charles allowed the silence to linger for a moment before continuing. "Why did you ever carry them if you never had to use them?" he asked with raised eyebrows.

Carol hesitated. "Just in case..." she began, finally realizing the point Charles was making "...we had to."

Her answer seemed to reverberate around the courtyard as everyone grasped what Charles was getting at.

"You see, everyone, this training is no different," said Charles confidently as he gestured grandly with open arms. "It is purely just in case—just like with Carol's gun. It's better to have it and not need it versus needing it and not having it. Would y'all agree with that?"

There was a thoughtful hush as each person considered his words before grudgingly nodding in agreement; even Sean and his cohorts seemed impressed by his argumentative prowess.

Charles stepped down from the table, taking slow strides toward Duke. He gently draped an arm around Duke's shoulder and guided him away from the courtyard, their conversation so low that it could barely be heard by anyone else.

"I appreciate you taking my advice and not telling them. But it really isn't the right time," said Duke meekly. "You saw how the community just reacted, just imagine if they knew the truth."

"At this point, Duke, what exactly is the truth?" asked Charles with inquisitive eyes.

Duke's voice shook with a combination of fear and determination as he spoke. "We have to come to terms with the fact that the unrest outside these walls is only going to get more desperate. Eventually, that chaos will arrive at our doorstep. Mountaintop needs to be ready for that fight."

CHAPTER 17

It had only been a few days since Karl, Jones, and Patch arrived at Mountaintop to start their training program.

"So, how is it going, Chief?" Duke asked, already knowing the answer.

"Not well," Karl said as he looked across the teams practicing hand-to-hand combat. "It's been less than a week; this kind of training takes time and dedication."

"Yes, I am aware," Duke replied with a hint of stress in his voice.

Karl gave Duke an understanding nod before patting him on the back and letting him go off to check on the other groups.

As he walked around the village, all that Duke could see were volunteers too young or too old to do anything else. There wasn't enough help to finish all the tasks they needed done so instead everyone was either participating in Karl's hand-to-hand or Patch & Jones' militarized training, or helping build a firebreak up north to keep the wildfire from reaching Mountaintop. The council decided that they would rotate between the three teams every day—that way everyone could get some training while also getting their daily duties taken care of.

The closer Duke got to where Jones and Patch were working, the louder their firearms shooting and tactical maneuvers became.

"Ceasefire! Put your weapons on safe and stand next to

your targets!" Patch yelled, making movements with his arms along the firing line. He noticed Duke approaching and offered him a friendly smile. "Hey there, what brings you here?"

"Just checking up on everyone," Duke replied.

"Most of these people need some work with pistols," Patch remarked with amusement. "But their rifle skills are really good."

"That's great news," answered Duke. "How is Jones' group doing?"

A smirk spread across Patch's face. "Why don't you go ask him yourself?"

"That bad?" questioned Duke. "I'll talk to you later," he said.

As Duke approached Jones' training area, all he could hear was Jones shouting instructions.

"Come on, people! We just went over this!"

Duke grimaced. "Having trouble?" he asked.

"You think? I knew it would be bad, but it's awful," Jones replied, frustration evident in his voice.

Duke held out his hand. "I know, but please stay with them," he said. "This will help us be better prepared and let us be a quick reaction force for your group."

Jones shook Duke's hand firmly. "Yeah, I get it," he said.

Duke started to walk away, then remembered something else and turned back. "They need all the training they can get," he said, nodding toward the group.

Jones sighed heavily and shook his head before turning back to his troops and shouting, "No, wrong—try again!"

Duke felt the weight of his duties burden his shoulders as he trudged through Mountaintop in search of Charles to get an update about the fire. All he wanted to do was be with Julie and his children. Duke wanted to stop by the medical center and see Julie's smile. He wanted to find his children so he could hear them laugh. But his duty was paramount; they had to find out what was happening with the fire and prevent it from spreading farther south. Agigi and his crew were too close, and they had to find those caches before it was too late.

Duke always tried to think optimistically but knew sooner or later Agigi and his crew would find Mountaintop and do everything they could to destroy it. So they needed to find those caches before Agigi knew of their existence. Jake pointed out that he wasn't sure if Isaac even knew that he buried the caches, but everybody—including Colonel Campbell—thought it was better to be safe than sorry.

Finally, Duke arrived at the communication building and found Charles sitting amongst a group of men, including Sean.

"What's going on?" asked Duke.

"Duke, we need to talk about who we are sending out to look for the caches," said Charles.

"Good, 'cause I wanted to see what you thought about sending a handful of Jake's security team." Duke's eyebrows furrowed. "Also that we were going to keep the information about the caches quiet."

"Duke, time is of the essence." Charles took a drink of water. "So I decided that Sean and some of his men were best suited for this task. And Jake and some security personnel are already down there."

"You decided that without talking to me? This is an extremely sensitive and important issue," Duke said, his words heated with frustration.

"Like I said, we are short on time. Also, you seem to forget that I'm the one still in charge!" Charles took a moment to collect himself. "Sorry, Duke, I'm under a lot of pressure. You don't have to like this decision, but just hear me out. Sean and the other hunters know this area the best. They are out there daily, and they are well-trained with weapons. Okay?"

"Yes, sir, I hear you," said Duke reluctantly. He shot a wary look at Sean, never quite trusting the man but having to rely on him all the same. But Charles was right—they were indeed best for the task at hand.

Sean seemed oddly quiet, not uttering one of his silly remarks as he usually did. Maybe he finally realized this mission was serious.

Charles began briefing them on the firebreak up north and where the caches could possibly be located. It was decided the northernmost cache should be their first stop.

"All right, gentlemen," Charles said, "does anyone have any questions?"

Sean shook his head, but Duke had something on his mind; more of a statement than anything else. He looked Charles square in the eye before speaking.

"I'm going with him." His voice was heavy with purpose.

"What, you don't trust me, Duke? I thought we were past that," Sean scoffed.

"To be honest, no, I don't," Duke grumbled darkly. "But it's not about that. This is personal for me. I can't let those caches fall into the hands of that monster." His gaze hardened into a glare as if it alone could communicate all that he meant without further words needing to be said.

Charles looked back and forth at both men before leaning back in his chair. "I'm not sure if it's wise for you to be out there, but if you think you need to help, then that is fine with me. Link up with Jake when you get there and see if he can recall any memories of where he buried those things." He stood up from his chair with a sense of finality in both his voice and mannerisms.

Sean flashed Duke a smile. "All right, then, gear up, buttercup—we're burning daylight!"

***

Duke and Sean jolted from the truck, their feet crunching on the gravel as they were hit by a wave of sound. The backhoe was shrieking like a wounded beast. Multiple chainsaws skirled in the distance, their blades clanking against the bark of trees, smoke shrouding the sun. Visibility was getting compromised as the fire near Green Mountain Falls grew larger with each passing day.

The sweet smell of freshly cut pine mixed with the acrid scent of smoke filling the air. Duke strained to be heard above the noise as he surveyed the scene before them. "Looks like they've already made a lot of progress on this firebreak," he said.

Sean nodded in agreement and pointed out Jake at once, despite him being lost in the crowd of people scrambling around them. Jake's skin seemed to gleam with an alabaster light, his head newly shaven and beard red, draping off his chin like a lion's mane. Sean let out a loud whistle that pierced through all other hustle-bustle and got Jake's attention. He acknowledged them and made his way over to them with an apparent sense of pride radiating from him.

"Hey fellas, are we ready to do this?" he asked.

"Yeah, we're good, but what did you tell everybody that we are doing?" Duke questioned him intently.

"Told everyone they were sending up a roaming security team to make sure everything in the surrounding area was good," Jake replied with an air of importance.

"That's fairly smart, actually," declared Sean, impressed.

Jake flashed his teeth in a wide grin before taking charge; map in hand, he led them toward their destination—where he thought he had buried the crates not so long ago. As they walked into the smoky unknown, anticipation coursed through each of them.

Duke looked around at the forest, his heart racing with anticipation. The trees loomed like malevolent sentinels. He glanced over at Jake, who was staring up in concentration as if trying to read something written in the sky.

"Come on, man," Duke urged him, his voice shaking slightly with anxiety. "Anything."

"Think of anything you can remember," Sean chimed in

from behind them, a hint of desperation seeping into his tone.

"I know, hold on, give me a second," said Jake, face strained. "I think this is the one I did a pace count for!" He shut his eyes as he rummaged through his memories. "I remember the pace count being 420 because it would be easy for me to remember."

Everyone shook their heads like disappointed parents, except Dale, who grinned and gave him a thumbs up.

Sean cut in, "First we need to know, four hundred twenty paces from where?"

Jake answered, "I think there should be an old barn close by."

Sean nodded and motioned forward. "All right, then, lead the way."

Duke swallowed hard. They were actually going somewhere—it wasn't just a wild goose chase after all. As they walked, he felt a small flame kindling inside him; a sense of hope.

The group crept through the dense and dim forest, each step bringing them closer to the unknown. Eventually, a collection of old barns and cabins came into view, built from rough logs that appeared haphazardly placed. It was clear these dwellings were hastily constructed. Sean deduced they must have been put together after the power went out—a sign of desperation.

The eeriness of the scene descended upon them like a fog. Duke muttered under his breath, "I don't like the feeling of this."

Sean nodded in agreement and glanced over his shoulder with a heightened sense of awareness. Looking over at Jake, he spoke with urgency. "Do your damn pace count so we can get the hell outta here." That's when he noticed Dale was missing, which caused his heart to race faster than ever before.

Standing there with his long salt-and-peppered hair pulled back in a low ponytail was a man with an air of authority about him. His clean-cut appearance made it obvious he was not some average Joe; he was a warrior leader of sorts.

He growled at the group with contempt as he adjusted

the blade against Dale's neck. "Y'all drop your weapons, nice and slow." His voice seemed larger than life, yet despite its booming resonance, there was something soft about it too. He didn't seem to want violence but rather to achieve understanding.

Duke responded first, trying to keep the situation at bay. "That's not going to happen."

Sean stood tall and firm and echoed Duke's words with certainty while glancing around him, assessing how many people now surrounded them with various weapons in hand—approximately two dozen individuals, including men, women, and even children, all standing at attention, waiting for commands from their leader.

"All right, take it easy, we mean no harm," said Duke, trying to sound calm.

"You Benny's boys?" asked the man.

"No, sir, we're part of the group that's creating that firebreak."

"If you're part of that group, why the hell are you over here on our property?" the man asked.

"We're just trying to find something, that's all," proclaimed Duke with desperation.

This time anger laced the man's words. "Yeah, I bet you were." His grip on Dale's throat tightened. "This one here just happened to stumble upon our distiller." There was something in his eyes—sorrow, maybe, or regret—as if somehow he knew what was coming next. He adjusted his hold on the blade and spat out menacingly: "Tell Benny he messed up for the last time."

The stranger stood motionless, but the cunning in his eyes betrayed an impressive level of intelligence. Everyone shifted nervously in place, wishing they had never stumbled into this man's domain.

"Like he said, we don't know who Benny is. We're just looking for something put around this area many years ago,"

Sean said, his voice edged with frustration.

"I don't know what you have in this area, but this is Crawford property. It has been for the past few years."

"Just let that man go, and we'll walk away," said Jake nervously.

"You know where we are now—don't think I can just let you walk away," the man said bluntly. His words cut through the air like a knife.

"You have my word; we mean no harm, and you'll never see us again," said Duke.

"Your word, huh? That used to mean something. A man's word was everything. Then, slowly but surely the American culture changed into the garbage that it has become. Used to be able to rely on a man's word and handshake. But those customs and culture are long gone, even more so since the world has gone to shit! This here is all we have. Those children are all we have. So, excuse me if your word doesn't hold weight with me!" the man shouted defiantly.

Duke stepped forward, his face painted with determination as he gazed at the emblem on the man's forearm. A Marine Corp emblem.

"Were you in the service?" he asked, already knowing the answer.

The man seemed to find a newfound respect as he sized up Duke. "Twenty-two years recon," he finally replied.

Duke nodded solemnly. "Yeah, me too. Did ten years in the Army as an infantryman."

"So you were one of those undertrained bullet sponges, huh?" said the man, unmoving.

"Hell yeah, I was. Better than being a robotic jarhead," said Duke, trying to match the insult.

The man said nothing as his mouth curled into a smirk. A gangly family stood behind him, their faces hollowed with fear and worry.

"So grunt to grunt, I give you my word," Duke said, his

voice low but clear.

"Crawfords, lower your guns. Looks like we have ourselves some guests," said the man, waving off his family. He released Dale, who quickly moved to stand next to Sean.

"Name's Kyle, Kyle Crawford." He extended a weathered hand toward Duke.

"Duke Hollander." Duke clasped the man's hand tightly, sealing the agreement between them.

Dale glanced up, eyes wide with confusion at the strange exchange that had just taken place. "What the hell just happened?"

Jake gave a relieved smile. "Duke just saved our asses, that's what."

"They insulted each other and made everything better?" Dale asked incredulously.

"Unspoken language," Sean chuckled softly.

Duke knew then he had made the right decision. Most military personnel had a few things in common. A dark sense of humor and an understanding that insults were part of military camaraderie.

Gesturing to the forest beyond them, Duke reminded Kyle of the danger they all faced. "Not to insult your intelligence, but you do know there's a fire coming your way, right?"

Kyle shifted. His face, previously full of optimism, now slackened, disheartened by the hopelessness of the situation. "Twenty-two years on reconnaissance," he sighed heavily. "We know about the fire. We simply have no other option to try to fight it. With our best men aiding the Woodland Park folks to create a firebreak further up north, all we can do is try our best."

For about twenty more minutes, Duke and Kyle asked questions and gave each other answers. But their conversion was cut short when a gunshot rang out nearby. Duke and Kyle instinctively snatched their weapons up, simultaneously exchanging looks of understanding.

"Crawford men, on me!" Kyle shouted, his voice reverberating through the mountainside. No orders needed to be issued; the group was already running with him. Duke's squad hurdled toward the sound, the echoing shots slicing through the crisp air like an axe. More gunshots filled the mountainside, sending reverberations throughout the valley. Wildly discharging firearms took a heavy toll on the inexperienced community.

"You two stay here. Keep an eye on this side," he shouted to Jake and Sean before shouldering his weapon and motioning for Kyle alongside him.

With urgency, Duke and Kyle weaved between pine trees and boulders using military technique called bounding overwatch, covering each other along their path. It seemed as if they had descended into an apocalyptic battleground; over a dozen bodies lying lifelessly on the ground. The two men made their way to Karl's black ops group, who managed to find some semblance of cover from the fury.

Duke wildly whirled his head in disbelief, unable to make sense of the chaos before him. He bellowed, "What the hell is going on?!"

A man growled in response: "Someone took a shot at us, and your security squad started firing off without hesitation. The noise galvanized workers into a fit of blind panic—everyone began randomly shooting at shadows."

"Where's it coming from?" Kyle asked, his voice barely clearing the clamor of war.

"We spotted some muzzle flashes up on that cliff edge. We lit it up like a bonfire! Ain't seen those flashes since."

"Then what's your people shooting at, Duke?" Kyle inquired, perplexed.

"Nothing!" Duke barked out amid his inexperienced community members.

"The only thing they're doing really well is wasting a shit load of ammo," added the soldier grimly.

A chorus of whistling and shouting arose as Duke, Kyle,

and Karl's men desperately called for a ceasefire. Gradually their pleas were heeded, and all fell still once more as they tended to the wounded. A few men volunteered to climb up the cliff face in search of any clues left behind by the shooters.

Duke roared out orders with authority. "Get the casualties on the trucks!"

"What about our dead?" someone hollered out from behind him.

"We'll come back for them later," he said firmly, knowing full well they had no choice but to leave them behind in order to ensure no one else was killed that day. Just then a whistle pierced through the air from the cliff ledge where the assailants were believed to be hiding. A special forces team waved frantically, indicating for Duke's party to join them.

Duke's voice boomed over the din of the wounded. "Jake and Sean, come with me; everybody else keep helping the wounded."

"I don't take my orders from you," Dale snapped, defiance flashing in his eyes.

"Do what he says; we don't got time for arguing," said Sean, turning to Duke with a nod, a glint of steel in his gaze.

Duke nodded back, appreciating the support. He led Jake and Sean around to a small footpath leading up to the cliff ledge where Karl's men were waiting for them. The acrid smell of smoke filled their nostrils as they drew closer, and Duke could see two dead bodies lying crumpled on the ground. Their faces were twisted in agony, their clothing slick with blood. Hunting rifles lay discarded near their feet.

Sean immediately recognized one of the men he had seen when he encountered Agigi in the woods. His heart quickened as he stared at the familiar face, lost in thought.

"You all right, man?" Duke asked him, concern creasing his forehead.

"Yeah, I'm good, just one of these dudes looked familiar, is all," said Sean gruffly.

"Someone you knew?" Duke probed gently.

"Nah, just familiar," Sean lied.

"We got a blood trail over here," one of Karl's men said, pointing. "Looks like one is injured. They're bleeding pretty bad and took off that way."

"We should catch up to them; see who the hell did this and why," growled Duke, his anger palpable.

"Honestly, man, I think that is a bad idea," said Sean cautiously, knowing where that blood trail was likely to lead.

"So we're supposed to sit here on our hands?" countered Duke hotly.

"We got it. They couldn't have gone far from the amount of blood," assured another of Karl's men.

Without another word, three of Karl's men moved out and took off down the footpath, following the blood trail.

"All right then, we need to get back and help as much as we can," said Duke with a hard look at Sean.

"What about the firebreak?" asked Jake worriedly.

"Honestly, the firebreak will have to wait," Duke replied gravely.

"Yeah, that fire is not gonna wait for anybody," Sean said, his voice carrying through the smoke like a bellow. "But it's hard to create a firebreak without workers. We have two other groups in the rotation. They're just going to have to rotate in."

Duke stood at the cliff's edge, looking down upon their group with sorrow-filled eyes. His words seemed to sting as he spoke them. "They need to get here fast to gather the dead and then get back to work. Otherwise, that fire will kill a lot more people."

"Let's get moving," Sean urged, his face grim and stoic like a marble statue. "I have a feeling the medical station is going to need all the help they can get back at Mountaintop."

When Duke arrived at Mountaintop, the once peaceful community was in complete disarray. People darted to and fro, their actions haphazard and panicked.

Duke bellowed to Jake, "Go find my kids! Make sure Sarah stays with them and that they are not watching!"

Jake gave a hasty nod and took off without hesitation.

A bedraggled Charles ran up to Duke. "What the hell happened out there? People are saying we were ambushed!" he wheezed, sweat dripping off his brow.

Glaring, Duke replied, "Exactly that; I don't know who did it, though. But I can give you a few guesses."

Charles shuddered as realization sunk in. "Lord help us."

"Also, we need to rotate the other group back out there to collect the dead and finish that firebreak," Duke commanded gravely.

Charles sighed wearily. "Already being done, but a lot of people are too scared to go out there."

Duke regarded him sternly. "Tell them that if they don't go out there and finish that firebreak, we are going to burn to death."

Charles nodded resignedly and as Duke made his way toward the medical center he felt Charles grab his arm tightly. With trepidation Charles said, "There's something else."

"What now?" Duke said impatiently.

"It's about Sean," Charles whispered hoarsely.

Duke swallowed uneasily as he glanced at Charles—whatever it was had rattled Charles to his very core.

The air split with a sudden, deafening CRACK—the sound of gunshots echoing close by, as if a giant had clapped its hands.

People were screaming in terror and some were crying out, pleading to the heavens for mercy. Duke jumped onto a nearby table, trying to instill calm, but his words failed to penetrate their panic, only a small handful heeding his pleas.

Swiftly, Duke descended from the table and spoke with Charles. "Sounds like another firefight nearby. We need to get around to calm everyone down." His gaze shifted to the medical center. "I'll go help them out."

Charles blurted out, "But what about Sean?"

Duke uttered calmly but firmly, "That's going to have to wait, Charles."

The sun hung low in the sky, a dull orange blaze that provided some much-needed warmth to the traumatized community. Duke spent most of the day helping Julie and the medical staff tend to the victims, while Charles busied himself organizing volunteers for a firebreak team. With their missions accomplished, they returned to their temporary campground just in time to see the last of the teams come back. The sight was heart-wrenching; people mourned as each body brought back from the front line was identified; it was a reminder to all that death could lurk around any corner.

Charles stood there silently, shaken but trying to maintain a stoic composure as he watched people carry their fallen family members home one by one. Duke offered him an understanding glance and a pat on the back; he knew when someone needed space and when they needed comfort.

"Go get some rest, Duke. First thing in the morning, we have a lot to talk about," said Charles, regaining his composure.

"Yeah, I know," Duke said with an exhausted sigh before wiping himself down with a wet rag.

It wasn't long until Julie finally walked through the door into what felt like another lifetime. She looked despondent; Duke put aside the rag and enveloped her in his arms as she softly sobbed against his chest.

"I can't stay long. Dr. Kelly told me to sleep for a couple of hours, but I can't leave her for too long," Julie said with puffy eyes, determined to keep going despite her own exhaustion.

Duke's heart felt like a lead weight in his chest, his brow heavy with exhaustion. He had to keep his strength up if he was going to help Julie and all of the people that called Mountaintop their home. He lay down next to her, but neither of them found solace in sleep that night. The darkness that surrounded them seemed alive, as if it were the embodiment of every fear they had and not just an empty void. Duke tossed and turned, trying desperately to ignore the feeling of dread deep in the pit of his stomach.

CHAPTER 18

Colorado | July 2035

Light poured in through the tiny cracks of the doorway of Duke's shelter. Julie stirred and slowly got up from her bedroll. She and Duke had been taking turns attending to the wounded over at the medical center, each of them barely getting any rest. Despite her bravado, Julie was worn out from the unyielding stress and trauma that soiled their days, leaving traces of anguish in its wake. The thought of having to face another day—talking about casualties, digging mass graves—was almost too much for her to bear.

Duke went over and kissed her on the top of her head before mouthing an unspoken word of love. No words could describe the emotions he felt inside; his body ached with fatigue and worry as if it were made out of lead instead of flesh and bone. He knew, despite all his efforts to keep everyone safe, there was only so much he could do as Mountaintop struggled with their own fears.

"I need to get back to the medical center," Julie said grimly, getting dressed.

"Yeah, I know, I need to get going too," said Duke in a tired voice.

Julie left, but not before taking one last glance over her shoulder with hope written all over her face. "We're going to get through this, right?" she asked, waiting for a positive answer.

Duke quickly stood up and held her in his arms. "I promise you, I'm going to do everything in my power to keep you, my kids, and this community as safe as possible," he said, again kissing her on the top of her head.

With a heavy spirit shadowing their goodbye, Julie departed to attend to the day's tasks while Duke prepared himself for whatever might come his way.

The cool air bristled against him like icy needles as he stepped out into the open air, where mist hung like a shroud accented by the smoky smell lingering in every corner. In an almost silent plea, Duke whispered under his breath an earnest prayer: "God please, if you can hear me now, then put out this fire, I beg you ... I'll give you anything."

Duke's relationship with the Lord was a distant and dismal one. His faith remained, but his relationship had been tarnished over time. He wasn't sure if he felt guilt for breaking his promise to never take another life—or perhaps it was something else.

As Duke trudged toward the communications building, he spotted Sarah making her way to the shelters. "Hey," Duke said, relieved, as she approached him. "How are you and the children holding up?"

Sarah scoffed and rolled her eyes at his question, the worry pressurizing her already fragile nerves. "Are you serious? We're having a blast. What do you think?"

"I'm asking seriously, Sarah, I just want to make sure they're doing okay," Duke replied desperately.

"They're scared out of their minds, Duke," Sarah finally admitted, her shoulders slumped in defeat. "Believe it or not I understand that everyone needs you, but these kids need you more now than ever." She cleared her throat. "I know you're not my husband anymore but I need for you to be their father still."

It was obvious that Sarah's resentment of Duke going to prison was still fresh. It didn't help that being married in the military wasn't exactly an easy lifestyle. Instead of building his relationship at home he was off training or on deployment in other countries, barely seeing his children grow up and leaving Sarah feeling isolated and alone while raising them by herself. In a desperate attempt to fill the void in his life, Duke tried alcohol, toys, gadgets—anything to keep from facing the emptiness inside him. Eventually this led him down a dark path ending with Agigi, something he could never take back now no matter how hard he tried.

Duke looked around at the once happy-go-lucky Mountaintop community; it seemed it had finally tasted the outside world's reality. Children were nowhere to be seen and adults stood still with fear and fatigue. His every footstep seemingly echoed louder than usual as he approached what used to be the community's communication center, now surrounded by gaunt figures coughing from the thick smoke that filled the atmosphere with its acrid stench.

Tears of sorrow stained many faces as memories of lost loved ones hung heavy in the air, only broken by low murmurs that hushed as soon as Duke arrived, all eyes on him with questions: "What are we going to do?" "Will they send more troops?" "Where did our safety go?"

The situation quickly boiled over, and soon the crowd erupted into chaotic rants and wild accusations. Curses were slung at Duke and Charles while others desperately tried to defend them—all whilst trying their best to make themselves heard above the din.

"People! Please! We must calm down!" shouted Duke, but it appeared his efforts fell on deaf ears, for if anything, the shouting and name-calling grew louder.

Suddenly, an ear-piercing whistle cut through the tension like a hot knife through soft butter, accompanied by a familiar voice: "Everyone stop this nonsense NOW!"

It was Charles Ferguson—usually so full of energy and optimism, but now heavily burdened by grief and distress. His red face made evident the gravity of what was happening in Mountaintop, and no one could deny his absolute authority at that moment.

"My friends, I am sorry for your losses and your fears," said Charles gravely. "When we ventured out of Mountaintop it seemed like a necessary risk to take. We had no idea that such destruction would ensue, yet nevertheless we managed to build the firebreak that we needed." He paused for a moment, letting the fact sink in. "In times as these it is easy to let our fear overtake us—but courage does not mean being without fear! Be brave and use that fear to prompt you into action," he implored them. "Today will be sad, and even though it is hard we must continue forward. What do you say?"

A majority of the crowd silently nodded their assent. However, some of them still mourned their loved ones before reluctantly returning to their posts as Charles exhaled in relief.

"Thanks, they were about to eat me alive."

Charles sighed nervously, glancing at Duke. "Duke, I'm afraid there's something much larger and more sinister that we have to deal with ... and I'm not sure how to go about it without it blowing up."

Duke scrutinized Charles' choice of words, furrowing his eyebrows in worry. "Worse than this?"

Charles nodded gravely. "Honestly, just about as bad if not worse."

The older man had piqued Duke's interest; he leaned forward eagerly, curiosity burning in his eyes. "Okay, you got my attention; what is it?"

Charles paused for a moment before answering, his brows knit together in thought. "I want you to meet someone." He motioned for Duke to follow him and started walking briskly down the hallways lined with a tired and overworked security detail. Duke could almost feel their exhausted stares on his back as he passed them by. The atmosphere seemed heavy and oppressive, like the air was filled with unspoken secrets and despair. It felt like whoever or whatever they were protecting here was something truly harrowing and dark.

They eventually stopped in front of a door and Charles

pulled out a key to unlock it. As soon as the door opened, Duke recognized the young man sitting at the table in the middle of the otherwise empty room: Timmy, one of Sean's men, whom Duke had met at one of the night fires—the night he and Sean made a truce.

Timmy looked at Charles with apprehension written plainly on his face. The older man gave the boy an encouraging nod. "Go ahead, son, tell him exactly what you told me."

Duke felt a chill wash over him as those few words sunk in—this conversation would be far from pleasant or comforting. He took a deep breath and calmed himself.

Timmy stammered out his sentence. "The animal meat that we have been bringing in ... it's not really animal meat."

Heat flushed through Duke's veins as he tried to comprehend Timmy's words. The idea slowly engulfed him like a suffocating fog and before he could say anything he noticed tears streaming down Timmy's face.

"We've been bringing in meat from dead people," the boy said, his voice barely above a whisper and yet piercing Duke like an arrow.

A cold wave swept through Duke as though an icy gust of wind blew directly through his body—his vision narrowed into a tunnel, nothing but darkness all around him. His thoughts ran haphazardly through his mind like tiny firecrackers exploding one after another in chaotic patterns.

A thick silence shrouded the room as Charles and Duke sat in uneasy contemplation, their attention fully locked on Timmy's quivering form. An involuntary shudder coursed through Duke's body, his knuckles whitening as he clasped them together.

"Duke ... Duke, did you hear him?" Charles asked, breaking Duke from his trancelike state.

"I definitely heard him," Duke spat through clenched teeth, rage radiating from his face.

Timmy shrank back into himself, tears streaming down

his cheeks. "I'm sorry, I wanted nothing to do with it, but my Uncle Dale threatened to disown me. Sean convinced me we'd be kicked out if anyone found out, including me, but he said we were all going to starve if we didn't start bringing in meat for Mountaintop," he croaked through sobs of desperation.

"That's no excuse! He has been feeding the whole community, including my children!" Duke yelled, electricity crackling in each word.

Timmy cowered back further, mumbling an apology between broken sobs. "My Uncle Dale and even Sean are good guys," he pleaded desperately.

Duke scoffed before screaming "Bullshit!" and launched the table toward the wall with an animalistic roar.

Charles winced as splinters of wood flew around them and finally shouted out to Duke. "Stop that! If it wasn't for Timmy, we would know nothing!"

"They really are good! Just rough around the edges is all. They really do mean well. They even turned down that man in the forest who was eating people. I think that's where they got the idea from. That man offered Sean to be his second but Sean refused—said he couldn't bring himself to eat people— but the pressure of having to feed the community became too overwhelming."

"What man in the forest?" Duke asked, his thunderous voice reverberating off the walls of the tiny cabin.

"Some dude with a crew," Timmy answered meekly. His face strained with the effort to recall details. With a click of his tongue, he continued, "His name? No wait—can't remember."

Duke stepped closer to Timmy, looming over him like an angry giant. "Was it Agigi or Isaac?" he barked out harshly.

Timmy jumped at the sudden outburst of noise and nodded quickly before realizing what he had committed himself to. He stuttered, "Yeah! That's it! He said his name was Isaac!"

Charles' brow furrowed with concern as he looked to Duke

for more information on this unknown man. Before either of them could ask any questions, Duke took a step back and growled, "Someone you should have reported back to us about ... someone dangerous."

Timmy's face drained of color and his voice cracked nervously when he spoke. "I didn't know—but I do know my place. I'm the low man on the totem pole."

Charles lightly put his hand on Duke's arm, bringing him back from whatever faraway place his anger had taken him to. "Duke," he implored. The look on his face showed distress but also understanding—an attempt to remind Duke that violence was not the answer here.

Duke rolled his shoulders back and held up two hands in surrender as he exhaled sharply through his nose in a fit of resignation. He spun around and headed for the door without another word, leaving Charles no choice but to chase after him.

"Let's not do anything irrational, Duke," Charles panted as he struggled to keep up with Duke's brisk pace. "We don't want this thing to go sideways."

Duke and Charles stopped dead in their tracks, fear knotting deep within their guts. As they approached the large cooking station, they could make out Joe's beefy figure amidst four steaming cauldrons. He was adding herbs and spices like an alchemist, tasting each difference with a spoon as he stirred.

"Hey, fellas! Wanna try today's soup?" Joe said with a booming voice, his enthusiasm seemingly unshaken by Duke's seething anger.

"Hell no!" Duke snapped.

Charles stepped closer to Joe and spoke quietly. "No. Did you know what Sean has been bringing to you?"

The jovial look on Joe's face melted away, replaced with a frown of confusion. "Geez, a simple no would have— What do you think he's been bringin' me? Everything from rabbits to squirrels to elk," he said defensively.

"So you didn't butcher them yourself?" Duke asked through gritted teeth.

"No, not anymore," Joe replied, disbelief tainting his voice as he caught the hint of suspicion in their words. "We used to, but we're busy enough, so Sean and his group volunteered to butcher the animals themselves. What's going on?"

A menacing silence ensued for several tense moments before Duke spoke again. "Make sure nobody eats this!" He pointed at one of the colanders with conviction and something akin to horror in his eyes, as if whatever lay inside the container was too terrible to be spoken aloud.

"Are you kidding me? I've been slaving all morning!" Joe protested indignantly.

"Believe me, you do not want to be serving … that," Charles said softly yet gravely.

Duke grew hot with rage as he watched Charles urge caution, desperately trying to contain the situation. Anger rose in his throat and threatened to lash out. He wanted these people to know what was being kept from them.

He could feel the eyes of a crowd on him, like a weight pressing against his back. All of them eager for answers, but none daring to ask until Duke's voice boomed through the area.

"Low key? Sean has been feeding this community dead bodies! Dead people! Humans!"

The collective breath caught in their throats and apprehension filled the air as one person stuttered out a reply. "What kind of lie are you trying to sell?"

The answer rippled through the crowd as everyone shifted at once and all eyes fell upon the hunting party gathered nearby. Without thinking Duke leapt onto the table, standing defiantly before them.

"You've been lying to all of us! You've been feeding us dead bodies!" His voice echoed through the crowd like thunder.

They stared at Duke with shock, even horror, guilt, shame, and remorse. As if these hunters knew that they had done wrong and were now ready to face justice for their actions.

Suddenly a wave of nausea rolled over many of those gathered around as they realized what had been done to them. A few even fled in an effort to quell their stomachs.

Someone spoke up from the agitated mob, their trembling voice barely audible. "Dead people? Humans?"

"Don't listen to him!" Sean shouted. "He's just trying to get me into trouble because he doesn't like how I conduct myself and my crew. He wants to control us, and we won't let him! But I never thought he would stoop this low!"

A cacophony of voices echoed as tempers flared and accusations flew. Some people believed Duke's claims, while others voiced doubts. Questions swirled around like a maelstrom, and everyone wanted proof before they could accept what he said. Charles let out a sigh of frustration and glared at Duke.

"Everyone shut up!" roared Timmy from the back of the room. His voice had gained an octave and took on a ferocity that only someone with extreme conviction could possess. Every eye in the room fixed onto him like moths to a flame. He stood tall, his face burning red with rage and defiance. "You want proof? I'm your proof!" he declared, daring anyone to challenge his words.

The crowd hushed into an eerie silence as Dale shot Timmy an incredulous look. "What the hell are you doing, Timmy?" he shouted, clearly not expecting this turn of events.

Timmy's lip quivered with emotion and tears began streaming down his cheeks. "What I should have done when y'all started bringing back those dead bodies."

"Don't listen to this kid," Sean warned. "He's had a rough time growing up without parents and Dale here took him in, trying to do what was best for him even if it meant being tough. Now it seems like the kid is telling lies as some sort of payback."

The crowd observed the spectacle between Timmy and Dale with rapt attention, waiting to see how it would all unravel.

The crowd was a maelstrom of rage and disbelief. Timmy stood in the midst of it all, tears streaming down his face as he shouted at Dale. "I'm not lying! You may have been a douche to me, but I still thought of you like a father—until you agreed to eat dead people!" His voice quivered as he finally said the words that had been gnawing at him for weeks.

Dale's face paled in shock. He approached his nephew with caution, barely believing his own ears. "You ... you think of me as your father?" he asked, voice soft and filled with sadness.

"Yes, I did," Timmy replied meekly, tears falling from his eyes faster than ever. "But after this ... I realized you're not a father." He paused for a breath, and his mouth quivered as if the weight of this realization was almost too much to bear.

Sean couldn't take it anymore. Irritation laced his tone as he yelled out at the crowd. "So now what? You still don't have any proof!"

While some members of the crowd seemed angry, others simply looked skeptical, searching for something more tangible than Timmy's word on which to judge Dale's actions.

It was Duke who spoke up first, interrupting Sean's tirade with an ominous response. "You need to be dealt with."

Enraged, Sean bellowed back at him. "So, you get to decide we need to be punished based on zero evidence besides one young kid's testimony? That is bullshit! Our country may be devastated but this is still a democracy, is it not?"

The crowd roared in agreement. They wanted justice—they wanted their vote to mean something.

Charles stepped in before Sean could say another word. "People," he addressed the group calmly yet sternly, "of course we'll take a vote. We are not tyrants; we just want what's best for our community."

Sean huffed slightly but conceded nonetheless. He knew better than to fight against the will of the people in such uncertain times. With a grumble, he asked Charles, "What's the consequence for a majority vote?"

Charles answered without hesitation: "You and all those who participated in this monstrosity will be banished from Mountaintop."

The tension in the air was palpable as Sean's crew and the crowd of onlookers exchanged glances. Tense whispers bounced around their heads like balls in a pinball machine.

"That's fine, but under one condition," Sean declared, his voice dangerously low.

"What condition?" Duke asked, looking from one face to another.

Sean's lips curled into an evil grin, and his eyes flashed with a malicious glint. "If we get the majority vote, those who falsely accused us get punished. You, Charles, and Timmy get banished. After that, Mountaintop holds another election for new leadership."

Onlookers erupted into a chaotic chorus of loud chatter, some questioning what they heard while others were unsure if it was true or not.

"So ... what do you say?" Sean asked, again looking at Duke expectantly.

Charles pulled Duke aside with a heavy hand on his shoulder. His voice was a loud whisper in Duke's ear as he spoke. "Are you sure you want to do this? There is no proof, and the community holds that crew in high regard for supplying them with meat. This could backfire on you!"

Charles' words made Duke hesitate; he glanced around, searching for Sarah in the crowd, wanting to make sure his children were not close by as they would be affected by all of this drastically if things went wrong. He sighed heavily before turning back to Timmy, who seemed almost scared of what was happening among them.

"Are you sure? Are you telling the truth?" Duke asked, genuinely trying to weigh out whether this was the right decision.

Timmy nodded slowly before answering shakily, "Yes, I

promise." His brown eyes pleaded for mercy and understanding as he watched Duke turn to Charles, who shrugged unconvincingly, throwing his hands up in despair. There wasn't much else they could do but hope that everything would turn out okay in the end.

"All right, fine, you have a deal," said Duke.

"All right, then … if you believe that we feed everyone dead people," Sean gestured mockingly, "raise your hand."

Before anyone could vote, though, Duke held his hand up once more. "Before you answer that I want to talk to Sean's crew."

"What the hell are you doing?!" Sean bellowed. "Quit stalling and let's get this over with!" He stood proudly, sneering at his accusers, chest puffed up and seemingly indignant.

"If anyone involved comes forward and confesses now," Duke began, "I promise that you won't be exiled."

"Using fear as leverage to make my crew turn me in? Good luck with that!" Sean scoffed.

"It's a genuine offer," Duke defended himself.

"Sounds awfully tyrannical to me," Sean shouted back.

Charles weighed in, looking at Sean's men. "It's just a second chance."

Duke repeated, "So what's your answer?"

"Go ahead! Answer the man!" Sean declared confidently.

But then something unexpected happened: one of his men stepped forward.

"What are you doing?" Sean questioned in disbelief.

Two more men stepped forward. Another five followed suit until there were over a dozen members from Sean's crew who had come forward.

Charles asked their leader, "Are these true confessions? Have you all been serving human meat to this community?"

They all nodded in unison.

Duke gestured for them to stand by him and said, "Let's vote: raise your hand if you find them guilty." Everyone in the room agreed—except those loyal to Sean—and raised their hands unanimously.

"You can't do this!" shouted the accused.

"People have voted, Sean," Duke stated coldly, "even your own people. Time for you to go."

"Fine," Sean spat out viciously. "But we're taking our stuff: food we supplied to the community and our vehicles too."

"The hell you are. Jake, have your security team escort these people out," said Duke.

Sean pulled his gun on Duke, causing a domino effect of multiple guns being drawn and pointed. Jake's security team and Sean's crew faced off. Duke could feel his heart thudding in his chest, adrenaline pumping while his blood rushed through his veins. He felt the urge to run but he was frozen like a statue. The crowd around them screamed and ran in panic, some even trampling others in their haste to escape.

Sean held his gun firmly, aiming straight at Duke, then spoke in a low voice that made Duke's skin crawl. "Without these supplies, we're dead anyway, so if you want to keep everyone alive, it would be wise to let us take our share."

Charles stepped forward, hands trembling with nervous energy. "We aren't monsters here. Let them take what is theirs. No more people need to die."

✻✻✻

The next hour proceeded in an eerie silence as Sean's crew loaded up five trucks with their designated fuel and food supplies—sacks of rice and beans plus guns and bullets. Finally, when they were done, Dale spoke for the first time since Timmy had confessed. "That's it, boss man," he said to Sean.

"I hope you're happy now, Duke," growled Sean coldly. "You just doomed everyone here."

Duke shook his head slowly and answered confidently, "No, your own actions will lead to your demise. Mountaintop will survive this."

The silence in the air was deafening. Everyone's gaze was focused on Duke and Sean. Duke could feel a tingle of fear run down his spine as he watched Sean staring him down.

"See you around," Sean said, his voice low and menacing.

"I'm sure we will," Duke replied, not taking his eyes off Sean for a second.

Duke then noticed Dale cautiously approach Timmy and embrace him. Timmy stumbled back from Dale with a pained expression on his face that caught Duke's attention. He quickly strode toward them, Charles one step behind him.

"What is it?" Charles asked when they reached Timmy, worry in his voice.

Timmy didn't say anything, but held up his hands, and to their horror, they were covered in blood. Before Duke had time to react, Timmy crumpled to the ground like a ragdoll with a loud thud.

Panic swept across Duke and Charles' faces as they looked up and saw Dale slip a large Bowie knife back into its sheath.

"Help! Medic!" Duke screamed frantically into the stillness of night, his voice echoing in the total silence of the onlookers. People from Jake's security team rushed to help Timmy, who was now soaked in blood from his stomach wound, clutching it tightly as if it would stop the pain that radiated through him.

The air seemed to press down on Duke and the rest of the group as they stood, nervously watching Charles stomp, veins bulging in his neck, toward Dale. They had all seen Charles angry before, but never like this—never so red-faced and wild-eyed with fury as if he were some kind of ancient beast awakened from slumber.

"You murderous coward!" Charles shouted. "That boy is probably going to die!"

People stepped back at his words, a clear look of surprise on their faces. Dale, however, remained completely stoic, finishing up packing his things without so much as glancing at Charles.

Charles' steps never faltered nor did his voice diminish as he yelled again, "You hear me?" He quickly followed up the statement with an unexpected punch to poor Sean's nose. Everyone gasped at the sight of their usually calm community leader exploding with anger. But their shock was quickly supplanted by terror as Dale finally faced Charles' challenge, pointing a revolver directly at him. Without hesitation, Dale fired one shot at Charles' chest; the abrupt sound silenced the crowd.

Charles fell to the ground in front of them and Sean yelled, "What are you doing?" in disbelief.

Dale stood above the fallen man and coldly replied, "What we should have already done." Then with menacing calmness, he walked over to Charles and held the revolver pointed directly at his face.

Duke sprang into action. Adrenaline-driven fury began to boil inside him as he tackled Dale to the ground. As they wrestled in the dirt, a second shot fired off, burying itself inches away from Charles' feet. The gun flew free of Dale's grip, causing him to lunge for it, but was beat by Duke's hand, which quickly snatched it up.

The heat of the moment took over; his tunnel vision only allowed him to see the enemy before him. Duke pounded on Dale's face with the revolver in a gruesome fashion. Someone grabbed Duke from behind. He could feel them on his back, tugging at his shirt in urgent desperation, yelling words muffled through his rage-filled trance. He instinctively elbowed them away as hard as he could and spun around, only to find Jake collapsed on the ground in pain. Furious memories of Jake's betrayal with his wife flooded his mind like a silent film reel.

Just then, he heard a gut-wrenching scream from behind him and spun around to see both of his children standing there in horror, eyes wide and mouths agape.

Michael croaked out a single word: "Daddy ..."

Duke realized he was now aiming the revolver directly at Jake. Blood had spattered across Duke's swollen hands and face like paintbrush spots on an artist's canvas. Sarah quickly ushered the children away with a look of utter terror on her face. Duke scanned the crowd around him; everyone stared back at him with looks of horror, shocked at what they had just witnessed.

He watched Sean as he loaded Dale up into the back of a truck. Dale's face was bloody and battered.

"Duke, you got to believe me when I say that was not the plan." Sean sighed heavily. "I didn't care for Charles but he didn't deserve that."

Duke felt like the weight of the world had landed on his shoulders. Charles, his friend and leader of Mountaintop, had been shot down in cold blood. He surged forward through the crowd, his feet feeling like lead with each step he took toward Charles' body. As he arrived at the scene, all sound seemed to fall away. Duke was overcome with a terrible sense of dread as his eyes adjusted to the dim light and laid upon his fallen comrade. The gray shirt that Charles wore was now stained crimson around the bullet hole in his chest. It was too late for any heroic attempt at saving him; he had gone beyond this world.

As Duke knelt next to his friend, he thought of all the words he wished could have been said between them before they parted forever, but it was not meant to be. There would be no heartfelt goodbyes or insightful thoughts shared—just death. Duke stood back up and turned around to face the questioning crowd, noting how quickly they moved out of his way, as if afraid of him. His mind raced with questions of how he could possibly lead them now when he himself was filled with so much pain and doubt.

Exhausted, Duke made his way back to his shelter alone. He paused in front of the mirror and looked at himself. Blood spattered his face, beard, and clothing—no wonder his children had been so scared when they saw him pointing a gun at

Jake. Taking a steadying breath, he said aloud to his reflection, "Get a grip, Duke ... you have to keep it together."

It had been hours since Julie had come home. Duke was too drained emotionally and physically to even greet her, let alone explain what happened. Her presence comforted him, but he refused to move or speak, ashamed of his own lack of control during the altercation. The scene at Mountaintop had been catastrophic; Sean feeding them human flesh, Dale stabbing Timmy, and Charles getting shot right in front of him. Everyone was terrified of what they had seen.

"Duke?" Julie murmured cautiously. "You okay?" she asked, worry curling her expression.

Duke spoke plainly and with a heavy heart. "No." After a brief moment of silence he spoke again. "How is Timmy doing?"

"Timmy is in critical condition," she said quietly, "but actually may survive."

A small glimmer of hope lit up Duke's face as he heard this news—it seemed that some moments were still salvageable amongst all the destruction he had caused.

Julie looked up at Duke, hesitating before asking her next question. "People said you kinda lost control and almost beat Dale to death then pulled a gun on Jake. Is that true?" she questioned gently, searching his eyes for the truth.

Duke swallowed hard before answering her softly. "Yeah, it is." His head hung low after admitting this fact.

"I can at least understand that," Julie replied thoughtfully as she stared into his despondent face, perfecting the moment with a gentle kiss on his forehead.

"I know; I am scared too. Sometimes I just ... lose it. When I was in prison they kept it under control with meds, but now I'm on my own," said Duke.

"No, you are not," said Julie, looking Duke in his eyes and giving him a kiss.

She cradled him in her arms as his tears began to fall once

again—this time due to relief and not shame or sadness—knowing he would never be truly alone if Julie was always there beside him.

CHAPTER 19

COLORADO | JULY 2035

A week after Charles and another eighteen citizens had been brutally murdered, Mountaintop reluctantly agreed that cremating them was the best option. No one had seen Sean and his crew at all.

The raging fire from the north steadily advanced, leaving a suffocating blanket of smoke over the area. Training the community became priority number one for Mountaintop. Everyone knew they had to be prepared after all that had happened to Charles and those in the ambush. Mountaintop finally woke up and realized that their community, country, and possibly even the world had changed forever.

Duke was the primary leader of Mountaintop, even though many people in the community were still apprehensive about the way he lost control. Duke knew he could not do all this by himself. He needed to find a second in command soon. Until then, Duke did everything he could to ensure Mountaintop's safety, his morning rounds being one of them.

"How's it going, fellas?" Duke said, trying to sound chipper.

Eric and Patrick just stared at him for a few seconds.

"Oh, ummm, it's good, what's up?" said Patrick.

"Come on, guys, that's it? I usually can't shut you two up. How's your master's dungeons campaign coming along?"

"It's Dungeons and Dragons, and if you must know, it's going great, even when my metagaming turd of a brother tries to ruin things," Eric said, looking at Patrick with an exasperated expression and furrowed brow. His glare could cut through steel.

Patrick chimed up with defense in his voice, "Oh, quit your whining, and excuse me if my gnome wizard has super high intelligence. Mr. McDoogle just knows things!"

Duke let out an awkward chuckle before saying, "Okay, enough of this Master Dragon talk."

"Dungeons and Dragons!" Eric and Patrick said in unison.

"Okay, my bad—any updates on Agigi?" asked Duke.

"Not really, but we heard more radio chatter from the FEMA camps," said Patrick.

"Like what?"

"Like they are running out of food or having a hard time resupplying. They are running out of fuel. Oh, and Fort Carson is not responding to their calls anymore," said Eric.

"Fort Carson?" A deep frown etched itself onto Duke's face as he contemplated the situation, trying to make sense of it all. "I bet they just have too much going on. The military has finite resources, so everybody is feeling the pressure by now. But I would think they would be able to hold out longer than a few months. The majority of military vehicles should have been shielded from an EMP. So fuel and transportation shouldn't be a problem for a while."

"Maybe they're doing fine and choosing not to supply FEMA anymore," Patrick said, his voice gritty with cynicism.

Duke's brow furrowed, his features contorting with moral outrage. "Maybe, but that would be super unethical," he exclaimed.

Eric's face twisted into a grimace of mocking disbelief. "What? The government doing something unethical? No way!" he said, sarcasm dripping from every syllable.

A satisfied smirk crossed Duke's lips and he nodded slowly in agreement. "Yeah, I suppose that's true." He exhaled heavily and rubbed at the back of his neck. "All right, I appreciate the update, guys. If anything changes with Agigi, just let me know."

"Will do, boss man," Eric replied as he adjusted a hand-painted figurine.

Duke stepped outside into the oppressive smoky haze. His eyes burned, his throat scratchy from repeated coughing, but he carried on; it was his duty to keep up with these daily rounds.

He shuffled over to the cooking station where Joe stood stirring a giant black pot, his head bowed sullenly. Duke knew something had shifted in him since he realized what ingredients he had unknowingly served the community.

"Hey, Joe," Duke said gently, "how goes it?"

Joe shrugged disinterestedly. "Same as yesterday. Rice and beans soup."

"No, I meant how are you doing?" Duke persisted, trying to make Joe look up at him.

Joe's voice thickened with emotion when he said, "Not that great. Do you know how guilty this makes me feel? It's my fault we've been eating contaminated meat for a month!" He slammed the spoon down hard in defeat.

"It's not your fault—nobody else could tell either," Duke quickly reassured him, hoping to lighten the mood.

But Joe would hear none of it. "I should have known better!" he lamented loudly. "I should have known not to let them handle the meat themselves!"

Duke placed a comforting hand on Joe's shoulder. "Have you heard any news about the hunting party recently? Are they managing to bring back some actual meat?"

Joe shook his head and replied despondently, "Only rabbits and squirrels so far—haven't seen the hunting party in a few days though." He stared gloomily into the depths of the pot.

"Maybe they've gone farther out looking for game—somewhere unaffected by the fire and smoke," Duke suggested hopefully.

Joe gave another sad shrug of his shoulders instead of responding.

Seeing Joe so devastated made Duke want to give him some

words of encouragement, so he smiled warmly and said, "Don't worry, buddy—this community loves and needs you."

This seemed to finally break through Joe's despair and he returned Duke's smile with a weary nod.

Duke trudged through the walkways of Mountaintop, feeling the weight of every death they had recently endured deep in his bones. He felt responsible for the safety of these people and he intended to do whatever he could to make sure they all made it out alive.

Tracy's house was up next. As he approached her, she seemed so far away yet ever-present. A feeling of dread hung in the air like a thick fog rolling in from the riverbanks.

Tracy caught his gaze, and she gave a nervous laugh. "Oh, Duke, you scared me," she said with an uneasy energy.

Duke, perceptive of her fear, remained composed. "How are you doing, Tracy?" he asked gently.

Tracy replied with a hesitant stutter, masking her nerves with over-emphasized cheerfulness. "I'm good, really good, exceptionally good ... How ... are ... you?"

"You okay?" he inquired.

Tracy's voice quivered as she insisted, "I'm...fine." She forced a smile. "Well...it's..."

Duke felt a chill run down his spine as he encouraged her to go on. "Yes? What is it?"

"This whole week has been really an eye-opener for me." The terror was evident in her shaking voice. "My husband and I thought we had prepared for anything, but no one could have predicted something like this happening. Every day brings about news of someone else gone or leaving us forever and all our important decisions rest on your shoulders now." Her eyes filled with tears. "When Charles died ... it was scary. I'm sorry—I'm just scared is all."

Duke pulled Tracy into a hug. "Hey, that's perfectly normal to respond that way," he said into her hair. His voice was comforting yet bittersweet with memories of his late friend

Charles.

Reluctantly pulling away from him so as not to linger too long, Tracy looked into Duke's eyes for comfort, but instead saw a battle-worn soldier trying to remain strong despite the hardship of recent events.

"I guess I should ask how you are doing," Tracy said.

He gave her a fake smile, one which hinted at years of practice covering up moments such as these when tough decisions needed to be made. "I've been better, but we'll all pull through. I promise you that."

She reciprocated the gesture and they settled into awkward silence until Duke changed the subject.

"So be honest," he began with a newfound determination setting in his gaze, "how are we looking with the numbers?"

Tracy took a step back and surveyed him for a moment before speaking her mind. "Well, not bad but not good either," she said cautiously. "Our supplies are based on a hundred people for one year if we are supplemented with wild game, but Mr. Ferguson took in about fifty more people after the power went off." Her voice trailed off as she started recalling all those newcomers showing up within days after word got out about Mountaintop.

Duke sensed her worries and probed further. "I know Charles was generous," he said reluctantly, seemingly trying to get past his own grief over his friend's death, "but how are we looking, Trace? What do you expect our future to be like?"

Tracy swallowed hard before responding somberly. "Well, after Sean and his crew are left with their share ... I'd say at this rate if we don't start rationing, we have six months of food left."

To Duke it seemed like time itself stopped. "Does that include our crop?"

After a few seconds, Tracy shook her head solemnly. "No," she said dismally, "not counting that because it may not grow."

"What does farmer Ed say about his potatoes? What does

he expect he'll be able to harvest?"

Tracy blinked her almond eyes as she glanced around the desecrated land. "He says it should produce about three months of food if it grows as expected and we ration it. He said we should be able to harvest it for sure by September."

Duke thrust his hands into his pockets and took a few steps forward, kicking up a cloud of dust behind him. He looked out across the horizon, optimistically commenting, "Well, that's not great, but it could be worse."

Tracy furrowed her brows in worry, beads of sweat trickling down her forehead as she posed an all too grim question: "Duke, what do we do next year?"

Duke turned to face her, confusion on his face. "What do you mean?"

"Food. This year we have food we stored. Rice, beans, and some random things. We have potatoes as well, but next year ... what are we going to do for food?" Tracy asked somberly.

Duke shifted uneasily from one foot to another before offering a half-hearted solution—one that neither of them truly believed would come true.

"Best-case scenario," he started with fake confidence, "it's not as bad as we thought and the government comes in and helps us out before we run out of food, okay?" He tried to make his tone seem more certain than he actually felt, fooling no one other than himself.

Duke had already begun to turn away when Tracy spoke up again. "Worst case scenario?"

Duke hesitated before resigning himself to answer her question honestly. His usually strong jawline seemed tense as he stated plainly, "We take a portion of the potato crop and replant on a bigger scale. Hope the animals come back and repopulate. But hopefully it's not the worst case," he concluded without emotion, searching his mind for any sort of hope he could offer her but coming up empty-handed each time.

Tracy mustered up a faint smile as she went back to her

tasks; Duke was aware that this only masked the apprehension she felt. As if it was inextricably tied to an undeniable fact: no one knew what would happen in the future.

Next up were Julie and Dr. Kelly. Duke's knuckles rapped sharply against the aged wood of the door mere moments before it reluctantly squeaked open. Dr. Kelly opened it from the other side, her face gaunt and eyes lined with shadows. There was a weariness about her that he'd become all too familiar with since the ambush.

"Hey Duke, Julie is in the back." Her pleasantries were forced and contrived, yet Duke smiled in understanding.

"Are you doing okay?" he asked.

"I'm great," said Dr. Kelly with a forced smile.

Duke knew better than anyone that she was anything but all right—exhaustion painted itself across her features in what seemed like an endless cycle of sleepless nights.

"I'm trying to find more helpers for you, but right now we're tapped out for medical talent," he responded.

"I know, I know," came her sigh of resignation. Though by no means alone, between Julie and herself, it felt like they were treading water in an ocean of other people's pain and suffering with nothing but their own strength to keep them afloat.

With a wave of her hand, Dr. Kelly invited him inside.

"How is Timmy doing today?" Duke asked gently.

She glanced back at the room of survivors; a reminder of the horrors of war that still lay upon them. Steeling herself, Dr. Kelly managed a somber reply: "Same as yesterday, still in critical condition. But I think Timmy will pull through. We had several people donate his blood type." She crossed her arms tightly in an effort to keep what little hope she had alive.

Duke and Dr. Kelly moved into the room where they discovered Julie leaning over Timmy's bedside like some kind of angelic figure amidst the chaos and despair. The sight caused Duke's heart to swell with love and admiration; hers was a strength unmatched by those twice her size. As if sensing his presence, Julie looked up with a tired but genuine smile that felt like only a warmth that can exist between true lovers.

"Julie, you got this? I'm gonna lay down for a few hours," Dr. Kelly said with an exhausted sigh.

Julie nodded and waved Dr. Kelly off before she took Duke's hands in hers and led him away from Timmy's bedside and into another room across the hall. Before Duke had time to speak, Julie began kissing him with such vigor and passion that he felt swept away by the moment, swept away by love itself. When their moment of passion ended, Duke smiled at Julie with sparkling blue eyes full of wonderment and joy.

"Well good morning to you too," he teased playfully.

Julie shyly looked down at her feet before replying apologetically, "Just missed you ... I know I haven't been around a lot since everything happened, but we really don't have a choice."

Duke noticed the redness in her eyes and knew she had been crying. "Hey, no need to apologize, Jules—this community needs you now more than ever," he said softly. She smiled in response, but Duke keenly observed the slight tremble of her lips. He could sense something was troubling her. His brows furrowed. "What's up? You have something on your mind?" he asked inquisitively, trying not to prod too much into her personal space.

Julie lifted her gaze and looked into Duke's eyes for a long time before answering. "Yeah, sorta, but can't talk about it right now. But maybe we can talk about it tonight?"

Though Duke was eager to know what was going through her head, he also knew not to push for an answer if she wasn't ready to give one yet. Thus, he simply nodded and replied calmly, "Yeah, of course."

"Okay, then I'll see you tonight," said Julie, and she gave him a kiss before turning and leaving without another word.

Duke watched her from the corner of his eye as she went back to Timmy's bedside. Despite not knowing what haunted her spirit, he couldn't help but feel a heavy weight in his heart whenever she left his sight. He finally shook off his worrying thoughts and returned to his rounds.

Duke approached the workshop with some trepidation. The sound of Mr. Colfax hammering away had been constant all morning, a stalwart figure standing amidst the orange glow of a forge, sparks cascading from his heavy anvil as he hammered out glowing pieces of metal. Duke braced himself for the usual one-word answers he had grown used to.

He cleared his throat and asked, "Mr. Colfax, how are you doing today?"

The large man stopped pounding at the metal he had been shaping and looked up at Duke with blank eyes. Then he continued working as if Duke wasn't there, and the desperation Duke felt made him almost turn around and leave, but he pushed on.

"Give me something," Duke pleaded.

Colfax simply replied, "What do you want from me?"

"I don't know," Duke said desperately, "your first name, what you've been making all this time, who you are or where you're from. I mean give me something."

Colfax stood there and glared at Duke. Without saying a word, he waved Duke over to an old conex in the corner of the shed and swung open the rusty doors. As sunlight poured into the space, Duke found himself awestruck by what lay before him; various hand-forged tools and weapons all tucked away in neat rows—knives, spears, and machetes, but also shovels and garden hoes.

Duke gasped in amazement while asking questions in rapid succession: "What is all of this? Why are you making all these? Who are—"

Once again, he was cut off, this time by Mr. Colfax's booming voice. "Are you going to talk some more or will you listen?"

Duke stood there anxiously waiting to hear what this man had to say.

"My name is Kazim Colfax," the smith said slowly. "I was born and raised in Sudan, Africa." His voice was deep and gravelly, like stones rolling down an empty mountain pass. "My parents were murdered in front of me—my brother and I were kidnapped when we were young and forced to fight as child soldiers in the Sudanese civil war."

Duke could feel his stomach twist at these words; something about them stirred something deep within him. The man continued speaking, only now his voice had become so quiet it was barely more than a whisper.

"We grew into young men," Kazim murmured. "My brother did not make it through the war—I ran away from the rebel forces and the fighting." He paused then, lost in thought as if revisiting some distant memory before continuing, his words coming faster. "I was only saved when American missionaries found me and took me in."

For a moment they stood there in silence, two strangers bound together by pain yet separated by worlds beyond comprehension. Duke could almost feel death seeping out from Kazim's eyes like a thick fog, engulfing him until he felt suffocated by the sheer weight of their experiences.

Kazim looked up then and met Duke's gaze for what felt like eternity before finally breaking it and saying gruffly, "I've lived and breathed war my whole entire life—I know war when I see one. The bullets will only last for so long." He stared steadily for another beat before adding with an ironic smirk, "Is that a good enough explanation for you?"

"Ahhh, yes," said Duke breathlessly, almost regretting asking him anything. He swallowed heavily before continuing nervously. "So ... what other talents do you have?"

Kazim shifted his weight, a hint of pride glinting in his eye. "Many," he stated firmly.

Duke's boots thumped against the hard ground as he made his way back to the command building. The sun was sinking lower and lower in the sky, but Duke didn't feel tired, only invigorated—the conversation with Kazim had left him feeling more alert than ever.

Nearing the command building, he saw Jake. "Hey, man," he said, trying to sound nonchalant despite the anxiety coursing through his veins.

"Hey," said Jake, though there was something in his voice that made Duke suspicious.

"I just wanted to say again that I'm sorry about..."

"I know, man, I get it," Jake said with a wave of his hand. "You didn't know it was me at first."

The understanding in Jake's voice was unmistakable and Duke couldn't help but reach out and give him a slap on the shoulder.

"Again, thanks for understanding."

Jake let out a short laugh followed by an inquisitive look. "Anyway, forget all of that stuff and tell me what I just witnessed," he said. "You and that mute of a blacksmith. It actually looked like he was talking to you."

Duke took a deep breath before answering. "Yeah, that was weird, shocking, and awesome all at once."

"What?" asked Jake.

"Never mind about that right now," Duke replied quickly. "But I'll explain some things later on. Definitely going to need your help on some things."

Jake raised an eyebrow but nodded nonetheless. "Okay... What is this all about?" he asked with a hint of frustration in his voice.

"Right now I need you to help rally up a meeting after dinner. Have Patrick or Eric call in Karl as well."

Jake crossed his arms as if bracing himself for bad news. "Karl, Patch, and Jones should be on their way already for community training. You wanna tell me what's going on?"

A sly smile crept onto Duke's lips as an idea occurred to him—one that could possibly take away some of this overwhelming stress they both felt crushing them from every side. "Can't right now," he said with a wink, walking away while calling out over his shoulder, "but I'll explain later at the meeting."

The distant report of gunfire echoed off the mountains, reverberating through the air like a thunderous drumbeat. Duke surveyed the camp, watching with a sense of admiration as the soldiers sparred and practiced their formations. Karl, Patch, and Jones seemed unusually focused and intense, uncharacteristically devoid of their usual banter.

"What's going on?" Duke asked with assertive curiosity.

"Nothing," Karl spat back.

"Cut the stoic crap, Karl. Something is up," Duke persisted.

"Well, our search team hasn't come back since ... the ambush," Karl exclaimed, his voice full of veiled rage.

Duke thought for a moment before replying. "You didn't find any bodies? I thought we accounted for everyone after that attack—dead or alive."

"You remember that small group that headed down that trail chasing after the ambushers?" Karl continued, his tone now more urgent and pained. Duke nodded, knowing what he was getting at without needing an answer. "They never made it back." Karl paused briefly before adding, "People die in war but it's especially hard when they are likely eaten by Agigi's men."

Only then did Duke begin to imagine the inner turmoil that had been brewing inside his comrade-in-arms.

"Sorry to hear about your people, Karl," he replied sympathetically. "How are Patch and Jones holding up?"

"That's tough on them both—they were close to those who are missing. I heard you were calling a meeting tonight; anything special to discuss?"

Duke nodded affirmatively. "A few things need addressing and backup plans ... but I'll explain more later tonight."

Taking his cue, Karl muttered a quick word of acknowledgment before turning away from Duke and continuing his training mission with newfound zeal and intensity.

The pall of exhaustion hung heavily over the training ground; Duke joined the others in their drills but even the usually enjoyable hand-to-hand combat was becoming a chore. Karl, the gruff instructor, had begun to take great pleasure in pushing Duke further and further until his body begged for respite. With a loud thud, Duke landed on the ground again as Karl looked down on him with a smirk.

"You good?" asked Karl.

"Oh yeah, that was a good one," replied Duke, trying to catch his breath between ragged gasps.

"You need a minute?" Karl asked.

Duke managed to nod before he felt Karl's hands grip his shirt and pull him back up into a standing position. Before he had time to react, the seemingly ageless man forced him down onto his back and pinned him there with a wooden training knife pressed against his throat.

"What the hell, Karl!" Duke grunted in pain.

Karl's gaze burned like fire into Duke's eyes as he spoke grave words of warning. "Do you think Agigi or any of those turds who follow him are gonna give you a break? I'll answer that for you—No! You need to train as if your life depends on it—no, no, not just your life, but your children's lives too! Don't expect mercy in training when your enemies don't have mercy to give."

The words rattled around inside Duke's skull like a bullet in a chamber and something inside him snapped as if finally unleashed from its bonds. He roared with fury and with all his might bucked Karl off of him and kicked hard with both feet, sending Karl flying backward.

Karl quickly recovered and gave Duke an approving nod. "That's more like it," he said with a smile. He readied himself, eyes narrowing as Duke advanced. Karl was fast, dodging each punch Duke threw with ease. He even slapped Duke with an open hand, letting him know he could have been taken out if he were quicker.

"Good energy, Duke," Karl said calmly, "but you must use your head—not your emotions." His words fell on deaf ears as Duke charged forward, tackling him to the ground in an instant. But Karl was quick, using all of his strength to launch Duke up and over his head. Duke landed hard on his back and staggered up, rage written clearly across his face.

"All right, enough!" Karl shouted, breaking Duke from his trance-like state.

"Sorry, Karl, I didn't mean to get out of control," stated Duke, face beet-red from exhaustion.

"No need," Karl responded gently, his voice laced with understanding. "We just have to figure out a way to harness those emotions without letting them control you."

Trying to catch his breath, Duke watched as Kazim passed. He waved at him, but Kazim didn't gesture back.

"What's his story?" Karl questioned.

"He was a child soldier in some civil war in Sudan," Duke replied, reminiscing about their conversation.

Intrigued, Karl approached Kazim. "Hey, sorry, guy, I haven't introduced myself yet. My name is Karl," he said, extending his hand for a handshake.

Kazim simply looked at him and spoke abruptly. "What do you want?"

"Why haven't you participated in training yet?" Karl asked.

"I don't have time for this," Kazim said, trying to walk past but blocked by Karl.

"Training is mandatory, Colfax. Or do you think you don't need to train?" asked Karl.

"Get out of my way," demanded Kazim.

"All right, sorry to bother you. At least shake my hand, please," Karl said as he held his hand out.

Kazim just scowled at him and finally shook his hand before walking away. As he did so, Karl turned over Kazim's wrist to examine it and noticed a large burn scar there.

"What used to be there, Colfax?" Karl asked, but Kazim

pulled his arm away violently and left Karl and Duke standing dumbfounded.

Duke looked at Karl questioningly. "What was that all about?"

"He must've burned off a branding or tattoo of some kind," Karl replied thoughtfully. His eyes narrowed in concentration as he spoke. "My guess is that he really was a child soldier."

Duke leaned forward with interest. His brows furrowed as he asked, "How do you know that?"

Karl exhaled and closed his eyes briefly. "I've done special operations in Sudan. We saw a lot of kids with AK-47s ... they were either tattooed or branded like cattle to show ownership."

"So," Duke's voice dropped to a low mumble, "what do you think of all of this?"

Karl opened one eye and glanced up at Duke, his features now hardened in determination. "If he is who say he is, then that man has been through hell and back. As a result, his personality might have taken more than its fair share of beatings—I mean, it's no surprise; training and fighting since the age of eight or nine would make anyone into one pissed-off badass." He paused for a moment. "So if your meeting tonight talks about him, I'm all ears."

✳✳✳

Duke's body ached from training, but it was nothing compared to the pain of his racing mind. Thoughts swirled like a storm in his head—thoughts of Julie, his children, Mountaintop, Agigi. He couldn't help but wonder what was happening outside their small community. Was the rest of the world fighting for survival like they were? How long until NATO arrived to lend a hand?

As he sat on the worn wooden bench with his thoughts tumbling, Julie snuck up on him, her footsteps silent as death.

"Hey stranger," she teased, causing Duke to jump in his skin.

Barely catching his breath, he replied, "Oh, hey, Jules."

Julie's eyes flitted over him in concern as she asked, "Are you doing okay?"

Duke let out a humorless laugh. "Okay? I haven't been okay since this whole thing started."

Julie nodded sympathetically. "I know what you mean. Dr. Kelly's been working around the clock. She hasn't even gone back to her shack. Set up a cot at the medical station."

The gravity of their situation weighed heavily on them both, and Duke could sense that Julie had something else on her mind.

"What's going on, Jules?" he asked gently.

She hesitated before answering. "I need to talk to you about something."

The setting sun cast eerie shadows across their faces as they began their hushed conversation.

Julie opened her mouth to speak, but before she could get a word out, the sound of someone running in their direction caught their attention. They watched as Patrick shambled up, stopping abruptly when he reached them. His chest heaved as he tried to catch his breath desperately.

"There you are! I've been looking everywhere for you!" he exclaimed, eyes wide and voice charged with urgency.

Duke raised an eyebrow, his gaze shifting from Patrick to Julie and back again. "Relax," he said calmly. "What's up?"

Patrick swallowed hard and gave Duke a worried look. "Someone is on the radio for you and said it was really important."

"Who is it?" asked Duke, curiosity flickering across his face.

Patrick glanced around uneasily before replying, "He called himself inmate 95557. Said you would know who it was."

A stunned silence fell over the group as Duke stared off into the distance, his mind reeling at what this could mean. After several moments of contemplation, he finally spoke up. "No way! You sure? Inmate 95557?"

Patrick nodded, watching as Duke jumped quickly to his feet and began jogging away without so much as bothering to say goodbye. After a few steps, however, Duke realized that he had left Julie without addressing her issue and he came to a halt, turning slowly back toward her. "Sorry," he said sheepishly. "What was it you were wanting to tell me?"

Julie forced a smile onto her face and waved him off good-naturedly. "Not that big of a deal," she replied dismissively. "Just wanted your input about something."

Duke released a sigh of relief before responding in turn with an offer of sorts. "Okay, well, I'll see you later tonight after the meeting?"

"Yeah," she replied softly with a nod of her head. "Sounds good."

Duke planted an affectionate kiss on her forehead before turning and bolting toward the communication building. He could already hear the excited murmurs from inside as the majority of Mountaintop's council awaited his arrival. As he stepped through the door, a myriad of lanterns illuminated the room with a ghostly light, their flames making shadows flicker across the walls like they were performing some intricate dance. Duke made eye contact with some of the members before settling his gaze upon Eric, who was stationed by the radio. Duke grabbed the microphone from Eric's hands and took a deep breath.

"Are they still there?" Duke asked warily, his voice quivering slightly.

"Oh yeah, and he's getting impatient," Eric replied.

"Sounds about right," Duke said, steeling himself for what lie ahead. He switched on the mic. "Roberts, you there? Over."

Static crackled for a few seconds before someone responded. "Holy shit! It's true, you made it! You skinny sack of shit, you made it! Over."

Duke recognized John Roberts' unmistakable voice and a smile crossed his face. "John freaking Roberts! Son of a bitch!

Wait, how?" he exclaimed in utter astonishment.

"Wow, take it easy, potty mouth," came John's sarcastic chuckle, "don't think your buddy Jesus would approve of that type of language. Over."

Duke couldn't help but let out a short laugh at his old friend's joke. "Yeah, well, things change," he replied softly after regaining his composure. Anxiously he asked again, "But still, how did you find me, John? Over."

"Well, long story short. When I found my children, their mother had been with a fella for a few years. The dude is a fucking idiot, but thankfully he was somewhat of a prepper type. He had food, water, and supplies, but they were not expecting me, break...

"I didn't exactly receive a warm welcome, but they were using my property, my preps, so with some ... convincing, they let me stay. My kids are happy. Feels good to be able to be in my kids' lives again. But anyway, to get to your question, break...

"My ex-wife's dumbass boyfriend did manage to have a ham radio. I've been listening to what's happening around the country and around the world. Which, Duke, the world is falling apart. We can talk more about that later. Anyway, hundreds and hundreds of ham radio operators are updating people about what's happening in the country, break...

"Our local radio operator guy said his contact in Colorado, the Voice of the Mountains, has been updating him on the army and air force bases. Said there was a huge forest fire wrecking a part of the state of Colorado. Then I chimed in asking about survival communities in that area, and my guy came back saying his Colorado contact said there were a few, but there was a larger one he heard of. He contacted you guys then contacted me. Now here I am. Over," said John, sounding proud of himself.

"Thought you said a long story short? Over," Duke said, his voice reverberating through the still air.

John's response came back loud and clear, filled with laughter. "Fuck you, Hollander. But yeah, you know me, I like to talk. Over."

Duke smiled despite himself. This man had been a friend for years, and it was good to hear from him again; like he had come back from beyond the grave. He shook off those thoughts and continued talking into the mic.

"Yes, yes you do. Hey, I have a meeting to get to. People are waiting on me. But I want to catch up some more later. Over."

The fondness in John's voice came across the line as he replied, "All right, man, talk to you soon—oh, and Duke, I really am glad to hear from ya. Over."

Duke's throat tightened at the sincerity of his friend's words, and a chill ran down his spine as he pressed the button one last time and spoke into the microphone. "Yeah, you too, brother," he said into the static space between them before pausing and ending with a gruff declaration: "Mountaintop out."

He handed the mic back to Eric and slowly turned around to face those in the room who were glaring at him with questioning looks that seemed to be saying "What exactly was that about?" His chest felt tight as he let out a nervous laugh and answered their unasked question. "Yep, old friend." He cleared his throat and tried to refocus on the task at hand, turning away from old memories and toward new challenges.

"We have a lot to talk about ... the fire, cache update, picking a second in command ..." Duke paused for effect, "... and some strategy for training and security." The intensity of his gaze swept across each person around him as he announced with authority: "Which brings us to our first thing to talk about—you know him as Mr. Colfax."

✳✳✳

"All right, man, talk to you soon—oh, and Duke I really am glad to hear from ya. Over."

"Yeah, you too, brother. Mountaintop out."

Agigi turned down the radio volume.

"Well, ain't that just the cutest thing you've ever heard? Tweedle Dee and Tweedle Dumb have been reunited," Agigi said sarcastically.

"When are we gonna make our move, boss man?" one of Agigi's men asked.

"Be patient. As I said before, since we found out there are caches of my weapons still out there, that is our priority," said Agigi, glaring at the man.

"But how do we find them?" the man inquired timidly.

"That's where our new friends come in," Agigi said as he glanced over at Sean and Dale.

CHAPTER 20

COLORADO | JULY 2035

* knock * knock * knock *

Duke sat up in a quiet panic, unsure if he heard knocking or not. He realized Julie was not in bed with him.

*knock * knock *

The banging startled him. "Who is it?" he asked, still tired and confused.

"Will you let me back in?" asked the voice.

Duke didn't recognize the voice, but it felt familiar. "Who are you?" he asked, growing more concerned.

"It's your father, please let me back in," said the voice.

"My father? What the hell?" Duke mumbled to himself. There was no way his sixty-five-year-old father would be able to make the trip from his family farm in Iowa to Colorado. Plus, his dad didn't know about Mountaintop.

"Nice try, you are not my father!" Duke yelled.

"I promise you, I AM," the voice proclaimed.

Intense light started shining through the cracks of the door. Duke felt compelled to open the door. As he walked through the opening, the intense light dissipated. Duke stepped out of his shelter and noticed no one was around. Everyone was gone, but everything seemed very peaceful. There was no smoke in the air, and all the negative energy that made the air seem heavy was gone. Even though he was alone, Duke felt an overwhelming sense of joy.

"Hello, my son," said a voice behind Duke.

Duke turned around and saw a figure of pure light. "What are you?"

"You know who I AM..."

"Oh, I get it, I'm dreaming and I'm talking to God. Awesome!" Duke said sarcastically.

"But that doesn't make this any less real."

"Yeah? Why would God want to talk to me?" asked Duke.

"You are on a path of self-destruction, and these people need you. Your country needs you. Your children need you. Let me back in."

"Well, if you're really God then you should have thought about that before you let all of this happen! You could've stopped all of this! But instead, you are letting people suffer! What kind of God lets His own creation suffer? And spare me the whole free will speech," Duke said with tears in his eyes.

"I understand your frustrations. I need you to let me back in to help you from this path of destruction."

"Why? What has being a Christian ever done for me? It made me weak, made me feel guilty, filled me with anxiety, and gave me crushing depression for never amounting to what I'm supposed to be. But for the first time in a long time, I only recently have felt truly free," Duke said with saddened anger.

"No matter what, I will always love you."

Black clouds started rolling in as the wind picked up gradually. Lightning danced across the sky, getting closer and closer. A slight drizzle began, then suddenly, as if someone turned on the faucet full blast, grew into a torrential downpour.

Duke noticed the figure walking away. "What's happening?" he yelled over the claps of thunder.

Even though the combination of rain, wind, and thunder made it seem impossible to hear anything else, when the figure spoke it was as if it was whispering loudly in Duke's ears.

"Giving you something in good faith; all I ask in return is that you let me back in."

"A storm? How's this a good thing? Plus, this is just a dream!" Duke yelled, confused.

"I guess you should wake up then."

Duke went to follow the figure but was struck by lightning. The powerful jolt knocked him off his feet.

Duke awoke with a start, the sweat on his forehead like an icy film. He took a moment to acknowledge that he was no longer dreaming. Though Duke knew it was a dream, it felt incredibly real. He felt as if the icy fingers of electrifying lightning still coursed through his veins. He even felt the lighting strike; something he wished to never feel again.

His movements jostled his beloved Julie awake.

"You okay?" she murmured, her voice thick with sleep.

"Yeah, I'm fine," Duke breathed.

"Another bad dream?"

"Yeah ... I think so."

Duke noticed there was a storm raging outside their shelter. The heavens had cracked open, thunder bellowing as rain poured from the sky like tears from an anguished mother's eyes. To Duke it seemed like an omen of things to come, casting its pall on their refuge in the mountaintops. Trying hard not to cower, Duke opened the creaking door and peered out into the darkness. As far as he could see, a bright flash illuminated the distant mountainside like a vengeful spotlight—a reminder of what lurked in his mind—followed by a deafening clap that rattled his bones.

"How long has it been storming?" Duke asked.

"Not sure." Julie yawned. "An hour or two," she replied groggily, rolling onto her side to burrow deeper into the sheets. "Sounds really bad out there."

"Yeah, it is, haven't seen something like this here in Colorado for a long time," Duke claimed.

"Really? In Kansas this happens all the time. We even have a tornado season."

"Oh, I know, I lived in Kansas for a little bit."

"When did you live in..." She paused for a moment. "Oh, yeah. Sorry, I didn't mean to bring—"

"It's okay," he assured her warmly, "I'm just glad to be out. To be with my kids. And to be with you."

"Even if it's the end of the world?" Julie asked playfully.

The rain thundered down like a harsh decree from an ancient god, each drop appearing malevolent in the eerie silence that followed. Duke smiled as he tenderly placed his lips onto hers. They lay there on their bed as if suspended in time, allowing the electricity of the night to fill them. Eventually, they surrendered to the communion between them and nature as a lullaby of thunder lulled them both into a deep sleep.

The inky night sky faded away as the first hints of sunrise illuminated the Mountaintop community. Julie planted a gentle kiss upon Duke's forehead. He tried to cling to the moment, but he knew Julie would have to leave soon. Reluctantly, he opened his eyes and gazed at her. He tried not to think too much about how empty their shelter felt without her sweet presence; instead, Duke focused on her blue eyes sparkling in the pale morning light.

As if sensing his reluctance to part with her, Julie let out a sigh and tenderly kissed him goodbye. "I got to get over to the med bay," she mumbled before making her way out of the shelter. But just seconds later, she came dashing back inside with an expression of urgency across her features. "You might want to get up, Duke, that storm made quite a mess," she said breathlessly.

Duke jumped out of bed and followed Julie—as soon as he stepped foot outside of their shelter, however, the unbelievable scene lying before him quickened his heart with dread. The small mountain community had been reduced to shambles in a matter of moments; branches and debris lay scattered on the ground with trees toppled over like lifeless corpses in battle. A cacophony of chainsaws could be heard as people sliced through fallen trunks and limbs.

Duke stood there for a moment in stunned silence before noticing Jake walking toward him in a daze. "How are the kids?" he asked solemnly.

Jake shot him an exhausted glance before responding wearily. "They're fine, but the storm freaked them out."

"How's Sarah doing?" Duke asked.

Still fighting off his weariness, Jake scowled at him. "Are you asking as a community leader or as an ex-husband?"

"How about a decent person who has been friends with her for a long time?" Duke replied coolly.

Jake gave him an almost imperceptible nod and then answered: "She's doing okay ... a bit more depressed these days but she's doing fine."

Duke raised his gaze skyward. "I guess that is to be expected."

"Yep, everyone's world was turned upside down." Jake let out a long sigh. "And I don't think it will ever be the same again."

Duke nodded in agreement. "Hey, can you rally up the council so we can assess the total damage? I want a meeting within an hour."

Without hesitation, Jake nodded and took off running.

"Daddy!" Duke's children both cried out.

"Hey, buddy, hey, Ava Wava. You two all right?"

"Yeah, we're okay," said Michael.

"It was so loud, Daddy, like a big boom!" Ava exaggeratedly mimicked the sound of thunder.

"Hey, kids, I wanted to talk to you about last week when I got into that fight."

"It's okay, Daddy, Mama told us he was a bad guy and he deserved worse," said Michael.

"Yes, indeed, but I shouldn't have drawn my gun on Jake," replied Duke in a gentle voice.

Michael responded with assurance: "We know, Dad, Mama said Jake just scared you and you didn't know it was him."

Duke held his children tightly. He noticed Sarah a few feet away, looking like she wanted to say something.

"Hey, kids, let me talk to your mama for a second, okay?"

"Okay, Daddy, love you!" said Michael and Ava before they ran off.

Duke trudged up to Sarah, feeling the weight of his guilt settling on his shoulders. He nervously cleared his throat, trying to find the courage to express himself.

"I wanted to thank you," he finally managed.

"For what?" she asked gruffly, weariness in her eyes.

"For talking to the kids about last week."

She shook her head dismissively. "I didn't do it for you—I did it for them."

"Well, either way, thank you," Duke said with a soft smile.

Sarah shook her head and exhaled roughly through her nose in frustration. "Duke, even after everything, I've never made you out to be a bad person. Just someone who made mistakes."

There was a moment of silence between them.

"It's just that you were not the only one to pay for your mistakes."

"I know." Duke looked at his feet with embarrassment before looking her in the eyes again. "The guilt from making you have to take care of the kids by yourself never left me."

"Good, because I still haven't forgiven you," Sarah barely managed to say with a quivering lip.

"Well, hopefully one day I'll earn that from you." Duke smiled softly.

Sarah smiled back. "I hope so too." She turned and walked away from Duke, making him feel strangely humbled.

He stood there for a few moments before calling out, "Hope you all have a good day."

Sarah stopped and looked over her shoulder. "You too, Duke."

The moment was interrupted. "You guys made it!" Patch said sarcastically.

Duke squinted and rubbed his chin before replying, "Yeah, we did, but not without damage. How'd y'all make out?"

Patch scoffed and rolled his eyes at Duke's question. "Come on, Duke, our place is bombproof."

Duke shifted in place and looked down at the ground, a grimace tugging at the corners of his mouth. "Chief told me about your friends going missing. Real sorry to hear that, brother."

The color drained from Patch's face and his mood seemed to darken by the second. He just nodded his head, thankful for the sympathy but unable to form any words of gratitude.

"How are you and Jones holding up?" Duke asked.

"Well, how do you think? Our friends are dead and most likely they were eaten."

An awkward silence filled the air until Patch broke it again with a gentle pat on Duke's shoulder.

"Hey, I'm sorry, man, it's just hard. But soon as we can confirm Agigi was behind this ... him and the rest of his minions are gonna die real soon." Patch's voice was cold and penetrating like an icy winter wind sweeping through Mountaintop; determination seemed to radiate from him in waves.

Duke put up his hands in surrender, feeling slightly intimidated by Patch's intensity. "I get it, he has a lot to answer for," he replied softly. "Wanna come with me to the meeting?"

Patch shook off the darkness that had enveloped him and turned toward Duke, giving him a slight nod of approval. "Yeah sure, Jones and Chief should already be there."

They began their short walk-through Mountaintop, people staring in their direction with dejected expressions, searching for answers they would never receive from these two men. In minutes they arrived at the command center where Duke addressed the assembled with authority. "All right, people, what's the damage?"

Dr. Kelly's voice rang out like a bell. "The medical center's power is off. I think some of the panels on the roof were damaged. We have the generator up and running but that will only last so long."

An unnerving pallor fell over the group as they realized the gravity of the looming crisis.

Duke turned to Greg, who was rubbing his temples from an obvious hangover; even in crisis he was ever dependable. "Greg," Duke said, trying to keep his own fear at bay, "how's the shop looking?"

"Besides a little water, it's fine," Greg replied gruffly.

Duke sighed with a breath of relief. "Good to hear. Gonna need you to go and take a look at that generator and those panels ASAP."

Greg took a swig from his flask before replying, nothing but fearless defiance in his gaze. "Sure, I can take a look at it." He raised the flask higher in emphasis and Duke shook his head silently in response.

Everyone looked around for more news but there was only silence until Farmer Ed spoke up, words spilling out from between lips weathered by too much sun and work.

"Crops are fine," he said confidently. "Actually, I won't have to run the irrigation pumps for a few days because of all that rain." He glanced sideways when he mentioned the broken lines, but everyone understood his meaning; unbowed despite the mounting pressure they all faced.

Duke smiled tiredly and asked if there was any more news. Dr. Kelly spoke up again, her voice strong yet gentle in its reassurance.

"No one was hurt last night."

The tension broke immediately as everyone rejoiced in gladness for each other's safety.

"I also think Timothy is going to make it just fine as long as we can prevent infection in his stab wound," Dr. Kelly continued.

"I feel like I can speak on behalf of Mountaintop when I say that you and your team are all invaluable to this community," said Duke, clapping slowly and deliberately, each clap echoing through the room.

Dr. Kelly looked exhausted as her gaze followed Duke's hands, her eyes heavy but her expression stoic. She replied in a weary voice, "Thank you for your kind words, but we are running ourselves into the ground here. We need help."

Duke nodded. "Maybe when things slow down a little bit more, you and Julie could teach some volunteers from our community basic medical care so they can assist you both."

Patch chimed in eagerly, "I have almost twenty years' experience in the medical field—I'd be more than happy to help teach!"

"Okay, let's see if we can make that happen," said Duke with a nod toward Dr. Kelly and Patch. "So, Chief, do you guys need anything?"

"We'll make it."

"Good, because we wouldn't be able to help anyway," Duke said with a smirk.

That made everyone chuckle.

"Oh, you got jokes now," said Jones, chuckling.

"Good to know," Karl said, smiling back.

"Anything else?" Duke inquired.

"There's still no sign of that backhoe," Greg said.

"What do you mean?" Duke inquired.

"I went out to retrieve it and it was gone. Thieving bastards," Greg grumbled.

"Whoever took it after we got ambushed probably doesn't plan on giving it back," stated Jones.

Patrick suddenly spoke into the mic. "Voice of the Mountains, this is Mountaintop..." His voice then rose in decibels as he exclaimed, "Holy schnikes! I have some extremely good news, everyone! You gotta hear it from the horse's mouth." He pulled off his headset and continued speaking louder, without needing the extra microphone boost, "Voice of the Mountains, tell everyone what you just told me!"

"From my sources, and can confirm from my position in the mountains, that the forest fire has turned and has mostly dissipated from last night's storm. The fire is no longer a threat to your area!" the man said with excitement in his voice.

Everyone, without hesitation, jumped up and cheered. Hugs and high-fives were exchanged around the room.

"Wow, that is good news. Thank you!" said Duke, keying the mic.

"You are welcome. Voice of the Mountains out."

The room was suddenly alive with ebullience, the sheer energy providing a stark contrast to the previous agony of their situation. Even cranky old Greg Arrowood couldn't contain his elation as he broke into a rare smile. Duke turned to Jake and stuck out his hand, offering an earnest handshake. Jake accepted it without hesitation, mirroring Duke's expression.

"All right, I know we are all excited with that news, but we need to move on," Duke said, resuming the meeting. "The next order of business is finding me some help. I need a number two. Any volunteers or know of anyone that wants the position?"

The long stretch of silence felt like an eternity, until finally someone raised their hand. Jake stepped forward and nervously cleared his throat.

"I'll do it if everyone will have me … if you would have me, Duke?" He looked around at everyone anxiously, as if at any slight movement he might break into pieces.

Nobody said a word at first; all eyes were focused on Duke, who looked almost surprised by Jake's offer. He paused for a moment before responding with a small nod of approval.

"Actually, I think that's a great idea. You're well known, well liked, and respected around here as the security leader," Duke said, carefully choosing each word. "I think you would do well. But of course, we got to put it to a vote even if there's no one running against you."

"Yeah, of course," Jake said with a look of surprise on his face.

"We'll put it to a vote tonight," Duke confirmed. "After our community is back in order, training will start, which includes weapons training with Mr. Colfax. We'll divide into groups to make it more manageable and split the tasks among us like this: Chief will teach hand-to-hand combat, Patch will be responsible for marksmanship, Jones will cover tactical movement, and Mr. Colfax will handle primitive weapons.

Additionally, we'll use trees that were blown over by the storm for firewood. Any questions?" He let his gaze wander across the room. "Good—let's get to work, people."

"Man, you seem to be finally getting into the groove of running this place," stated Karl.

"What do you think of Kazim?" asked Duke.

"Well, one thing's for sure: the man is the real deal. I finally got him to spar a few times, and we mostly stalemate. I've beat him but he has beat me as well. It's been a while since I've met someone who's at his level of skill—he'll make an excellent training partner for me."

"You don't say." Duke grinned.

"Yeah, I'm on the same level as him when it comes to knife fighting, but with his other weapons, he defeated me quickly," Karl replied joyfully.

"That's great news for us. It means you can improve your fighting skills."

"I suppose so," Karl said, then looked pointedly at Duke as he spoke again. "We must discover these caches to rest our minds in peace."

"Right. Any updates on our search for them?" Duke queried further.

"It's a slow process—all we can do is use metal detectors and keep narrowing down those broad search areas that Jake marked down."

"Hey Duke, that loud and rude guy is back on the radio," Eric interrupted with a frown.

"Who?" Duke asked.

"Inmate 95557," Eric replied.

"Tell him I'll be there in a minute," Duke said, turning to Karl and shaking his hand. "I'm off to the radio—you can start training now."

"Sounds like a plan." Karl smiled.

Duke was intrigued by what John Roberts wanted to discuss. He never knew what could come out of that man's mouth.

"Hey, can you two give me some privacy?" Duke asked Patrick and Eric.

"Yeah, no problem. I can get the daily Agigi update with the drone," Patrick replied.

"I'll just … not … be here," Eric muttered, leaving the room.

Over the radio, Duke heard John call out: "Mountaintop, this is Inmate 95557, over. That you, Duke? Over."

"Yes, it is, what's going on, John? Over," said Duke.

"You know me, kinda getting bored over here, over."

"John, I can appreciate that but I'm a little busy to be just chit-chatting, over."

"Yeah, I know…"

There were a few moments of silence.

"John? You okay? Over."

John sighed loudly over the radio before replying. "I don't want to sound like a little bitch but I'm worried, man, over."

"Worried about what? Thought you weren't the worrying type. Over."

"Fuck off! I just don't think we're gonna get our country back anytime soon! I knew things would get bad but hell, brother, it's really bad! Over."

"Yeah, it is bad, man, but we still have our military, and we still have our allies, right? Surely they are planning on something as we speak. Over."

"No help is coming, Duke!" John's sigh was heavy and long. "I've been listening to reports from people all over the planet," he said. "All of Europe has lost power. Break …

"Since most of the NATO countries' electrical grids were taken out, Russia has taken Ukraine and other eastern bloc nations with little resistance. We haven't heard much from Canada or Mexico … Over."

"Lord, help us …"

"Yeah, don't think Jesus is gonna be saving us anytime soon."

"I suppose not, but a really bad storm did put out that forest fire that was heading for us, over."

"Well, congratu-fucking-lations—oh, and I forgot the worst one. North and South Korea is gone."

"What do you mean? Over."

"I mean like it's glowing to the nuclear level."

Duke stood at the radio, stunned into silence.

"So, like I said, brother, no one is coming. We're on our own," said John solemnly.

A few moments of silence went by. Duke's head swirled with this new information.

"All right, enough crying about shit. I just thought you should know. Over," said John, sounding like he was perfectly fine.

"One day at a time, John."

"What?"

"We just gotta take it one day at a time, over."

"Yeah, I know. Anyways, I got mouths to feed. You take care of yourself, Duke. Over."

"Yeah, you too, brother. Over."

"Inmate 95557 out."

Duke sat, his mind spinning. All of the worries he had before seemed so insignificant now that he knew the truth about the world. He sighed heavily as he tried to make sense of it all when suddenly he heard Eric's voice behind him.

"The world is screwed?! Nuclear war?! Holy moly!" Awe was written on Eric's face.

"Shh," Duke commanded sternly. "Not a word of this can get out. You hear me? We have enough problems on our hands without this getting out and causing a panic." The urgency of the situation was almost palpable in the air around them.

Eric slowly nodded. "Can I at least tell my brother? I've never lied to him before—well maybe not ever." He paused for a moment, then added with a sheepish grin, "There was that one time I may have borrowed his car and ..."

Duke narrowed his eyes but nodded reluctantly in agreement. "Yes, fine, you can tell Patrick, but nobody else. You hear me?"

Eric nodded hesitantly, still processing what they were dealing with. "Nuclear war, huh?" he asked again in disbelief.

Duke slowly nodded, looking out a window into the horizon as reality set in.

Eric cleared his throat. "You think ... that over time ... the bugs and things would mutate or anything? I mean, that would be awesomely terrifying, could you imagine having to fight a flying ..."

Duke rolled his eyes and cut him off immediately, trying hard not to laugh despite the severity of their situation. "Okay, and this is over," he said firmly as he stepped away.

Just then Patrick came in with a somber expression, putting Duke instantly on alert.

"How's it looking? Same old same old?" he asked cautiously, hoping for some good news amidst all the madness.

"Actually no," Patrick replied gravely, going on to explain there were around 500 people instead of 100 at the nearby FEMA camp.

"Just keep an eye on it," Duke said. As he walked away from Eric, he reminded him, "Remember: nobody else."

Patrick looked around, confused, before turning back to Eric with a questioning look on his face. "Nobody else what?"

And without missing a beat, Eric replied with wide eyes and a mysterious smile, "Dude, one word: giant mutated Korean cockroaches."

CHAPTER 21

Colorado | July 2035

Gordon and his family of four trudged wearily up the steep road, their breaths labored and their limbs heavy with exhaustion, their clothes dirty and sweat-stained. As they climbed higher, the air grew thinner.

Danielle, Gordon's twelve-year-old daughter, lagged behind them, heaving her seven-year-old brother Tyler in his Radio Flyer wagon behind her. Without any food, Tyler had grown increasingly weak over the past week, too feeble to move on his own anymore. His sunken eyes flitted desperately around for something familiar—anything that would reassure him that they were going to be safe soon.

Gordon glanced back at Danielle every few moments, his heart heavy with guilt as he registered the look of determination on her face as she towed Tyler along.

"Here, honey, let me take him." Gordon grabbed the wagon's handle from Danielle.

He could sense Susan's anxiety too—she was fighting hard to keep it together for the kids' sake, but he could see the fear in her darkened gaze as she surreptitiously studied Tyler's frail form.

"How much longer, Dad?" Danielle asked eagerly, her voice hoarse from exhaustion.

"Just a little farther," Gordon said determinedly. "We'll be there soon."

"Gordon, the kids are tired," said Susan.

"Susan, it's only ten more miles to Cascade," said Gordon.

"Yeah, uphill going into the mountains," she retorted.

"Susan, I understand your worries, but that guy said the meeting—this chance at salvation—is today," Gordon gasped, pushing back his exhaustion to find a spark of hope in his weary eyes.

Danielle peered into the depths of the wagon and tried to comfort her little brother. "Hey, buddy, can you sit up?" she asked softly, carefully handing him a bottle of water.

Tyler weakly nodded and managed a few sips before asking Danielle, "Where are we going?"

"We're going to get help," she assured him, mustering up the courage she needed to sound confident. "There's going to be food and medicine. I promise."

Gordon pulled the wagon with renewed energy and strength. They'd been walking for what seemed like an eternity and he could see progress just ahead. He could see it. Through labored breaths, he muttered, "Just a few more miles..."

"It better be worth it. The kids haven't eaten anything in a while, and neither have we. Tyler might not..." Susan trailed off, fighting back tears.

"Don't finish that sentence; my boy is going to make it! You hear me?" Gordon said with glassy eyes.

Susan's hands trembled and her lip quivered as she steeled herself against the rising tears. She inhaled a shuddering breath before bravely lifting her chin, her lips forming a courageous but feeble smile in an attempt to beat back the wave of emotion.

"We have to try; all the FEMA camps are already over-packed and out of supplies. We have to do something," said Gordon desperately.

"I know we do," said Susan solemnly. She turned to Danielle. "How is he?"

"He's still in and out."

After about an hour of hiking up the steep mountain road, suddenly Gordon heard it—a faint murmur that grew louder and more distinct with every step closer. He looked forward with renewed vigor, pulling his son close to his side. The din of the gathering swelled around them as the amassed group of people came into view.

"Here, this has to be it," said Gordon breathlessly. "See? I told you guys!"

He approached an old man with wary eyes with urgency.

"Hey, man, what's going on here? Is this where they said there was going to be food and medicine?" Gordon asked, his voice strained with desperation.

The stranger gave a slow nod. "Yeah, I guess some guy is gonna be speakin' to us about it here in a few minutes."

"Come on." Gordon beckoned to his family, motioning toward the front of the crowd. They forced their way through until finally reaching the front row just as a short, stocky figure ascended onto the platform, bald and with a tight expression, gripping a bullhorn in one hand like a broadsword. A wave of hush swept over the assembly as everyone leaned forward expectantly.

"I want to thank you all for making the trip to join me here today," the man announced, his strong voice echoing out across the audience. "My name is Isaac Agigi. We are living in tough times. We are all doing our best to survive—food is scarce, medicine is gone ... supplies dwindling while our loved ones are dyin'. The FEMA camps have failed us! So what do we do? Give up?"

Answers flew from the throng like hailstones—dissenting cries full of anger and fear rang out from every corner before Isaac silenced them with one final declaration: "Hell no! Our government may have failed us, but we shall not fail each other!" He held his ground as he finished speaking, sternly scanning each and every face.

Agigi hushed the clamoring crowd and began to slowly ascend the steps of the makeshift platform. He surveyed the group before him; men, women, and children, pale and malnourished from a wretched existence on the run for so many months.

He stretched his arms out wide, like a great prophet determined to inspire confidence in his flock. "Friends, today marks a new beginning," he declared, his voice strong and sure. His hands pointed to a distant mountain beyond the horizon. "There lies a large survival station up yonder—a community of resources, food, supplies, and shelter which we can use to help each other survive."

A dull roar erupted from half of the crowd, but it was quickly followed by rumblings of disbelief and resentment from others.

"So, there's no food or medicine here? We were promised food!"

"Who said that?" Agigi called out.

A man raised his hand. "I did."

Agigi hopped down from the platform and moved swiftly toward the man, standing next to him, as powerful as a lion yet calm as a gentle breeze.

"What's your name?" asked Agigi.

"Gordon, and this is my family."

Agigi took a minute to look over Susan, Danielle, and Tyler, still in the wagon but awake.

Agigi cocked his head slightly with empathy before responding. "Don't be so pessimistic, my friend." His baritone voice was soft yet steady, deliberately muffled to avoid further unrest amongst the crowd. "Your lovely young daughter and little boy, who's not looking so great, need you to use your head." He paused for a moment to let his words sink in. "There is food; it's just in that community. That community also has medical supplies that your little boy will need."

Gordon was unconvinced. "Feels like you want us to storm a community in mass numbers and steal other people's food and supplies," he spat back at Agigi defiantly.

Agigi chuckled softly as though amused by Gordon's accusation. "Is that what you think? Oh, man, not at all! This is what you all think? I promise we are not stealing anything from anyone," he said into a bullhorn as he addressed the concerned crowd once more. "I'm good friends with the leader there; this is a message from him—he's a good man with an even bigger heart."

"What's the catch?" someone in the crowd yelled out.

"No catch ... well ... there is a small catch," Agigi said slowly, almost savoring the words. "Everyone here is going to get food, but that group's leader will not take everyone into the community." He paused. "If I were in charge, I would take you all in, but I'm not. So, you will be at the mercy of Duke Hollander. He says he'll take people that he sees as useful. Doctors, hunters, mechanics. People like that."

The crowd buzzed with conversation, a cacophony of voices filling the air as the implications of Agigi's words sank in.

Gordon glanced at Susan and saw fear etched on her face. He put an arm around her shoulders and tried to offer some comfort, but she seemed beyond it; the thought of what might happen made his stomach churn with worry. He then looked over at his son, Tyler, who had already appeared pale before all this started and now looked even worse.

"We leave first thing tomorrow morning," Agigi called out.

Most of the crowd just slept right where they were standing. Gordon looked up at the crystal-clear night sky; the stars shone brightly like diamonds scattered across a black blanket as the family of four huddled together against the unpredictable night. Even after finding some shelter beneath one of the trees, Gordon found himself unable to sleep, too many worrisome thoughts running through his mind.

The sun had only just begun its ascent above the mountains when Gordon awoke, his aching back protesting. Scrutinizing the area with apprehension, he saw Agigi talking in hurried whispers on a portable radio and the group of people starting to slowly make their way up the road ahead. He took Susan's hand firmly in his own as they joined the procession, both of them aware that something wasn't quite right but unable to do anything other than follow along.

Tyler seemed even paler this morning, Gordon noticed with concern; perhaps sensing the tension in the air or being pulled by an unseen force. The sound of hundreds of cheering people quickly diverted their attention, and they looked around to see what was going on.

"Good morning, folks! Who's ready to get fed?" shouted Agigi.

Just then Danielle glanced up in wonderment. "What is that sound?"

Tyler pointed into the heavens, still laying in his wagon. Gordon could hear a strange buzzing noise emanating from high above them—like a swarm of bees—and questioned Susan with uncertainty. "Yeah, what is that?"

"It looks like a big drone," Danielle replied with awe, shielding her eyes from the rising sun as she peered upward.

"It's super high up," exclaimed Tyler weakly.

Gordon raised his eyebrows in confusion. "Who in the hell has a working drone these days?"

"Maybe there's some truth to what that guy was saying," Susan said, hope stealing into her voice. As she finished her sentence, Gordon felt dread flood through his body—were they walking into a trap?

His heart raced as they approached the immense survival community that Isaac Agigi had promised them. He couldn't believe his eyes; towering walls of brick and mortar, coiled barbwire spiraled at the top like a candied treat. Two security towers loomed above them, two faceless men from within pointing weapons at the group—at Gordon's family. He anxiously shot a glance back at Agigi, who was still intently speaking on the radio. Abruptly, but without explanation, the men pointed their guns away, aiming them downward, and allowed the motley crew to pass by. As they trudged warily through several barricades woven together in a winding serpentine pattern, Gordon instinctually pushed his wife and children to the front of the line, though it elicited complaints from those behind him.

"Seriously, pal, there's gonna be plenty for everyone!" a gruff voice cried out from somewhere in the crowd.

Gordon gave a faint smile of assurance before continuing forward toward a gargantuan metal gate secured with steel bolts blocking the entrance. It seemed impossible that anything would dare penetrate such walls, yet Susan asked, "So now what?"

"I guess we wait," Gordon replied gingerly, unsure what else could be done.

Murmurs began amongst the group, soon followed by whispers of awe and admiration. Daring glares were lifted skyward toward an overhanging battle platform with three figures standing atop it: A tall and slender blond man whose beard barely touched his chin held aloft a megaphone, flanked by a bald Irish-looking fellow with a wild reddish beard and a massive Native American man who seemed to dwarf all around him. The crowd stood silent as they prepared themselves for what they knew could be their only hope for survival.

"My name is Duke Hollander," boomed the deep voice of the blond man through the megaphone, addressing the haggard crowd of people. "I don't know what you've been told, but it was probably a lie."

His words sparked a flicker of fire in the pit of their bellies—one by one they erupted into an angry mob, shouting for vengeance and justice, pounding relentlessly at the gate blocking their path.

Duke Hollander stood on the platform with a sawed-off shotgun pointing in the air. The abrupt crack of a gunshot echoed throughout the mountains. The air suddenly felt heavier, as if all life in the valley had been frozen in time by the noise. Even the birds in flight seemed to hang suspended for a few brief seconds, their wings mid-flap.

Duke shifted his weight from foot to foot, hands clasped around the megaphone in front of him like a shield. His face was lined with regret, but his eyes sharply surveyed the group before him. "Listen, we do not want anyone to get hurt! But I am sorry—we are struggling here as well. We do not have extra food, supplies, or medicine. I can't express enough how sorry I am that I have to turn you away. Please go back the way you came," he said firmly. "And do not push on those doors again, or you will force us to have to protect our community."

"What can we do now?" Susan asked.

Desperation built within Gordon as he peered at his children. "Duke, take my children, they are sick and need help—you don't need to take us, just take them," he shouted, waving his arms around frantically.

"What are you doing?" Susan yelled.

Gordon hoisted Tyler into the air; the child was pale and barely conscious. "Please, take them! Please!" he begged, clinging tightly to his son. He could tell Duke was looking at him.

Duke exchanged words with the Irishman and the big Native American for what seemed like an eternity before loudly whistling.

"Listen up, I got a proposal," Duke announced.

CHAPTER 22

Colorado | July 2035

"So, it's between you two," said Agigi, looking back and forth between Duke and Roarke. "I thought it was Duke here—part of me still does. But then I heard about Roarke planning to get out of our deal. How would he do that? The only way is to make a deal. You little shit!"

Agigi's men pulled Duke out of the hole before pointing their guns at Roarke and his girlfriend.

"Wait! You don't need to do this," begged Duke. "He might be innocent, and she certainly has nothing to do with this."

Agigi raised an eyebrow while still keeping his weapon trained on them. "Yeah? Is there something you want to confess, Duke?" he asked, still staring at his prey.

Duke contemplated for a brief moment; his features twisted with shame before he gave an adamant shake of his head. Agigi pointed his pistol at Roarke and Amber. But Duke could see something pass behind Agigi's eyes before he lowered the weapon.

"You know what, I have a better plan," Agigi declared with a sinister smirk.

Duke awoke in a panic, the sweat drenching his sheets as he jolted upright. Julie's gentle voice filled the room, her eyes full of understanding.

"Another bad dream?"

Duke couldn't bring himself to answer, only nodding slowly as he rose from the bed and began to dress. His movements were robotic, almost like he was trying to tell himself that the nightmare wasn't real.

"Where are you going?" Julie asked softly.

"Need an early start and some fresh air," Duke murmured in response, his voice still tinged with fear.

"Are you going to be okay?" She seemed hesitant to let him leave on his own so soon after his nightmare.

"Always will be," Duke replied with a forced smile, bending down to give her a kiss before heading out into the pre-dawn darkness.

The devastation around Mountaintop was evident but the community had worked tirelessly together to make repairs and clean up the aftermath of the storm; children even helped with the burden of tasks. It was a stark reminder of how different life could have been if society hadn't become so lazy and unprepared for anything—especially the end of the American Dream. Everywhere Duke looked there were people working together like a functioning organism. He smiled fondly at their camaraderie, thinking to himself, *this is how it should have been all along.*

The Mountaintop community had much to be thankful for, with hardworking people and experienced teachers in multiple disciplines. Kazim was an expert in the art of combat with primitive weapons, even though his teaching methods were harsh. His ideas on fortification and security were bizarrely brilliant; training with spears, machetes, and knives was not something out of a fairy tale, but it happened every day under Kazim's supervision. As Duke watched from the sidelines, he felt content seeing Kazim interact with others instead of staying at his anvil, and Karl seemed to be enjoying himself as Kazim's training partner.

Duke saw Jake doing his rounds as second in command. Having Jake as his second took a lot of stress off Duke's shoulders. At that moment, Duke remembered his dream. His heart constricted with guilt and shame thinking of the events that had transpired years ago. It was time to confront what happened head-on and talk about it.

"Hey, boss man," Jake said with a wide grin plastered across his face.

"Hey, man, I just wanted to say thank you again for stepping up as my second," Duke replied, trying hard to sound sincere.

A mischievous glint shone from Jake's dark eyes and he quipped, "Well, you're welcome, I guess." His smile widened, and he added, "I should get back to my rounds."

Duke shifted uneasily. The words were stuck in his throat. He knew this conversation would be difficult, but it was something that needed to be done.

"Before you do that, there's something we need to talk about..."

Fear crept into Jake's expression. "That doesn't sound good." He could tell from Duke's expression that whatever was coming next would not be pleasant. All traces of mirth vanished from his persona, and he folded his arms protectively across his chest. All he could hear was the blood pounding in his ears and the ticking of the clock on the wall like a countdown to Armageddon.

"No, no, it isn't," Duke said nervously.

"Okay, you have my attention now."

"Wanted to tell you the truth about..." Duke said before being cut off.

Eric came busting into their conversation, his chest heaving and sweat dripping off of him. "Hey, Duke! There you are!" he gasped. "Patrick said he needs you at the command room ASAP!"

Jake shook his head in disapproval. "Y'all really need to exercise more," he said with a smirk.

"Hey, shut up, I'm brains, not brawn," Eric shot back with a scowl.

"Okay, we'll be right there. Are you coming?" Duke asked Jake.

"Oh, yeah, of course," said Jake, and together they set off toward the Mountaintop command building. Up ahead they could see Patrick already setting up his drone controller and head display as they approached.

"Hey, Patrick, what's going on? Eric said you needed me. Said it was urgent," Duke called as they drew nearer.

Patrick nodded gravely and handed Duke the goggles. "Here, put these on."

Duke's stomach dropped as soon as he put the goggles on; in an instant, he understood what Patrick meant by "urgent." Hundreds of people were marching slowly closer to their camp—only a few armed among them, but their sheer numbers were enough to cause serious damage. His heart hammered against his rib cage as he removed the goggles and turned toward Jake and Eric, wide-eyed with worry; the two of them had already noticed something was wrong judging by their pale faces and tight lips.

Jake spoke first, breaking the heavy silence that hung in the air. "What is it?"

"That whole group of people at the FEMA camp that Agigi was at is coming up the road as we speak!" Duke stated nervously, trying to make sense of the situation as he talked about it out loud.

"How many people?" Jake asked nervously, though deep down everyone knew the answer would not be reassuring— especially given how close it felt.

"Honestly it looks like over five hundred," Patrick said after another moment of uncomfortable silence. His voice trailed off, but no one seemed to want to ask any further questions, all too aware of what this meant for them.

Jake swallowed hard before asking, "Are they armed?"

Duke scanned their faces, seeking solace in Jake's determined expression—but found none there.

Patrick shook his head hesitantly, revealing what no one wanted to hear: "Looks like only a few; the majority are just carrying gear. It looks like a massive group of regular people."

Jake cursed under his breath but quickly regained his composure. "Okay, so how long until they get here?"

Patrick glanced at his watch. "At this pace, probably thirty minutes or so."

Duke sighed, looking around anxiously for ideas, when suddenly Patrick spoke again. "Actually, I might have an idea." He walked into the command building, the rest of them following.

"Okay, we're all ears," Duke said. He rubbed his forehead with one hand and swept his finger along the jagged scar with the other, a daily reminder of the events that had led him here.

Patrick began to speak in hushed yet confident tones. "I have done something similar in one of my Dungeons and Dragons campaigns..." His gaze shifted around the room before finally landing on Jake, who was fidgeting uncomfortably.

"We don't have time for fantasy or games!" Jake yelled, his voice filled with fear.

Duke ground his teeth together, his face stoic but his eyes flashing with anger. "Patrick, this better be good. Lives are at stake, and we don't have much time."

Patrick swallowed hard before continuing. "I know, I know, just hear me out. Jake, isn't there a whole bunch of Tannerite in storage?"

Confused, Jake replied, "You mean the exploding targets?"

"Yep." Patrick's lips curled into a smirk.

"Whoa, hold on," Duke interjected before Patrick could explain further. "We're not gonna blow up those people."

Patrick held up a hand to calm Duke down and responded confidently, "And I'm not suggesting that—it's gonna be non-lethal. Just got to talk to Joe."

Karl walked in then, not having heard what was being said beforehand. "Hey, what's going on?" he asked Duke.

Jake took over, speaking rapidly in an effort to provide an accurate description of the situation despite his fear-filled voice: "Oh, just your typical group of 500 survivors being led by a murderous sociopath heading our way." He threw his hands up in exasperation and continued in a louder tone than intended, "You know, your typical day in the apocalypse!"

Karl's expression hardened as he processed this information before quickly springing into action. "Agigi is coming? I'll tell Kazim and my guys to get everyone in place." He dashed off down the hallway.

"Good news is it seems like it's mostly just non-combatants," Duke called after him, hoping for a bit of reassurance.

A hollow laugh echoed from down the hall as Karl responded without turning back around. "Doesn't matter, Duke; got to treat everything like it's a threat."

Duke let out a sigh and returned to the conversation at hand. "You said they are not even close to being ready," he said, looking from Patrick to Jake and back again. His voice was strained with desperation.

Karl reentered the room and with determination declared, "We don't have a choice, Duke; it's time."

"Can you call in reinforcements from your group?"

Duke hung his head low, shaking it back and forth slowly. "Duke," he pleaded for understanding as he stood face-to-face with him now. "We've been over this. The colonel said no—that's the end of it."

Eric burst into the room, pale as a ghost. Words tumbled out of his mouth in a wild panic. "Duke, he's on the radio asking for you!"

"Who?" Duke asked, narrowing his eyes suspiciously.

Eric looked around the room with an exaggerated expression and lowered his voice to a whisper. "He who shall not be named."

Everyone stared at each other in confusion as Eric rolled his eyes.

"Really? You all need some old-school pop culture in your life." His frown deepening, Eric continued: "I'm talking about Agigi."

Sarah walked up to Karl. "What did he just say?

Karl barreled past Sarah, shouting instructions. "Handle

this, I'll get everyone ready and in place."

Sarah spun around, trying to keep up with Karl's movements. "Handle what?" she demanded urgently.

"Get yourself and the kids to the shelter; there may be a big fight happening," Jake said gravely.

"What? Between who? What's going on?" Sarah questioned frantically.

"Just go get the kids and get in the shelter," Jake said desperately.

With no time to lose, Duke grabbed the microphone aggressively and spoke hastily into it without any formalities or introduction.

"Agigi, it's Duke."

There was a long pause before a chuckle came over the waves. "Ah, there he is, the man of the hour!" The sinister glee in Agigi's laughter hung heavy in the air like dark clouds gathering overhead, heralding a storm that they all could feel inevitably coming closer by the minute. "All right, Dookie, I know by now you've seen my new friends. Now don't be alarmed, we're just coming by to say hi." His tone became light and casual now as if mocking Duke's current predicament despite knowing exactly why they were here—what they wanted from him and how he didn't have a choice in complying. "Maybe borrow a cup of sugar... Or maybe you can give us a tour of Mountaintop or something." There was a long pause before Agigi finished off with an unsettling statement: "Don't worry, we'll think of something. We'll be there shortly."

"What do you want, Isaac?" asked Duke.

"Don't play dumb with me! You know goddamn well what I want. To watch you squirm. I like to play with my food before I eat it."

"Isaac, you literally gave me no choice back then," said Duke.

The room seemed to tilt as the gravity of Duke's situation sunk in. The hidden truth was revealed like an executioner's blade, unwinding a thick carpet of lies smothering the air.

Agigi spoke in a harsh whisper into his microphone. "Was I the one in debt? Was I the one trying to figure out how to make extra money? Did I hold a gun to your head to make you mule for me? No, that was on you. You made that choice."

"I didn't know what I was getting myself into, then I got caught. What did you expect me to do?" Duke spat back, desperation coating his words like oil on water.

"Yeah, you didn't ask questions, which I appreciated by the way," Agigi conceded reluctantly. "But you've always had a choice. Including Roarke."

"No, with that you definitely didn't give me a choice," Duke argued weakly.

Agigi's voice grew colder as he said, "Oh yes, you did—let me refresh your memory. When I put all four of you in that hole, I knew from the beginning that you were the rat. I knew Roarke and Jake didn't do it; they didn't have the balls, but you, Duke, did. I knew as soon as you got caught. I gave you a few chances to come clean and save Roarke's life, but you didn't."

A look of defeat fell upon Duke's face as he was confronted with his own cowardice—he had chosen himself instead of saving his friend's life. His shoulders slumped and he looked at the ground with shame.

Agigi allowed a few moments of quiet reflection before continuing: "Nothing to add, Duke? Doesn't matter, it wouldn't change the facts." He chuckled darkly before adding, almost as an afterthought, "Oh yeah, that's right—I almost forgot another minor little detail which was never said to the cops or brought up in court. They think I was the one that shot Roarke but in fact it was you who shot him."

Duke's tortured screams pierced the air as he was wracked with guilt and pain. Tears streamed down his face, staining his cheeks, each one a reminder of his friend's death. He pleaded to an unseen force for absolution, his voice growing steadily more desperate. "You didn't give me a choice; you were going to kill him anyway!"

"Wait, what is he talking about?" asked Jake.

Duke looked at Jake in horror, having forgotten Jake was in the room. Jake finally heard Duke's dark secret. That he was the one that killed their friend Roarke.

Agigi's voice crackled. "Well, I guess we'll never know because you pulled the trigger, Duke. Not because I forced you, but you wanted to save your own ass. Roarke would be alive if you told the truth. You could have saved him, but you chose to save yourself. Then you blamed me for your choice. You took a plea to what, five years? That's a drop in the bucket to the multiple life sentences I got!"

Duke dropped the receiver and sunk into himself, over-come with guilt and shame. His secret had been revealed—he'd killed Roarke to save himself—and now Jake knew too. Jake slowly turned around and looked at Duke with fury in his eyes as Agigi continued to speak.

"I can't imagine what that felt like, though, having to kill one of your friends to save your own skin. Super brutal, Dookie, but don't worry, your secret's safe with me. Well, we can talk more here shortly. Can't wait to see you."

Duke dropped the microphone in defeat. "Jake, I was try-ing to tell you this morning," he began, but he was interrupted by Jake hitting him.

He wanted to protest, yet he felt too remorseful and just accepted the blows.

"Was it you?" Jake shouted angrily.

"Jake, get off of him," Sarah cried out.

Jake slowly got off him. Duke rolled over, bleeding from his nose and mouth, trying to stand up.

"You stay the fuck down!" screamed Jake.

"Stop! I heard the whole thing, Jake. You were part of that?" asked Sarah.

Jake reluctantly nodded.

"You took advantage of me. Lied to me. Made me believe that someone like you would never do what Duke did." Sarah looked from Jake to Duke with tears in her eyes, shaking her head in disgust. "You killed Roarke?"

"Wait, Sarah!" Jake called out, but Sarah left.

Duke pulled himself up, his face dripping with blood. "We'll discuss this later—we have a problem headed our way now," he said.

"You had the audacity to treat me like I'm the bad guy this whole time! You may not have turned us into the feds, but you killed our friend to save your own ass," Jake growled.

"He would have killed him anyway!" Duke muttered loud enough for Jake to hear him.

"Is that what you tell yourself?" Jake shook his head. "How do you even sleep at night?" he seethed.

"I don't..."

"Good," Jake said coldly before turning away and leaving with an emphatic final statement: "You and me are done."

Eric and Patrick stood in disbelief, unable to say a word. Patrick handed Duke a damp cloth for his bleeding nose.

"Thanks," said Duke through the fabric. "Eric, can you give me a Harris radio with a portable backpack so I can take it with me?"

"Sure thing, man," said Eric.

Duke then asked Patrick, "How's your Tannerite plan coming along?"

"It's all set up," Patrick replied with a smirk.

"That was fast," observed Duke.

"It was pretty basic—I only had to make one," Eric commented.

Patrick walked with Duke to the gate, to the overhang where people could walk along the wall overhead. Karl approached them.

"Chief, is everyone in order?" Duke inquired.

"They're a little anxious but they're nearly in place. Patch is on the Ferris wheel platform with other long-range snipers." Karl dropped off as they ascended the stairs above the gate.

"Duke, here's your portable radio!" Eric shouted from below, throwing the backpack to him. Duke caught it midair and adjusted it upright on his back.

"So where's this nonlethal Tannerite?" he asked Patrick, who gave him a pair of binoculars before pointing past them.

"Holy cow, Patrick! You put a five-gallon bucket there? How much did you put in there?"

"Well, around twenty pounds," Patrick answered hesitantly.

"Twenty pounds!? Do you know how big of an explosion that would be?" asked Duke incredulously.

"It should be far enough away ... I think," said Patrick doubtfully.

"Let's hope so; I wouldn't want anyone getting hurt." Curiosity stirred in Duke's mind as he asked, "So what makes it nonlethal anyway? What's its purpose?"

"Well, it's more than just a distraction. I put, like, two big things of cayenne powder in it. Think of it as a giant powdered pepper spray ... bomb," Patrick said with enthusiasm.

"I hope no one gets hurt," Duke replied. Then he instructed Karl, "Chief, please tell Patch to set off the bucket, but only if things get out of control."

"Will do," Karl responded as he walked away and spoke into his handheld two-way radio.

No more than ten minutes later, Duke saw the first signs of Agigi's group gathering at Mountaintop's security towers.

"Come on, Dookie, you can do this without any violence," Agigi taunted over the radio.

Duke refused to answer him.

"The guard towers are asking what they should do," Jake informed him with a handheld radio in his hand.

"Let them pass," Duke said, taking a deep breath.

The large group of people slowly made their way through

the serpentine barriers that led up to the main gate. A foul odor from the crowd filled the air. Duke thought back to what life was like during the 1700s and 1800s when people weren't able to bathe regularly; he guessed that this smell was similar to that era. Most of the watchers on top of the wall held their noses in response to the pungent smell.

"Good boy, Dookie," Agigi mocked again.

"Why don't you show yourself?" Duke demanded of him.

Agigi laughed as if he were playing a game. "You'll have to find me first."

Jake angrily muttered something under his breath.

"Patch is asking where Agigi is," Karl said, handing Duke the handheld radio.

"Patch, this is Duke, over."

"Yes, go ahead."

"I'm sure he's in the midst of the crowd. I'm not willing to put anyone in harm's way. Over."

"Copy, over."

"Wait for Chief's signal and fire off the canister. Over."

"Copy that, Patch out."

"Are you ready?" Duke whispered to himself.

"Here, take this." Patrick handed Duke a megaphone.

"My name is Duke Hollander."

The crowd finally went silent.

"I don't know what you've been told, but it was probably a lie," Duke said.

The crowd instantly exploded, screaming and yelling, and rushed forward, smashing into the gate, making it bend inward horrifically.

"Get ready!" Karl yelled down to Kazim and Jones.

"Duke, Patch says he sees the man with the bullhorn. You want him to take him out or shoot the bucket? But if he shoots Agigi, the bullet will probably hit somebody else," Karl stated.

"Shoot him!" Jake screamed.

"No, neither!" Duke cried out, picking up his sawed-off

shotgun. He pointed it skyward and fired off one of its rounds.

The horde of people immediately stopped pushing against the gate.

"Listen, we do not want anyone to get hurt! But I am sorry—we are struggling here as well. We do not have extra food, supplies, or medicine. I can't express enough how sorry I am that I have to turn you away. Please go back the way you came. And do not push on those doors again, or you will force us to have to protect our community."

Duke slammed another round into his shotgun as the people shouted and begged.

"Good job, Dookie; they shouldn't have called your bluff. I should know better than anyone, since I know you'll do anything to save yourself," Agigi remarked.

Jake shot Duke an angry stare. Suddenly, a man standing in the crowd started yelling.

"Duke, take my children, they are sick and need help—you don't need to take us, just take them," screamed a blond-haired man at the front of the crowd. He picked up a little boy from a wagon and held him in the air. The little boy was barely responsive.

"Please, take them! Please!" the man pleaded, holding his son in the air.

Duke stared at the man with a broken heart as the man's wife and daughter pleaded with him.

"We got to do something! Jake, please help me with this. I know you don't want to talk to me right now, but please help me with this," Duke pleaded with Jake.

"Right, well, we definitely can't take everyone, but maybe we can help the sick children and take in people with useful skills. Like hunters, carpenters, and medical personnel."

"Okay, sounds like a plan. Now execute it, Duke, before shit gets any crazier," hollered Karl.

Duke raised the megaphone to his lips. "Listen up, I got a proposal," he called out.

The crowd roared as one, a deafening cacophony of misery. Duke's amplified voice cut through the noise and commanded their attention. "We can only take a few people. So as of right now, we are only taking medical personnel," he bellowed, "as well as sick children and their parents!"

Like a line of dominoes being toppled by an unseen hand, almost half of the throng simultaneously raised their hands into the air in despair, crying out that they had either sick kids or were medical personnel.

"That's going to be too many people, Duke," Jake yelled over the frenzied din.

Karl shook his head skeptically and replied, "Looks like everyone and their mama went to medical school today."

"Well, goddammit, we're gonna help and save at least a few people!" Duke glanced around the multitude of desperate faces until his gaze settled on the man carrying the little boy in his arms. Something inside him stirred and without hesitation he pointed directly at them and shouted above the chaos, "You there! You four can come on in!"

Karl surveyed the situation and interjected uncertainly, "Duke, I don't think that is wise!"

But Duke was undeterred. He began screaming at the crowd to let them pass. His words fell on deaf ears as the throng started pushing on the gate again. It bowed and cracked under the intense pressure.

"Duke, we got to do something!" Karl yelled frantically.

Duke froze for a moment before barking into his two-way radio: "Patch, shoot it!"

Instantaneously a shot rang out followed by a massive explosion that shook the entire compound of Mountaintop to its core. An acrid cloud swiftly rolled through the crowd, engulfing everyone within its path. People screamed and coughed violently from the caustic fumes while Jake and Patrick struggled to remain standing from its sheer force. Even Karl was affected as cayenne powder infiltrated his eyes, causing him to blink profusely to ward off the pain. The sound of desperation was almost deafening as the survivors clambered to reach the imposing castle walls. Just when it seemed that their efforts were in vain, time abruptly stopped. Suddenly, a faint rumbling filled the air and all eyes turned to the doors. Then, in one unified crash, the wooden parts of the heavy gates began to splinter as if they had been suddenly struck by an invisible force.

Karl's voice seemed to boom in Duke's ears as his yell resonated through the air: "Duke! Make the call!"

Before Duke could even process what was going on, he fell back and hit the ground below as a gunshot pierced the stillness. He lay there with everything moving in slow motion. When he tried to get up, his head throbbed in pain, and he stumbled back down again.

Suddenly, Duke was being lifted into the air by strong arms and gently brought to the side. Then he heard it—the deafening sound of the gate bursting open from the force of an incoming mob.

"Fire!" someone yelled out. Panic began to take hold of Duke before darkness clouded his vision.

As the crowd poured in, bullets ripped through them. Dozens of people dropped to the ground. The gunshots sounded like small explosions underwater. Duke struggled to stand; his body gave away and he fainted once more. When he came to, the shooting had already stopped. People were screaming and crying in terror. He realized he was staring into the lifeless eyes of the blond-haired man he'd tried to help. He lay there in silence, not moving nor saying a word.

The sandman's heavy hands descended upon him, crushing the life from his bones. He was trapped in a swirling vortex of unending exhaustion as he tried to retain hold of consciousness but was swallowed by its depths. His lids lowered like old marble doors, and he stood no chance against the irresistible pull of slumber.

CHAPTER 23

COLORADO | JULY 2035

The group of men huddled around the fire, its light casting an eerie glow upon their hard faces as they cleaned and loaded their weapons. The clouded sky was illuminated by a macabre orange hue, a reflection of the atrocity that had occurred earlier that day. Dale, ever the optimist, glanced at Sean and spoke excitedly.

"So, seems like everything went better than expected," he said, his voice sounding hollow in the night air.

Sean's face darkened as his mind shot back to the massacre. "If that was better than expected, then you are a freaking idiot," he spat venomously.

Dale looked taken aback by his words. "How you figure? You shot and took Duke out; we have the numbers now. How's that not a win?"

Sean shook his head with disgust. He stared down at the group before him, taking in how little they had actually accomplished this night despite their great loss of life. His voice lowered into a ghostly whisper. "They took out almost a quarter of that group."

Agigi lit up a cigarette and exhaled slowly, resting his hands on his knees while glancing up at the two men sitting across from him. "What could possibly be a problem on such a beautiful night?" he asked casually.

"No problems here," Dale replied hastily.

But Sean refused to let it go so easily. "I didn't sign up for women and children to be killed," he said softly yet firmly.

Agigi stayed quiet for a moment before responding, his tone harsh and uncaring. "No one held a gun to their head. They made a choice, just like you made a choice. Just like Duke had to make a choice to fire upon them." His sunken eyes met Sean's as if challenging him to disagree.

Sean swallowed hard before replying resignedly, "Well, I didn't think that—"

Agigi cut off Sean mid-sentence. "What? You didn't think that Duke had the balls to make that call, to kill all those people?" He leaned forward slightly and spoke slowly as if trying to drive home every syllable of his words: "It's funny how people will react when you back them into a corner … they'll surprise you." An evil grin spread across his face as he continued to stare at Sean from across the fire, unblinking in the darkness. "Duke is no exception."

Sean's voice was laced with dread as he asked, "So we knowingly led those people into a slaughter?"

Agigi's eyes were like two deep pits as he stared at his new subjects aimlessly walking around their camp. "No, no, no! Don't you see the big picture?" He pointed his cigarette at a few of his new people. "We led those people into an opportunity," he said, enunciating each word with calculated precision. Through the smoke clouding his face, Agigi held out one long arm to emphasize his point. "A chance for a better life, for a few more months! Without us, they'd be nothing but pathetic organisms waiting to die."

Agigi stood up, jutting out his chest in pride. He spread his arms wide as if embracing all of them in his unstoppable optimism. "Don't you see? We gave them purpose. We gave them hope!" His voice swelled like thunder. "We promised those people food, and Duke Hollander helped us deliver that promise. All those we lost will not be in vain—they will feed this army for a month or two!" he finished with a predatory grin spreading across his face.

"Well, Sean here took out that son of a bitch," Dale eagerly interjected.

Agigi leaned forward then and roared with laughter, a sickening sound layered over an eerie stillness that had settled after his words. Dale's brows knit together, unsure why Agigi found this so amusing.

Agigi moved closer to him, looming above like an inquisitor intent on eliciting a confession. He squatted down and grabbed Dale's face in both hands while fixing him with an intense stare. "Dale, do you know anything about cockroaches?" he rumbled softly.

Dale shook his head slowly, mesmerized by Agigi's concentrated gaze.

"Have you ever tried killing a cockroach?" Agigi persisted, now squeezing Dale's cheeks even tighter between his bony fingers.

At this point everyone in the room held their breath, uncomfortably awaiting Dale's response.

He managed to mumble, "No."

Agigi released Dale's face from his grasp and stood tall again, looking around at each of them expectantly before finally continuing: "It's hard—you can step on them, drown them, burn them, shoot them. Hell, you can even hit them with a nuclear bomb. They'll be battered, bruised, and broken—and somehow, they'll manage to just limp away." He said as if he was describing something admirable rather than sinister. "I say that to say this—Duke Hollander is a cockroach ... you can beat him ... stab him ... shoot him ... but that man will survive and just limp away somehow ..."

"Okay, if he's not dead," Sean snarled, "how do you suppose we get rid of him then?"

Agigi leaned back in his chair and answered coolly, "Well, the question should be how do you get rid of cockroaches? The answer is simple: you get rid of its home, their nest. Then, you got to cleanse the area of the infestation."

Sean's eyes widened in disbelief. "So what? Are you suggesting we kill all the people in his community?" he asked incredulously.

Agigi shook his head solemnly. "Of course not. Not everybody." He paused for a moment before continuing, searching Sean's face for understanding. "Dictionary states that peace is the absence or the end of war. So one could say peace cannot exist without war. Just like life cannot exist without death. Good without evil, up without down." He leaned forward, an amused glint in his eye as he quoted Roman General Vegetius: "If you want peace, prepare for war."

Feeling suddenly sick to his stomach, Sean argued weakly, "There has to be another way. I may hate Duke, but there are innocent, good people in there, Isaac."

Agigi smiled slowly at this, as if he had expected it from Sean all along. "Trying to provide them with peace," he whispered ominously, "but in order to obtain that—war is inevitable. To put it more plainly, can't have an omelet without cracking a few eggs," he said with finality as he sank back into his chair and whistled loudly for two of his men.

They came over and set something down at Agigi's feet as anticipation thickened the air between them like fog on a cold night.

Eyes widening further in disbelief, Sean choked out, "Is that ..." But before he could finish his sentence, Agigi nodded with a sinister grin curving his lips upward.

CHAPTER 24

COLORADO | AUGUST 2035

The cacophony around Duke swelled as the crowd surged in. His heart pounding and sweat dripping, he heard someone yell above it all, "FIRE!" Bullets ripped through the air like hot knives into the unsuspecting masses below.

"No!" Duke screamed as he plummeted to the ground, body after body thudding against him until he finally landed atop a pile of motionless corpses. He could taste the coppery tang of blood on his lips.

With a heavy heart, he gazed down at the body directly beneath him. A man with bright yellow hair and sapphire eyes seemed to be looking back up at him. In that instant, Duke was gripped by an overwhelming guilt and grief so immense it felt physical. He heard a voice inside himself whisper in sadness, "It's all your fault, Duke."

Duke awoke with a start, his heart pounding in his ears. Every breath brought stabbing pains from his wounded shoulder—the one that had been grazed by a bullet days before when the horde had broken through the gate. He felt like he was moving through thick syrup as he tried to move his left arm; the pain was almost too much to bear. Dr. Kelly had insisted Duke wear a sling, and though he yearned to use both hands again, for now he would have to settle for being conservative with his movements, and rely on her advice.

Julie had been checking in often on Duke's condition since the incident. In a moment of weakness, he asked her how many people made it through the gates alive. Her answer was not one he wanted to hear—thirty-five dead inside the gate, ten more succumbing to their injuries after, and a few more still in critical condition. Even worse was that there may have been seventy-five to one hundred people killed outside of the gate. Eventually someone from security reported that no more bodies remained—they had either been taken by Agigi's mob or scavenging animals. None of them would ever know for sure because any time they tried venturing out past the entrance there were gunshots fired at them.

The guilt that Duke felt was overwhelming. He told himself it wasn't his fault those people were killed; it was Agigi's. But in the back of his mind, Duke knew he was responsible not because he ordered those people to be shot but because he allowed Agigi to live when he had the chance to kill him.

Duke stepped out of his shelter like an old man, the sun blazing unmercifully down on him. His eyes slowly adjusted to the bright light, nausea coursing through his body as it had for weeks in his dark retreat. He wanted to turn and go back inside, but he remembered what he had come outside for—to face the challenges that awaited him as leader of Mountaintop and put to rest all that had happened. Duke noticed the air was no longer thick with smoke from the forest fire. The only smoke that lingered was from random campfires around Mountaintop.

The thought of the forest fire brought Duke's dream of God to mind. He felt angry and confused; why would God let all those people die if he had helped put out the fire? Was it just a dream? Or perhaps God didn't exist at all anymore. These questions swirled around Duke's head as he made his way across Mountaintop.

The first person he saw was Sarah, the last person he wanted to talk to. He tried walking away, but she intercepted him before he could make good on his escape.

"Finally, you're up and about. The kids have been asking about you," she said.

Duke's lips parted to speak, but froze before the sound of his voice emerged. His gaze dropped to the ground. "Didn't think you would want to talk to me," he muttered.

Sarah stepped closer. "Why, because of you and Jake? I really don't know what to think about all of that." Her voice caused Duke to flinch, as if her words were sharp knives aimed at him. Sarah swallowed. "I'm still shocked about it all, but to tell you the truth I'm more mad at him than you."

There was a slight pause during which Duke nodded slowly. He ran his hands through his hair and opened his mouth again. "So what are people saying about how I handled the mob?"

Sarah sighed and took a seat on an old log nearby. "Honestly, Duke," she said solemnly, "no one truly blames you for what happened. You tried your best in a very shitty situation."

He offered her a small smile of appreciation before asking, "How's Jake doing?"

Sarah shifted uncomfortably. "Crazy busy, especially with your absence," she replied wearily. "Roarke was his best friend—hell, he was your friend too." She paused, suddenly overwhelmed by emotion. Images of Roarke flashed across her mind—them gathering around a fire late into the night or laughing hysterically over some stupid joke—and then just as quickly vanished into smoke. "I don't know how I would react if I were put in your shoes," she continued quietly. "Or in Jake's."

She searched her mind for something else she could say, anything that might break the suffocating silence that had befallen them both. And then it came to her.

"Life is too short," she said softly, looking around them at the brambles that had taken over this place once so familiar to them all. "As cliché as that sounds, it's true. Ever since the power went out, losing our way of life ... then all these people dying—I've just started to see things differently." Tears prickled at the corner of her eye and she blinked them away quickly before continuing. "Things in the past need to stay in the past." She reached forward and placed a gentle hand on Duke's arm before looking directly into his eyes and speaking firmly: "All we can do now is look to the future."

Duke looked at Sarah with a glimmer of hope, a sliver of optimism that, perhaps, they could reconcile their past and rekindle the friendship that had once flourished between them. For a moment, Duke thought he detected a spark of understanding. But whether it was real or imagined remained to be seen.

"Daddy! You're awake!" Michael and Ava squealed in unison, throwing their arms up in excitement.

"Hold on, kids, why don't you let your daddy rest," Sarah said, her voice strangely soothing despite the edges of sadness that seemed to permeate it.

Michael looked up at Duke with his big eyes and asked, "Is it true that you were shot?"

Duke let out a small chuckle and tousled his son's hair with one hand. "Yeah, buddy, but I'm okay now."

Ava looked up with wide-eyed innocence and asked curiously, "Can we see it? Is it bad?"

"No, sweetheart," Duke said with a smile, trying to push away any fears she might be having. "It's all bandaged up nice so I won't get hurt again and there's nothing to see. Besides," he added, winking at Michael, "I'm tough, remember?"

The two children laughed and Michael asked, "Did it hurt?"

"Nah," Duke said, shrugging one shoulder, forcing himself not to grimace at the pain radiating from his wound. "It wasn't so bad, just tickled a little bit." He tried scooping both children up into a hug but felt himself become lightheaded after only managing to get one arm around Ava before having to put them back down.

Michael gave him a concerned look. "You all right, Daddy?"

"Oh yeah, kiddo," Duke said, giving him a reassuring smile. He was obviously far from all right but he wouldn't worry his son by saying so. "Just a little tired is all." He gave them both an affectionate pat on the head. "Why don't you two go play and I'll see you later?"

"Okay, we're going to try to play with our new friends,"

said Ava, running off.

His gaze returned to Sarah, who watched the kids run off with a sad expression on her face. "New friends?" Duke asked, knowing full well what she was implying without needing to ask further questions. Understanding crossed over her features as she nodded slowly.

"Yeah, only a few people survived from breaking through the gate," she started explaining. Her sorrowful demeanor made it clear that there hadn't been many survivors. "A couple of adults and five kids..." Her voice trailed off as sadness radiated off her like a palpable force field. It was obvious that the parents of those children hadn't been so lucky in surviving whatever tragedy had befallen them. With typical selflessness, Sarah had decided to take care of these unfortunate souls as if they were her own children. Knowing how much Sarah loved being a mother, it didn't surprise Duke that this would be her course of action in helping others during such hard times.

Duke's mind raced with questions. "What does Jake think about that? Taking on new kids?" he asked cautiously.

"Well, it was his idea and I of course supported it. He feels guilty for making the call." A somber note tinged her voice.

"The call for what?" Duke prodded. He could already feel the dread seeping into his gut like an icy river, traveling ever so slowly toward his heart.

Sarah averted her gaze and her words cut like a knife when she spoke again, "The call to open fire on that crowd."

The air went quiet as Duke looked around, searching for something that could make sense out of it all—an answer, a light in this abyss of darkness. But none would come, and it all boiled down to an empty void of shock surrounding them both.

Sarah tried to fill the silence with some soothing words. "So, like I said, just give him some time." Her footsteps echoed softly as she walked away, leaving Duke standing there in place as if frozen in time, dazed and paralyzed by the news he had just received. No one had told him how hard Jake had been hit by having to make such a call.

Duke's shoes scuffed the concrete pathway as he made his way to the medical station. A cold sweat drenched his forehead, and a lump rose in his throat when he thought of what Sarah had told him—Jake was responsible for calling the order to open fire on that crowd.

His heavy steps slowed further as he neared the doorway to the infirmary, dread clinging to his chest like an anchor. Duke trudged inside, greeted by an overwhelming blanket of worry and fear from the sick and injured. Every bed was occupied—some with people he recognized, others strangers in a foreign land.

"Oh, wow, you should not be walking around, Duke," said Dr. Kelly with surprise when she laid eyes on Duke.

"Good morning to you too, Doctor. Is Julie around?" Duke managed a pained smile.

"Yeah, she's changing Dr. Bailey's bandages; they're in the back." Dr. Kelly gestured vaguely with her hand.

"Dr. Bailey?"

"Yeah, luckily one of the survivors was a doctor—not someone with some medical experience but an actual doctor." She shook her head in disbelief. "That's a huge amount of pressure and time taken off Julie and myself."

"Wow," Duke gasped at this news, "that's amazing."

Duke slowly made his way to the back room where Julie was working. As he shuffled closer, he could hear Julie's laughter ricocheting off of the walls like rain against a tin roof. He opened the door and saw Julie busily wrapping up what must have been Dr. Bailey's forearm; he was tall and darkly handsome. Despite himself, Duke felt a spark of what could only be described as jealousy flame inside him; it was different from his feelings for Sarah and Jake—this was raw, and uncharted territory.

Julie immediately rushed over to Duke and said, "Oh my God, Duke! You're up! Oh, honey, you honestly should still be in bed resting, but I know better than to even try to convince you otherwise!"

Dr. Bailey stood up and reached out his hand in greeting. "Hi, I'm Dr. Bailey; I appreciate you guys taking me in."

Duke replied nonchalantly, "Don't thank me, it wasn't my call," feeling oddly threatened by the presence of this stranger who had entered their lives so suddenly.

Julie tried to break the awkward tension. "Soooo, isn't it amazing that we have some new help?" She smiled at both of them before carrying on with her work.

"Yeah, it's really cool; I'm happy for you, Jules," said Duke with a forced cheerfulness.

"You okay?" Julie asked, her voice gentle and concerned.

"Yeah, I'm just tired and in pain," Duke responded, reality sinking in deep within him.

"Okay, well, you need to get your bandage changed," She looked at Dr. Bailey with a warm smile. "Now might be a good time for Dr. Bailey to see his first patient here."

Duke gave a half-hearted smile before slipping into the chair opposite them both. His eyes held that same solemn glint they always did when he was dealing with physical pain—and perhaps something deeper—as Dr. Bailey began to unwind the fabric from his arm.

"Well, I'm going to help Dr. Kelly and leave you to it," Julie said to Dr. Bailey.

"So you're the head honcho, I hear," Dr. Bailey said, taking off Duke's bandage.

"Yep, I'm trying to be," said Duke flatly. "So Bailey, how old are you?" he asked after a few moments of silence, trying to distract himself from the growing discomfort radiating from his wounded limb.

"Thirty-five." Dr. Bailey squirted saline onto Duke's wound, causing him to wince slightly, before changing the bandage with practiced hands.

"Really? We're pretty much the same age," Duke remarked incredulously. "You look a lot younger than that."

"Yeah, I get that a lot." Dr. Bailey let out a gruff laugh as he finished tending to Duke's wound.

"You lived here in the Springs?" Duke questioned, ignoring the sharp stinging sensations still emanating from his arm.

"No, from LA," came the answer after a pause. "Flew into Denver for a medical conference. Then when everything turned to crap, I migrated down here with a bunch of people to the Springs," said Dr. Bailey as he put a fresh bandage on Duke's arm and helped him back into his sling. "Think that should do it. Just let me know if you have any questions or concerns." He shook Duke's hand.

Duke nodded as Dr. Bailey got up. "How long do you plan on staying?" he inquired nonchalantly.

The doctor slowly turned around. "I just assumed I could stay," he replied cautiously, his gaze flickering toward an uncertain future. "Is that not the case?"

Duke regarded him quietly for what felt like eternity before finally responding, "All depends if you can pull your own weight." He spoke with finality and strength before adding in a more friendly tone, "We'll decide all of that at a later date. You married? Single? Kids?"

Dr. Bailey's jaw clenched as his eyes narrowed at Duke. "Why do I suddenly feel like I'm being interrogated?" he asked, barely controlling his voice.

"Just fairly simple questions," Duke replied with a weak smile, "and you are still a stranger."

Dr. Bailey said with a hint of sadness in his voice, "I have no idea if my wife and children are dead or not. Is that good enough for you?"

Duke immediately regretted asking such intrusive questions and hastily offered an apology. "Listen, I'm sorry, just under a lot of pressure is all."

Dr. Bailey seemed to relax somewhat after Duke's apology

but there was still an underlying tension between them.

Duke cleared his throat before continuing, "Also, I'm sorry about the whole..."

"Being almost killed by your people?" Dr. Bailey interjected wearily. "Really not ready to talk about that," he replied curtly. After a pause, he spoke again, snuffing out any hopeful glimmer of reconciliation between them. "I don't blame you for what happened. That had to be a hard call." His voice softened as he continued, "I think a good number of us knew it sounded too good to be true. I was extremely lucky that this is all that happened to me."

Duke stayed silent, feeling immensely guilty for the part he played in the doctor's fate and merely nodded in agreement as a show of sympathy.

"Well, that should do it," Dr. Bailey said, referring to Duke's bandage and thus ending their conversation abruptly as if nothing had ever gone wrong between them.

Duke paused before leaving the medical station, struggling with a turmoil of emotions within him. Embarrassment was at the forefront, and he knew he could not control how he felt but could rein in his reactions. He tried to push away the jealousy that bubbled up inside when considering Dr. Bailey. Duke knew the doctor would be an excellent asset to Mountaintop, yet he still felt threatened by him.

Duke trudged on to the command building. As he sauntered past, he caught sight of Jake helping the community spread ashes which Duke assumed were of those killed in battle. Ever since Mountaintop had been ambushed for the first time, it had become policy that each body must be cremated and placed into the wooded area among the pines and evergreens to make the soil acidic. Some people didn't take kindly to this practice at first, until Farmer Ed explained how beneficial it was and even Dr. Kelly pointed out that the burning and spreading of ashes would prevent disease from spreading as well.

The people of Duke's small community were still train-ing, though now it seemed with a newfound intensity. Duke watched as the trainees labored in earnest, every action taken with an urgency they had not previously possessed. Some yelled commands back and forth, while others swept their gazes warily about, as if at any moment some new enemy might appear. Everywhere there was trepidation, a sense of fear that seemed to grip them all—it was clear they were aware of the gravity of their situation and that failure would be unacceptable.

Duke stumbled forward, his vision blurring and head in agony. He could still make out the figure of Patch standing ahead, overseeing the training of Kazim and Jones' troops. When Patch caught sight of Duke, he grinned widely.

"Hey! There he is—how you feelin'?" asked Patch with a mischievous glint in his eye.

"Like crap, but could have been worse," Duke answered, wiping the beads of sweat from his forehead.

"Ain't that the truth," chuckled Patch.

Patch yawned and stretched out his arms lazily. "Oh yeah, Karl wanted to talk to you. He's in the command center." His grin widened as he spoke, though Duke had no idea why.

Mustering all his strength, Duke got up and trudged toward the command building. As soon as he entered, he saw Karl furiously speaking on the radio mic before flinging it aside with an audible thump onto the desk. Eric winced vis-ibly at this display of anger and tried to explain something about backups, only to be silenced by Karl's menacing glare.

Duke cleared his throat timidly and asked, "What's up Chief?"

Karl focused on Duke with blazing eyes before finally calming down enough to answer him: "Well, I had good news ... It's still good news, just not exactly what I wanted."

"Okay," Duke replied hesitantly as he slowly lowered him-self into a chair.

"Our team found the most southern weapons cache." The excitement in Karl's voice was clear and contagious; Duke jumped up excitedly then quickly slumped into his seat due to pain ricocheting through his skull.

Karl continued: "I just talked with Colonel Campbell again and he said that he's not going to authorize its use for Mountaintop's cause."

"Well, it's better for you all to have it rather than Agigi. It's not exactly what we wanted, but we just keep training and preparing," said Duke, trying to sound optimistic.

Karl stood silently for a moment before speaking. "That's the other thing. The colonel just pulled us from helping Mountaintop any further. Said we were getting too attached. That we were wasting the company's time and assets," he said with an edge of bitterness in his voice.

"What? Wait, I thought we…"

"Trust me, this is not what I wanted," Karl said, his voice thick with emotion.

Anguish and frustration rooted deep within his chest, the reality hit home like a punch to the gut. "So when do you have to leave?" Duke asked despondently.

"He wants us back right now," Karl said through gritted teeth, barely containing his outrage.

✳✳✳

Duke walked Patch, Jones, and Karl out the gate. As they said their final goodbyes, Duke thought to himself, *There goes our best chance at beating Agigi.* Losing Karl and his men was not only disheartening to Duke but utterly demoralizing to the people of Mountaintop. However, there was still one silver lining—Kazim remained in their corner.

Duke had only made it halfway back to the command room when Eric's frantic shouting roused him from his reflections. "Duke! Radio!"

With a heavy sigh, Duke trudged toward the radio. Picking up the microphone, Duke asked wearily, "Who is it?"

Eric replied with reservation: "He who shall not be named."

"What?" Duke asked, confused.

Frustration was evident on Eric's face. "Oh never mind, it's Agigi." He threw his hands up in the air in defeat. "A perfectly good Harry Potter reference gone to waste," he mumbled to himself.

"What do you want, Isaac?" Duke spoke into the radio mic.

The radio crackled to life, and a gruff voice spoke through the static. His adversary's response was half laughter, half taunt: "Holy shit, I knew it. Told everyone that you would be hard to kill." Agigi's voice thundered over the speaker.

"Yeah, your sharpshooter skills are a little rusty, pal," Duke replied matter-of-factly.

"Sorry to disappoint, but it wasn't me who took a shot at you; that was my new buddy Sean. I believe you two know each other," Agigi said with smug satisfaction in his tone as he reveled in the moment.

Duke closed his eyes and shook his head. "... that turd would team up with someone like you," he sighed wearily

"Can't blame him," Agigi chuckled mockingly. "Our company provided an opportunity for promotion—we're a bit more forward-thinking, and our retirement plan isn't half bad."

A wave of rage swept over Duke as he glared into the darkness of the room beyond his viewport. "Get to your point!" he snarled between clenched teeth.

Agigi seemed to take immense pleasure in the moment as he continued goading Duke on. "Oh, Dookie, do I sense some sass in that voice?" He chuckled again before replying in an almost singsong manner, "Relax, just wanted to let you know that I—no, WE all appreciated the meals you provided for us; it's going to feed this army for over a month. Well done!"

"You're a monster," Duke spat into the mic.

"No," Agigi corrected him coolly and almost reverently,

"you have me all wrong, Mr. Hollander. I'm no monster; I'm an opportunist." He paused for dramatic effect before adding menacingly, "That's where you and I are very similar. We're willing to do whatever it takes to survive." His words hung heavy in the air as the truth settled on Duke's conscience like an oppressive fog. "Making tough decisions, like shooting dozens of people bum-rushing your community or having to shoot a close friend. You see, survivors are the ones who can make the tough calls—you, Duke, are a survivor!"

Duke's fingers were trembling now; he could barely contain himself anymore. With a shaking voice full of rage and fury, he spat, "You're going to pay, asshole! You wanna know what we found today? Hmmm? We found one of the weapon caches! So, what are you waiting for? Huh?"

Agigi's deep breathing lingered in the air like a noxious fog, growing thicker and more intense with each passing second.

Duke clenched his teeth in frustration and let out an enraged scream into the radio microphone. "Not feeling so confident anymore, do ya?"

Agigi's voice slithered through the speakers, breaking the stillness. "Well, this is going to be interesting, then."

"Oh yeah, why's that?" Duke asked, his heart sinking as a sickening sensation of dread wrapped around him.

"Because—" Agigi spoke slowly and ominously, "—so did we."

CHAPTER 25

COLORADO | SEPTEMBER 2035

The oppressive air of the waning summer hung like a weight on Duke's shoulders. It was officially fall and it had been a month since Agigi had shared his news—yet Mountaintop had not come under attack. Had Agigi been bluffing? Or was he simply waiting for the right moment to strike?

Duke's suspicions were aroused, and he sent Patrick to do some reconnaissance. Armed with his drone, Patrick flew out toward the central and north cache locations. When he got there, it was clear that Agigi had not been lying. To the north, Patrick spotted a large crater on Crawford's property and Kyle Crawford himself arrived at Mountaintop shortly after, confirming what they had seen. He described how he had watched hundreds of people armed with shovels, pickaxes, and a backhoe unearth dozens of wooden crates heavily damaged from being buried in the ground for so long. Duke explained the situation to Mr. Crawford, who sadly refused to get his family involved despite their dire circumstances.

Karl's voice crackled over the radio, checking in with Duke every week. Colonel Campbell had remained adamant that Karl and the others stay away, no matter how much they wanted to help. Training was never quite the same without Karl, Patch, and Jones, yet the people of Mountaintop refused to give into despair. They carried on without their beloved friends like a well-oiled machine, each doing their assigned tasks with even greater strength than before.

As Duke gathered the group, he glanced over at old Greg.

His clothes were stained and his breath reeked of alcohol. The others had to train, but Duke knew that was impossible for him. Dr. Kelly and Dr. Bailey weren't allowed to be a part of any battles if it came to that; however, they were given pistols as backup. Julie insisted on being a field medic regardless, and Duke couldn't help but feel his heart sink at the thought of her in harm's way. But even he could admit that someone like her would be invaluable. It was also clear that she was getting good with a pistol—something that brought Duke both relief and envy.

Michael and Ava asked to start training too, but Sarah only agreed to physical training for Ava and limited weapons training for safety reasons. Duke felt Michael was old enough, though, and taught him basic marksmanship and safety, then gave him a .22-caliber long rifle for practice. To Duke's surprise, Michael learned fast, quickly becoming deadly accurate at fifty yards, filling him with pride.

Duke sighed as he thought about Sarah taking in Tyler and Danielle, two orphaned children who lost their parents to the tragic gate massacre. Though life at Mountaintop had been hard for them, Michael and Ava still managed to get them to open up and act like normal kids—though Duke could still see grief lingering in their eyes.

With a heavy heart, Duke admired how far Mountaintop had come. He knew that it took courage and consistency to succeed during times of danger. But looking over at Jake only reminded him of the sorrow brought on by his actions. Jake didn't share jokes or attempt small talk with him anymore. Instead, there was nothing but an uncomfortable silence between them; one that spoke volumes about Duke's actions without saying a word. Jake would never forgive him for killing their friend.

Jake still was not talking to Duke on a personal basis. Their relationship was entirely on a professional level. Jake no longer cracked jokes with Duke or attempted to make small talk.

Duke and Jake decided it wasn't safe enough for the hunting party to go beyond the gate anymore, even if it meant no more extra meat for their food stores. The decision was made: no more risking lives for food.

Duke tossed and turned in his bed, the day's events replaying in his mind. Even when he finally did drift off to sleep, the memories haunted him with each nightmare, causing fear to trickle through every inch of his body.

Suddenly, Julie's voice rang out. "Duke, you up yet?"

Duke sat up with a start. "Yeah, I'm up. Is everything okay, Jules?" he asked cautiously.

"Good," she said as she tossed her tattered notebook onto the floor. "What the hell's the matter with you?" she yelled as her icy eyes pierced Duke's very soul.

"What's going on? What did I do?" Duke asked, bewildered.

"For the life of me, I couldn't understand why Dr. Bailey didn't ask questions about you or why he acted like he didn't like you. Or why you never included him in your daily rounds." Her words reverberated off the walls of the small room, adding to his discomfort. "So, I had to ask, and he finally told me about the interrogation you gave him last month." Her voice grew louder with each syllable. "You did that right after we almost killed him, and all those other people and you couldn't cut him some slack!" Her face was red with rage at the thought of what Duke had done.

He hung his head low in shame before answering her in a timid voice. "I apologized immediately to him for that."

Julie looked confused; this wasn't like Duke at all. "Then why do you act like you don't like him or whatever?"

"Like I said, I apologized for that. I know he's a great asset to have here."

It was then Julie noticed something else stirring beneath Duke's cold façade—jealousy. She asked cautiously, "What is it, then?"

Duke suddenly felt exposed and embarrassed as he mumbled his confession: "I mean ... you two have so much in common; you're always laughing and having a good time with him." His words were barely audible as his cheeks blushed deep red in humiliation.

Julie stood speechless for a moment before finally asking, "Duke, are you jealous?"—a question that only served to deepen his shame further. All he could offer was a faint nod of confirmation. "Duke, I could never ..." Her words trailed off. "I would never leave you for somebody else! Plus, I'm pregnant!" she blurted out, burying her face in her hands.

The room fell silent as Duke's mind reeled with the news. *A child? Now?*

"How do you feel? Happy ... sad? Please say something," Julie begged.

"Well, it's not exactly the best time to be having a kid," Duke muttered, standing up to pace.

"Yeah, no shit," Julie said bitterly, turning her head away.

"But the thought of having a child with you makes me happy, excited, and frightened all at the same time. But to hell with how I feel—how are you taking this?" Duke asked finally.

"Scared, and I've been trying to tell you but at the same time I was worried that this would add to your already over-filled plate," said Julie nervously.

"I know I've been busy; I'm sorry that I haven't been there for you lately like I should have been."

"It's okay, I just didn't know how you would react. I've always wanted to have a baby, but like you said, this isn't the best time to have a baby."

"Yeah, I know ... So, what did you decide to do?" Duke asked warily.

"I haven't; I wanted to talk to you first."

"Well, that decision is completely up to you. But know that whatever you decide, I'll support it," Duke assured her.

"Okay." Julie took a deep breath. "I decided, then. I think

I'm keeping it." Her voice was soft.

Duke's eyes swelled with emotion. "We're having a baby?" he whispered, barely able to believe it.

"We're having a baby," said Julie with a nervous smile, taking Duke's hand in hers.

For a few seconds, Duke was weightless and free from the crippling fear that had been weighing him down for so long. In these few blissful moments, even his fear of having a baby in this perilous world didn't seem to matter.

Then there was a loud banging, shattering Duke's momentary peace. He leapt up and darted toward the door, heart pounding in his chest.

"Duke, you in there?" Jake called out.

"Yeah, what's up?" asked Duke, stepping outside into the dimly lit night. The distant stars twinkled coldly in the sky above them.

"We have a problem. Follow me," Jake said in a ragged whisper, already turning away and heading off into the darkness at a slight jog.

Duke blew Julie a kiss goodbye and hastened after him. He eventually caught up to Jake, who seemed eerily unruffled.

"What's going on?" asked Duke breathlessly.

"You'll see," Jake responded cryptically as he led Duke into the command building, where Kazim, Eric, Patrick, and two of Jake's security personnel waited inside with grave expressions.

"Jeremy and Carly, tell Duke what you saw," said Jake solemnly as they entered the room.

A chill ran down Duke's spine as Jeremy recounted their discovery: "As you know, this morning is the first day we are going back out to the security towers..."

"No, I didn't know, actually," said Duke, surprised, looking at Jake.

"I made the call; we needed extra security," said Jake.

"Ooookay, please continue," said Duke, not wanting to argue.

"We were walking to the towers when we saw it lying there on the serpentine barrier—a head! It was so horrific—flies buzzing around it like a morbid halo."

Duke swallowed hard against the lump in his throat and asked quietly, "Where is it?"

"It's still out there, sir … and there was something written on its forehead, but we didn't stick around to look closer."

Duke took a deep breath and let it out slowly, resigned to whatever fate awaited them outside the walls. "Okay, let's go take a look," he prompted reluctantly.

Kazim peered out toward the gate as he said, "It's probably a trap."

Duke grabbed a duffel bag from the corner, slinging it over his shoulder. His brow furrowed in thought as he replied, "Could be, but it's an obvious message, and I intend to hear it."

Jake marched toward the door, rifle in hand. He was determined; there was no room for doubt. He took the duffel bag from Duke. "We'll put it in this. Then we'll bring it back here."

Duke looked apprehensive as he protested, "We? I'm doing this alone; there's no need to jeopardize someone else's life going out there too, but like Kazim said, it could be a trap."

Jake simply nodded and continued walking away without a word. Before he left, Duke grabbed his sawed-off shotgun off the wall and followed after him with Kazim close behind.

Outside the gate stood an eerie silence; even the wind seemed to have ceased its whispers. Jake took off at a sprint while Duke crept slowly forward, every fiber of his being alert for danger. Jake ran ahead toward the barrier they had been told to investigate. When they got there, sure enough, the head was where they said it would be—cradled between blades of grass. With practiced precision and not an ounce of hesitation, Jake opened the duffel bag and rolled the severed head inside before making his way back toward the gate.

Duke watched incredulously as Jake passed by him with nonchalant steps and made his way out of sight. They returned through the gate without incident. But before he entered the communication building, Duke yelled for Jake to stop. Turning around with irritation etched on his face, Jake demanded to know why Duke had stopped him so abruptly.

With conviction Duke replied, "What the hell was that all about?"

"We needed to get the head," Jake replied matter-of-factly as if that were explanation enough for his reckless behavior.

The air was thick with tension as Jake, Duke, and Kazim stood outside the communication building. Jake's face was a mask of stoic rage as he stared at the ground, fists clenched tightly by his sides.

"Yeah, I see that," Duke said cautiously, taking a step backward. "I don't know exactly what's going on inside your head, but I still need you. I need you to use your head."

"It's a little too late for that, isn't it?"

Back inside the command center, the stifling musty air clung to Duke's skin like heavy velvet curtains—all the windows were shut tight.

"Where's Jeremy and Carly?" asked Jake as he looked around, expecting them to jump out of one of the darkened corners.

"They didn't want to stick around for this," said Eric, his voice dripping with disdain as his eyes locked onto Duke's.

As Jake dropped the duffel bag heavily onto the ground, a thick silence descended. He tugged on the zipper and a swarm of flies escaped, along with the smell of smoke and decay. All four men put their hands over their mouths and noses to block out the smell. Jake pulled something from within the bag, raising it until it was facing up. The rippled skin clung tightly to its skull, as if it had seen too much death in its life. Its features were twisted grotesquely into the picture of eternal sleep. Burned into its forehead was "F.E.A.R."

"What does F.E.A.R. mean?" Eric asked, his voice barely audible.

"Forever Enduring Always Ready," Kazim replied. "It was

Agigi's domestic terrorist group; they trafficked military-grade weapons for clients across the United States."

Patrick frowned in confusion. "Why doesn't it stink as bad as it should? If this was from those bodies last month, shouldn't it be almost liquified?"

Kazim shrugged his shoulders. "Because it was smoked," he said matter-of-factly.

"Smoked? Like barbeque?" Eric asked incredulously.

"Makes sense," Duke interjected gravely. "How else do you preserve dozens of bodies for an extended period of time?"

Eric scoffed and groaned, "Well, that's ruined now—that psychopath ruined barbeque!"

Patrick nodded slowly, understanding dawning on his face. "Well, that explains what we saw them doing last month." He glanced around nervously before continuing. "Remember the day after the attack I said I thought I spotted one of Agigi's big FEMA tents on fire but it never burned down?"

Duke nodded, prompting Patrick to add with a look of disgust, "They must have used it as a giant smoker—hanging dozens of bodies like some kind of meat locker."

Even thinking about such a scene made Duke's stomach turn.

Jake cautiously stepped closer to the head, his curiosity overcoming his fear. He examined it more closely, and a chill ran down his spine as he noticed an odd shape inside its gaping mouth. "What's this?" With shaky hands he pulled out an old shoelace holding onto a plastic sandwich bag with a note inside. As he pulled out the object, Jake heard a revoltingly dry and sticky sound that turned his stomach. His face twisted in horror, yet compelled by a morbid curiosity, he opened the bag. Taking out the note with trembling fingers, he handed it silently to Duke, who read it out loud: "Let's talk."

Duke's expression hardened as he made his way to the radio, an oppressive heat rising from within him. His voice was cold and calculated as he spoke to Agigi on the other end of the transmission. "Agigi, this is Duke, you got my attention."

CHAPTER 26

Dale anxiously asked, "When then?"

Agigi's grin widened. His eyes suddenly blazing with determination, he bellowed over the sound of wind whipping around them, "I love your enthusiasm for killing, but I have a plan. Everything I do is for a fucking reason!"

Dale shifted on his feet, visibly nervous. He tried to maintain composure as he stammered out his response. "Even if they do have one of the weapon caches, we have the numbers, don't we?"

Sean impatiently scolded him. "Yes, obviously we have more people, you moron."

Agigi's attention piqued. One eyebrow raised in curiosity, he said, "But?"

Sean forced himself not to show any emotion as he spoke. His voice trembled slightly; he knew what he was about to say would risk consequences if Agigi didn't agree. He hoped his words could justify the way Duke acted at Mountaintop, but even Sean wasn't sure Duke's actions could be justified.

"But Duke is smart and obviously very ballsy. Didn't think he had it in him to fire upon all those people." He paused and drew in a deep breath. "So I'm a little hesitant about marching on Mountaintop like we did. Plus I don't see any reason why we have to kill all those people."

Agigi looked him up and down skeptically. "Are you getting soft on me or is there a reason for you saying that?"

Sean almost choked on his reply, years of pent-up fear

gushing forth from his mouth like a broken dam: "I'm saying killing all those people would be a wasted resource—children grow to be strong and helpful; women can reproduce; men can work."

Agigi slowly nodded in approval. A sly smile played on his lips as he said, "Ha! Indeed! Bravo, Sean—see, this is why you are my number two. Our thoughts almost align." His gaze shifted away from Sean toward the horizon beyond them before turning back. "I've only shared with everyone my plan B—the tactical plans if plan A fails."

Confusion filled Dale's face; he couldn't help but ask the obvious question: "What's plan A then?"

Just then one of Agigi's men strode over, bearing a radio. "It's Duke."

A mischievous smile spread across Agigi's face and he grabbed the radio mic, speaking into it dramatically. "Well, you're about to find out." He beamed. "Speaking of the devil! That was some fantastic timing, Duke. I was just sharing my plans with your buddy Sean here."

Duke's familiar gruff voice came through the speaker, replying without preamble, "I got your message. You know you could have just called me over the radio. What do you want?"

A gust of laughter exploded from Agigi's chest as he replied playfully, "What would be the fun in that? Was wondering when you were going to get my message. It was pretty genius to be able to smoke and preserve that many bodies, Dookie."

Duke's voice crackled. "You're sick."

Agigi hissed a sarcastic laugh. "No, I'm quite healthy, thank you, but you're missing the point. They were awesome! I'm more of a hickory man myself but who knew some scrub oak smoke, a little salt, a little pepper would be so tasty."

"Cut the crap, Isaac! Are we doing this or not?" Duke bellowed.

Agigi didn't flinch at Duke's rage. His words dripped with

menace and he seemed to take pleasure in tormenting Duke. "Whoa, pump the brakes there, killer. So eager to spill more blood, so out of character—or is it?" He paused, allowing his suggestion to settle like a cloud of toxic gas. He chuckled coldly.

Duke's voice exploded through the radio speaker. "Screw you!" he screamed.

"I have a proposition for you," Agigi said. "Give me Mountaintop without bloodshed, and in exchange, I get to kill you in front of everyone. Scout's honor." His tone was eerily calm considering the stakes at hand.

"Bullshit! What's gonna stop you from hurting anyone else if I agree to something like that?" Duke retorted.

Agigi's voice was like a roll of thunder, booming with reverence as he spoke. "Genghis Khan was a master strategist, and went from being betrayed and left with nothing then rising to power and having thousands follow his commands. Scavengers that roamed the plains of Mongolia in search of basic necessities, and Genghis Khan provided them food, shelter, and protection in exchange for their loyalty."

Duke scoffed. "You're nuts."

"Am I? Duke, if you say no then dozens of your people will die—possibly even your children. Right where you have the power to keep everyone alive." There were a few seconds of silence. "You have twenty-four hours to give me your answer. Give yourself up to save your community or go to war. The choice is yours, Dookie."

Dale nervously looked over at Agigi. "What now?"

Agigi sighed before murmuring quietly, "We wait."

∗∗∗

The radio static chirped, leaving an awkward silence. Duke slowly spun around and met the eyes of his ragtag group, each one trying to hide the fear behind their grim expressions.

Eric finally broke the spell of quietness. "So, uh, you think you know what your answer is gonna…" His question ended abruptly as Patrick jabbed his elbow into Eric's chest with a whisper of "Really?"

"What? Just want to know if I'm … if *we're* gonna die or not is all," Eric said flatly.

"I guess you'll find out in twenty-four hours," Duke said as he forced himself past the group, heading for Julie, but Jake reached out and grabbed his arm.

"You're not going to actually give yourself to him, are you?" His voice shook slightly and Duke felt guilt wash over him like a torrential downpour.

"Do I really even have a choice, Jake?" he muttered hopelessly.

"Yeah, you do. Plus it shouldn't even be your choice. No matter what you choose, it's going to affect everybody here! That includes your children," Jake said gravely.

Duke felt tears prick at his eyes. "You don't think I know that? But I spared my life once before in exchange for someone else's. I'm not going to do that again—and this time it will be more than one person that dies if I choose to save myself," he spat out angrily.

Jake took a step back as understanding dawned on him. "I get it now, I really do," he said softly. Tears swelled in his eyes. "I understand what true guilt feels like. Yes, you may have shot Roarke, but you didn't make the call that slaughtered dozens and dozens of people."

Duke hung his head and exhaled deeply. "You didn't have a choice, and you did what you had to do," he replied sadly.

Jake nodded. "Neither did you… Kill or be killed isn't much of an option. I may be mad, but believe it or not, I get it now, and I forgive you." Tears started streaming down his face as he spoke earnestly. "But, Duke, please don't make this decision for everyone; let Mountaintop make the choice for themselves."

Duke paused for a moment before responding quietly, "I'll think about it." As he walked away from Jake, his mind raced with possibilities—all led to a somber outcome.

Duke felt the crushing weight of his words bearing down on him. Julie's silence was so absolute and oppressive that it seemed to fill the entire room, its presence acting like an icy vice around Duke's heart. He looked into her frightened eyes, wide and unblinking like a deep abyss reflecting the pain and despair he had just inflicted upon her.

Suddenly, Julie let out a whimper, followed by a piercing wail of anguish. Tears cascaded down her face in a desperate plea for mercy as she begged for his reprieve. "Please, Duke, don't do it," she pleaded, her voice trembling with unbearable sorrow. "You can't do this to me!"

Sarah had almost the same response, pleading Duke not to go through with it. But she agreed not to say anything to Michael and Ava.

A heavy burden weighed on Duke's shoulders like never before. He couldn't muster the strength to eat or drink. Instead he lay in his bed, tortured by visions of Michael and Ava growing up without him; of Julie and their unborn child living a life without knowing their father. As these thoughts swirled around his head, he eventually succumbed to exhaustion, drifting off into a deep sleep.

*****

Pale orange began to pour through the tiny gaps around the door of Duke's shelter. The light cast a ghastly reflection across his drained face, reminding him of the decision he had to make that morning. Tugging on some clothes, he stumbled toward the entrance, rubbing his eyes as he went.

As he stepped outside, a riot of conversation filled his ears and he squinted against the harsh sun reflecting off the snow-covered mountaintop. Everywhere Duke looked, people stood in clusters with worried expressions. He felt lost and disoriented in an unfamiliar sea of fear and dread. Finally, Duke saw Jake walking toward him.

Jake stepped forward from the crowd, his hands shoved deep into his pockets. "Duke," he said solemnly as their eyes met. "You haven't made your choice yet, so I thought I'd give them one. I didn't tell them everything but I did mention that we might have to fight today and you would be the one to address it this morning."

"But I haven't had my coffee yet," Duke replied meekly, a hint of sarcasm in his voice.

Jake shook his head. "I appreciate the attempt at humor but this is serious, Duke."

Duke sighed heavily, knowing there was no turning back now. Resigned to his fate, he made his way through the crowd as Julie reached out for him. Tears welled in her blue eyes as she grabbed hold of him tightly.

"No matter what happens," she whispered between sniffles while caressing her belly, "we love you."

A gentle kiss grazed Duke's cheek before he made his way to a nearby picnic table. An eerie hush fell amongst the community members waiting for him to speak. His heart thundered in his chest as reality set in: he had to make a choice that would change everything.

With resolve glimmering in his determined gaze, Duke bellowed out loud for all to hear, "So I'll get straight to the point—we don't have much time left. Yesterday I was given a choice: go to war or give myself up to save you all."

The crowd fell silent. It was as if the air itself had grown heavy with anticipation, or maybe dread. Onlookers shifted and mumbled to themselves, unsure what to make of Duke's words. He stood there regally, his hands clasped together in front of him like a king pleading for an answer from his subjects.

"For me, this was an easy decision. I chose to save you all," he declared.

A wave of emotion filled the atmosphere. Some cried out in sadness while others clung to their anger. Duke raised his hand and motioned for them all to hush.

"But I was reminded by an old friend that it should not be my choice, but rather yours. Though America is in shambles and things are much different now, it's true. No matter what it turns into or what it gets built into, freedom needs to remain at the forefront when rebuilding communities and this country again. Personal choice matters. Personal freedom matters." He paused, scanning the faces before him with piercing eyes as he spoke his last words: "So please, when you make this decision, make it for yourselves and not for me. Know this: no matter what you choose, I love you and will respect your decision. I'll go willingly with no regrets."

Kazim stepped forward onto the picnic table, raising his voice to make sure everyone could hear him.

"Duke is right; freedom is EVERYTHING! But it comes at a price!" he shouted. "If you choose to sacrifice him, you will still be choosing death. You'll be alive, but you will give up your personal freedoms. You will be choosing slavery. You will experience what it is like to be dead and alive at the same time!"

His voice echoed off into the horizon, and all was still for a few moments. Duke noticed Kazim had tears in his eyes, filling him with emotions he could scarcely contain. Kazim's words touched a chord in all of their hearts as they had seldom heard him speak outside of training. The blazing sun shone yet the crowd's eyes were transfixed on him.

"You will not be an individual or a person anymore. I should know. I was enslaved as a young boy in Sudan." He paused and looked at each of them in turn, almost daring them to stand behind him. "I know what it feels like to be a number, an instrument, and an expendable asset. True freedom comes at a cost, so I'd rather die as a free man than live as a slave!"

"All those who feel the same, all who choose freedom; stand behind us," Kazim said, pointing behind himself.

Julie and Jake immediately rushed over to stand behind them.

Some were scared—not wanting to face the consequences of standing up for what they believed in—yet many more found courage enough to walk over to Kazim and Duke without saying anything; they simply nodded in agreement.

"I choose freedom," said the cook, Joe.

"Shit, I guess I choose freedom too—I'm about out of liquor anyhow." Greg Arrowood smiled and winked at Duke as he walked by.

The air hummed with electricity. Duke felt the weight of his decision and the consequences it would have on those he loved dearly. He watched, stunned, as an unstoppable force of people began to march forward. Dozens of people coming together for a common purpose—to choose their own freedom. At this sight, Duke could not contain himself any longer; tears streamed down his face as he beheld the courage and love that these people showed him.

Michael and Ava ran up to Duke. "Daddy!" they cried out, their little arms reaching toward him.

"Are you leaving us?" Ava whimpered through her tears, clutching her brother's hand.

Duke brought them close into a hug and kissed their heads reassuringly. "Doesn't look like I will be, Ava Wava," he said softly. "Mikey, I'll never leave you two ever again, you hear me?" His voice was strong and unwavering.

Duke pulled away from them reluctantly to see Sarah standing nearby, her face wet with tears and surrounded by Tyler and Danielle, who she now lovingly referred to as her own.

"Take them to the shelter and do not come out. Only open the door for Jake or me," Duke said.

She nodded and walked away with all four kids.

"So it looks like I'll get a few more hours with you after

all," Julie said through tears and a smile.

"I guess so. Jules, are you sure you want to still be a field medic while carrying this baby?"

"I thought about it and yeah, I do. I'm needed, and this is bigger than the both of us."

Duke continued to stare at her for a few moments, his voice soft and reassuring like a balm from the cold air. "Okay, be careful out there, Jules."

She nodded slowly, finally managing to form an answer amidst all the chaos in her mind. "I will, and Duke ... I love you."

"I love you, too."

The moment seemed frozen in time, giving them both just enough time to take solace in one another.

Duke felt it deep in his soul, as if he had been granted an epiphany. He was truly in love with Julie, and nothing would ever be the same again. He wanted to stay and bask in the glory of his newfound emotions, but he noticed Kazim motioning him to get back up on the table. He moved swiftly, planting a gentle kiss on her plump lips before ascending.

Duke let out an ear-splitting whistle that reverberated through the night sky. His voice was like thunder, booming with pride as he shouted: "Thank you for choosing freedom!" The crowd exploded into cheers and whistles. "And thank you for your sacrifice," he said solemnly, knowing that many of their lives would be lost in the coming days. "We need all the help we can get, but to those who cannot fight or choose not to be a part of this battle, we will not judge you for that decision—instead, we will respect it."

The atmosphere shifted from one of rambunctious excitement to hushed reflection as Duke continued.

"Folks, time is ticking away; we have a lot of work to do and a long, hard fight ahead of us—look around you now and cherish all the things and people you have in your life, because this time tomorrow everything will be different," Duke said somberly.

The hushed stillness that descended upon the crowd was suffocating. They felt the gravity of the situation settling on their shoulders, fear and trepidation slowly creeping up their spines. Despite it all, a spark of hope lit in their eyes.

"But do not let that sadden you or scare you. We have been training for this moment. If anything, they should be the ones who are scared, and I assure you they are. They may have the numbers, but we have the high ground. They are taking the fight to us on our turf!" A jolt of electricity surged through the crowd as Duke continued. "What they don't realize," he said, his voice rising as if to call on the heavens for strength, "is that we are willing to fight, to bleed and die for what we have! Most importantly, this community remembers what this country once stood for!" His hands clenched into fists, and a fire burned in his eyes. "Our bodies might die, but those principles will not die today! WE are willing to sacrifice everything to keep it that way—WE are willing to die for freedom!"

With a raised fist, Kazim screamed, "Freedom!"

Cheers rose from the people, and many of them were overcome with emotion. They knew that Duke was right—that no matter the cost, they would sacrifice everything in order to remain free.

Duke's blue eyes burned as he spoke his last words of encouragement. "Get your mind and your bodies ready! Get into your positions. Let's give that son of a bitch and those who follow him a history lesson on why you don't want to back a freedom-loving community into a corner!"

CHAPTER 27

COLORADO | SEPTEMBER 2035

Karl stood defiantly, trying to mask his face from betraying a maelstrom of emotions hiding underneath. His hands were clenched into tight fists and he remained steadfast as Colonel Campbell loomed over him menacingly. The large man was almost oppressive with his towering presence, as if he could physically squash those who opposed him like an insect.

The colonel walked back and forth, his heavy boots pounding the floor like a death march, his hands clamped around the half-full glass of scotch which clinked mercilessly, silver cubes matching the rhythm of his march like some twisted metronome. The amber liquid sloshed and swirled, threatening to spill out its secrets.

The colonel's gaze was one of pure ice as it swept across the room, searching for something that would never come. He stopped abruptly, the metal toe of his boot striking the large wooden table with a loud thud that made Karl jump in surprise. The table was made of a deep, dark mahogany that seemed to pull all the light in the room toward it. It was topped with a computer screen that glowed like an ethereal beacon from another world. It displayed an intricate digital map with blinking red dots that rose straight up, hovering in mid-air like ghostly apparitions.

"Again and for the last time, Chief—no! I don't care who's marching on who. That group may have found one of the caches but they are no concern to us." The colonel uncorked another bottle of scotch, raising it up into the air as if offering a toast. "Now I can appreciate you wanting to help your little friends out there, but we have rules and guidelines to follow. We need to maintain and preserve every resource possible. Remember, the program is looking for the survival of the fittest. Your buddy Duke is looking fairly promising."

Karl shifted his weight from foot to foot in response, knowing full well that any other sign of disagreement would be met with swift retribution.

Colonel Campbell took a long swig from his drink before continuing. "But tell you what, though—you can go and help them if you want. But don't come back, and if I ever see you again I'll kill you myself! Is that what you're wanting, Chief?" His voice lowered into a deadly whisper, icy and dangerous as he cocked an eyebrow at Karl.

A heavy silence filled the room as Karl weighed his options before finally letting out a resigned sigh. "No, sir."

The colonel nodded knowingly before strolling around the room again, this time taking longer strides as he looked Karl over with contemptuous eyes. His gaze lingered without mercy on every corner and crevice; Karl's every movement seemed to make him angry.

Finally halting in front of Karl once more, Colonel Campbell sneered. "You went and got yourself attached to this damn group. You've gotten soft in your old age. Have you forgotten our mission—what we are doing here? I know you were locked up in that prison for a while, but nothing has changed besides the length of my ballsack!" He gestured toward himself wildly with one arm, still clutching firmly onto his glass with the other, sloshing its contents all over the floor without care or remorse.

"No, sir," replied Karl honestly. "It's kind of hard to forget the mission." He tried hard not to show any emotion but he could feel anger bubbling inside him; anger directed at both himself for being so foolishly trusting as well as toward Colonel Campbell for being so unfairly cold-hearted.

Karl felt the colonel's hypnotic and judgmental gaze pierce his very soul, not unlike a predatory beast sizing up its prey. He had a smirk on his face as he casually swilled down the last drops of his scotch, setting it down with a clack that resonated throughout the room.

"You really care about them, don't you, Chief?" Colonel Campbell said mockingly, his raspy voice like gravel.

Karl blinked once then narrowed his gaze, trying to appear calm even though he felt the heat of anger coursing through his veins. He could feel the weight of Colonel Campbell's stare burning into him.

The colonel sighed heavily, shaking his head before continuing in a gruff voice, "It's time for your head to come out of the clouds and get back into the game, Chief. Are we clear?"

Karl forced himself to say, "Yes, sir," with no emotion on his face.

∗

The oppressive atmosphere in the command building seemed to strangle Duke, squeezing away any hope within him. He sat motionless, his gaze fixed on the radio as if it were an eerie talisman that could unlock some dark secret.

"Sorry, Duke, I've tried my best," echoed Karl over the comms before they cut off into static.

In frustration, Duke hurled a Dungeons and Dragons figurine across the room.

"Hey! That was my Eldar Wraithknight!" cried Eric from his corner of the room.

Duke gave Eric a piercing glare.

"Whom ... I don't need anymore," Eric said nervously.

"It's okay, it's okay, we don't need them," Duke muttered to himself.

As if on cue, Kazim and Jake entered the room dressed in full combat gear.

"How's it looking out there?" Duke asked warily, trying his best to suppress the nervous energy that seemed to be propelling him forward.

"Everyone is nearly in place," Kazim replied firmly. "We've got long shooters set up on the Ferris wheel platforms, while everyone else is in their strategic locations."

Duke hesitated. "And what about the non-combatants? Are they accounted for?"

Jake nodded solemnly. "They're good, but you might want to stop by and see your kids first. They're terrified, Duke."

Duke felt a wave of guilt washing over him as he stumbled upon this thought—for how could he possibly focus on the task ahead while knowing that his children were suffering?

"How much time do we have left?" asked Jake.

"Couple of hours until the deadline."

"Okay, what's the plan? How do you think he'll attack?"

"I'm not sure," Duke started slowly. "It all depends on what kind of weapons they have, but I'm gonna assume their best route is going to be either the main gate or the rear emergency door." He paused, contemplating. "If I were them, I'd try to overwhelm us by throwing a massive force against the gate and then send some force in via the emergency door—which is hard to find if you don't know what you're looking for, but we have to assume that Sean told them about it. He used it all the time when he went on his hunting trips. Everywhere else is surrounded by super steep cliffs and ledges. Charles definitely knew this would be a great place for a survival community."

"Yeah, they would have a really hard time trying to climb these walls," Jake said.

"Do you want me to send a portion of our fighters to that emergency door now or hold off just in case?" asked Kazim.

"We don't want to spread ourselves too thin if we can help it."

Kazim nodded.

Duke turned his attention to Eric, who had been standing nearby. "Eric, did you make any more of those boombuckets?"

A mischievous grin crept across Eric's face. "Yeah—this time with something a bit more ... explosive," he said proudly. "We've got two five-gallon buckets filled with Tannerite and Greg's old stripped-out nuts and bolts. Should do some serious damage wherever we need it."

Duke's eyes darted around the room like a hunted animal, sweat pouring down his forehead. "Well, we're gonna need to put those somewhere it won't hurt our structures or people," he muttered, shaking his head.

"Yeah, I have the perfect place for one of them."

"Where's Patrick?"

"He's flying the drone to see when there is any movement from Agigi. He also plans on hiding on top on the building to be out of sight and do reconnaissance for us," answered Eric, his fingers fidgeting nervously.

"That's actually a great idea," said Duke, trying to hide the tremble in his voice.

"Why does everyone have white strips of cloth on their arms?" asked Eric.

"That reminds me ... you and Patrick need to put them on your arms as well. If Agigi's group gets inside, we are going to need a way to tell everyone apart," said Duke grimly.

"Really?" asked Eric, his eyes widening in fear.

"It's not like we have uniforms to identify each other with. So the white strips of cloth will have to do," Duke responded with a sense of finality. "Make sure all squad leaders have a two-way radio. Also start packing up all of our main radio equipment and try to hide it in one of the conexes. And make sure Patrick gets a radio too."

"I'm on it, boss man," replied Eric as he hastily started rummaging through equipment crates.

Duke and Jake held each other's gaze for an uncomfortable beat.

"We're going to get through this, right?" said Jake, desperation creeping into his voice.

"For everyone's sake I sure hope so. Julie is pregnant," said Duke, taking a deep breath to steady himself.

"Oh my God! That's going to be tough, but that's awesome, man," Jake exclaimed, his eyes widening with excitement.

"Hey, so I was thinking … if I don't …" Duke began, but Jake interrupted him harshly.

"Shut the hell up, we're going to get through this," he gritted out, his jaw set with determination.

"I know, but if I don't, will you please look after Julie and the baby for me?" asked Duke, his voice barely above a whisper.

"Of course I will," Jake promised fiercely as he placed a comforting hand on Duke's shoulder.

"Good. Time is running out and I need to go talk to the kids," said Duke.

"Okay, I'll get into position." Jake took off into a jog.

The sun shone with a bloody hue, and time seemed to slow as Duke trudged forward. He had to be brave now more than ever; no matter what he would do everything in his power to protect his own. With each step, a cold wash of dread consumed him.

He headed for Sarah's shelter where she would be with Michael, Ava, Tyler, and Danielle. Duke saw everyone getting ready or already in place. Some looked prepared, but the majority looked terrified. But that was okay. Duke knew that it took courage to be scared of dying yet willing to sacrifice one's self, all in the name of freedom.

Duke knocked on Sarah's door, and he could hear all the children scream. Hearing that broke Duke's heart.

"It's me, it's Duke."

"Don't worry, it's Daddy," Duke heard Sarah say from inside the shelter. The door creaked open a sliver until Sarah's wide eyes were revealed; she looked petrified yet her face held a strength that made Duke proud.

"Just want to talk to them before everything starts," Duke said gently, knowing what risks they all faced.

She nodded slowly as she welcomed him inside. Duke knelt and Michael and Ava ran up to him with tear-streaked faces. They both clung to him like vines.

"Daddy, I don't wanna die!" Ava cried out between sobs.

"You'll protect us, right, Daddy?" Michael asked.

Duke set his jaw firmly and looked into their eyes. "That's right—no matter what, as long as your daddy has a breath left in his body, he'll do everything he can to keep you safe." He pulled his babies close as tears streamed down his cheeks. He held them tightly for a few moments while fighting back the fears raging inside of him.

Though Duke was confident, he truly didn't know if he would survive the day. With one last embrace and kiss upon his children's foreheads, Duke closed the shelter door behind him. A war was coming, and courage was essential if there was any chance of victory.

Duke shuddered, forcing back the trembling in his hands. His heart fluttered in his chest like a frightened bird, but he refused to succumb to the fear. The graveyard-like silence made it hard to ignore the ominous feeling pressing down on him. Taking a deep breath, he strengthened his resolve. He clenched his fists and determinedly set forth toward the battle ahead.

The tower guard's voice crackled over the radio: "This is tower one, we have a vehicle approaching. What should we do? Over."

Duke responded swiftly. "How many are there? Over."

"Just one," came the reply. "It's an old pickup truck. Hold on ... they're getting out!"

A wave of anticipation swept through the crowd around him as Duke waited for a response from the tower.

Finally, it came: "It's Karl!"

"Everyone stand down! Let him through!" Duke shouted on the radio.

He felt a surge of excitement shoot through his veins as he ran toward the gate. He smiled widely when he saw Karl walk inside, wearing traditional Apache war paint—red streaks across the lower half of his face and a single white stripe bisecting his nose—and eagles' feathers on his tactical vest fluttering in the wind. His piercing gaze demanded respect.

"It's about damn time you got here, Chief," Duke said sarcastically with a smirk on his face.

Karl simply smiled and replied, "Didn't feel right not to be here."

"What's all this?" Duke pointed to Karl's face paint.

"Apache war paint. If I'm going to return to the earth I'm going to do it as my ancestors would."

A relieved smile spread across Duke's face as he replied with appreciation, "Good to have you, Chief. So does this mean Colonel Campbell changed his mind?"

Karl shook his head. "Not exactly. Do you think you have room for one more at Mountaintop?"

"Of course." He shook Karl's hand firmly once again. "Thank you, Chief. Good to have you here."

A voice from the radio speakers cut through their conversation. "This is tower one, we have another vehicle approaching. It looks like a military Humvee."

"Is that yours?" Duke asked.

Karl shook his head.

Duke offered his own interpretation with a heavy hint of sarcasm. "Maybe Colonel Campbell sent someone to come get you. Not happy that you disobeyed him."

Karl chuckled darkly. "Oh I certainly know that he won't be happy about my decision, but I doubt he would show up here."

Jake's voice came over the radio next. "What's happening? Who is it?"

Tower One replied, "Wait one. They're getting out with their hands up. It's Jones and Patch!"

Adrenaline surged as Duke and Karl raced to meet their unexpected allies in the parking lot past the communication building.

Karl surveyed his comrades; Jones was dressed in a camouflage jacket with a bandolier of shells slung across his chest, while Patch stood empty-handed, the corners of his lips tugging into an eager smile.

"So much for it being just you, Chief," Duke said, slapping Karl on the back.

"What the hell are you guys doing?" asked Karl.

"Well, we saw you putting on your makeup and thought either someone forgot to mention it was Halloween or you were going to go party without us," Jones said, his face set in an amused grin. A chorus of laughter erupted from the group.

"I appreciate it, guys, but you know you just screwed yourselves, right?" Karl snickered.

"Yeah, we know. We overheard you talking with Campbell," Jones admitted sheepishly.

"We know we are not gonna be welcome back, especially after we took this," said Patch, pointing to the Humvee.

"Nice," said Duke.

"Wait, that's not all." Patch stepped forward, gesturing behind him to the open hatchback door of the Humvee. "We took this on the way out as well," he said proudly. He paused for dramatic effect and reached inside to pull out a large, black machine gun, which glimmered menacingly in the moonlight.

"A 240 Bravo, a 7.62 by 54 belt feed piece of sexy," Duke said triumphantly with a wide grin splitting his face. Everyone couldn't help but smirk at the giddy excitement radiating off of him as he stared lovingly at the gun. "What? I remember my first deployment," he quipped.

Karl shook his head in disbelief but couldn't help but feel admiration for his friends' brazenness despite knowing full well they would never be welcome back to their unit.

The air stilled with a palpable tension that seemed to hang

over the motley group of survivors like an anvil waiting to be dropped. Together they planned out their defense strategy, and it was decided that Patch would take his sniper rifle to the top of the Ferris wheel to provide overwatch for the community. Then when he ran out of ammo he would help Julie as a field medic.

Jones was going to be the first line of defense for the main gate. He would be stationed at the back of the parking lot in the Humvee, manning the machine gun. Karl suggested that they bring back the plans they'd originally come up with. Duke, Karl, Kazim, and Jake would take command of separate groups. The plan was etched in stone, each member of the community bracing for what lay ahead.

The radio crackled. "Duke this is Patrick, over."

Duke's brow furrowed as he issued a gruff response. "What do you got, Patrick? Over."

The radio hissed and then Patrick spoke again, his words thick with tension. "Agigi is already moving, over."

Duke clung to hope. He had to know more if his team was to have any chance at success. "What else can you tell us? Direction, size, weapons, vehicles? Over."

"All I caught was the first movement making its way our direction on Highway 24. Didn't see any vehicles yet, but it looked like most people were carrying some type of weapon in their hands. I got to dock the drone and get it charged up; I thought we had more time. Over."

Duke cursed under his breath as he spoke into the mic again, urgency dripping from each word. "So did I. Get it charged up and get that thing back in the air ASAP, over."

"Roger that," replied Patrick.

Duke let out a deep sigh of frustration. "Dammit, thought we still had over an hour left."

Jones chimed in, his voice weary but determined. "Looks like he's done waiting. See ya on the other side, boys."

Duke didn't need to ask what would happen if they failed—

they all knew the stakes were high and failure meant death or worse.

He keyed his radio once more, only this time his voice was filled with fire and purpose. "Team leaders! Get your people ready, it looks like it's game time!"

337

CHAPTER 28

Colorado | September 2035

Duke's heart hammered in his chest as he peered through the dust-covered gate. He looked back to see Julie crouching behind a makeshift fort, her eyes wide and filled with fear. His stomach lurched at the sight of her, but Duke turned away and squeezed his rifle tight. It was time to focus on the mission.

"Tower two, they did what? Over," Duke said into his radio.

"They walked into the woods across Highway 24 on the opposite side, away from us. Over," came the reply.

"What is he doing?" Duke muttered.

"Havoc, you see anything?" Karl called over the radio.

"Negative, all quiet by the gate," Jones replied.

"Patch? You got anything?" Karl asked.

"We saw what tower two saw, but they are already out of sight," Patch answered from his vantage point atop the Ferris wheel shooting platform.

The tension was killing Duke. He could feel everyone's nervous energy. He almost wished that the shooting would just start.

Suddenly, someone shouted over the radio. "We got smoke coming in!"

"Where at?" Duke demanded.

"Out front," came the reply. "I can't see anyone."

"Both towers open fire into the smoke," Duke barked into the radio.

Shots rang out from both towers, firing in rapid succession.

"Hold fire until you can see a target," hollered Duke.

There was an eerie moment of silence throughout Mountaintop. Then the air turned into a living, breathing creature—the sound from dozens of gunshots going off simultaneously. The rounds ripped through the gate with a deafening crack, punching holes in the communications building and whizzing by their heads, causing them to duck down instinctively. Jones retaliated with his machine gun, spraying an onslaught of bullets at the enemy. Panic took over as Duke's radio crackled and he barked into it: "What's going on, towers?"

A single word trembled through the static: "Pinned."

"Havoc, have we been breached?" Duke pressed.

The only sound was the eerie hum of gunfire filling the air. Through the clashing sounds of battle, Patch's voice warbled out like a beacon—"If you must know, there's around 150 to 200 people pressed up against our walls. Havoc is blind but hitting quite a few of them! Over!"

"You damn right!" Jones exclaimed.

***

The earth trembled beneath Jones' feet as an ominous rumbling pierced the air. The hairs on his neck stood up while he watched as plumes of black diesel smoke could be seen just beyond the gate.

"Oh shit, they're bringing up a backhoe! It's heading right for the gate!"

The aged gate groaned in protest as the rusty yellow backhoe thrust forward, its front bucket lifted defensively. A throng of desperate men and women crammed through the space between the gates, only to be mercilessly cut down by Jones' gunfire.

Watchtower one collapsed suddenly, like an axe-felled tree. Jones witnessed as its guard leapt out just before the wooden beams engulfed him in its death throes. In horror, he watched as tower two's guard attempted to cast away a gre-nade that had been thrown into her tower. Before she could fling it away, it detonated in her hands, blasting her and her post into a cloud of pink mist.

"Both towers are down; both towers are down!" Patch radioed.

People finally stopped rushing through the gate, hesitant after their counterparts were mowed down by Jones' machine gun fire.

"Patch! Reloading! Cover the gate!" Jones screamed into his radio.

"I got you, brotha," said Patch.

Jones knew he had to quickly get his machine gun reloaded. He knew he was the only thing standing in the way of people rushing in.

He heard the menacing growl of the backhoe's engine as it gradually came back to life and lurched forward with a hunger for destruction. It was heading straight for him, as if homing in on its prey. The pitch of the growling grew louder until it was almost unbearable, like some sort of creature straight out of his nightmares come to life.

"I don't mind covering your ass, but hurry up, man!" Jones could hear Patch say in the background over the radio.

"I'm coming, I'm coming."

"Here they come!" Patch screamed.

Jones peeked through the windshield quickly only to see dozens of people pouring in on both sides, sprinting down the parking lot. People on the left side turned off into the wooded area. Others ducked behind the backhoe for cover as it marched mercilessly forward.

From his right side, Jones heard an exchange of gunfire; it was Duke's squad moving in for an attack on the people try-ing to rush that side. But it seemed like no matter how many bullets fired, there were just too many to stop them all.

Just as Jones closed the feeding tray on his machine gun he heard another voice yell out over the radio: "AT4!"

"Oh shit," Jones muttered to himself.

***

Duke peered at Karl with a grimace that conveyed his urgency. "I'm moving up to help cover Jones."

The air was heavy with chaos and ruin as shots were exchanged between Karl's squad and the opposing force. In a desperate attempt to keep Duke alive, Karl pleaded with him, "Duke! There's no cover out there—stay here and let them run into us! That's the plan so stick with it!"

Before any reply could be given, Patch yelled out in warning, "Here they come!"

Through gritted teeth, Karl again begged to Duke not to move an inch, knowing that if he did, he would surely be killed. But his words went unheeded as Duke responded with fervor and declared loudly to his squad, "On me!"

With every stride toward their foes, battle cries from both sides filled the air in a chaotic chorus. Seeing an opportunity for strategic advantage, Karl made a sudden call to Kazim. "Kazim, take your squad over to the west end and try to cut them off to the left!"

"I'm on it," Kazim shouted.

The order resonated through the warzone as Duke ran alongside his squad toward certain death. Upon reaching their destination, they frantically scrambled for cover. Raising his rifle to his shoulder, Duke cried out with determination while simultaneously shooting wildly and rapidly into the approaching horde. Several fell dead instantly, but it was almost too late—the wall of people had already returned fire, hitting nearly half of Duke's squad within moments of beginning combat. All around him, bodies dropped like rag dolls as screams echoed throughout the mountainside.

"AT4!" came Patch's voice on the radio.

Duke watched in horror as Jones attempted to leap from the vehicle, but it was too late. A violent blast reverberated through Mountaintop, sending Duke careening to the earth. Everywhere, time seemed to stand still—not even a flutter of wind or a distant bird's cry could be heard as the survivors gazed upon the unthinkable destruction wrought before their eyes.

Rising dazedly from his spot on the ground, Duke staggered through the thick blanket of smoke spilling from the twisted metal remains of the Humvee. He made his way toward Jones, who lay motionless several feet away amid a sea of blazing debris. Duke's stomach lurched as he noted with horror that one of Jones' legs was gone, while the other looked hideously mutilated.

Duke searched the parking lot for any sign of danger. His heart thumped in his chest as he spied more people approaching and a menacing backhoe looming in their midst. The machine stood like some malevolent metal beast. And then something caught Duke's eye—a bright orange blur bobbing near an old pickup truck. Eric's boom bucket. A low growl escaped Duke's lips as he barked into the radio, "Patch! Hit that damn orange bucket!"

He quickly spun on his heel and faced his squad, his expression grim and determined. "Get down!" he bellowed, motioning them toward cover. Then, without another word, he charged headlong into the communications building.

The force of the explosion reminded Duke of his deployment in Ukraine when Russian artillery shells rained down on Duke's position. The ground quaked around him as if the whole mountain would collapse upon them. His ears were bombarded by a thunderous roar and all he could see were fragments of nuts and bolts cast in every direction. The communications building was suddenly filled with shards of glass, raining down from the violently shaking windows at its crown. Duke watched helplessly as Eric cowered in the corner, whimpering as he desperately clamped his hands over his ears, shielding himself from the deafening screams and explosions. His eyes were tightly shut, hoping in vain that he would awaken from this living nightmare.

Duke reached out a hand, his face twisted in anguish and desperation. "Get up," he rasped hoarsely, "we have to go."

The two men slowly ventured past the destroyed walls of their once-safe refuge. Duke's senses reeled in abject horror; everywhere he looked there was death and destruction, with hundreds of corpses scattered across the battleground and agonizing cries of pain from all around him. Some people had seemingly been frozen by fear while others ran amok, trying to flee the devastation. Still more attempted to crawl away, desperate for safety.

Duke tried to radio Karl to inform him they were on their way back, but saw that his radio had taken damage. Duke pulled Jones off the ground and dragged him back with one hand, using his other to hustle Eric along. Jones had briefly regained consciousness but only long enough to pull out his pistol and fire a few futile shots into the crowd. All around them bullets whistled through the air like angry hornets, but none could touch them.

When Duke rounded the corner to Karl's position, he heard shots being fired at him and wood splintering right beside him.

"Whoa!" Duke exclaimed in shock as Karl barked out, "Hold your fire!"

Karl's face was strained with worry as he hurried over. "That was too close!"

"Sorry I couldn't call you back on the radio—it got damaged earlier," Duke responded.

Suddenly Patch's panicked voice burst on the radio. "Can anyone see Jones?"

Karl replied firmly, "We have him here. Keep your eyes downrange, Patch!"

Duke's breath was labored as he dragged Jones the remaining feet to Karl. The air around them still held the scent of gunpowder, and smoke hung like a veil in front of them.

Karl let out a long sigh as he knelt on one knee next to his brother-in-arms. "Damn it," he muttered.

"How bad is it?" Jones asked weakly, his voice barely audible through the ringing in their ears.

Karl smiled tightly, trying to exude some semblance of confidence. "Oh, not bad, brother, you'll be fine in the morning," he lied.

"Get tourniquets on that now," Karl tried to say quietly to Duke.

Jones smiled feebly. "You always ... were bad ... liar, Chief."

As the light faded from Jones' eyes, Karl looked away in quiet agony—everyone knew what had just happened, but no one wanted to speak the words aloud.

"Chief, how is Havoc doing?" Patch asked.

Without missing a beat, Karl replied coolly, "He got lucky—he'll pull through."

Though he had answered confidently enough for his friend to accept this statement as truth, Duke knew better than anyone Karl was merely trying to keep Patch focused and determined during such a time of crisis.

Karl closed his friend's eyes and calmly keyed his radio. "Patch, how we are looking out front?"

"There are still people out there, but it has died down. Most of them are fleeing or hiding."

Duke pointed to Patrick's position. "Eric, go link with Patrick on top of that building."

Eric didn't say anything as he ran off as fast as he could.

"Patrick, where we at with the drone?" Karl asked over the radio.

"It's not ready yet," Patrick replied.

"Well, make it ready," Karl retorted.

"We would have like ten to fifteen minutes of flying time."

An explosion ripped through the air behind them.

"Don't care, just make it happen; we need eyes in the sky now!" Karl yelled.

A deafening blast rocked the ground beneath their feet. Time seemed to pass slowly, as if suspended. From behind them an ominous cloud of smoke and debris rose into the sky.

"The rear entrance has been breached!" Patch cried out.

Thirty seconds stretched like a hundred years as Karl and the rest of them strained for some sign from Patrick's monster drone.

"Come on, Patrick, talk to me!" Karl shouted into his radio.

The reply sent a chill through their bones.

"Jesus! Two hundred coming in from the back way!"

Karl immediately began snapping orders. "Kazim and Jake, take your teams southward and hold them off!" He turned to his mixed-up crew and spoke with raw authority. "Listen good, everyone! We'll keep 'em from coming in from the front! If anything happens at south, then we're ready to back 'em up!"

Patrick's voice came through again urgently. "There's a group of people with some kind of shoulder-mounted system!"

Seconds later a sound like thunder shook the earth followed by a blazing orange light that lit up the sky. The air was thick and electric as an enormous boom resonated through the valley like a giant's fist pounding against solid steel. In the center of it all was the Ferris wheel; in mere moments it had been freed from its moorings and slowly began to roll downhill gaining speed as it went.

Duke cried out in anguish. "Patch!"

But only emptiness answered his call.

Karl implored frantically, "Patch ... come in, buddy ..."

Duke watched as Karl closed his eyes and knotted his fists in rage. He could only listen helplessly as Kazim and Jake's squads stymied the ingress at the south entrance. His thoughts turned to Agigi—this time Duke wouldn't let him go unscathed if given the chance. This time, Agigi would suffer for what he'd done.

"Jake," Duke broadcast in desperation, "how're you guys doing?"

"Not good, man ... too many of them and our ammo is running low! We're taking serious losses, Duke!" Jake shouted back.

"We're running short on ammo here too," said Duke to his squad. Then, to Jake, "Just get your way back here!"

"Roger that, we're almost at your eight o'clock."

Karl began to walk away, knife and pistol drawn. His eyes looked determined and his jaw was set.

"What are you doing?" Duke asked.

"I'm not losing any more friends," Karl answered and then took off toward the left-hand side where Jake and Kazim were supposed to be. Duke watched Karl press against a brick wall and peer around the corner. Suddenly his arm came out from behind the wall as someone whirled past. His knife caught the tall man in his chest, clotheslining him off his feet. The man writhed in agony on the ground as Karl brought up his gun and sighted it against the man's skull, letting off one single shot.

"This is Patrick! Get ready, that group that had been circling is finally heading your way from the front! They have big machine guns!"

"This is it; everyone ready up!" Duke yelled to his squad.

"Hey, they've halted halfway! They're readying their guns! Dammit! There's another large group coming out of the woods north of the gate, probably another fifty or so!" Patrick reported urgently.

Duke watched Julie move among the wounded, heedless of the carnage around her. He felt a strong urge to get her out of the maelstrom.

"Julie!" he shouted at her. He rose and ran toward her, waving his arms in a frantic gesture. He broke through Jake's squad, which had retreated to their positions, heading in the opposite direction.

"Julie! Get down!" he cried desperately.

At last he got her attention, but she was too far away to hear him.

The air suddenly seemed full with scores of machine guns firing all at once. Duke threw himself on the ground as bullets ripped through the small community, shattering buildings and felling trees as bits of asphalt flew everywhere.

When Duke dared to look up again, Julie had vanished. Crawling slowly over fallen comrades, he made his way downhill until he was safely below the path of fire. There he saw Joe's cooking station and Mountaintop's food stores being plundered by a raiding party, some making off with bags of rice and beans while others carried clothes away in their arms. Helplessly, Duke watched as his community's chance of survival unraveled before his eyes—yet there was nothing he could do.

The gunfire stopped as suddenly as it began. The sound changed from the angry buzz to single shots. Duke hesitatingly raised his head above the crest of his cover and saw Karl, Jake, Kazim, and what was left of Mountaintop in a savage hand-to-hand fight with their enemies. The remaining Mountaintop community fought with desperate intensity. Karl wielded his knife and pistol with deadly accuracy; Kazim chopped people down with a strange cold-blooded efficiency; Jake clung onto someone he was pounding with powerful blows.

Duke took the opportunity to go find Julie. He broke into a run the moment he spied the building smashed by a great pine tree. He leapt through the gaps in its shattered walls and there Julie lay on the floor beneath a pile of ceiling debris. Her hair was soaked in blood, her breathing slow and shallow. His stomach sank with terror.

"Julie, baby, open your eyes," Duke pleaded in a soft voice, though in his heart he knew she wouldn't answer. He slapped her face gently then felt helplessness consume him. Despite better judgment, he lifted her over his shoulder and climbed up the fallen tree, towing her away as quickly as possible. At the medical bay he found an intruder trying to break in and swung his sawed-off shotgun into the man's knee, felling him with one blow. Duke walked closer, finished him off with a second shot, then banged urgently on the door.

"Dr. Kelly! Bailey! It's Duke!"

Dr. Bailey threw open the door, thrusting a pistol in Duke's face until he saw who it was and lowered the gun. He and all within shook with fear.

"It's Julie!" cried Duke.

"What happened? Set her here," said Dr. Bailey.

The medical room was filled with blood and men and women alike.

"A tree fell on the building she was in," said Duke. "Is she going to be all right?"

"We won't know now," answered Dr. Bailey.

"Well, I'm not leaving until I do!" shouted Duke.

"Duke, you can't help her here but you are needed out there," said Dr. Kelly softly.

Duke nodded, wiping tears from his eyes as he looked upon Julie's seemingly lifeless body. He noticed some people had white cloth on their arm, while others did not.

"Julie wanted them seen the same—she never saw them as the enemy, just humans in need," said Dr. Kelly. "Go. We got her."

Duke left the medical bay. "Karl, how are we looking? Jake?" He keyed his radio mic only to remember it was broken.

"Don't move!" a voice called out then, and Duke slowly looked around to see a middle-aged man holding a gun, desperation in his eyes.

"Please don't hurt any more people! I need your meds! My kids are sick!" the man pleaded, pointing the gun at Duke.

"Then don't—walk away, leave us alone," said Duke.

"I can't do that either. All I have left are my children, but they're sick and hungry. I need food and medicine!"

"So my kids have to suffer because you weren't prepared? Why?" asked Duke.

"I know, I'm sorry, but what else can I do?" Tears rolled down the man's face.

"We all make choices," said Duke.

"No! I won't sit here and watch my kids starve—"

The man was cut off by a shot in the side of his head and slumped over, twitching on the ground.

Patch limped around the corner, his body cut and bruised, hands clasped about his ribs.

"Are you all right?" asked Duke. He helped Patch stand as best he could. "We thought you'd had it. You're alive! But how? We saw the Ferris wheel go rolling away."

Patch almost laughed. "Simple, jumped to a tree as it started to roll."

"Simple? It looks like you didn't make it."

"I said jumping to the tree was simple—grabbing on to the tree without breaking several branches on the way down is another thing." Patch laughed at himself but winced at the pain in his ribs.

"Let's get you to Dr. Kelly," Duke insisted.

"Piss off," scoffed Patch, "my trigger finger still works."

A little unsteadily, Duke led Patch away from trouble's path until they were back where Karl stood waiting. When Karl spotted Patch he rushed up and hugged him tight.

Patch rolled his eyes and said good-naturedly, "Don't go getting all weepy on me now." But Karl just kept smiling.

Duke drew near to a mass of folk unknown to Mountaintop clad in old-style desert and woodland camo, lacking the white strips on their arms that betokened them as kin. It was only when he'd gotten close that Duke recognized Kyle Crawford at the fore of his band and several more besides.

"Took you long enough!" Duke said, clasping Kyle's hand

in greeting. "Didn't realize you had such a large family."

"Half are mine; the other half here are some of your other neighbors," Kyle replied. "Seems Agigi has been raising trouble around these parts and folks looked to me for solution. Since you invited us once before I hoped we were welcomed again."

Duke's lips curled into a smile. "Indeed you are."

Karl bellowed, his voice filling the air like thunder. "We appreciate you taking out that firing squad out there, but we still have a lot of shit going on here."

"Good news is most of them are taking off; the bad news is they are taking off with food and everything they can get their hands on," hollered Duke.

"Kyle, take your group and circle around to try and cut anyone off from leaving through the front," Karl commanded.

"Roger that. Crawfords, follow me!" Kyle yelled as he and his men pounded away to fulfill their mission.

"Everyone else follows me; we're going to try and clear out the stragglers," Karl roared.

Duke's children came to mind like a tidal wave, and he felt an urgent need to make sure they were safe. "I'm going to check on the shelters and see how Sarah is doing," he said.

Jake nodded as a range of emotions crossed his face. "I've been thinking about doing the same. I'll come with you," he responded, his mouth turning down into a determined frown.

Duke and Jake tore away from the group, running as fast as their legs could carry them, desperation driving them forward. When they arrived at the shelters, an eerie feeling filled the air; it seemed like something had happened here. Duke's shelter was in shambles; everything was tossed around, and it was clear someone had broken in.

Dread suddenly filled their hearts when they got to Jake and Sarah's shelter—the door was wide open. Jake pushed past Duke and ran inside, his heart throbbing loudly in his chest. He immediately saw Sarah and Danielle on the floor. Sarah's face was unrecognizable, swollen and battered beyond belief. Danielle's fourteen-year-old frame was limp and broken.

"Honey, please wake up," Jake pleaded, patting her face gently.

Sarah groaned faintly, making both men's shoulders slump in relief. Duke bent down and tried getting her attention. "Sarah, where are the kids?"

No answer came from Sarah, who was too messed up to speak.

Rage bubbled within Duke before screaming, "Sarah, where are the kids?!"

From under the bed a voice spoke up: "That man took them."

Jake eagerly crawled over to Tyler—a weary seven-year-old who had tears streaming down his dirty face—and comforted him. "It's okay, buddy, you're safe now. Who took them?" he asked gently.

"The bald man and the long-haired man took Michael and Ava. My sister and Sarah attacked him," said Tyler.

Jake stood, his body shaking with rage as tears streamed down his face. His voice was ragged and broken, but still held all of his fury. "I'll stay here with them. Go get them. And Duke, make that bastard pay!"

***

"Stop squirming, you little brat!" yelled Dale, smacking Ava in the face.

"Leave my sister alone!" hollered Michael as he swiftly kicked Dale below his belt.

Dale bellowed in agony as he bent over, clutching his pulsating pain. Agigi seized the opportunity and grabbed ahold of Michael's hair with an iron grip, yanking his head back. He peered into Michael's eyes—eyes that radiated terror.

"Now, Dale, we don't want to be hurting our bargaining

chips," Agigi said coldly as he dragged a whimpering Michael further away from Dale. "These two have so much potential, so full of life," he added with admiration, betraying his otherwise merciless demeanor.

"There you are—what the hell are you doing?" asked Sean as he ran up.

"This is plan D. In case you didn't realize, we lost! Those cowards are just taking loot and running! They didn't see things through and won't get to reap the benefits of what we were trying to do!" Vengeful rage stewed in Agigi's veins. "Then those backwoods rednecks came to the rescue and fucked everything up! So Sean, what you are seeing is plan D."

"Didn't know we had a plan D," said Dale, confused.

"That's because we didn't have a plan D, you idiot!" countered Agigi harshly as he slapped Dale in the back of the head.

"We're not going to hurt these kids, are we?"

This query was met by Agigi's mocking laughter. "Why? Would that bother you there, Sean? Is that big ole soft heart of yours gonna not like that?" he taunted.

"Well, I didn't sign up to kill kids," murmured Sean meekly as he surveyed the carnage before him—bodies of good men and women who'd been cut down in their prime simply for being in the wrong place at the wrong time.

Agigi cocked an eyebrow mockingly at him. "And why would that bother you, Sean? Is your heart so soft that you couldn't bear to see these two come to harm?" He laughed malevolently as he took in the look of horror that crossed Sean's face. "Don't worry, my friend; we can still accomplish what we set out to do."

"What is that, exactly?" Sean looked around at all the dead bodies. "Because I'm not so sure anymore."

Agigi's voice lowered conspiratorially. "We can finally destroy Duke."

CHAPTER 29

Colorado | September 2035

The acrid stench of gunpowder hung in the air. Duke used to savor the smell, fondly recalling all sorts of memories from his many visits to the shooting range with his troops over the years. But here and now, those hazy images were quickly replaced by a more harrowing reality; dead bodies scattered at his feet while he feverishly searched for his two children.

"Michael! Ava!" He could barely choke out their names between gasps for breath, trembling with fear. He listened intently for the sound of his children's voices, then heard Agigi call from nearby: "Oh, Dookie!"

He stumbled over debris and bodies as he ran, struggling to make out what was ahead in the dark. When he finally made it to the bridge where Agigi stood, flanked by Dale and Sean, Duke saw Michael standing before Agigi while Dale held tight to Ava.

"Daddy!" they called out in unison.

"I'm here, kids; Daddy's here," Duke croaked, trying to offer them some comfort.

Agigi spoke with snarky glee. "There he is! Mr. Hollander! Glad you could join us. Today is a very special day."

"Let them go and take me. Just don't hurt them, please," Duke begged.

Agigi scoffed disdainfully. "No shit, Duke, what do you think this is—family time with Uncle Isaac?"

Ava's shrill voice cut through the darkness: "Let me go, you big jerk!" She clawed at Dale's face, leaving scratch marks on his cheek and nose.

In a rage, Dale lifted her off the ground and shouted, "You little shit! I oughta throw you off of this bridge!"

"No!" Duke yelled in vain.

Dale sneered. "Oh shut up, the fall wouldn't hurt her any."

Ava wailed in terror. "I can't swim! Ya big jerk!" Tears streamed down her face as her cries echoed off the walls of the canyon.

Agigi's voice morphed into mocking curiosity. "What about you, young man? Can you swim?" He turned toward Michael.

Michael shook his head rapidly.

"Well, that makes things a little more interesting, doesn't it?" Agigi's smirk widened.

"What? No, no, no, just take me and let them go! Isaac, please!" Tears streamed from Duke's eyes as he begged for mercy, but Agigi only grinned wider.

"Listen to how pathetic you sound! Children make people so vulnerable. That's why I killed my pregnant wife," Agigi said as if reminiscing. "Well, mainly to get the insurance money, but I also could not allow myself to have such a liability. She was sooo adamant about not getting an abortion, so I took the matter into my own hands, literally. Do you actually know how long it takes to suffocate someone with a plastic bag? A lot longer than you think."

"You're a sick son of a bitch," Duke spat with disgust.

"Oh, you have no idea," Agigi replied. His grin returned as he waved his gun toward Duke. "Just you wait, Dookie, just you wait!" He chortled darkly. "So we're gonna play a game. A game called 'who daddy loves more.' His son or daughter? This should be interesting."

Panic surged through Sean and he pointed his gun at Agigi. "Stop!" he yelled emphatically.

But the twisted man only responded with more mockery. "Well, well, well, look what we have here. We got ourselves a hero! Mr. I Had a Change of Heart."

"I told you this is not what I signed up for! Not his kids, not anyone else! It was supposed to be just him!" yelled Sean desperately.

Agigi coolly replied, "If you kill me or Dale, one of these kids will die no matter what," and both men placed guns against the children's heads.

"You're right—then I'll stop the game," Sean responded bravely and stepped between Agigi and Dale, pointing his gun at Duke instead, when suddenly Agigi whacked him on the back of his head with his pistol, sending him into darkness instantly.

"No, you will not! Duke has things to learn!" bellowed Agigi with maniacal laughter. "Sorry about that, Duke, I might have to fire him. We might be heading in a different direction. Where were we? Ah yes, which kid do you love more? Let me quickly explain to you the rules. The kid you name lives, the other gets thrown into that pond. You get to listen to that kid drown. If you try to jump in and save them I will shoot the other kid. So no matter what, one kid is dying today, and you have to live with that."

Duke felt like his world was crumbling around him as the words penetrated his consciousness. His tears flowed freely, and his body trembled with fear. He could feel his chest tighten further with each word that came out of Agigi's mouth; it was becoming more difficult to breathe. Agigi stood before him, an evil glare in his eyes, causing Duke to feel even more helpless than before.

"Please no, please—"

"Yes! Yes! This is the only way, and do not make me choose for you, Duke, because I'll choose both," Agigi said with an evil glare.

Duke shuddered violently. Tears burst forth like a storm and spread down his face, mingling with the stream of mucus that had made its way out of his nose and onto his upper lip. His cheeks ached from the pressure he felt bulging inside, as though his face was about to explode.

"Tick tock, Dookie," Agigi said with a sinister smirk as he sized up Duke's two children. "Will you look at that, children—your father truly loves you two, but I wonder who he truly loves more."

Duke felt the weight of the situation bearing down on him. He had to make a choice—one child would live while the other would not, and if he refused to choose, then both of them would die.

"I can't! I'm sorry, I can't! Let's work this out a different way!" His voice cracked as he pleaded desperately for another solution.

"Well ... that's unfortunate, Dookie. Because I'm a man of my word." Agigi spoke with dark, emotionless eyes. Without hesitation, he viciously threw Michael over the edge, sending Dale into a frenzy as he followed suit by tossing Ava over the side like she was nothing more than a sack of garbage.

"NO!" Duke roared, whipping out his gun and firing with reckless abandon. Dale was struck in the arm, and the force of the bullet knocked the weapon from his hand. But before Duke could reload, Agigi retaliated, sending a shot into Duke's leg and causing him to tumble onto the ground. Struggling against two adversaries, Duke attempted to rise and rush to aid his children, but with both men on top of him, he felt all hope slipping away.

Desperate cries of "Daddy!" echoed from within the depths of the water. Michael and Ava were frantically swimming, their voices weakening with each passing second, fading until there was nothing but silence. Duke howled in anguish at being unable to save them.

Agigi's maniacal laughter reverberated as he glared at Duke. "See, Duke, I told you all along that there are things in this world worse than death! Now do you believe me? Huh? Do you finally comprehend the horror?" he spat with sickening pleasure, foaming at the mouth, the words spewing out of his lips like molten lava.

Duke shrieked in terror and agony, the sound echoing through the whole mountainside. "No! No!"

A sadistic smile crept over Agigi's face as he witnessed the fear that had taken hold of Duke. "Their screams mixed with yours … is almost euphoric, don't you think? Now you'll truly understand what pain is."

Duke's vision was blurry, but he could make out Sean, who had staggered to his feet and regained control. With a primal roar, Sean lunged at Dale and Agigi, bowling them away from Duke and giving him enough time to stand.

Without a moment's pause, Duke flung himself over the railing into the cold depths below, kicking and gasping for breath as he pushed himself toward the unknown. He dove deep, searching for Michael or Ava in the murky waters, desperate for one of them to appear.

A sharp pain shot through his leg with each powerful stroke. Despite the agony that came with every kick of his legs, he stayed underwater until his lungs burned, only to come up empty-handed.

"Help me!" he screamed breathlessly. His throat felt raw from shouting. "God, please, help me! Please!"

Suddenly, a few people started diving into the water. Before long, dozens of people had joined in the search and rescue effort.

"Got one!" shouted a man struggling with a limp body under the surface. It was Ava.

A few seconds later, someone quickly tugged Michael out of the murky water before laying them on the bank next to each other, both lifeless and blue as ice.

"Someone perform CPR on Michael!" Duke shouted as he closely hovered over his daughter. "Two breaths then thirty compressions! You got it?" He began giving two breaths followed by compressions to Ava.

"Ava Wava, please wake up, please wake up," he mumbled desperately.

The group continued with CPR until Dr. Kelly and Dr. Bailey took over performing CPR on the kids.

"God, if you are listening, make my babies wake up," Duke prayed aloud.

Dr. Kelly spoke softly, her voice encouraging as she performed CPR on Ava. "Come back to us," she begged. "You can do this, Ava."

"How long have they been not breathing Duke?" Dr. Kelly asked.

"I don't know—a few minutes?" Duke replied, his voice shaking with fear and despair.

"They were probably in the water almost five minutes and at least two or three minutes out of the water," someone in the crowd replied.

Dr. Kelly stopped and looked at Duke tearfully. "I'm so sorry, Duke, we're already past the ten-minute mark; even if they regain consciousness, there is a high chance they'll sustain permanent brain damage."

"No! We must keep going!" Duke sobbed as he shoved Dr. Kelly aside, sending her crashing to the ground. He frantically took turns giving CPR to his children while wailing in distress.

"Kelly ... Bailey ... please don't stop!" he begged hysterically. "My babies! Not my babies!" he shouted in anguish.

Dr. Kelly hugged him from behind, tears streaming down her face. "Duke, I'm so sorry, but they're gone," she said softly.

He embraced their still bodies, crying uncontrollably until his voice went quiet, frozen with pain and grief. Finally, Dr. Kelly wrapped her arms around him and his children and wept with him until there were no more tears left to cry.

Karl, along with a few other people, escorted Agigi, Dale, and Sean to Duke. Their hands had been bound behind their backs. Duke's thoughts turned dark very quickly. He squatted down and looked at Agigi, drained of emotion.

Agigi spoke in a soft voice, inquiring, "So tell me, Duke, do you understand? Do you believe me now when I say there are things in this life that are worse than death?"

Duke regarded him with an expressionless face.

Agigi continued, sarcasm dripping from his tongue. "Ohhhh, Dookie, what's wrong? Come on, you can tell me—what's bothering you?"

Dale shuddered and Sean hung his head in shame. Duke left then returned with a post-hole digger, digging three holes and firmly placing three four-by-four posts in them.

"Can I have some help here?" he asked meekly.

"I got you, brother," Karl answered as he approached. "I know they deserve to die but not like this, not in front of everyone," he said cautiously.

"You gonna stop me?" Duke questioned without looking at him.

"No, it's not my decision; all I know is that it won't fix anything, but it will change you forever."

"That was a good speech, Chief, think you finally made an impression," Agigi joked.

"It's too late now," Duke focused his gaze on his children lying under the blanket. He then bound his antagonists across their chest and legs tightly to the upright posts with their arms still behind their backs. He left again only to come back with an axe and Dale's nephew, Timmy, who was still recuperating from the injuries Dale had inflicted upon him.

"Where's Dale's knife?"

Karl stepped forward, handing Duke the large buck knife. Duke passed the blade off to Timmy, who walked over to his uncle as tears streamed down his face.

"Come on, Timmy, I'm sorry, I didn't mean to do it—I was angry—I love—"

Timmy started sobbing as he plunged the knife into Dale's midsection and twisted it harshly. Dale howled in pain while cursing his nephew out. Timmy removed the knife and began stabbing relentlessly.

"Is that really your brilliant plan, Duke?" Agigi jeered.

"Well, I'm all right with that! Bring it on, pal! When I die, I'll be content knowing you'll have to live forever with the fact that you weren't able to save your children."

Duke studied him intently. "You're right," he said as he walked away.

It took Duke a long while of tugging and pushing to move the aging, rusted woodchipper in front of his rival. He positioned the chute so that it was facing Agigi. For the first time ever, Isaac Agigi was silent. Duke snatched the knife from Dale's corpse and went over to Sean.

"I'm sorry, Duke," Sean mumbled, hanging his head in shame, "I never intended it to turn out like this. I wanted you dead—but not this way. I deserve whatever is about to happen."

"Yeah, you do," Duke admitted. "But you're not gonna die today." He cut through Sean's bonds. "You stood up to Agigi and tried to help me save my kids and that's the only reason why you're not dying. Agigi is right; having to live with oneself can be far worse than death. So leave now and never come back. If I ever see you again, I'll put you back on that post until you starve," Duke finished, his eyes cold and lifeless.

Sean looked at Duke with understanding. He stepped through the crowd of angry onlookers who glared at him as he passed.

Duke reverted his attention to Agigi, who still said nothing, trying to put on a brave face. But Duke could finally smell fear on him.

Duke turned to address the crowd. "If you want to see justice served, then stay and watch, but if you don't have a strong stomach I'd advise you to leave."

Duke switched on the woodchipper. The steel jaws and rotating blades hummed to life with a rumbling growl. He cut Dale off of his post and picked him up. Most of the crowd walked away, sick to their stomachs. Duke held Dale in his arms like a child. He walked him over to the chipper and threw him in headfirst. The machine struggled to chew and grind up the body. It produced a nauseating sound with its efforts. The air was quickly dominated by a heavy metallic scent. People in the crowd screamed in horror as blood, guts, meat, and bone spewed out of the chipper, splattering Agigi's face and body. Agigi seemed to struggle to breathe, waterboarded with buckets of gore. Eventually, the woodchipper finished its horrific task. Duke shut the machine down and walked over to Agigi, who trembled in shock as bits of bones and meat, covered in hair, slid down his face.

Agigi's eyes bulged as he stared ahead, his face a mask of shock and horror. A low, guttural noise escaped his throat as panic spread and twisted his features into something unrecognizable. He gagged and coughed, spitting out chunks of Dale from his mouth onto the ground. The stench of iron and copper wafted from the blood that accompanied it, coating his tongue with its metallic taste. His shoulders shook with the force of his shuddering breaths.

"Good, you look finally ready," Duke whispered in Agigi's ear.

Duke picked up the axe. "This is for what you did to the people of Mountaintop!" he said, severing Agigi's right leg at the knee.

Agigi screamed at the top of his lungs.

"This is for Mikey, and Ava!" Duke screamed, taking a couple of swings to sever Agigi's left leg.

Agigi's body was no longer supported by his legs. The rope that was fastened around his chest was the only thing holding him upright against the wooden post.

"Oh no, don't pass out on me yet," Duke said, slapping Agigi's face. He paused as if he had just had a revelation. His words echoed with a strong sense of relief and closure as he spoke, his gaze unwavering. "And most of all. This is for me, you son of a bitch." He took off Agigi's head with one swift stroke.

The axe stuck in the post as Agigi's head rolled to the ground with a wet thud, his face frozen with a pained expression. Duke walked through the crowd, leaving them shocked and silent.

CHAPTER 30

COLORADO | OCTOBER 2035

A month had passed since the battle, and repairs were still being made to the damaged buildings from bullets or fire. Some structures were too damaged to fix, so they had to be demolished and their materials repurposed. One of the most crucial buildings on Mountaintop, the communications building, rose to priority status in terms of restoring it.

Duke wouldn't accept his children being cremated. Instead, he laid them to rest at a desolate area of the Mountaintop estate. Every day, he took a somber stroll to his children's graves and every time he encountered them, his body and soul were wracked with heartache and anguish.

The community was mourning. Mountaintop had lost its spirit. Dozens of people in the community were killed, among them Greg Arrowood and Pete Smith. Greg's body was found riddled with bullet holes at his mechanic shop. He was cremated while wearing his Vietnam veteran hat.

Tracy, the storage manager of the community, was another casualty. Her corpse had been found guarding the food stores. She had taken down multiple people before succumbing to them when her ammunition ran out. Sadly, nearly all of the rice and beans had been plundered. What little remained was consumed over the last month, so it was now up to Farmer Ed and his potatoes to save the fifty or so survivors left at Mountaintop.

Joe was also found dead trying to protect his wife, Diane. Diane survived and said her husband's responsibility as

Mountaintop's main cook fell on her. She said she was the only one who could probably replicate her husband's cooking.

Karl and Patch remained at Mountaintop. They said they honestly couldn't go back to their unit unless they wanted to face Colonel Campbell and the consequences of leaving. Kazim, Karl, and Patch were put in charge of Mountaintop's security and defenses.

The battle with Agigi left Mountaintop nearly dry of all its ammunition. With bullets becoming a rare commodity, they were spared for only the defense of Mountaintop. Spears, knives, and machetes were primary sources of protection. Kazim and Karl showed the community how to make bows and arrows, but that had been a long and tedious process.

There had only been a few times people came looking for asylum or for food, but they were turned away without question or argument.

The animals had just about disappeared—the large game animals especially. They'd become almost like legends, something out of a storybook, since no one had seen them around in a long time.

Duke was still healing from the gunshot wound to his leg. It had to be packed every day as Dr. Kelly advised him not to walk on it at all. Mentally, Duke felt like he was hanging on by a thread and he couldn't just sit around and do nothing. He wanted to help his community, but in reality, he was of little use. Thoughts of his children consumed his day and visions of their death filled his nightmares, so Duke stayed away from sleep as much as possible despite how badly his body needed rest.

Julie was his only source of comfort. Every night he'd shed tears in her embrace. The only motivation to keep going was Julie and their unborn child. Luckily, she had not been seriously hurt; Dr. Kelly gave her a complete examination and said the baby's heart rate sounded normal, but they wouldn't know for sure until delivery.

***

Daddy's here, nothing bad will happen, I swear! I love you, kids. Daddy is here to help! No! You can't trust me?

Duke jerked upright in bed, ending his nightmarish sleep. Julie put a comforting hand on Duke's face and gave him an affectionate look. She knew it was pointless to ask what his dreams were about; the line of questioning felt unnecessary and too sensitive to talk about. Duke sat up without saying a word, feeling like his head would burst at any moment.

Julie tried to put on a brave face. "Guess what we get to do today?" she asked with an artificial brightness.

Duke shrugged his shoulders, not bothering to respond.

"We get to listen to our baby's heartbeat," Julie persisted, hoping for some enthusiasm.

Duke didn't seem interested. "That sounds great and all, but Farmer Ed needs everyone in the fields. We can't afford to miss a day."

Julie stood up and walked over to Duke, determined to make him see reason. "I know you're hurting, but we're all hurting. Our family, our unborn child, this community—they all need us. We have to stick together." She squeezed his shoulder before calmly walking out of the shelter.

Whenever Duke left his shelter and walked through Mountaintop, he turned away from anyone's gaze to avoid seeing the pity in their eyes. He felt guilty for not being able to help more with his injured leg and crutches. As he arrived at Farmer Ed's potato field, all the able-bodied citizens of the community were already hard at work. Every person was taking turns digging and pushing wheelbarrows.

"Duke, nice to see you," said Ed.

"So what do you think, Ed? Will this be enough food for us?"

"At this rate, yes. We should get around twenty to twenty-five thousand pounds," replied Farmer Ed coolly.

"Good news then. But why don't you seem so pleased?" asked Duke curiously.

Ed took a deep breath and looked concerned as he replied, "We may survive this winter but I'm worried about what comes next. The potatoes were only supposed to supplement our stores, not be our main source of sustenance. I've done the calculations and it doesn't seem promising unless we figure out how to get more calories outside of the gardens. We need to start thinking about not just making it through the winter but making it through to this time next year."

Jake joined the conversation. "But we still have the milking goats, right?" he queried.

"Yes, but it won't be enough." Farmer Ed shook his head. "I need to save some of this crop for seeding two acres next year. We're looking at only 600 to 800 calories a day per person for the entire year."

As they glanced at each other surreptitiously, they realized the gravity of their situation: it seemed that they were doomed to a slow starvation.

"We'll make it work," Jake sounded hopeful.

"No other choice," Duke grumbled before departing.

"Hey, wait up. How's it going?" Jake asked.

"Like my kids were murdered last month." Duke was frustrated and sorrowful. "Julie and I will have a baby in a few months, but with this food shortage, I can't help but think we'll all starve to death."

"I understand." Jake felt uncomfortable. "I'm just trying to stay positive."

"I know, I'm sorry. Cannot stop thinking about what happened. Everything just seems so hopeless now. What is happening on your end?"

"Tyler and Danielle are coping better, but still shaken," Jake sighed. "Sarah hasn't said much at all; she blames herself and keeps saying if she was stronger, Michael or Ava wouldn't have been taken."

"Yep, know the feeling," Duke agreed quietly, still blaming himself.

"The only thing that's made her smile these past few weeks is when I told her how Agigi and Dale died."

Duke kept silent, his mind plagued by the memory of killing them. He knew he was capable of violence, but what he did to them exceeded anything he expected from himself.

The room grew thick with silence before Jake spoke again. "So, how's Julie doing?"

"She's trying—she really wants this baby. She's at a checkup right now," Duke said as he scratched at his scraggly beard.

"Why don't you join her?" asked Jake.

"I'm scared. I can't lose another child," Duke murmured as tears gathered in his eyes.

"We're here for whatever you need—we'll do our best to help." Jake patted Duke on the back.

Forcing a joke, Duke asked, "Do we dig potatoes now or cry some more?"

"We can handle it, don't worry about a thing," said Jake. "Go be with Julie."

Duke nodded and left, walking toward the medical center. The air was heavy with body odor and rubbing alcohol; many were still healing from battle wounds as Dr. Bailey worked swiftly to tend to patients and clean surfaces with an antiseptic spray bottle.

"If you're looking for Julie, she's in the back," Dr. Bailey said without emotion. He had strong opinions on what happened to Agigi and Dale—as did many others—yet Duke didn't acknowledge it; he didn't regret it either, just regretted everyone else having to witness it.

"Am I too late?" Duke wondered as he approached Julie and Dr. Kelly.

"We were just about to get started," Dr. Kelly said, brandishing a handheld fetal doppler.

Julie didn't reply, just smiled, indicating for him to sit by her side.

"Jules, I'm really sorry—"

"Shh!" she hushed him, still smiling.

Dr. Kelly searched around on Julie's stomach for several minutes but couldn't locate the heartbeat.

"Is everything okay?" Julie asked, anxious now.

"I can't hear anything," Dr. Kelly uttered with trepidation.

Duke was overtaken by fear at her words. "What does that mean?"

"It means I can't find the heartbeat right now," Dr. Kelly explained nervously. "Sometimes they move locations and make it difficult to hear. This home doppler isn't the best either … but it could also mean something I don't want to mention yet."

Duke felt a wave of panic wash over him.

Daddy's here.

I won't let anything happen to you.

I promise, kids.

You're a terrible father.

"Aha, there it is!" exclaimed Dr. Kelly.

The rhythmic thumping of a heartbeat snapped Duke out of his trance. He peered at the contraption in Dr. Kelly's grip and was dumbfounded.

"That's our baby, Duke," Julie said joyfully, wiping away her tears.

"Based on what you told me and your appearance, I'd guess you're around four or five months pregnant. So that means the little one should arrive sometime in February or March."

✳✳✳

December 2035

The food shortage was taking its toll on all the Mountaintop survivors. Everyone was already thin from subsisting on such limited rations, yet they still managed to carry out their duties.

It was a major challenge to keep everyone warm now that winter had come, but each shelter or building housing someone had at least some kind of fireplace. One of the biggest issues discussed was what would happen when the firewood ran out. Collecting more fuel would be difficult with so few calories in people's bodies.

Jake and Sarah stayed together with their orphaned children despite all they'd been through—Sarah's face held a look of perpetual spacing out; Duke couldn't tell if it was grief or hunger that caused it. He thought about Michael and Ava constantly, mulling over what could have been done differently. Despite the snow, Duke regularly visited his children's graves, apologizing and expressing how much he missed them.

Kazim continued his work at the forge despite his lack of food intake; he mentioned it kept him warm and strong. He often volunteered for security shifts whenever someone else was too weak or likely to fall asleep on guard duty. Karl and Patch also helped out wherever they could in the security rotations.

Patrick and Eric continued to spend their time playing tabletop games and listening to the radio. Patrick tried repairing his damaged drone but lacked the spare parts and energy to do so.

Julie whined about feeling like an invalid, yet she had to remain in bed most of the time so that her caloric output wouldn't be too high. Dr. Kelly was concerned with Julie's health during the course of the pregnancy; she feared that a woman eating so few calories could cause complications for her baby.

Kyle Crawford and his family were fighting the same battle as Mountaintop. Mountaintop and the Crawfords decided to make a pledge of mutual protection. To alleviate the boredom of consuming only potatoes and goat's milk daily, they tried exchanging calorie for calorie with each other on an individual basis. Their specialty trades consisted of bullets, bread, and booze. When it came to foodstuffs, a person could barter their own portions, but when it came to material possessions to swap, that was decided by majority vote.

The radio operator Voice of the Mountains informed Mountaintop that help was on the way. A radio broadcast said that the Chinese were coming and giving humanitarian aid to U.S. survivors: "Though China and America may be adversaries, it was said that turning away from helping innocent American survivors would bring about China's downfall. Karma is of utmost importance in Chinese culture; a person will experience corresponding rewards or punishments for all their actions, as sure as their own shadow follows them."

John radioed Duke mentioning the broadcast. Duke wanted to be optimistic, but John said he didn't trust it. Asked his opinion on the situation, Karl put on a brave face, but Duke knew his thoughts were different.

***

February 2036

Duke observed Julie's feeble frame as she dozed off, her bony figure now so slender that he could make out every rib on her body. Her protruding belly looked oddly out of place with her emaciated form. Her golden locks of hair were noticeably sparser than normal and her complexion had taken on an ashen hue. Dr. Kelly believed that she had become anemic.

Everyone in Mountaintop was weakened by hunger—they had little energy to move or even stay warm. Sick people in the medical center were dying, possibly due to their lack of nutrition. It was a hard decision but eventually, it was voted for the security detail to take extra rations from those that passed away. There were complaints, but also volunteers for security rotations.

Duke wanted to remain by Julie's side, but he had to check

on others, so he decided to go to the communication building. Most likely, he would find Eric and Patrick there with their Dungeons & Dragons dice and surrounded by their handmade boards with miniatures spread out randomly. Although they had started with some pounds to lose, they were already thin and unhealthy.

As Duke came in, he saw Karl and Patch involved in a quiet argument.

"Hey, Duke," Eric said, looking up from his game. "What's going on?"

"What's going on with them?" Duke tilted his head and narrowed his eyes in the direction of Karl and Patch.

"They've been at it for a while now," Patrick offered.

"Over what?" questioned Duke.

"Not sure," said Eric, glancing at Karl and Patch.

Duke walked over to Karl and Patch. "Is everything okay?" he asked.

Patch stormed off in anger.

"What the hell was that about?" asked Duke.

"Duke, there are things too hard to explain," said Karl.

"Try me," declared Duke.

"I can't; the less you know the better," murmured Karl.

"That's such BS! No more secrets! You must know something!" shouted Duke.

"Christ, lower your voice." Karl quietly motioned him away to where Patrick and Eric couldn't hear them speak. "It's not that I don't want to tell you; it's for your own good."

"You got to give me something," pleaded Duke.

Karl hung his head low in defeat. "Very long story short, I was an SF baby. Came in as an 18 XRAY and loved every minute of it. When I came up on my second reenlistment, a few years later, two men from very important places offered me a job to work undercover in a black ops unit. I found myself without choice accepting the offer and taking on missions without questioning why or what for."

"You were part of a regular Special Forces unit when you killed one of your own, right?" Duke asked.

"I was doing a counterintelligence mission undercover in an SF group. I was sent to find an American mole who had been selling info to the Russians, and when someone in the unit tried to rape a Ukrainian woman, I made a split-second decision and shot him. My handlers did nothing to stop the murder charges. They washed their hands of me and walked away. But they must have got spooked thinking I was going to open my mouth about the unit in order to save myself. To protect themselves, they would send people to try and kill me."

"That's why there were all those stories about you being a big scary guy who was getting into fights and severely hurting inmates. That's why they kept you in solitary confinement," Duke said with surprising clarity.

Karl nodded.

"So what about Patch and Jones?" Duke queried.

"Same type of story, except they were in SF units long after I got locked up. They ended up in the same black ops outfit. They heard the stories, but never met me until I showed up here," said Karl.

"So, what about this group you are all a part of? What about Colonel Campbell?"

"That should be obvious by now that it is more than it seems. It's a deep black ops unit. Only a few people know what goes on in that place. Like Colonel Campbell, whatever the hell his actual name is. I happen to know a lot more than I should. Jones and Patch were given low-level info," said Karl.

"What was Patch so upset about?" asked Duke.

"He wants to go back no matter the consequences. He says the punishment will be better than starving to death. But he doesn't know what I know. They won't kill us; they've dumped too much money into us. But they definitely will figure something out. Patch will eventually learn the truth—well, some form of the truth. I eventually learned what my part is in all this. But I refuse to be a part of it anymore."

"The truth in what? Your part in what?" Duke asked.

Karl let out a heavy sigh. "Project Reset," he declared solemnly.

"Project Reset? What exactly is Project Reset?" Duke questioned.

Karl paused briefly, a look of concentration on his face as he summoned thoughts from the back of his mind.

"I was on a mission interrogating an individual with a trusted partner of mine. That individual ended up giving up a clandestine operation by the name of Project Reset. I pushed the man for more details but my partner immediately put a bullet in his head. When I asked why he did that he just told me to forget the name Project Reset. Of course that only piqued my interest. I went out on my own to gather intel on this operation. And I ended up coming across information that made me wish I never dug so deep. But knowing what it was, I felt an obligation to our country to keep digging. But very important people caught wind of me snooping around. They were impressed with me, so instead of getting rid of me they used me to help with their goals in Project Reset."

"What, are you going to tell me that our government did this to our country or something?"

"No, they didn't. But they didn't prevent it either. They came up with a plan to help offset the end of the world, or the end of the United States."

"But that sounds like a good thing, Chief," Duke stated.

"You would think that, but—"

"But what? Does this have to do with the Chinese coming and helping us?" asked Duke.

With an air of urgent secrecy, Karl leaned in and whispered to Duke, "I'm uncertain about what lies ahead, but I am certain that everyone will be confronted with a critical decision..."

Suddenly, their conversation was interrupted by a loud,

jarring clanging sound, the deafening sound of a large metal bell.

After their battle with Agigi, someone had discovered an old bell in Charles' storage and decided it would be a great way to get the attention of everyone on Mountaintop. They all had a predestined position to take when the bell was rung.

Duke and Karl raced to investigate what all the commotion was about. Patrick was standing there, frantically ringing the bell and setting off a series of events that saw the people of Mountaintop scramble back into their defensive positions.

"What is going on?" Duke asked Patrick.

"A guard on the wall said a troop of military vehicles were outside our gates," he replied.

"Why?" asked Duke.

"Campbell must be coming to reclaim his belongings," Karl said.

"No way!" Duke snarled.

"We can't do anything here," Karl stated calmly.

Duke knew Karl was right. Mountaintop was in no condition to fight anybody, let alone some type of black ops unit.

Eric sprinted out with a small ham radio in hand. "He's on the line," he said.

"This is Duke," Duke said into the mic.

"Ah, there you are, Duke. Colonel Campbell here. Do the right thing and open your gates up."

"What do you want?" Duke replied.

"Don't play games, kid! Open those doors now!" the colonel shouted through the radio.

Karl put his hand on Duke's shoulder to reassure him before he could answer. "It's all right, Duke, just let 'em in."

Duke glanced back at his people; they were worn-out, cold, and fearful. He had no choice but to give in and ordered for the gates to be opened.

"It's okay everyone, you can relax now," Duke called out to his community.

At least a dozen vehicles filled the large parking lot. The air was thick with the smell of diesel and oil, and all of the vehicles had mounted machine guns. One door opened and Colonel Campbell emerged, cutting through the silence that followed when all the engines were turned off. All Duke could hear then was the bitter Colorado winter wind and Campbell's feet crunching against the snow.

"I figured you'd be a reasonable man, Hollander. Especially since I was asked to come here," declared Colonel Campbell.

Duke threw up his hands in confusion and exclaimed, "What the hell are you talking about?"

Karl spoke bluntly. "I've made my decision. Sir, nobody called you."

"Actually, I called him," Patch revealed.

Karl angrily whirled on him. "You what? Why?"

"Don't get me wrong, I fell in love with Mountaintop and its people. But I refuse to sit here and starve when I don't have to, and neither do you, Chief. So whatever fate awaits me, I won't fight it any longer," Patch declared.

Colonel Campbell gestured to his Humvees, nodding to Patch. He headed toward the vehicle in response and got inside. "Chief, let's keep this simple rather than going on with cinematic dialogue or longwinded threats. Karl, you ARE coming with us," Colonel Campbell stated bluntly.

Karl lowered his head and looked back at Duke before he began walking toward Colonel Campbell. "I'm sorry, brother."

The colonel sneered. "Good man, Chief."

"Karl, you can't go," Duke protested.

Karl stopped and returned to Duke's side. "I don't have any other choice; either I go or he'll tear this place apart," he explained. "Then he'll need to find someone else as a replacement."

Colonel Campbell stepped in smugly and quipped, "It's like you know me, Chief."

"Replacement?" Duke uttered in confusion.

"Yeah, Duke—you see, I'd be forced to kill Karl here and find a replacement. But the problem is he's just so damn unique and would be hard to replace." Colonel Campbell smiled sarcastically.

"Take care of yourself, and remember what I said. Everyone will have a choice to make," Karl whispered in Duke's ear. He embraced Duke before getting into the colonel's Humvee.

The colonel regarded Duke with an impressed smirk. "You've definitely proven your worth, Mr. Hollander," he said. "Chief told me about your experience in Ukraine—quite impressive for a man of your age. And now you've demonstrated yourself to be a strong leader who led his people to victory despite heavy odds."

"What are you getting at?" Duke asked warily.

"I'm giving you an offer to join us, Duke," Colonel Campbell stated plainly. "It beats starving, that's for sure."

"I think I'd rather take my chances without you," Duke replied as he eyed the Humvee Karl had gotten into.

"That's too bad," Colonel Campbell said. "You could have been one heck of a team player."

The colonel drove off with Karl, leaving Duke alone with conflicting emotions and unspoken words.

CHAPTER 31

Colorado | March 2036

Duke heard a noise near his shelter and decided to investigate. As he neared the entrance, the door to his shelter opened electronically, revealing a brilliant light. He stepped out into the beam and felt the cold air become warm. When the blinding light dimmed, Duke found himself standing in a grocery store. His vision was blurred until he blinked away the confusion. All around him were boxes of food untouched by human hands. Suddenly, "Lollipop" by The Chordettes wafted through the loudspeakers. Duke began walking along the aisles, running his fingers along the packages. Inexplicably, he could no longer contain himself and grabbed what he could find: chips, candy, beef jerky, and a beer and Gatorade for good measure. As he chewed on this bounty, Duke thought about Julie and how she should be here too.

Duke awoke to the frigid cold in his shelter. He was even hungrier than he had been before he fell asleep. The absence of light revealed that no fire was burning. With a heavy sigh, Duke threw off his covers and got up to throw more wood into the fireplace. Thankfully, hot coals still burned beneath.

It had been almost a year since the power had gone out. One year since Duke fled prison to get back to his family. One year since the ruination of the United States of America. The winter temperatures had finally started to relent. Seemingly all anyone could think or talk about was food. The lack of calories became more dire than before when half of the milk goats froze overnight due to the unforeseen extreme drop in temperature.

Mountaintop seemed empty without Karl and Patch. Duke

felt conflicted when considering the two of them; while he was relieved they now had enough to eat, he also knew they were facing whatever punishments Colonel Campbell could come up with.

Duke visited his children's graves daily, even as the bitter cold seemed to threaten him each time he ventured out. Julie's pregnancy was not going well; she wasn't getting nearly enough calories. The hungry ache in Duke's stomach paled in comparison to the sight of Julie slowly dwindling away. Her face became hollow and her skin sank into her bones, yet her belly continued to swell. Dr. Kelly and Dr. Bailey had given their full attention to her, although they too were gradually losing strength. They estimated the baby would arrive sometime around March. Everyone in Mountaintop watched cautiously for Duke and Julie's child—some with hope, others wary that it was another empty mouth to feed.

The loud knocking on the door abruptly jolted Duke back to reality.

"Duke, sorry to wake you," Eric said softly. "But Inmate 95557 is on the radio. Said it was important."

Grudgingly, Duke leaned over to kiss the only spot on Julie's head that was visible above the covers. The path to the communication building seemed longer than usual, as if his exhaustion had dulled his movements.

"John?" he called into the receiver.

His friend's reply came with a slight delay. "Yeah, I'm here." John Roberts sounded despondent.

"It's been a while, my brother. Are you managing all right?" Duke asked.

John replied in a strained tone, "Everything's good over here."

"What is happening?" questioned Duke, puzzled by John's reluctance.

"I got an update on those Chinese troops coming your way."

Duke pushed further, "What news have you heard?"

"It looks like they are actually helping people out—giving them food, providing medical attention."

"That actually sounds positive," Duke said in surprise.

John responded slowly. "I thought so too until I heard they were setting up permanent structures."

"Damn ... well, maybe they are sticking around for a while to help fix things," Duke speculated.

"I don't know what to think, but something is not right. Just not going to trust them."

"I think he's right, Duke," said another voice over the radio.

"What? Who was that?" asked Duke.

"I don't know... Who the fuck is this?" John demanded.

"Sorry, bad habit. This is the Voice of the Mountains."

"Okay, what can we call you besides the Voice of the Mountains? Over."

"I guess it doesn't really matter a whole lot anymore." The man audibly sighed over the radio. "You can call me Harvey. Over."

"Okay, Harvey, what do you have to add? Over," said Duke.

"Reports are coming in that they are putting in permanent structures like FEMA lookalike facilities and humanitarian aid stations. But it also looks like they are sending in branches of their military, putting up structures to house their soldiers. They also are going around putting out signs, radio transmissions where to find the local food depot. Break...

"They came with the promise of food. Apparently it is only given after their face and fingerprints are scanned into a device. But it seems like they are taking care of people. They are administering medical treatment and giving people lots of food and water. Over."

"Yeah, fuck that!" growled John.

"Sounds better than starving, John," said Duke.

"To top it off, reports are coming in that a Russian Naval fleet is heading for the East Coast," said Harvey.

"What the hell! Dammit! Oh, fine, let those sonsabitches come!" John yelled.

"John, we got to keep our cool, you hear me?"

The radio stayed silent.

"Roberts? If the Russians are really on their way I pity them. They're up against a bunch of hillbillies like you. Over," Duke said.

A few moments of quiet passed.

"They have no idea what they've gotten themselves into. I gotta go—and Duke ... take care of yourself," John said.

"Yeah, you too, man."

The radio sank into silence again.

"So Harvey, what did you do before all this started? Over."

"I was a radio host. Heard of my show? Hanging with Harvey? Over."

"No, can't say that I have. Over."

"Figures. My demographic was mostly seniors who still listened to the radio. Over."

"What do you make of it now?" Duke asked. "Do you really think they're invading us or something else? Over."

"Unfortunately, with the evidence we have, it doesn't look good. So yes, that's what I'm going with. Over."

"What in the world are we supposed to do? Over."

"Don't know—just try to stay alive maybe or give up and give in to whatever they want us to do, fight back, maybe, not sure at this point. God help us." Harvey answered grimly.

"God? At this juncture after everything that's happened I don't think He exists anymore, and if He does then He definitely is one spiteful SOB," Duke muttered darkly.

"I'm sorry you feel that way. But if the Chinese are really heading this way and their intentions are not good, we should probably make this our last transmission. Over."

"I suppose you're right," said Duke.

"Take care of yourself, Duke."

"Yeah, you too, Harvey. Mountaintop out."

✳✳✳

"It's all right, Jules. Try to breathe," Duke said, trying to remain calm himself.

"Duke, this really hurts—is that normal?" Julie asked in a quiet panic.

Duke glanced at Dr. Kelly for an answer.

"Julie, these are labor pains and yes, they are very common and incredibly uncomfortable," the doctor stated.

"How long ago did her water break?" Dr. Bailey inquired.

"We're not sure; it was sometime during the night," Duke answered. "Why does that matter?"

"When I used to work in labor and delivery, we typically wanted the baby born within twenty-four hours of when the water had broken to reduce infection risk," Dr. Bailey replied.

A few hours passed before Dr. Kelly advised Julie to start pushing. She seemed weak and pale from exhaustion, needing breaks between her efforts. Despite all this hindrance, she continued pushing with determination. Duke looked down at her with such pride filling his eyes.

"Ready for another round, Julie? Let me know when you're ready." Dr. Kelly spoke softly and reassuringly.

"I feel another one coming on," Julie said through gritted teeth.

"Go ahead and push," Dr. Kelly urged her on.

"It burns! It burns!" Julie screamed.

"I understand, sweetheart, just keep pushing—you got the head out already," Dr. Kelly encouraged her once more.

"You're doing great, Jules, I'm so proud of you." Duke kissed her forehead tenderly. "Just one last push now."

Julie let out a loud scream as she strained against the waves of agony. A moment later, Dr. Kelly held up a tiny bundle and exclaimed, "Congratulations! You have a baby boy—he's small as we expected, but he's here!"

In that moment, tears flowed freely down Duke's face as memories of Michael's birth flooded back to him. "Are you feeling okay?" he asked Julie.

"I'm dizzy and feel like I just pushed watermelon out of my vagina," Julie said sarcastically, sweat dripping down her forehead and her blonde locks wild and untamed. "Can we see him?"

"Give us a second; he's not breathing yet," Dr. Bailey said, grabbing the newborn from Dr. Kelly.

"What is wrong?" Duke inquired.

"We just need a moment, Duke," Dr. Kelly answered.

Dr. Bailey started rubbing the newborn's chest.

"Please do something!" Duke demanded.

"We are, he's just not responding!" shouted Dr. Bailey.

Duke felt faint and his head began to swim as the room began to spin around him. He could see the ghostly expression on Julie's face while she silently wept. He couldn't bear the thought of losing another child. Suddenly, his trance was broken by the sound of a life crying for attention—his new son's beautiful voice filled the room with joy and relief.

"He's breathing now! Oh, thank God!" Dr. Bailey cried out.

Duke stood quietly in amazement as Dr. Bailey handed Julie her son for the first time.

"Hi, my sweetheart—your mama loves you." Julie spoke through tears of joy as she held her baby close to her heart.

"Hey, buddy," Duke greeted his newborn child, gazing into his bright blue eyes.

"What's his name gonna be?" Dr. Kelly asked.

"Lucas," Julie said without hesitating.

"I guess Lucas," Duke said with a smile.

"It was my father's name," Julie added softly as she stifled a cry of emotion that threatened to burst through her lips.

"I love it," said Duke.

"All right, we need to get your placenta out now," said Dr. Kelly.

Julie passed Lucas over to Duke.

"I love you, Jules," said Duke.

"I love you, Duke. I'm so exhausted, I think I'm just gonna

rest my eyes for a bit."

"Julie, I am sorry but we have to deliver your placenta right away."

Julie didn't respond.

"Julie? Honey, wake up." Duke adjusted Lucas in his arms and shook Julie. "She won't wake up! What's wrong with her?"

"Bailey, she is losing a lot of blood," Dr. Kelly shouted.

"Oh no, she's hemorrhaging," said Dr. Bailey.

Duke leaned closer to Julie and pressed his forehead against hers.

"Wake up! Don't leave me, Jules! Please wake up."

***

When Duke tried to dig a burial site for Julie, the ground was too hard due to the weather. So he built a pyre and spread her ashes across the mountain and hills of Mountaintop. Looking at his son in despair, he felt defeated and helpless. But Charles had told him that lots of babies were expected at Mountaintop with mothers who wouldn't produce enough breast milk, so plenty of baby formula was in storage for Lucas.

"I don't know if I can do this without you, Jules," Duke said softly, gazing at his son.

***

April 2036

It had been a month since Julie passed away, leaving Duke wholly shattered. He was just a walking former shell of his old self. He had a hard time looking at Lucas because he was reminded of Julie and Michael and Ava every time he did. Sarah often volunteered to watch and take care of Lucas almost every day. Her orphan children were reasonably self-sufficient—Danielle took care of Tyler, so Sarah said she wasn't really needed anymore. But when she was with Lucas, it seemed to give her purpose and joy.

Duke didn't talk to anyone very much. The community whispered about him. Said that he was not fit to lead anymore. Duke knew they were right, but he didn't care to address it. He figured there was no reason to. He had nothing to say and nothing to give. Duke's will to survive had faded, as had his will to live.

Duke dropped Lucas off at Sarah's one morning and returned to his shelter. As he sat, he thought about everything and everyone. Duke finally understood what Agigi meant; there were worse things in this world than death.

Duke crossed the room and faced his reflection in the mirror. Grief etched lines of torment across his face. His once vibrant blue eyes, now dull and lifeless, betrayed the weight of his sorrow. A six-inch beard covered his gaunt cheeks, framing a mouth that had long forgotten how to smile. His disheveled hair, matted and unkempt, mirrored the chaos that had consumed his soul.

As he gazed at his reflection, memories flooded back like a tidal wave, crashing against the shores of his shattered heart. The laughter of Julie, the innocence of his children, their voices echoing hauntingly in his mind. Julie's gentle touch, the warmth of his children's embrace, all lost forever in a cruel twist of fate.

A tremor coursed through Duke's weakened body, the weight of his grief unbearable. With trembling hands, he reached out to touch the mirror, tracing the lines of his face. How had it come to this? How had he survived the unimaginable loss, only to find himself trapped in a desolate existence?

Duke's weary gaze shifted from his reflection to Julie's grandfather's shotgun leaning against the wall in the corner of the room. For a moment, his eyes locked onto the weapon, its cold metal taunting him, promising an end to his suffering. The temptation to succumb to the darkness clawed at his soul, whispering promises of relief from the relentless ache that consumed him.

Duke held the old shotgun to his chin, feeling tears streaming down his face as his cheeks turned red and he started to shake. He just wanted to be reunited with Julie and his children—to end all his suffering. "You win," he said softly, squeezing the trigger.

Click.

Duke gasped for air, still shaking from a new burst of adrenaline. Even in the chill of his shelter, sweat and tears poured down his face. He put the gun down on the bed and opened its chamber: there was a small mark next to the primer. The weapon had finally misfired. Duke wasn't sure if it was luck or another thing he failed to do.

The sound of the alarm bell filled Duke's ears. He immediately ran to the communications building, where Jake was ringing it with vigor.

"What's going on?" Duke shouted.

"Security just called; they reported military vehicles at our gate," Jake replied in an anxious tone. "Do you think it might be Campbell?"

Duke grabbed a handheld radio and tried to reach the colonel. "Campbell, this is Mountaintop. Over." A wave of silence spread.

"Just let them in," Jake said. "What other option do we have?"

"You're right," Duke agreed, resigned.

As the gates opened, military vehicles came in slowly. Duke did not recognize any of the vehicle's makes or types. Quickly he became aware that this was a foreign military. The vehicles parked, then an Asian man wearing full military dress stepped forward from the convoy.

The man shuffled toward Duke and Jake, who looked back to see the citizens of Mountaintop preparing themselves for an unpredictable danger.

"My name is Han Weiguo, and I'm a commander of the People's Liberation Army," said the man with a soft accent. "We're here to assist survivors in the West."

"Assist how?" Jake questioned.

"We are working with your government to help provide food, water, shelter, and medicine," Han answered.

"Oh my God! We made it! We're saved!" Jake shouted before sprinting off to tell everyone.

Duke stood silent, scrutinizing the Chinese commander. The man patiently returned Duke's piercing gaze.

"Let me be clear: we really are here to help you, Mr....?"

"Hollander," Duke replied.

"Yes, Mr. Hollander. Please go get your people so they know they are safe now. Our escorts will take all of you to receive medical assistance and food."

Duke's spirit was broken. He no longer cared to know the truth; he just wanted the pain to end. No more fighting, no more decisions or needing to look after people—he didn't even care about living himself.

Everyone boarded large cargo trucks. Duke had Lucas wrapped up tightly in blankets. They traveled down the road to what Han called a rescue center. Duke stared at Lucas, again reminded of Julie and his dead children. How would he be able to take care of this baby? His mind was in shambles. Then he saw Sarah sitting with Jake, cuddled with Tyler and Danielle. Sarah stared at Lucas with loving eyes. Duke always thought she was a good mother and Jake a good father despite what had happened between them. Lucas deserved better than a crumbling father.

"Sarah, I have to talk to you about something," Duke said solemnly.

"Of course," Sarah replied, looking at him and Lucas intently.

"I need you to take Lucas and raise him."

Sarah looked at Jake in disbelief before turning back to

Duke. "But ... we can't do that, Duke ..."

"Please," he begged desperately. "You have to help me. Please?"

Jake and Sarah exchanged glances before she opened her arms wide. "Okay, Duke, we can do that."

"I love you so much, buddy," Duke choked out as he kissed the top of Lucas' head. "But I can't take care of you right now. I will forever be your daddy." His tears fell onto Lucas' blanket as he passed him over to Sarah, his heart aching from the loss. He knew she was a better caretaker for Lucas, but it didn't make handing him off any easier. Duke felt like he had given away a piece of himself.

The truck eventually pulled over, and Duke stepped out to see a huge line of folks. Some were nibbling on food, while others had medical professionals attending to them. There were also large sleeping barracks set up.

Despite what everyone had been through, people's faces were lit up with grins of relief. All they needed to do was queue up and submit themselves to the scanner.

The Chinese collective ran their checks, taking Duke's fingerprints, facial features, and eyes for a retinal scan.

"Name, age, occupation?"

"Duke Hollander, thirty-six."

"And occupation?"

"Retired U.S. Army," replied Duke.

The man mulled it over, then exchanged hushed words with another person.

"Is something wrong?" inquired Duke.

"No problem, sir." At last the man announced: "Next!"

At the sound of Lucas' cry, Duke spun to catch a glimpse of him receiving an injection.

Duke saw his picture and information being uploaded on a computer screen behind the man who scanned him. Jake and Sarah had already received the same injection as Lucas and it was now Duke's turn. He stood in front of the man who was giving out the shots. On closer inspection, it appeared that the man was using a big hollowed-out needle with a beveled tip—similar to what they'd used when having their family dog chipped—and inserting it into people's hands.

"Hold out your hand," the man commanded.

Duke could hear Kazim and Karl's words echoing in his mind:

I'd rather die free than live as a slave.

Everyone will be confronted with a critical decision.

Duke's pulse skyrocketed as he shook his head. "No," he asserted.

The man exchanged a mystified glance with his peers. "What do you mean?"

"I don't want that thing in me," Duke declared.

"It's a drug; it will heal you," the man responded.

"I don't need medicine. I don't want it!" Duke yelled, gaining the attention of everyone in the area.

A high-ranking Chinese officer approached them and asked, "What seems to be the problem here?"

The medical personnel giving the injection spoke to the officer in Mandarin.

"So I'm being told you are refusing the injection, is this correct?" the officer asked Duke.

"That's right," confirmed Duke.

"If you deny this medicine, we won't provide you with food, water, or shelter. Do you understand?"

"That's fine too!" Duke shouted.

The man's face distorted into an unpleasant expression. He banged his fists on the table. "You will take the shot! You have no other choice!"

"Bullshit!" Duke shouted defiantly.

From across the room Jake cried out, "Duke, what are you doing? Just get the shot." Sarah stood next to him, holding Lucas, who had started wailing in her arms. At that moment Duke regretted giving Lucas away and reached out, begging for him back.

"Sarah, I am sorry—I was wrong—I must get Lucas back!"

Sarah was confounded by what was happening. "Duke ... What? No! Just do what they say so we can all take care of Lucas together—please?"

Duke surveyed the people around him. Some were trembling in fear, while others looked at him incredulously. He wished that he could undo what he had done and be reunited with his son again. But it was too late to turn back now. Instead of speaking the words aloud, Duke silently said goodbye with a meaningful look to Jake, Sarah, and Lucas. His whole body ached for him to escape. With one last glance back at the Chinese rescue center, Duke dashed across the street.

"阻止他! (Stop him!)" yelled the officer.

Duke bolted into the nearby woods, hearing people trailing behind him. As he dashed through the wilderness, he felt more alive than ever before. He couldn't understand why he was running. For months, Duke had been feeling as if he were already dead. But running through the Colorado wilderness with his adrenaline pumping and sweat pouring down his face, he had never wanted to live more than he did at that moment. Emotions flowed through Duke like floodwaters rushing down a mountain valley after a sudden rain break. A newfound determination sprung up inside him that he knew would never go away; he was going to get his son back no matter what the cost.

EPILOGUE

The Chinese soldiers had been hunting Duke for the better part of the day, and they had hit him several times with their rubber bullets. The sting of each round was agonizing, but that was nothing compared to Duke's exhaustion; his body was already broken from months of not having enough food. Adrenaline and thoughts of his son provided Duke with the drive he needed to keep going, but then he twisted his ankle while trying to cross a stream.

Desperately, Duke ducked behind a large boulder, holding his injured ankle tightly as the soldiers approached. He did his best to stifle any noise.

"他去哪了? (Where did he go?)" a Chinese soldier yelled out.

"我发誓我看到他走这条路 (I swear I saw him go this way)," another soldier replied.

Duke held his breath as the three Chinese soldiers slowly waded through the stream. There was no more time for running away, so he just waited. His heart thudded in his chest when the first two crossed by him. When the last one came into view, Duke snatched the gun out of his hands, gave him a kick in the chest, and pointed the weapon at the leader. He pulled the trigger but all that emerged was a red light accompanied by a buzzing sound.

What the hell?

He hurled the rifle at the soldier with both arms raised above his head like he was wielding a tomahawk. The gun smacked the man's face and sent him tumbling to the ground. Duke hastily attempted to grab the other rifle, but his sprained ankle caused him to stumble.

"举手转身! (Hands up and turn around!)"

Duke spun around quickly and tried to fire off a shot. The

gun again made a buzzing noise and lit up with red lights. The Chinese soldiers cackled in amusement.

Through his combat mask, one remarked, "那是一把智能枪, 你这个白痴 (That's a smart gun, you idiot)."

With little enthusiasm, Duke raised his hands, but he still managed to throw a punch at the soldier coming to apprehend him. The three guards swiftly subdued him after one of them fired several rubber bullets into his legs. They secured Duke's hands behind his back with zip ties and forced him to kneel.

The Chinese soldiers abruptly paused upon hearing the sound of someone running through the woods.

"那是什么?(What was that?)"

"展示你自己! (Show yourself!)"

The stillness of the mountain forest was broken only by the rustling of the leaves and chirping of the birds. Suddenly, out of the shadows emerged a mysterious figure wearing dark clothing and with a burning determination in their eyes. They tightly grasped a shining knife.

Startled, the Chinese soldiers immediately pointed their weapons toward the stranger. But before they could speak, the warrior sprung into action; they closed the gap between themselves and the soldiers in an instant. Their movements were a fusion of accuracy and agility as they evaded bullets and weaved through them with purpose and precision.

The stranger then flung their knife with remarkable accuracy. The first soldier stumbled back, clutching at his arm as blood seeped from his wound. Unfazed, the remaining two increased their attack—but it was no use. The figure ducked and dodged with uncanny grace, never losing control or balance. They skillfully disarmed one soldier before engaging in an intimate fight between blades and guns.

The final soldier stumbled backward, terror clearly visible on their features as the determined figure advanced. The soldier fell with a resonant thud after one decisive hit.

The mysterious figure stood tall and proud, surrounded by the defeated enemies. After a brief moment of silence, the forest seemed to breathe a sigh of relief. The figure approached Duke, and he felt their eyes upon him. He looked up expectantly to meet the figure's stare.

Duke squinted as he tried to make out the figure in front of him. The sun was blinding, making it difficult to see anything. Then the figure moved to Duke's back and undid his binds. As soon as Duke turned around, he recognized the face of the person who had freed him.

As Duke rose to his feet, bewildered yet thankful, he inquired, "Kazim? What are you doing?"

"As I told you before, I'd rather die a free man than live as a slave," said Kazim.

END

A PREVIEW OF...

STATE OF CONTEMPT

REFORMATION

PROLOGUE

Pre-Takeover

World War Three pitted China and Russia against the United States and NATO. The vast expanse of the Pacific Ocean bore witness to an epic showdown between the naval and air forces of China and the United States. Meanwhile, on the battle-scarred grounds of Ukraine, Russia locked horns with NATO forces in a fierce and unyielding struggle.

As the war raged on, both sides faced heavy losses and widespread devastation. Despite their best efforts, neither China and Russia nor the United States and NATO could gain significant ground or make decisive progress. The once-steady march of military seemed stalled in a quagmire of relentless opposition.

Desperation seeped into the decision-making, and the use of tactical nuclear weapons became a haunting reality. The objective was to achieve strategic strides, yet the outcome proved catastrophic. Instead of shifting the tide of war, the deployment of these nuclear weapons only served to escalate the threat of even deadlier strategic nuclear strikes.

The world watched in trepidation as World War Three evolved into a new and chilling era—the second Cold War. The threat of mutually assured destruction casted a chilling shadow over the international stage. The once volatile geopolitical landscape now held the world in its icy grip, every move carrying the weight of potentially cataclysmic consequences.

During the second Cold War, Chinese intelligence had picked up information that North Korea was planning an assault on the United States. In response, the Chinese authorities put together a concealed plan that would benefit them while still keeping the U.S. in the dark. To start, China supplied North Korea with EMP technology to construct a formidable EMP weapon and conceal it as a satellite. They promised to intervene if America attempted any kind of retaliation.

The economies of China and Russia had dwindled to an unprecedented low due to the expenditures associated with World War Three, as well as US and NATO sanctions. To remedy this, the BRICS Nations (Brazil, Russia, India, China, and South Africa) managed to rope in over a hundred and thirty countries into their system of using a centralized digital currency, the CBDC. This gold-backed digital yuan displaced the United States dollar as the global reserve currency, resulting in a sharp decline in the American economy.

As the United States fell out of favor with the global market, China seized the opportunity to incentivize nations within and outside of the BRICS community to invest in their Silk Road Initiative. This project was dedicated to increasing connections and improving economic cooperation between China and other nations worldwide. The initiative included constructing roads, railways, ports, and pipelines to create transportation and energy infrastructure.

In order to ensure China's place as the number one global superpower, they established a contract with the most powerful nuclear state, Russia. This deal was known as the Sino-Russian Treaty. Outwardly, the treaty was designed to promote military collaboration, foster technological progress, and ensure nuclear safety between the two nations.

However, there was a far more sinister plot brewing out of sight. This treaty was but the beginning of their strategy to exploit North Korea's hostile nature. China and Russia knew North Korea would eventually attack the United States, and thus supplied them with technology and resources to build an EMP satellite weapon. To further encourage them, they promised to protect North Korea under the Sino-Russia nuclear umbrella. Their collective goal was to take over U.S. land and its resources, including people as slaves. Both countries vowed to help each other rebuild the regions in the former United States that they had previously asserted sovereignty over. Unbeknownst to North Korea, Russia and China had no intention of rushing to their aid when the time would come.

Years 1 & 2

North Korea enacted their end of the plan and successfully destroyed the United States' power grids with a satellite-based EMP weapon. China and Russia, contrary to North Korea's expectations, denounced them on the world instead of supporting their actions. In retaliation, the U.S. Seventh Fleet targeted North Korean leadership and military structures. Before they could complete their mission, North Korea unleashed a monumental bombardment against South Korea and American military bases. The United States responded with low-yield atomic weapons, leaving sections of the Korean Peninsula desolate and uninhabitable.

Russian hackers manipulated data to make it seem like Iran had caused a crippling cyber attack on Israel and other middle eastern countries. The same thing happened to NATO countries across Europe. The consequence of this attack was catastrophic, leading to economic ruin for NATO countries and allies.

China claimed all the land west of the Mississippi River as its own, while Russia declared ownership of all the land east of the Mississippi River. The Chinese military used food and medicine as bait to lure the remaining Americans into their control. On the other side of the river, Russians rounded up all the surviving Americans without any promises or deception—just sheer strength. This spurred those Americans east of the Mississippi River to unite in an attempt to fight back against Russian forces, but their efforts were ultimately futile. Despite the occupation, some American militias remained and fought back against the Russian army.

The remaining citizens of the United States were sustained, cared for, and returned to health. Then, they were implanted with a chip from a Chinese firm called Deep Thought. China and Russia had their own versions of the microchip featuring the same technological capabilities in order to tell who owns which chip. The device was produced commercially for human use as an identification tool, similar to a wireless barcode or dog tag. It also monitored vital data such as health, activity levels, and location. The chips were no bigger than a grain of rice and were surgically implanted under the skin; they would last for twenty-five years.

China and Russia combined forces, enlisting the labor of Chinese, Russian, and American slaves to reconstruct the broken infrastructure of the former United States. China loaned Russia money, food, and manpower when needed. West of the Mississippi, China started the process of replacing the damaged and outdated power grid with thousands of independent microreactors operated by advanced AI systems.

The two nations began constructing a place known as "The Farm" where the American survivors were made to labor in re-education work camps. This huge area was formerly known as the Midwest and became China and Russia's main source of food. The Americans were also forced to learn their captors' language.

The Farm served to provide sustenance for both countries, but that was only a fraction of its purpose. Individuals were divided into camps and sectors based on their abilities and behavior—agriculture, manufacturing, carpentry, and so on. Those deemed valuable by the authorities received preferential treatment compared to others.

On the Chinese side of the Farm, the Americans could work toward "freedom" if they stayed out of trouble, learning basic Chinese commands and responses for the betterment of Chinese society. They could be bought or gifted as a sub-class citizen. The Russians did not do this. Americans who the Russians caught remained at the Farm.

The Farm was managed with AI technology to ensure that the Chinese and Russians could maintain control. The two countries ran their camps differently, but both enforced American restock laws. These laws required any American survivors to reproduce, which would replenish both countries' slave stock.

The Farm also had sectors dedicated to raising animals to be released into the wild in mass quantities. Both China and Russia reintroduced several species of their homeland to the former devastated and overhunted regions of the United States. The Chinese shipped the animals from their native land on massive boats called fāngzhōu (arks).

Years 3-5

A border was erected entirely around the old U.S., isolating the newly formed superpowers from the outside world. The Mississippi River served as a natural border marking the boundary between Russian and Chinese territories. In order to limit movement between the two countries, most bridges spanning the Mississippi River were destroyed, replaced by massive structures deliberately placed in strategic locations.

Government personnel and businesses from both parties took up residence in the new areas, and new seaports were built to manage the increased level of imports from each nation.

China built multiple large cities that housed up to five million people each. Both countries consumed twenty-five billion metric tons of concrete on an annual basis.

Russia had 100 million citizens migrate to their now vacated cities, creating a population surge with incentives for having children. Duties like military service were imposed on all fifteen- through fifty-five-year-olds.

Through compulsory abortions, legislation against having more children was enforced by China. Numerous factories were erected across both nations, where technology of various kinds was exchanged between them.

China deployed weaponized drones to provide surveillance throughout its cities and regions.

China and Russia constructed the Yuán dǐng (the Dome), a huge sports stadium capable of holding over 250,000 people, located at the convergence point of the former states of Missouri and Tennessee in the middle of the Mississippi River. The structure stood on large concrete pillars, allowing the river to flow underneath it. Aside from hosting mass entertainment events, they used it for sporting competitions between the two nations. Nonconforming prisoners were made to fight each other to the death.

Years 6-10

The Sino-Russian Treaty came to an abrupt stop when the power struggle between the two nations escalated and promises were left unfulfilled. Both countries had similar technology and weapon arsenals, leading to a stalemate. From then on, a Cold War took place between China and Russia. Outsiders—such as media, networks, and companies—were prohibited from entry into either country.

The Mississippi River was divided between both countries, with reinforced boundaries and walls like the DMZ of North and South Korea.

The two nations devised a plan for maintaining peace and avoiding nuclear conflict. Both countries agreed to continue to run the Dome and the Farm together. They still ran competitive sports, but it was a testing ground for new AI technology and weaponry. Each country was starting to outdo each other with AI technology. The ultimate goal was to create a symbiosis between humans and AI with upgradable microchips implanted in the brain.

The American survivors became extremely valuable to both China and Russia, so the two countries only used those who behaved badly or got into trouble as subjects for testing. The Dome also served as a form of punishment for Chinese and Russian citizens who were caught helping American survivors, committing treason, or partaking in other offenses.

CHAPTER 1

2045

It had been ten years since the power went out and nine years since the People's Republic of China (PRC) extended its borders and land to the United States, claiming all land west of the Mississippi River. They came in under the ruse of humanitarian aid. The Chinese military did provide the surviving American population with food, water, and medicine, but it was discovered to be disingenuous. Their real motives were more insidious; they wanted control and ownership of all land, property, and resources available. China was not the only country to take advantage of the once-great nation—Russia also took over the land and cities east of the Mississippi. Together the two nations rebuilt their acquired land to their liking.

Kazim taught Duke everything he knew about survival and fighting. The duo was very nomadic during their first year on the run after the Chinese invasion. Whenever the PRC authorities moved into the area in which they were camped, Duke and Kazim would find another location and build structures into the landscape to keep hidden. For the first few years, they lived off of yucca roots from the southeast plains and the forgotten fruit groves in the west. They refused to be enslaved. They refused to give up their freedom. But that came with a cost. They had to move from hidden shelter to hidden shelter for various reasons. The Chinese authorities were looking for surviving Americans. They gave rewards to anyone who offered information that led to the capture of an American "stray." Duke and Kazim were almost apprehended a few times over the years. Duke knew for sure that if they were caught, they would be sent off to the Farm like everyone else—or sent to the Dome to be made into an entertainment spectacle if they wouldn't comply.

The Chinese authorities reintroduced animals into the environment but they were unfamiliar to Duke and Kazim: kinds of Chinese deer, rabbits, bears, birds, leopards, wild hogs, and even some giant pandas. The wild hogs took over several areas but provided an abundant food source for Duke and Kazim. They still saw animals native to America, but the forests were much different than before, especially at night.

After the power went out, tens of thousands of fires ravaged across America. Hundreds of millions of acres and over a million homes were destroyed, but their owners were already dead more than likely. The forest fires went unchecked, with no firefighters to help combat them, and the plant, tree, and animal ecosystems shifted. Despite all this devastation, nature found a way to recover from this disaster on its own. But with assistance from the Chinese, it recovered even faster. The great fires cleared out low-growing underbrush and purified debris from the forest floor, which allowed more sunlight to nourish the soil. And without competition for nutrients in the soil's depths, established trees grew stronger and healthier than ever before.

In Duke's former home of Colorado, the Chinese set up cloud formation factories as part of their cloud-seeding initiative to bring rain to the dry land. They also planted millions of bamboo, empress trees, and other fast-growing plants and trees, which took over the environment, creating a unique ecosystem of American and Chinese trees, plants, and animals.

Duke and Kazim had to rely on the animals they hunted for sustenance, yet this changed with the introduction of Chinese surveillance drones. To avoid detection and being sent to the Farm, they chose to hide away and endure starvation rather than risk capture.

Despite Duke's deep-seated reservations about the Chinese, he found himself unexpectedly admiring their remarkable efficiency. Freed from the tangled web of American bureaucratic red tape, the PRC authorities had constructed millions of homes, structures, and buildings in just the first half-decade following their arrival. They not only revitalized the aging American infrastructure but also infused it with their unique touch. The Chinese government operated without the need for extensive consultations or burdensome paperwork. When the PRC authorities decided to act, their execution was swift, decisive, and unquestioned. To Duke's own astonishment, he had to concede that, in many ways, the country now seemed to be in a better state than it had been before.

Significant damage was done to the delicate grid system, technology, and gadgets that America relied on. In its place, the Chinese government erected an all-electric, automated society powered by thousands of micro-reactors the size of shipping containers. Cars, trucks, aircraft, and trains could all move without drivers. To get around certain areas of a city, people would use pilotless drone taxis that could be summoned for a fee by entering a name or address. Chinese citizens with enough money could buy their own personal drone vehicle.

Most businesses had been fully automated with minimal help from people. This technologically advanced society was connected by the PRC's AI software known as Nexus. It belonged to Míngxiǎng (Deep Thought), a Chinese tech company.

Daily, Duke ruminated on Julie, Michael, and Ava. His inability to save them still plagued his subconscious day and night. He also reflected on the awful day he had handed his son Lucas over to his ex-wife Sarah. For the past nine years, Duke had been haunted by regrets. He wondered what horrible conditions Lucas was facing on the Farm, kept as a slave working for the government. But his hope was renewed when

Duke saw Jake Anderson and Sarah getting off a truck at a depot in Shānchéng (Mountain City), formerly known as Colorado Springs. Although he didn't see any young kids or people with them, it gave Duke a glimmer of hope. He felt a renewed purpose: no longer an animal just surviving, but a desperate father prepared to do whatever it took to get his son back.

***

Duke lifted his gaze to the starless night sky, illuminated by brief flashes of electricity that ripped open the darkness with jagged claws. A dazzling display of lightning lit up the sky in brilliant blues and greens. Thunder rumbled from far off as if part of some eternal battle for dominance with the gods. He felt the faint misting of rain and heard its gentle pitter-patter on the trees like a warning whisper. Moonlight carved a path through the forest so he could pick out shapes in the shadows. He knew it was the best time for him to move; his footsteps were masked as he darted across the road into the waiting embrace of a forest that seemed foreign and familiar all at once.

He had grown accustomed to living in these woods, attuned to the noises and smells he encountered every day. Years spent living amongst nature had transformed him into an extension of it, focused only on basic needs—food, water, shelter, security—like any other animal. But Duke had something more than mere survival on his mind. He had a purpose—a mission that drove him further each day despite whatever dangers may have been lurking—to find his son.

Duke ventured deeper into the wilderness, pushing through bamboo patches through which he had cut a path wide enough for him to pass through. The hybrid forest was alive with sound and filled with secrets. He pushed through the night, uneasy fear running through his veins like ice. He could feel the oppressive weight of the PRC drones circling like vultures above, just waiting to swoop down and snatch up any American strays. He kept his head low and trudged forward, feeling only a little safer with every step he took. His heart thundered against his rib cage like a drum as thoughts of utter despair coursed through him. He knew he was risking every-thing but all that mattered now was reaching his destination.

Although it was almost pitch black out, Duke's sense of sight had become acute from spending years in the forest, enhancing his ability to move at night. Shapes, sounds, and pace count were integrated to form pictures in Duke's mind. PRC authorities had security drones roaming in shifts around the clock, reporting to the Chinese authorities. They helped find any American strays and kept a watchful eye on their new land. The drones could sense and read the biochips implanted in the Chinese population and the enslaved Americans. Nine years ago Duke had come to his senses and ran away from the Chinese soldiers before they could put such a chip in him.

Duke came to an opening framed by massive empress trees towering over a cliff that overlooked thousands of local homes below. Millions of tiny lights strobed throughout the bustling city. Hands shaking, Duke tugged at the string of his woodland-patterned poncho, creating a mini tent to shelter his red-lens flashlight from prying eyes. He pulled out a map he made months ago. Duke had been mapping out all those homes in search of Sarah, Jake, and Lucas. Each hour passed in a blur as he ran his finger along the crudely-drawn boxes rep-resenting the homes below, hoping against hope that some-where amongst those dwellings he would find his son.

Duke peered out from the folds of his poncho, straining to make sense of the papers in his hands. He double-checked that he had in fact taken the right one before slipping a long-range spotting scope from his leather satchel. Holding it to his eyes, Duke surveyed the landscape below, searching familiar figures. Memories flooded back to him as he looked at the homes he once knew so well, an existence that felt like a lifetime ago. It had been ten years since Mountaintop was destroyed, yet here he still stood, battered and emaciated after all this time on the run.

Duke began to study the targets within his scope's viewfinder but found nothing more than everyday people going about their lives—Chinese families having dinner or watching the latest competition at the Dome. With a sigh of exhaustion, Duke decided it was time to go; he promised himself he would not stay any longer than an hour lest the drone spotters get wind of him.

Just as he began to turn around and make for his exit route through the forest, Duke heard a twig snap behind him. His body tensed with anticipation as fear pulsated through his every bone.

"Ka?" Duke called out in a loud whisper. He strobed his flashlight in a particular sequence—a challenge and password that only Kazim knew how to respond to.

But Kazim did not respond. Duke decided he couldn't risk staying any longer, waiting for his phantom to show itself. With a determined face, Duke held onto his flashlight and strode forward. Muscles clenched with every step; he waited for something to reach out and grab him.

A shudder of relief rushed through Duke as he stumbled out of the dark, dense forest. His eyes searched like a lighthouse for any signs of Chinese drones before darting across the road as soon as it seemed safe. He found his way along an obscure path on the side of the hill, one that was well hidden from the skies above. The light rain had settled, but his footlong beard was still dripping with moisture. Rolls of thunder roared in the distance and the light drizzle resonated with the chirping of crickets.

Duke trudged up the long dirt road that led to his home. He hopped over the ragged fence line, the moon throwing deep shadows across his path. The wind whistled through the trees as if trying to speak a forgotten language. Duke tiptoed across the driveway, all the while scanning for any sign of movement.

A voice spoke from the darkness, a voice he recognized— "You're going to get caught."

Duke leapt back in surprise, his heart pounding, and before he could think twice, he drew his knife lightning-fast. He relaxed when he realized who it was. "Kazim! You're gonna get cut one of these times sneaking up on me like that!"

"You're going to get caught. Or even worse you'll lead them back here." Kazim's dark eyes shone in the pale light of the waning moon.

"We both know that drones don't go this far out," Duke said, a hint of apprehension in his voice.

"Yes, but you could lead them back here from the cliff edge you always go to," Kazim replied, his words thick with warning.

"So that was you watching me tonight," said Duke.

Kazim stepped forward, throwing a pair of small animals on the ground in front of Duke. "No, I've been here hunting and waiting for you."

Duke paused, his heart thudding in his chest like a black-smith hammering an anvil. The reality that something or someone else had been watching him tonight struck him like lightning. "Okay, but my son is still out there, Ka. What do you expect me to do? Sit on my hands and wishfully think my son home?"

Kazim was silent for a moment before replying, still shrouded in shadows, "No, but I imagine it will be much harder to find him if you're locked away at the Farm."

"The Chinese would find me much harder to apprehend than most of the American strays."

Kazim chuckled darkly. "It's true, you've gotten better over the years, but you're still just an emotional pup."

Duke's face hardened with an expression that was equal parts grit and grim humor. "Care to back those words up, old man?" he growled with a sly grin, daring his friend.

"Of course," said Kazim.

"First blood?" Duke asked, holding Kazim's gaze.

Kazim stepped out from the shadows. The moonlight caught his bald head, making it glisten like glass under the evening stars. His dark skin made him almost invisible in the night, but Duke had grown accustomed to picking up on small details over the past decade of their time together. He had heard stories about Kazim's childhood, having been kidnapped in Sudan and raised as a child soldier—since then Kazim had perfected his body into that of an expert killing machine. He had trained Duke for years in many ways—including in the art of settling disagreements with physical combat. The two men had developed an unspoken language over the past nine years—one of fistfights and knives, their bodies now riddled with small scars like constellations across their skin.

Duke was a stalking lion seeking out its prey, but he knew Kazim would not be an easy kill. With deliberate steps and movements, Duke slowly approached his target. He threw jabs of fury, but his friend gracefully stepped aside and drove his knee into the pit of Duke's stomach, reducing him to a winded heap in a mud puddle at his feet. As Duke gasped for air, he felt Kazim looming nearer, but was unable to make out his form in the darkness. A vice-like grip suddenly pulled him back by his hair, only to release its tension when Duke's elbow collided with Kazim's face with swift precision. Duke followed through with a powerful side kick that sent the other man reeling. As he stumbled away, Kazim flashed a malicious grin through the darkness, two menacing eyes and teeth hovering in midair. Duke stood there, panting, ready for whatever came at him next.

The moment of tension was suddenly shattered when a porch light flooded the yard. A petite, elderly Chinese woman emerged from the house.

"You boys fighting again?" Her voice carried a hint of amusement.

"Yes, Mrs. Li," they replied in unison.

An amused smile lit up her face as she spoke. "Okay, well, when you're done acting like jackasses, take your boots off and wash up. Dinner is almost ready and I need help."

"Yes, Mrs. Li," the men again said in unison.

Mrs. Li closed the door behind her with a creak as she turned off the light, leaving the two men standing in the darkness once more. Duke glared at his friend accusingly.

"What?" asked Kazim.

"You cheated, pulled my hair," Duke grumbled.

Kazim shook his head. "I told you that you are at a disadvantage with a long beard and hair. And the PRC authorities don't care to play fair."

Duke knew he was right but only shrugged before starting back toward the house. "Come on, let's go inside before Li makes us sleep outside again," he said, smiling.

Most of Duke and Kazim's problems were solved when they met Dr. Johnny C. C. Chan, a professor, and his wife, Li Yang, who had taken them in. Despite the danger such an act would bring upon them, the Chans chose to help the American strays, opening their doors with sympathy in their hearts. Dr. Chan and his wife were kind and understanding; they made sure Duke and Kazim were comfortable, providing them with shelter, a warm bed, and hot meals.

The Chinese professor had been bestowed an honorary professorship at the University of Hong Kong. He was charged by the PRC government with an ambitious task: developing and honing new artificial intelligence technology for their new land. A workaholic, Dr. Chan hardly ever left his lab at work until the authorities stepped in and offered assistance that would make his long hours possible at home: they built him a home laboratory, equipped with all of the cutting-edge technology and gadgets necessary for AI research and development.

The bathroom air was heavy with humidity. Fresh towels

hung on the marble walls like banners, unfurling as water cascaded from a golden spigot above the long granite sink. The black and white tile swirled around Duke's feet as he undressed, sliding out of his soiled and sodden garments before settling into the washbasin. His hands cupped warm water to rinse away patches of mud spotting his face and neck. He gazed into the mirror, focusing on the two scars that began at his left eyebrow and ran down across the bridge of his nose. He remembered how close he and Kazim had come to losing their lives when they encountered a black bear and her cubs several months ago—a battle for survival that they won, but with lasting consequences.

Duke's once vibrant blue eyes were now dull, as if life had been sucked out of them; gone were any hints of emotion or joy. All Duke cared about now was finding his son and nothing else mattered—neither his country nor God.

"Go tell my husband if he doesn't come and eat this time he's sleeping on the couch again," Mrs. Li scolded from the doorway as Kazim tried to stifle a smirk.

"Yes, ma'am," Duke muttered and trudged off to the basement. Opening the basement door, he flipped the light switch and descended an unpainted wooden stairwell that groaned with age. A single bulb flickered, casting a dim yellow aura upon boxes of junk labeled with Chinese characters that lay scattered around the damp room like forgotten treasures. Its foreign presence seemed to bring Duke back to reality, reminding him of all those years spent without electricity before Dr. Chan and Mrs. Li had taken them in. His eyes wandered along the walls until they found a full-sized mirror almost reaching up to the ceiling. It was encased in gold trim outlined with an intricate dragon pattern engraved with Chinese symbols.

As Duke's finger brushed the jeweled eye of the golden dragon, he pressed inward, feeling the warm pulse of energy surge through his skin as a halo of red light surrounded the edge of the mirror, then shifted to a solid green glow. Dr.

Chan's face appeared in the mirror.

"Yes? What is it, Duke?" Dr. Chan asked.

"Mrs. Li says it's dinnertime," Duke replied.

At five-foot-seven, Dr. Chan was nothing special in terms of height. But when it came to his intelligence, few could match him; even the bright minds of the younger generations paled in comparison to his razor-sharp wit. Every contour of his body—from the slender build of his arms to the tightness of every joint—seemed to awe those around him; it was almost impossible to believe such wisdom and experience were packed within his frail frame. His salt-and-pepper hair was groomed neatly and added a touch of distinguished charm to his persona.

Always on the cutting edge of technology, Dr. Chan often wore smart glasses with high-tech lenses that not only enhanced his vision but also served as a gateway to a world of data and information, enabling him to stay connected to the vast network of knowledge he sought to explore.

Duke's heavy footsteps echoed in the stairwell as he ascended to join Kazim and Mrs. Li at the dinner table. A few moments later, Dr. Chan emerged from the basement, his face drawn and solemn. His eyes were weary and sunken deep into their sockets as if he had been mining dark secrets of the underworld and never returned unscathed. He had a modest and practical fashion sense, favoring comfortable, well-worn button-up shirts in subtle earth tones paired with simple slacks or chinos. His clothing was chosen for functionality and ease of movement, allowing him to focus on his work without unnecessary distractions. He completed the look with comfortable leather shoes that had seen years of use but were meticulously maintained. On his wrist, he sported a classic analog watch that symbolized his appreciation for tradition amidst the modernity of his technological advancements.

Dr. Joo followed close on Dr. Chan's heels, a more imposing figure. Dr. Joo-Ho Lee stood tall at six-foot-two, his middle-aged countenance belying his true age with striking features that many would have described as classically handsome. His jet-black hair was styled in a neat cut, reflecting his obsession with order and discipline. But it was not the good looks nor the youthful façade that commanded respect—no, it was the intelligence that radiated off him like rays from the sun, an intelligence that had earned him a renowned reputation as one of the foremost minds in the field of android development.

Dr. Joo had pledged absolute loyalty to the People's Republic of China and served them selflessly, never letting his faith waver despite knowing they were watching him closely. His deep-set eyes were filled with contempt as they swept over Duke and Kazim, who seemed insignificant to him, their only worth being able to hinder his cause or offer a nuisance to trifle with. Dr. Joo thought Duke and Kazim were freed American slaves bought by Dr. Chan, but little did he know they were American strays—harbored fugitives hiding in plain sight from the long reach of the PRC.

Dr. Chan stared at the untouched food in front of him and braced himself for yet another round of taunting from his colleague, Dr. Joo.

"I find it distasteful that you sit and share your meals with your American pets," Dr. Joo spat, his words venomous darts.

But Dr. Chan rarely took the bait with Dr. Joo's anti-American banter. He simply shrugged and gave a small smile as he muttered, "Well, it looks like my food is getting cold."

Dr. Joo's unblinking eyes were cold and empty like a shark's as he took measured steps closer to Duke. His voice was low and menacing, but it still cut through the air like a sharpened blade. "Your kind are nothing but wasteful drains on China's resources. You're all so disobedient. Do you know what? One day, my androids will replace every last one of you." His words sent icy shivers up and down Duke's spine.

"So it is getting late. Are you and your team prepared to

do another symbiosis test tomorrow at Míngxi□ng headquarters?" asked Dr. Chan.

Dr. Joo slowly peeled his eyes away from Duke and let out an exhausted scoff. He pridefully stroked his chin and spoke with conviction. "Of course, I am always prepared for anything."

***

The heavy humming of Dr. Joo's drone vehicle echoed through the air as it descended from the sky and glided onto the pavement outside. Dr. Joo said nothing more before he turned on his heel and got into his flying machine. Its turbines whirred as it lifted off, leaving behind nothing but a whisper hanging in its wake.

Mrs. Li spat with quiet anger, "Such a pompous, narcissist jerk."

Dr. Chan's head hung heavy with fatigue; a deep, exhausted sigh escaped his lips as he shook his head. "Pay no attention to him," he muttered wearily, "His foolish plans will never come to fruition. He'll never reach the heights he desires so long as my AI remains non-sentient and fails to symbiotically merge with his androids. That will never happen, I'm making sure of it."

Duke shivered at the thought of Dr. Joo replacing the American people with his own creations. His gaze darkened like the clouds before a thunderstorm as he glared at Kazim, his body tensing with determination. Should Dr. Joo succeed in achieving his goal, all surviving Americans would perish, including Duke's only living son.

ABOUT ATMOSPHERE PRESS

Founded in 2015, Atmosphere Press was built on the principles of Honesty, Transparency, Professionalism, Kindness, and Making Your Book Awesome. As an ethical and author-friendly hybrid press, we stay true to that founding mission today.

If you're a reader, enter our giveaway for a free book here:

SCAN TO ENTER
BOOK GIVEAWAY

If you're a writer, submit your manuscript for consideration here:

SCAN TO SUBMIT
MANUSCRIPT

And always feel free to visit Atmosphere Press and our authors online at atmospherepress.com. See you there soon!

ABOUT THE AUTHOR

TYLER DEAN MILLIGAN is a dynamic author whose creative spirit thrives on exploring captivating tales of the end of times. With a decade of experience as an infantryman in the Army, Tyler is also a 100% disabled veteran. Currently, he and his wife, Heather, find solace in the breathtaking Mountains of Colorado, where they have built their own off-grid property. Embark on a literary journey with Tyler as he weaves compelling narratives of the apocalypse that will leave you on the edge of your seat.